Escort in Training

James Grey

Chapter One

My hands shake as they fumble at the keys on my phone. They're out of control. My angry fingers can't seem to hit the right buttons. I curse the gibberish I've put on the screen and slam the fucking thing back into my handbag. It'll only be an enraged Facebook status I'll end up regretting. I should have gotten further away. Now I'm falling apart on *their* doorstep.

Somewhere behind the screaming pack of thoughts roaring laps around my head, I can hear a little voice urging me to get out of here. But my legs have gone to mush. I can barely grip on the cigarette I'm trying to pull out of its box. I sit down, right there in the morning sunshine, on the office steps. Right there in my pencil skirt. Eyes welling up.

We're not supposed to smoke on the front steps. But who gives a fuck now? I've just pushed that snake's laptop right off her sad-ass desk. Slammed the door behind me before her *fucking* computer spilled its guts on the floor. They can't fire me for smoking a cigarette. Or swearing at my manager. Or for damaging their equipment. Because I quit.

That poison-dwarf bitch. She had it coming. Everyone except her couple of smarmy, ass-licking, suck-up cronies detests her from the inside out. Day after day we've mouthed off to each other about her bullying, her incompetence, her lying and her manipulation.

But nobody applauded when I lost it today. Cowards. Secretly wishing they had my audacity, but staring at the scene like rabbits caught in a goddamn industrial searchlight. I spoke for everyone out there when I called her a cunt. Yet the only voice ringing out loud was mine. The rest? They just look out for number one.

And now I'm just a tangle of rage. Too incensed to feel a heroine. Too trembling to hold a fucking ciggy between my lips. They had better not come near me.

I'm home. It's been a blur of tubes and buses, but somehow I've made it from Canary Wharf to Putney. I could navigate this commute in my sleep. And it's just as well, since I've been somewhere between stunned and comatose all the way from the office to here.

I wanted my apartment more than anything, but at the same time I didn't care if I got home or not. Oh well, I made it. At least I won't be playing this godawful London commuting game any time soon. For three years I've given three hours of each weekday just to go back and forth and pander to those blowholes. *Jesus, why?*

I am not a lot calmer. I just want to cleanse myself of that place, of *them*, in every way I can. As I slam my apartment door behind me, I'm overwhelmed with a need to get out these clothes. It's hot and sticky, and I feel the office's stench in the fabric.

I fling my bag on the floor and kick my high heels off in the living area. I don't care where anything ends up. But I feel a little lighter as I run my hand through my hair and wearily puff out my cheeks on my way to the bedroom. I'm already unbuttoning my ever-so-professional white blouse.

I'm pulling my arms out of it by the time I'm into my room. It, too, lands on the floor. Now I toss the skirt away. Better already! Off comes my bra. My panties. I'll figure out where to burn it all later. Right now I just want to flop down on my bed.

I dive onto the welcoming softness of my duvet. I'm panting a little, from my angry rush up the stairs and getting undressed so fast. I feel my heart bumping away somewhere beneath me, its rhythm tracking the fury still pulsing through me. At last, I can sigh as deep as I want. I don't need to move for a long, long time.

I haven't slept like that in months. This morning's outpouring exhausted me, but it lifted a weight too. I don't remember lying awake for long. The warm afternoon, the understanding mattress, having nowhere to be…they must have knocked me off like a switch.

My heartbeat is still there in my breast, but now it's like a chilled-out, comforting companion, urging me to take it easy. I smile to myself when I remember I'm nude. I strayed far from my meticulous routine when I got home today. But then it's not every day that you walk out of your job halfway through the morning.

I'm surprised at how good I'm feeling. The tension in my shoulders has evaporated. I flip onto my back and stretch my sleepy arms and legs. A sunbeam from the skylight streams across my tummy. I'm utterly comfortable, and there's nowhere I'd rather be right now. This is like a Sunday afternoon, only better, because there's no work tomorrow. No work ever!

I doze a little longer, sunbathing on my bed. I can see a sliver of sky. The usual London sounds fill the distance: police sirens, the dull rumble of a jumbo jet on its descent to Heathrow Airport. For once my mind is empty. I'm content. I'm not dwelling on my scene this morning. The feeling of closure is fantastic.

At last I sit up, still a little groggy. I'm so glad I live alone at times like this. My hair must look a mess and my eyes will be bloodshot from the tears. But I can sort myself out and find clothes in my own time. Where's my phone? I guess that'd be wherever I hurled my handbag. I pad through to the living room, grab the phone, and flop back down on my bed.

I've got messages. A few of the brave ones from work have congratulated me.

Well done for standing up to her, Emma.

Brave girl, hun, call me when you want to talk. x

She deserved that, the cow. xx

Wow, you went out in style, couldn't have put it better myself!

What exactly did I say? My memory of the detail is lost in the haze of rage. Maybe I should have held my tongue? Fuck, I'm pretty sure I won't be getting a reference out of them.

The sun has gone in and the room is sombre now. I pull a light blanket over me. All of a sudden, I feel a knot tightening in my stomach. Like the one I had before my first interview with them. *Pull yourself together, Emma. You did the right thing.*

Nobody else knows what's happened yet. God, I'll have to tell my parents and my friends. They'll bug me about my plans. How am I going to pay the rent, anyway? I've got enough saved for a couple of months, but then what? Back to Mom and Dad at 26? I feel my brow furrowing already. Christ, my unemployment honeymoon is over after one blissful afternoon nap.

I don't have anything planned for this evening. Not unusual. I've been coming home spitting mad most Fridays, not feeling much like activity. But staying in seems a bad idea tonight. I don't feel like telling a crowd of people what happened today. I just need a good friend and a glass of wine. Maybe two. I hope Martin's free.

"Emma, you *had* to get out of there. I just knew we'd be having this conversation sooner or later. You deserve better."

Martin looks right into my eyes, all wisdom and soft stubble. The wisdom of years: he's 42 but he's one of my best friends. We hit it off six years ago when we worked together at the library, and it has never been anything but platonic. He listens to classical music and reads *Vanity Fair*. He is one of those men who can always offer a willing ear and a new perspective on things. He's a fantastic friend for any girl.

"Yes, but still, I'm really not sure, Martin. I think I might have really blown it this time. The money wasn't bad, and was the job *really* that awful? I'm on five times the money I earned when you and I worked together."

"Emma, listen to yourself!" he chides. "Yes, it really *was* that awful! You've been close to despair for over a year now. Do you have any idea how many jobs there are out there? I don't think there's any excuse for being unhappy in what you do all week long."

I sigh and rest my chin on my hands. Martin's words make sense, but I feel more and more glum about the state of my life. "Sure, but times are hard right now," I protest. "It could take weeks to find something, and my rent isn't going to go away. You know, it would be a lot fucking easier if I had a man in my life right now."

"Listen to me now, Emma," says Martin, launching into his build-me-up routine. "You're bloody gorgeous, but you're talented too. You don't have to have a man to look after you. Nor do you need to work for some soulless, life-sapping, multinational consultancy firm unless you love the work. You really have got to stop worrying. You're smart, and things will work out."

I wish I could perk up. "You're sweet to say it, Martin. But there's so much more going on in my head right now. I'm not even sure I *want* another office job. There's going to be another useless manager at the next one, isn't there? More of this crappy commuting. Any company sucks you dry sooner or later. I'm only 26 and sick of the grind already. I'm turning into a bitter old woman."

"Emma…" He's trying, but I cut him off.

"Maybe it's time I finally went travelling! I never did get that gap year. That's it! Six months backpacking around South America beats grey old London any day. I'll be my old self again in no time!"

I can feel myself brightening. I take a sip of my wine and smile at Martin as if I've just solved all my problems with a Latin American travel itinerary. He raises an eyebrow.

"You should definitely travel, Emma. Everyone should experience the world. I just wonder though – "

"What?" I interrupt.

"Well, where's the money for that gallivanting going to come from? A couple of plane tickets and you're through your savings, as far as I understand. How's your Spanish? Can you work in those countries?"

Fuck. He always has to find the catch in any plan. I say nothing. Back to square one. We sip on our wine for a while. I do like this about Martin: silence is never uncomfortable with him.

At last he clears his throat and speaks. "Well, maybe marrying a millionaire wouldn't be *all* that bad an idea."

"I might as well do! I can't get anyone else to hang around. Guys keep on seeing me as a notch in their bedposts. It's not easy being a girl, Martin!"

"Well unfortunately that can go with the territory of being a stunning brunette," he says, massaging my ego just exactly where I need it. "But on the other hand, you could always turn it round to your advantage."

"Huh? What do you mean?" I really am in the dark.

Suddenly he looks embarrassed. "Never mind, it's nothing. A mad thought just crossed my mind, but I really don't know where it came from. Sorry Emma, let's just forget that I mentioned it, okay?"

"Martin, come on, you've made me curious now!"

Where the hell is he going with this? I'm obviously not going to let it go.

"I couldn't, Emma…"

"Martin, you're going to tell me what you were thinking. And right now, if you don't mind!"

"Bloody hell, alright darling! But don't bite me, okay?"

Surely he isn't going to be suggesting *that*. Is he? My mind tries to blank out the thought.

"No biting, I promise…" Though I'm not sure I mean it. He can't seriously think I'm going to be a stripper.

Martin leans forward and lowers his voice. He's getting all conspiratorial, and it makes me tingle a little. "As I've told you a hundred times, you're a real beauty. You *do* believe that, don't you?"

I nod. I'm telling him what he wants to hear, just so he'll get to his point.

"Do you remember my wealthy friend Charles? The one who met us for a drink a couple of weeks ago?"

"Yes, I remember him," I reply patiently. Does he want me to marry Charles now?

I look at him with a furrowed brow. He's one step away from proving he's gone off his rocker completely.

"Okay. So Charles is one of a couple of friends I've got who are into, you know, escorts. High-class escorts. I'm talking £500 an hour escorts."

I'm so taken aback that my snappy riposte never comes. Escorts? Woah! So really he means *hookers*. Not strippers. *Wait a second: how much again?*

I wasn't prepared for this. I gape back at Martin like a goldfish with special needs.

He goes on: "After he met you he told me how much he wished you were in that line of work. Something about you piqued his interest. I never gave it a thought at the time, of course, but – "

"Martin!" I almost yell. I'm starting to really see where he's heading with this. I'm indignant. He can't be serious! He really *has* gone off his rocker!

"Hang on," he says, raising his hand. "You made me start, so you have to let me finish."

"Jesus, Martin! Alright! I'm just…still reeling that there are people who will pay that much for a girl."

He raises his eyebrows at me and says with a smirk, "And there I was thinking you'd reel from the mere suggestion of you being the girl in question. I thought I'd have wine in my face by now."

"I'm not like that, Martin," I retort, folding my arms crossly. "Besides, you didn't say I had to be *that* girl, did you? Or did you?"

"Not yet, but I just thought – "

"Come *on* Martin, you can't be serious! I'm not some, you know…" I can't say the word. My voice trails off and I just sniff at him. Martin and his outrageous suggestions. Not that he's in the habit of proposing stuff like this, to be fair.

"Alright, I'm not going to push this," he says. "You're offended. Just one little thing I should mention, since I've come this far."

He pauses, and drops his voice to a whisper. He avoids my eye now. He's looking to the left, at a spot on the floor somewhere behind me.

"Do you know what Charles said to me after meeting you? He told me he would pay a thousand Pounds to spank you and have sex with you."

Oh my God. A grand? *To have sex?* One of my eyebrows shoots up before I can stop it. "With *me?* Don't be silly Martin. Stop winding me up. I'm not in the mood."

"Emma, it's God's honest truth," he says, looking me straight in the eye to show he's not kidding. "And he swears blind his chums would do the same. I was never going to say anything about it, but the way the conversation turned tonight, it just sort of came into my head. Sorry. You see why I didn't want to mention it."

I'm stunned. Words, which had sparked quick-fire from my icy tongue that morning in the office, fail me now. I recoil at the mention of prostitution. Such a thing has literally *never* crossed my mind. Not even once. How could it? I'm a decent girl, after all.

But part of me is flattered to be thought worth so much. I've been told I'm pretty, but *one thousand Pounds?* A surge of electricity runs down my legs. I'm intrigued. There is a long silence, and I avoid my friend's soft eyes as I take a gulp of my Rioja.

"Are you mad at me Emma?" Martin looks concerned.

"Yes. No. Well, not exactly. I mean, it's ridiculous to even talk about it, but I guess it's amusing to know these things, isn't it?" I pause for a while, chew on a fingernail and look at the ground. "I don't mind that you told me."

He smiles. "And you shouldn't be offended. A girl doing that kind of job can bring an empire crashing down, you know that? Just think how quickly you could retire and go travelling if you made that sort of money?"

My curiosity is definitely rising, in spite of myself. Sex. Money. I like those things, don't I? "So, there's some pretty exclusive stuff going on out there, huh?" I try to sound as if I'm just filling up a gap in conversation. Definitely not curious for my own sake.

"Yup," he smiles, clearly not fooled by my act. "We're talking super-rich clients. Hotel visits, mansion parties…that sort of thing. Fairly kinky stuff at times. I've never been tempted, but I've heard a few things. We're talking about the seriously rich and famous. All the money and power in the world, but they'll melt into helpless little boys when you put a perky, willing blonde or two into the room with them. Or, ahem, a brunette…"

"Right," I nod, genuinely lost in thought. I'm still not sure what to say. There are all sorts of crazy ideas swirling around my head. Talk of sex usually gets me a little hot under the collar. Now the talk is of insane amounts of money as well. I'm supposed to be appalled. But now that I've recovered from the bombshell, I'm feeling something unexpected inside.

Would I? *Could* I?

"Look," says Martin, taking my hands in his, in that rare never-more-than-friends way you almost never find with a straight guy, "I wouldn't lose the slightest bit of respect for you if you wanted to do something like that. Hell, I'd jump at the chance to have sex for a living. I know you're not a prude and judging by some of your drunken revelations, you're up for a bit of bedroom experimentation."

I blush all the way to the tips of my ears. "Shut up!" I hiss. "Alright, so it might be fun in theory…and I know you know it's been a long while for me. But it's a big leap to do…that!" I shake my head. "A *huge* leap. I really don't think it's me."

He nods. "Emma. I don't give a flying fig whether you consider this thing or not. It's just an option that could be there for you. If you want, I can set up a meeting with Charles and his agent. They could tell you more than I can. Definitely no strings attached."

"OK Martin. Let me think about it."

The words slipped out of my mouth before I could even stop them. How did that happen?

Ah well. I said what I said. It's not like I have any other plans for the rest of my life.

Chapter Two

I've got shaky hands again. Clammy palms too. But this time, five days later, it's not rage I'm feeling. I'm quivering somewhere between nerves and anticipation. Part of me wants to run away and hide in the bathroom. That part of me is ashamed to be here, and it's telling me that it's not too late.

"It's only a discussion, you silly girl!" Martin's reading my mind again. "Pull yourself together now. Honestly, there isn't a sign around your neck that says 'I'm here to find out about being a hooker.'"

I glare at him. Remind me why I agreed to this again?

"Sorry Emma. Just trying to lighten the mood! I know you feel like all the eyes in this bar are judging you right now, but they don't know you from Julie Soap, OK?"

I nod. He's right. It's not even like I've tried to dress sexy or anything. I'm in jeans and a tight-fitting t-shirt. If (God forbid!) I bumped into my mother, she'd have no reason to ask any awkward questions.

Yup, it's my take-it-or-leave-it outfit. If anything I'm pretty marginal for this place. It's a hotel lounge in Mayfair, and women far more elegant than me are coming and going. But that's cool. I'm only fact-finding today: it's not an interview. I don't want it to be.

I go to the bathroom, though, just to check on my makeup. I look at myself in the mirror, and see an attractive face returning my gaze. Even though my makeup is minimal. I've still got plenty of girlish appeal: the shiny lips of Emma the teenager remain. The dark eyes are still full of life, perhaps a little more soulful and alluring now than a year or two ago. My radiant hair, somewhere between jet black and auburn, curves gently in towards my shoulders, then stops. But it's growing: that crappy business haircut can definitely get out of my life now.

I like that I like my face. I know some girls aren't that lucky. And I like that it doesn't need much makeup. My skin isn't supermodel flawless, but it's only a few feint freckles that make it so. I've been told my natural look is girl-next-door in a good way, and if I'm feeling lazy I can get away with a naked face. I smile at my reflection. Sure, beautiful women can flick my jealousy switches out there, but I'm pretty pleased with what I see when I'm alone with a mirror.

I head back into the lounge and rejoin Martin, feeling a little more settled.

"So Emma, would it be easier if I left you alone with them when they arrive?"

I know Martin isn't going to be judging me, but this sounds like a good idea. I know him too well to have this kind of conversation with him around.

"I think that would be good, thanks Martin. You're always so thoughtful."

"No trouble Emma," he chuckles. He rises to his feet, gathers up his newspaper and nods to someone over my shoulder. "Then I'll leave you in Charles' hands now…he's right behind you!"

This is it. My nerves start doing backflips. I look around, feeling like some kind of dopey sheep. Martin is already making his way to a far corner of the room. I'm all on my own, and Charles is smiling at me.

"Hello Emma. It's a real pleasure to see you again."

This man would pay a grand to fuck you. And I'd never have known it. Christ.

"Oh. Right, um, hi…"

I stand up to return his confident handshake. And I register that there is a woman with him.

"Emma, I'd like you to meet Lucy Fulford. She's the agent I use."

Agent. He says it like she's some kind of business associate. But all three of us know why she's here. We all know what kind of 'agent' this Lucy Fulford is. This woman does not sell houses.

Lucy is surprisingly plain. Somehow I expected glamour. But her face is ordinary, and a little on the thin side. Her hair is brown and straight, the same length as mine. She wears dark-rimmed glasses that give her hazel eyes a certain authority. She presents herself in style, in a knee-length skirt and blouse. Along with her high heels, it's an outfit that could work at any time of day.

"It's lovely to meet you Emma," she beams. Her accent is a little posh – something that usually puts me off people – but I sense her warmth is genuine. This woman is already putting me at my ease. I'm glad she's here. Charles might be intimidating on his own.

He sits down opposite me, Lucy to his left. Only a low table separates us. We're in a floor-to-ceiling window bay and the street outside is still bustling with people and traffic. London simply never stops. Martin was right: none of these passers-by give a damn what our conversation was about. But still I squirm in my seat.

I look at Charles and smile weakly. He left an impression on me the one time we met. I've run into a few of Martin's wealthy friends before, but Charles had an extra edge to him. Something that spoke of untold wealth that could not, and would not, be taken away. More than that, he *knew* his place in the world. You could tell that by the way he carried himself. It wasn't arrogance at all. Just the assurance of a man completely accustomed to getting his own way.

He was a little older than Martin. Not unattractive, was my first thought. Perhaps not a natural beauty, but he could afford to look after himself and clearly did so. He was not quite greying yet, but there was perhaps for a hint of wisdom in his eyes.

Now, like the other time we met, he wears a five o'clock shadow. And he pulls it off well. His expensive shirt is open at the neck.

"I heard what happened with your job the other day," he begins, sitting back in his chair and steepling his hands in front of him. Nails tightly clipped, no rings. "From what Martin tells me, it sounds like that was the best thing that could have happened to you. I think you can do a lot better for yourself."

"Yeah. Well….I guess so. I just don't really know what I'm going to do now. I'm thinking of going travelling."

I'm too shy to broach the reason for our meeting. They're going to have to get this ball rolling, not me.

"To which end we are here tonight," Charles replies. He is not going to beat about the bush.

They're both looking right at me. It's quite unnerving. My mind starts tripping over itself in the glare.

He's not bad-looking actually. A thousand quid. *Would I?*

"Let me explain a few things to you, Emma," he continues. "I know you're feeling a touch coy right now, so I'll make it easy and do the talking."

I smile at him, letting a little pout escape, and nod. He seems a good man. He must be, if he's friends with Martin. He leans forward and lowers his voice so the next table won't hear us.

"At this very moment, Emma, a friend of mine is hosting a party at his flat. Only four of his closest friends are invited. I'll be joining them later.

"It's a special kind of party. It's not about drinks and snacks. We don't need drugs or any of that. It's about men enjoying women. There will be about a dozen hookers there. A couple too many, in my opinion, but more than enough to go round."

I glance at Lucy. She's unperturbed, a dreamy look on her face. I guess she's heard this all before. So…this is for real.

"The women who will be there are out of this world, Emma. They are the kind of girls most men dare not even dream about. They are better than any airbrushed model you see in a magazine, because they really *are* that perfect. They are out of reach for just about every man on the planet, unless he is extremely wealthy or stupendously attractive."

Perfect women? Well, that rules me out, doesn't it? I relax, feeling quite safe that this conversation and I are rapidly heading in different directions.

"My friend is a millionaire several times over," he goes on. "The women who will be there tonight will be exceedingly well rewarded for their sexual services. I understand he has booked them for the full evening, and they will be earning several thousand Pounds each for their troubles. Usually he pays them in cash."

He pauses. There's no way to tell if he can see the effect his words are having on me. He must be talking about the kind of upper-class orgies I thought only happened in books. I have a few books like that next to my bed. I try to stop my mind recalling some of the country house scenes I've enjoyed so much. I can't. *How much again?*

"There is a growing number of men, Emma, who have made a certain lifestyle choice. I am one of them. And I am entirely open about it because I prefer not to live a lie.

"In a nutshell, men such as myself have come to the realization that with our levels of income there is no good argument for agreeing to marry someone. Given that we can afford to satisfy ourselves sexually with an unlimited number of the most beautiful women on earth, what sense is there in signing up for a lifetime with someone who will lose their beauty as fast as they increase their nagging?"

I shrug. Because in this moment, I can't think of any good answer to his question. Thankfully, I get the feeling it's a rhetorical one.

"Emma, rare is the man who would choose to be monogamous in an ideal world. Most men settle for it only because they have neither the money nor the looks to live a sexually liberated life. My wealthy friends and I don't have to settle for anything of the sort."

I'm listening to him intently now. His words make crystal-clear sense to me. Everything I've ever experienced with men is falling into place. I'm supposed to be outraged by his views, so politically unacceptable, so many centuries outdated. And yet…surely a good argument should be allowed to trump political correctness? I feel enlightened.

"The ladies who work for us are exceedingly happy that we've reached the conclusions we have," Charles continues. "They live extraordinarily well. Sometimes they only work one evening a week. Usually more, though, because they love what they do. If there's one thing we loathe as escort customers, Emma, it's a woman who gives the impression that she's only there for the money. Those ones don't fool us for a second, and they don't get invited back."

Enjoy sex? *Why yes, Mr Charles. Yes I do.* Though it's been a bit of a drought lately.

Fuck, I wish my mind would shut up. It's got me going down on him now, champagne glass in one hand while my other massages his balls. I sense another man, of similar age, is about to enter me from behind.

It feels damp between my legs. He's talking again. *Wake up Carling!* Suddenly I'm very aware of just how long a drought it's been for me. Fourteen months and counting.

"Our girls are more powerful than we are, quite frankly. There are some who could have absolutely anything they want off us. For all our money, the girls could ruin some of my well-known friends if they were not discreet. The best of these women are so addictive that we cannot say no to them. Sometimes it gets to a point where they can name any price. And people say men rule the world?"

He shakes his head and chuckles. I'm dead quiet, straight-faced. Damn, he's right. He's absolutely right in everything he's saying. His words, so well-delivered, have found a willing believer.

And I've just taken him deeper. My tonsils are tickling his tip and my lips are inching towards his balls.

I'm jolted back into the room by Lucy's voice. She's suddenly business-like.

"Emma, my agency supplies most of the girls to Charles and his friends. We don't advertise. We don't have a website. In fact we don't even have a name. We are truly exclusive and have just a handful of clients. Only with a personal introduction do people even get my number. As a personalised service, I work alone: I believe I need to know my clients and know my girls. I couldn't trust anyone else to do that.

"I'm incredibly careful when recruiting. Rarely do I have more than 25 girls on my books. This is a difficult game, Emma – I am not looking for street-corner whores with a heroin habit. I need outrageously beautiful women with certain looks, personalities and proportions. Most of them need to speak superb English, carry themselves with ease in polite company, and be models of discretion. They have to be healthy, clean and hygienic, and it's my job to make sure they stay that way.

"My escorts obviously need to have fantastic sex skills. I'm sure I don't need to tell you all of the things they might be expected to do, but it's a fairly long list."

She looks right into my eyes. I feel myself blushing. I feel like I am meant to respond, but I'm still tongue-tied.

"Finally, but most importantly, is their attitude. As Charles mentioned, they cannot get away with pretending to be willing. They must *be* willing. They cannot just say 'Fuck me harder' without meaning it. I cannot stress this enough. Remember, I do not take on clients with wives or partners. I wouldn't be comfortable with that. I take on single clients like Charles, and for them my girls *are* their sex life. It needs to be perfect for them."

At last, they have both stopped talking. I feel my turn to speak has come. My pulse is racing away with me and I'm pretty sure my legs might not hold me up right now, but the wetness in my panties, thank God, stopped increasing when Lucy took over the conversation.

"That's pretty well explained," I mumble. "I'm not sure there's much else I would need to ask!"

They haven't really said anything about *me* so far, and I'm happy for it to stay that way.

"I haven't mentioned the money," says Lucy, smiling again. I swear there is a twinkle in her eye. "I take a fixed 25 percent of your earnings from a client. I work on a trust system, and so far I haven't been bitten. Anyway, the rest of the cash is yours to keep."

I notice that she's suddenly started talking about me as one of her employees. Not exactly a subtle switch. I'm about to protest that I haven't said I want to be one of her escorts yet, but Charles gets there first.

"Emma, let me come to the point. From what I've seen and heard of you, I feel that you would be a delicious addition to Lucy's cast of ladies. We've been looking for someone with your personality for a while, and it goes without saying that you look the part. You'd work very well with most of the other girls. But there's a little more to it, isn't there Lucy?"

I'm glad he's stopped talking. His words are making my heat rise once again.

"That's right," says Lucy. "I'm pretty sure we'll be thrilled with you, Emma, but I still can't risk trusting a hunch with such important clients. You will need to earn a relevant qualification first."

I start. "A *what*?" I begin to chuckle, glad the tension has dropped a little with this joke. "Come on…there are no qualifications for…are there?"

"There absolutely are, Emma. Well, actually, there's only one worth having."

She's deadpan. Shit, the woman's not kidding.

I wipe the smile off my face.

"There is an advanced course recognised by upper-class escort agencies the world over. A small group of you spend two intensive weeks at a special location in the countryside. The purpose is to test and hone your sexual skills, nail down your specialities, and finally to ensure that you walk out with the attitude and the ability I've spoken about.

"Most of the work is practical and it's a *lot* of fun! They have some really excellent teachers." She's smirking now. "I've never spoken to a girl who didn't love it. They all say it was essential preparation for her first client.

"Emma, Charles has offered to pay all your fees if you would like to attend the school. There is a course beginning on Monday. Can we interest you?"

Until now I have hardly said a word to them. My hands are still sweating, I keep looking at my shoes and I still don't feel ready to stand. I don't know what they see in me, but…this man wants to *sponsor* me now? Bloody hell. I'm thoroughly flattered. I'm singing inside. Is that wrong?

I won't show my pleasure. I can't. *Straight face, Emma, straight face*. I should at least say 'I'll think about it'. But then… fuck it! Who am I kidding? I have an empty diary and moist underwear. Oh yes, and a rapidly-diminishing bank balance too. I might have slammed one door shut last week, but these people are opening another right before my eyes.

"Okay," I say, finally looking Charles and Lucy in the eye as an equal, albeit with nothing approaching confidence. "Count me in."

I can't believe I just did that.

Chapter Three

No way am I going to sleep. The train is a slow one, drifting through the countryside like it knows it's a Sunday. The carriage is almost deserted. Afternoon sun pours in, making my knees pleasantly warm as it bakes the denim of my jeans. I should be getting drowsy by now, after the frantic few days I've had, but I can't keep my thoughts quiet enough. They're racing ahead of me, and just keeping up with them is enough to keep anyone awake.

Instead, I sit with my hands clasped together, hunched forward and probably frowning. I look at the soft black travel bag I've brought, which sits on the seat opposite me. There's really not a whole lot in there for two weeks, I think to myself for the twentieth time.

I'm paranoid that some stranger is going to want to chat, ask me where I'm off to, why my bag is so small. Ludicrous: this is England. Strangers do not chat. And anyway, there's only one other person in this carriage. An elderly man with a dog on a lead. Heading home from Sunday lunch and a walk in the fields, I'm sure. I glance at him, but his nose is still buried in *The Times*.

I sigh. Are we there yet? Do I want to arrive at all? I chew even harder on my gum and stare out of the window as Cotswolds idyll slides past in the softening summer light. Some sheep, the odd cow, plenty of yellow rape flowers. Even the horses are feeling lazy: I spot several lying on their sides in the paddocks. I wonder if they're judging me. *Shut up, Emma, you idiot.* Horses mount each other in full view of everyone, don't they?

There's a crazy nightmare thought that won't leave my head: what if my parents climb aboard? *For fuck's sake Emma!* Mum and Dad *never* take Sundays in the country by train. Dad will be watching the football and Mum will be badgering him to do some chore or other. Ugh. That whole image helps me. It makes me glad I'm doing this experiment: no way do I want to get into *that* kind of domestic bliss.

Only Martin knows where I'm going. Parents and friends alike have been sold the line that I'm taking a holiday on a *very* small Greek island. One that has no phone signal. My folks took some convincing that my cottage didn't have a landline or anything, but eventually they had to accept my incommunicado trip. I'd just lost my job after all – who wouldn't want to get away from everything for a couple of weeks? Whatever. My story will have to do. I'd rather die than tell my folks where I'm headed.

I keep wondering if any of the other girls starting tomorrow are on this train, but I've hardly seen a soul at any of the country stations we've stopped at. I wonder if they will have brought more than I have. But the letter said we wouldn't need to bring much clothing. Just a couple of casual outfits. It said most clothing would be supplied, 'where necessary'. Ever since I started packing yesterday, I've been wondering what that meant.

Apart from that, I've just got my toothbrush and toiletries, a couple of books, my phone and my iPad. But if this train ride is anything to go by, I won't be doing much reading in the next two weeks. I tried, but I just couldn't seem to focus. Images kept invading my head. Charles sitting in a plush, comfortable armchair, beckoning me over to him; my handsome high school maths teacher calling me to the front of the class and instructing me to bend; feeling the tight cling of a close-fitting black dress as I ring the doorbell of a Mayfair apartment.

The man with the newspaper folds it up and rises as we pull into another deserted station. His spaniel, head down, strains at the leash as they walk towards me. The gent nods casually at me as he passes, giving one of those awkward half-smile, half-grimace greetings we English like so much. I flush in response. What if he knows?

I'm alone in the carriage now. Next stop is mine.

The end of the line. Trains do not penetrate the Cotswolds beyond this station. I stand up and brush myself down. Silly, really: I'm only in a baggy black t-shirt and jeans, and my hair's such a mess I've simply tied it up and hoped for the best. If I wanted to impress anyone, it's way too late.

But still. I'm being met. By someone. And that nervous, first-day-of-term feeling has come back to me.

I take a deep breath as I gather my bag and make for the door. Cautiously, I open it and climb down the steep drop onto the platform. Only a handful of people are spilling out of the other carriages. The train's motor has been switched off, and the sounds of chirping birds are louder than the footsteps of my fellow passengers. The turbocharged trot of high heels that follow me everywhere in London is conspicuous by its absence on this gorgeous Sunday evening in the country.

I'm a long way down the train, and most people have reached the platform exit long before I do. From what I can see, most of the passengers are a lot older than me. The sort of people who might have gone to a museum in Oxford for the afternoon, or taken tea in one of the small towns on the way. But I notice one young woman who stands out like a beacon. She's my age…no, younger. Maybe only twenty. That's a *short* skirt. Fuck, she's drop-dead sexy. Oh my God. She's *so* one of us. I'm *so* not going to fit in here.

She's messing with her phone as she walks, but I can tell she's spotted me. She doesn't show it. She looks like she knows *exactly* what she's doing. She doesn't have the uncertain walk I'm sure I've got, nor is she curiously taking in her surroundings like I am. It's a mite intimidating.

I keep my eyes down. She reaches the doorway before me. I follow her through the small ticket office and blink as I emerge into the bright sunlight. There's little more than a patch of gravel outside. Typical rural station: they've built it well outside the village.

A car has pulled up just to the right of the doorway. It's a Jaguar, but I'd guess it's one from the sixties. British racing green. A smart chauffeur stands next to the passenger doors, both of which are already open. I'm relieved we're just about the last ones off the train: this is not the low-key pickup I'd have chosen for my arrival. I thought this school place was meant to be discreet?

"Miss Carling! Miss Stoycheva! Welcome!"

The chauffeur gestures towards the car doors. The blonde in front of me, whom I gather must be Eastern European, barely nods at the chauffeur, and makes for the front seat. She's carrying even less than I am. Still hasn't said hello. Hmm. I'm not getting a great vibe here.

"Err, hi…" I say.

"I'm Chris and I'll be taking you ladies through to the school. Pleased to meet you!" He offers a hand and I shake it. He's smart in his uniform, and his easy manner has a calming effect on me.

"Good journey?" he asks as he motions me towards the back door.

"Yeah, it was OK," I smile. "Probably did too much thinking though…"

"Ah, don't you worry," he says, closing the door after me and making his way to the driver's seat. "That's normal enough, although we get all sorts of reactions here."

He looks over his shoulders at me and rolls his eyes towards the bitchy blonde, still tapping away on her phone. I grin back at him. I like Chris already.

"This is already an unusual experience," I say to him as he turns the key and the engine bursts into life with a throaty rumble. "First time I've had a chauffeur or ridden in a car like this. I wasn't quite expecting it…"

"I'm not sure how much you've heard," says Chris as we pull out onto a narrow country lane. "But you can expect to be treated very, very well. It's all….you know….part of getting used to some of the circles you might be moving in when you're done."

I stay silent, not knowing how to answer these vague yet loaded words. The leathery interior is warm and comfortable, but I'm not quite ready to pursue this conversation with a man I've just met. There's still an overthinking part of me worrying that I've got the wrong end of the wrong stick, or that the whole school-for-hookers thing is one big, fat, practical joke.

I change the subject. "Lovely out here, isn't it? I'm a city girl really, never been out this way much."

"Oh, you poor thing! The countryside is gorgeous round here, and in this weather there's nowhere I'd rather be. I'm from these parts so I would say that, but I bet you'll agree soon enough! Where we're going is one of those well-kept secrets – a long way from any trains or big roads – you'll love it out there!"

I smile, roll down my window and nestle into the back seat. There's a sunbeam draped across me, and I feel better now than I did on the train.

"We've got about 40 minutes through the back roads," says Chris. "Just relax and enjoy the ride."

"Well ladies, we're just about here."

I sit up and take in my surroundings. True to Chris's word, it's gotten quieter and quieter as we've driven closer to our destination. We've been mostly on single-track roads, and passing traffic has been rare. Once or twice we've had to pull into a widening to let somebody squeeze by, but the few passing cars have mostly deferred to our stately Jag.

The road we're on now is very shady, with willow trees hanging low on the left hand side. They brush my window as we motor past. To the right, a hedge, and beyond that a field of sheep, still drenched in sunlight even after seven o'clock. Now Chris has his flicker on, and I feel a pulse rise in my throat. We must be *there*.

The car takes a left at a break in the willows, and pulls up in front of iron gates framed by two grey stone pillars. Curious, I lean forward between the front seats for a better view. There's a stone bird of prey atop each pillar. Our chauffeur presses a button somewhere on the dash and the gates begin to open.

We pass through onto a gravel driveway. Even the bitchy blonde seems interested now. Chris swings the car to the right and I gasp.

Holy shit! There's a mansion in front of us. No, wait, a château. It's built in a French style, not the usual Cotswolds way, although the masonry is as beige as the rest of the houses in this part of the country. Two wings extend out towards us, like big arms waiting to gather us in. The wings are longer than the middle section is wide. It's more eccentric than beautiful, but certainly imposing.

I can see two storeys of enormous windows, seven on the front and eight on each of the side wings. That's a lot of rooms. Now I notice more windows, small ones protruding from a dark roof, quite reminiscent of the Louvre's in Paris. Attic rooms, maybe. I even notice a couple of haphazard turrets, with tiny windows of their own. I wonder where I'll be sleeping.

This is no school. This is a manor house. A country place for someone very, very rich. Maybe even someone royal. And a lot of servants.

Chris lets me out of the door and I raise my eyebrows as I take in the full scale of it all while I stretch and try to look comfortable. I somehow expected something a little more institutional. If there really are only twelve of us then there'll be room to spare. I smile at the thought that this will be my home for two weeks.

"Welcome to Cranleigh House. Do you like what you see?" says Chris.

"It's like…well, it looks a lot more spacious than my place in London!"

"I think you're right there. And the grounds are endless. Just watch out for the ghost!"

I blanch. Even the other girl gives Chris a worried look.

"Only kidding, girls! Probably…"

He winks at me, but not her.

"But Chris, this looks like someone's home! Whose is it? Do they actually live here?"

"Ah, that would be telling. Actually even I don't know, Miss Carling. Honestly. These things are kept secret, and I'm sure you can understand why. But clearly he's not short of a penny or two. And he must like his home being used for…training purposes."

He clears his throat and beckons us towards the front door.

"I'll be leaving you here, ladies. You'll be in good hands."

Before I can say anything he touches his fingers to his cap, turns on his heel and makes for the Jaguar.

For a moment I am alone with the other girl, stranded on the doorstep and wondering what will happen next. I try to give her a smile, but her blue eyes flit past mine and look away. I am not even sure if she speaks English. She snorts impatiently and pulls out her phone again. I'm sure she's just avoiding talk: the letter made it quite clear there would be no signal out here.

The heavy door begins to open. It creaks, and all I can see at first is gloom. But now a woman appears. She has a kindly, bespectacled face, like that of a favourite aunt. She must be in her early sixties, and wears a long dress. If she's meant to look like a teacher, she's got it spot on.

"Hello girls! Lovely to see you – that's everyone now!" She beams with delight. "Come in, please! Both so beautiful! I'm Miss Honeywell, I'm the housekeeper. Now, which of you is which?"

I like this lady.

"I'm Emma Carling…" I volunteer.

She shakes my hand warmly. Then she looks at the other girl, who remains expressionless.

"You must be Petra then!"

"Yes." It is the first time I have heard her speak, and one word is enough to confirm that she does have a thick accent. There's absolutely nothing in her tone that makes me want to like her, and somehow I'm not surprised. They shake hands and we follow Miss Honeywell inside the mansion.

"You must be tired from your trip! I'd best show you two to your room."

Room? I have to share with *her?* I sigh inwardly as I bite my tongue. I'm not going to get into any arguments right now. I had my fill of those at my last job.

"The house is pretty empty tonight," continues Miss Honeywell as we head toward a grand central stairway. "The main staff don't arrive till morning. But you can leave your bags here. Wilfred will bring them up in a moment!

"It's my job to get all of you girls settled in. I'll be here throughout your stay, and I'm in charge of your day-to-day care. That means anything you need outside of your instruction, especially your food, is my responsibility. You can always come to me if you want anything."

We're climbing the staircase now. Petra is ahead of me, and I can't help noticing the golden strip of skin between the bottom of her close-fitting blouse and the top of her skimpy skirt. Her butt is right at my eye level, and it's undeniably cute. The cheeks bobble up and down in time with her leg movements. I'm feeling decidedly unglamorous, and wonder what the other girls have chosen to wear today.

We turn left at the top of the vast oak staircase, and then we follow the hall around to the right. It feels like we must be moving down one of the wings, but it's hard to tell because the doors are all closed and I can't hear a sound apart from our footsteps. And their echo. Not that Petra's Tinkerbell feet make any sound, I'm quite sure. We walk to the very end, passing beneath a couple of elegant chandeliers, and stop before a stout wooden door with a gold knob.

"Girls, this is to be your room," says Miss Honeywell as she pushes it open. "As you can see, there is plenty of space."

I stop and stare. Plenty of space? This room is, in all seriousness, bigger than my entire flat in Putney. I see two vast, four-poster double beds, deliciously made up with royal blue linen to match their canopies. Thankfully they're far apart. Petra quickly claims the one furthest from the door by trotting across and dumping her handbag on it. Somehow I'm not surprised. This could be a long two weeks.

It looks like we won't have to share very much, at least. There are two dressing tables, two full-length standing mirrors and two chests of drawers, one with an old-fashioned ticking clock on it. There's a tray of expensive-looking designer toiletries on it, and I feel like I'm in one of those hotel rooms I used to hear about from colleagues who travelled around Europe on work assignments.

I notice a beautiful free-standing bath in the corner near the window. Well, it's not so much a window as a French door with a cast-iron railing beyond it.

I walk over to the window and take in the view. I can see the willows, the road we came in on, and beyond that the verdant fields. Nothing but rolling countryside. I get the feeling we must be miles from the nearest neighbour. I shiver slightly at the thought. Maybe it's the evening drawing in. Maybe something else.

Miss Honeywell interrupts my thoughts. "I should point out the walk-in wardrobe," she says as we troop after her to a door between the two chests of drawers. "We have stocked it up according to the measurements each of you sent us last week. Everything on the left is yours, Emma, and everything on the right is for Petra. Starting tomorrow, you will always dress, where necessary, from this wardrobe. Please keep it tidy as much as possible."

There it is again. *Where necessary.*

Even from the doorway I can see it's like a small clothing shop inside there. I feel myself gaping at the sheer volume of it all. I'm not sure what I'm supposed to do. "You'll have plenty of time to look through all that this evening," breezes the housekeeper. "Let me show you your underwear."

She waves at the chests of drawers. "You're not to wear any of your own underwear after tonight. You will find everything you could ever need in those drawers. Again, yours is on the left, Emma. Everything in there is brand new…you're such lucky girls to be young enough to wear what's in there, that's all I can say!"

I smile at her. I like her style, and couldn't have asked for a friendlier welcome. Apart from my icy room-mate, that is.

"Girls, we like to let you rest on your first night. Wilfred will bring you your bags and an evening meal shortly. Tomorrow you'll get properly briefed and shown around. The bathroom you'll use is just at the top of the stairs. Please don't stray beyond there until after your tour tomorrow.

"I'll say good night to you for now. If you need anything, you can call Wilfred or myself with this buzzer button, but I should imagine you'll be alright getting to know each other. And get an early night: you've got a big day ahead."

Chapter Four

The door shudders closed behind us. I stand in the middle of the room, feeling awkward. Petra has abandoned her phone at last, and gazes out of the window.

I'll take one last stab at this. *Be the bigger person, Emma.*

I walk over to her, muster the most genuine smile I can manage: "Hi Petra, we haven't met properly yet! I'm Emma. It's nice to meet you."

She looks suspiciously down at the hand I've offered her. *Bitch.* But she takes it and shakes, after a fashion. Her grip is limp, even for a girl. She looks me up and down as she does so. She seems more than satisfied: is that a faint smile I see at the corners of her mouth?

"Hello," she says in a syrupy Slavic way. She tosses her head to one side. "Petra. How old are you?"

Strange way to start a conversation. But I'll go with it.

"Oh, um…twenty-six. What about you?"

"I am twenty-two."

She's still standing right in front of me, looking directly at me. It's making me feel uncomfortable. I wander, as casually as I can, to the window railing, and lean on it.

Looks like it's up to me to speak again: "Where are you from, Petra?"

"Bulgaria," she replies.

Of course she is. They're all stunning out there.

"And you…are English, yes?"

"Afraid so," I smile. "You East Europeans can't have a monopoly on the industry!"

Fuck. Have I just been racist? *Nice one, Emma.*

She doesn't react to my nervy attempt at a joke at all. Suddenly I'm terrified again. Terrified that I'm the only one here for the reasons I *think* we're all here for. Especially with this stern, strong, beautiful woman before me. A woman who knows she's already one up on me.

"Sorry, umm, sorry." I mumble.

She doesn't acknowledge this.

"Why are you here?" she asks.

Just the question I don't want. And she puts it to me with a tiny smirk. Great, this one wants to play nasty games. I don't think that can lead to good things.

I feel myself twisting my ankles like a shy schoolgirl and do my best to avoid the elephant in the room. That prostitution thing.

"I guess I just…want to learn. I lost my job last week. Time for something new. You know?"

She shrugs.

"And…you?"

Petra stays silent a moment. For the first time I sense unease in her, now that I've thrown the ball back into her court. Then she folds her arms in front of her chest and fixes me with her gaze again.

"Just some regular training for my work," she says, and looks away to her left.

I'm taken aback. "Regular training? You mean…you've been before? Are you…"

She cuts me off: "I am already three years a hooker. I have not been here before. Okay?"

A hooker already? Jesus. What's going on here?

The blonde Bulgarian stalks off in the direction of the walk-in wardrobe. The elephant in the room has been dealt with, but I get the sense question time is over. I turn to face the open window again. It's quiet outside. So quiet. The merry birds of daytime have abandoned their song as twilight draws in. I long for a breath of wind. Anything.

My mind is racing, though. Aren't we all supposed to be rookies here? Or did I just assume that? Now that I think about it, nobody explicitly said so. Suddenly I'm afraid that I might be the only one. Maybe this is a practical joke after all. A joke on me. But all I know for sure is that my room-mate just became a whole lot more intimidating.

And why on earth does an experienced escort need to come here for lessons?

No bitch is going to get *me* down. I taught my boss that just the other day. Petra can be what she wants to be. Yes, I'm curious. But I have patience. For now, she can do as she pleases. They all can. I'm going to check out that wardrobe.

I barely notice the rummaging Petra as I walk in and turn to my side of the well-lit closet. There must be a hundred different outfits in here! A cursory glance reveals glittering evening gowns, a few expensive-looking skirts and a variety of blouses. There's the smell of dry-cleaning. I spot a selection of handbags crammed onto one of the shelves.

And then my eyes fall upon the shoes. They fill the floor beneath the hanging clothes. There are more on the shelves, in shoe compartments. Oh my, what a trove. Mostly they are high heels. Red, black, blue. Decorated, jewelled, pure glamour. Some of those heels look uncomfortably tall. The thought of wearing them thrills me a little, though. Like the prospect of a roller-coaster ride.

I pick up a pair of black leather heels and hold them up to my nose. New. Definitely new. I sniff a purple velvet slipper and it's also got that never-worn smell. I feel woozy at the thought of the money that must have been spent on all this. A little guilty, too. Was all this really bought for *me?*

This closet is every girl's dream, but butterflies start dancing in my tummy as I look more closely at the clothes. The more clothes I find, the more I sense the expectation attached to them. Deeper inside the cupboard, at the far end of the railing, I notice some more unusual items. A couple of business suits in the style favoured by my cow of an ex-boss. And that flash of white hanging behind it? I unhook it: a one-piece nurse's uniform. It's small. In fact most of the clothes look like they'll be a little tight, come to think of it. They've erred on the low side of my measurements.

I pull more items down from the railing. I'm startled to find a slim-fit dress with two very deliberate holes in the front of the top section. *Hmm.* There are numerous skimpy miniskirts, a pair of riding tights and what looks to be a complete school uniform kit.

There's some decidedly militaristic stuff too: a couple of khaki uniform jackets with matching caps. A swastika catches my eye, and something from recent news items comes flashing back to me. Who was that big shot caught cavorting with fancy hookers in Nazi gear? I shake my head and try not to think about it, but the tremble comes. It's not hard to do the maths here.

I rummage once again. A couple of bathrobes, one of them highly transparent. There's an emerald-green one-piece bathing suit. I like the mermaid colour, and picture myself diving into fresh, clear water looking a million bucks as it hugs my figure. There are several bikini bottoms: some with matching tops, others conspicuously mono. Some polo shirts that pair with sporty tennis skirts. Curiously, there's even full-front apron. Several plump, fresh bath and swimming towels fill a broad shelf near the bottom. Some classic, wispy nightwear. They were right: we wouldn't want for clothing here. *Where necessary.*

Just when I think I've seen it all, I pull out a black, backless dress. Except it's more than merely backless. It takes me some time to understand it. There's nothing below the neck strap, apart from another strap to go around the waist. Anyone wearing this would be completely bare to anyone passing behind her.

I let out a low whistle, and hear Petra look around. I've almost forgotten her, but there she is, with what looks like a British Airways stewardess's uniform in her hand. She sees the dress I'm holding, and I hear her snicker for the first time. My bemusement seems to amuse her.

I'm full, and I'm drowsy already. We've just been served a simple but tasty meal in our room. It was only soup and thick, chunky bread, but the ingredients and preparation hinted at a kitchen that knows its stuff. Petra, who is only just the right side of anorexic, abandoned hers halfway through and started reading, but I wolfed down everything. Nothing keeps me from my food.

I put my tray to one side and sit up on my bed. It's dark inside now: I reach over to the lamp and switch it on. There's now a pleasant glow on my side of the room. I'm relaxed, but it seems a little early to sleep. What I really want to do is unwind in that big bath. Does it really have to be out in the open like that?

Hang on, no. If I want a bath, I'll have one. Screw her. She's not going to spoil my evening. She's not going to spoil anything. The new Emma has got no patience for attitude.

I start as another knock at the door interrupts my thoughts. I hear Petra say something in a foreign language, and another woman lets herself in.

I'm surprised to see another beautiful female push her way into the room. Visitors already? She's an absolute screaming babe with inky-black hair. She barely nods at me as she passes my bed *en route* to Petra's, chattering all the way in what I assume is Bulgarian. Here we go again. Petra rises and hugs her, smiling. So, she's not a complete bitch to *everyone*, then. Which just makes it worse.

I know they're talking about me. I can hear my name mentioned, and the new arrival looks over and chuckles at least once. They're hotter than me, and they know it.

"It's Lilia," Petra pipes up at last. I guess this is her attempt at an introduction. "We work together in London."

"Oh, yes, hi," I mutter. Another veteran hooker, no doubt. Can this get any worse?

Don't be so paranoid, Emma. Stop it, right now. You're gorgeous, they said you were gorgeous. Martin said you were gorgeous.

Lilia and Petra make their way over to the closet, evidently to have a little look at the clothes stash. They close the door, but I can hear them giggling inside. I wonder what they're trying on?

Soon enough they emerge together, talking non-stop. Lilia wears a schoolgirl's uniform which had better have come from Petra's side of the cupboard. She pulls it off brilliantly, of course. Her hair is only shoulder-length, but it shines like every strand has been polished. She's quite skinny, but her breasts are prominent in that tight blouse. Just right for a saucy schoolgirl. Her skin is quite dark, her lips full and red. A pretty picture, whatever the angle.

Only now do I notice Petra. She's stripped down to her underwear. Something a lot frillier than what I am wearing. They giggle their way over to the window. Lilia pinches Petra's ass on the way. I'm not sure if this is a show, or they're just enjoying their try-on session on what is still a muggy night. Either way, they both end up leaned out over the window railing, smoking.

Nice of you to offer. No, that's okay, I brought my own.

I try to keep my eyes off Petra, leant on the balcony rail with her forearms, but I can't do it. I have a great angle, rear three-quarter. Her long legs are mesmerizing, all the longer for that pair of very high heels. Black ones. The underwear is red, and it does almost nothing to hide the two shapely crescents of her creamy-gold behind. It sticks out, nearly naked, waggling proudly every so often. It is a work of art, and this woman knows it.

I gulp as I admire her tight stomach, which loses none of its poise while bent over. It's as if she bends without bending;

there's no seam and no apex between her torso and legs. Even standing still, the curve of her body is like one flowing movement. In the soft light of the bedside lamps, she is a goddess.

A bitch, yes, but a beautiful one. It makes me worry. *Shit. Look away. Now.*

Right, I'm having that bath. It's getting late, but I just need to chill for a while. Petra's friend is gone, and my room-mate is lying on her bed, reading something once more. Thankfully she's changed into something less sexy for sleep: a t-shirt and a pair of shorts. Very short shorts, but less troubling.

I get up, pad across the wooden floor in my bare feet, and try the taps. As you'd expect in a big old house like this, the warm water takes a while to emerge. But emerge it does, and the plug seems to be working. I smile to myself. This is going to be luxurious – and never mind the audience.

"I'm just going to use the bath before bed," I tell Petra, who hasn't even looked up since I started speaking. "I'll be quiet if you want to sleep."

"Yeah," is all she says, face still in her book. Couldn't be less interested. Still, am I going to undress right in front of her? I ponder this as I let the bath fill up until the bubbles almost spill over.

As I go to the closet to collect a towel, I remember the bathrobes. Of course! I close the door, switch on the light and pick out an orange, oriental robe with a blue dragon motif. It's a little gaudy, but at least it's not see-through. I quickly strip down, shove my clothes in a basket marked 'dirty washing' and don the robe.

I go back out into the room. Petra is unmoved. A thought occurs to me: I should lock our door. But I can't find a latch. I sigh. Oh well, so much for privacy. No visitor is going to see me under the bubbles anyway.

With as little fanfare as I can, I walk over to the bath, turn my back to Petra and drop the robe to the floor. Fast, before I can change my mind. I climb into the bath. It doesn't feel graceful. I'd swear blind I can feel her eyes on me.

But now I'm under the bubbles. I'm safe here. I lie back, facing the window. I can see the dark trees and the sky through the open shutters. A pale moon glows behind limp, skinny clouds. There's still no breeze, the curtains hang lifeless. The soft chirp of a cricket is all I can hear. This is as blissful as I'd hoped it would be.

Petra does nothing in particular to spoil my peace. I think back over the day. I've only met two other girls so far: nine to go! As for teachers, or whatever they call them in a place like this, I suppose I'll find out tomorrow. I hope that everyone is as endearing as Chris and Miss Honeywell. And I hope not all the other girls are veteran hookers.

Yes, there's plenty I can worry about if I think about it too much. So instead, I think of myself two weeks ago, psyching myself up for another maniacal week at the office. Sunday nights were always the worst, that ghastly time when I stood on the precipice of the real world again. Right now, my friends back in London are getting an early night for all the wrong reasons, or God forbid, even making a head start on their emails.

Now, here, I'm on the precipice of something, yes. But something exciting, a new world. Something *naughty*. No, I don't want to trade this. The Jaguars, the wardrobe, the huge bubble bath? The...*no Emma, don't think of that yet.* I'm a lucky girl, even if I have to have a moody room-mate. I'm going to give this my best shot.

Chapter Five

A ferocious ringing startles me awake. *Ding-ding-ding-ding-ding.* The sound is full and rich, shrill and insistent. Where is it coming from? What's going on? And where am I? *Ding-ding-ding-ding-ding.*

The infuriating noise stops abruptly. I groan as the echo subsides and my brain slowly reassembles reality, coming to terms with its unfamiliar surroundings. I'm groggy not just from the sudden wake-up, but because my fears that I would not sleep well were entirely misplaced. I've never known such a comfortable bed.

The satin-soft linen is fit for a princess. After that bath, it had no trouble lulling me to slumber in five minutes flat. I expected to toss and turn, arguing with myself all night. But I felt at one with myself, sticking to my bath-time resolution. I might get nervous in the company of glamorous females, but apart from that I'm feeling pretty comfortable in my own skin right now.

Hooker school! It's my first coherent thought. Holy hell, this is it. It's day one. And things are happening. *What have you done?! Why the hell are you here?!* My pulse quickens and that first-day-at-school knot coils in my stomach. What am I supposed to do? I roll over and glance across at Petra. She's not much more awake than I am.

I start as I hear the door open. It's a man! Perhaps in his fifties, but with a far more youthful air than that. Even through my crusty eyes I can see he's a satisfying six foot two, and there is something of Colin Firth about him. I follow him with my eyes as he enters the room, and I'm a mix of curiosity and apprehension.

He's a most pleasant sight to wake up to. His chestnut hair is gelled to perfection, almost reflective. He's very smartly dressed; his tailored suit fits him and his strong shoulders just right. It's almost over the top at this time of day. His outfit borders on black tie. Despite my bleariness I notice the intense shine of his shoes. They do not look cheap.

He does not introduce himself. Instead he walks in with the confidence of somebody who is used to being obeyed without a word. It's that x-factor I've noticed with some of the boardroom types at work. I smell him as he passes the foot of my bed. Musk and spice.

He seizes the curtains and pulls them open to reveal another blue-sky day. Then he turns to face us.

"Miss Stoycheva, Miss Carling. Good morning. You will report to the showers when you hear the bell in ten minutes. Bring your towels and toiletries only."

With that, he crosses the room again, walks out of the door and closes it behind him.

I feel my nerves begin to dance as I awake fully to what he said. And *how* he said it. Was he doing an impression of a piggish client? Or is this how the teachers will be? There was something in his authoritative manner that hinted at a testing morning. I fear we're not going to be easing in as gently as I hoped. If only someone will tell me what I'm supposed to do, every step of the way, I might survive.

I look to Petra. Her hair's in a bit of a state, but otherwise she shows almost no effects of sleep. Experience tells me I'm probably not so lucky. She's up and moving before I am; seems to have taken the orders in her stride. My room-mate appears unhurried but purposeful. She walks to the window and lights up one of her cigarettes, turning her back on me as she looks out over the countryside.

I sit up and look around the room, at a loss. The instructions were clear enough. The implication was that we'd undress here, wrap up in towels and then head down the hall to the bathroom. I just wish…I just wish Petra will do it first so I can copy what she does. She says she hasn't been here before, but she's in the game, *ergo* she's someone I might want to copy. My pride, though, won't let me ask that cow for help.

I yawn, stretch and tentatively step out of bed. Like Petra, I'm in shorts and a t-shirt. I guess there's not much to do but take them off. I make for the wardrobe, still wondering who that man was. I have a feeling we'll cross paths again. I know the question will play on my mind. I do wish I could shut down that curiosity of mine sometimes.

I'd prefer Petra not to walk in on me getting changed, so I'm quick once again. In just seconds I'm wrapped up in one of the big, fluffy, white towels. And now, I'm not really sure what to do with myself.

I idle some time away looking through the clothes again, and wonder what I'll wear today. What do you wear on your first day at school? Especially *this* sort of school? The school uniform seems logical enough, but isn't that just silly? Then again, it's one of very few things suitable for daytime use. This closet has been filled by a night owl, by the looks of it.

I'm startled as Petra opens the door. *Oh God!* She's already topless. She must have whipped off her t-shirt as she walked across the room. This woman is not shy. She gives me a cruel smile that says 'I know'. She seems utterly comfortable, but I feel I must look away. I quickly push past her, mumbling apologies. *Jesus, what are you sorry for? You're so fucking English, Emma.*

I sit on my bed, waiting. I did notice one thing: her breasts are not big. Of course they aren't: she's petite and perfectly-proportioned. But I smile to think that I have an edge on her in the chest department. Mine are ample and support themselves well: I've always been able to fill a tight top rather snugly.

Petra emerges, thankfully wrapped up in a towel just like I am. She comes over to my bed and sits down to wait with me. She doesn't speak, nor seem to care about the silence.

"He *did* say something about another bell, right?" I ask.

She shrugs. "Yes, I think so…so we wait."

"I wonder if it will be the same every morning?" I muse.

Petra takes this as a purely rhetorical question, not a chance to take the conversation further. She just plays with her fingers, waiting. What. A. Cold. Woman.

A few more awkward moments of silence. Then footsteps. We hear the bell come closer as it stops outside each room. A door slams in the distance.

We don't wait for the infernal *ding-ding-ding* to come any closer. We step out into the dim hallway. A couple of towelled women, only their shoulders and calves bare, are already making their way to the bathroom. So it's to be all of us, then. *Crap.* I keep my head down as we pass our waker and his bell.

The walk down the hall seems to take an eternity. I hear the sound of running water beyond the bathroom door. I popped here to use the toilet before bed last night, and I noticed then that this room was different to what I'd seen of the rest of the house. It was quite modern inside, and sparkling with cleanliness. It must have had a lot of work done and was one room that *did* look a little institutional. Including the open-plan shower area.

Fuck. Group shower. It must be. I pray I'm wrong.

I open the door ahead of Petra, glad that I'm not the first one inside. The showers have been switched on, clouds of steam billowing up from the black-tiled floor. And there, I assume, are the rest of my new classmates.

None of the girls has taken the plunge yet. They all seem to be waiting for someone else to go first. There's a nervous energy, an uncertainty, in the room as the others mill about near the benches that run along the wall opposite the shower entrance. There are towel hooks above the benches, and some of the girls are hanging their toiletry bags up.

My heart is absolutely pounding now. I can be very naughty in the company of someone with whom I feel comfortable, but I've always managed to avoid this kind of situation in locker rooms. Not that I mind women's bodies. It's just that I feel a bit shy and awkward about it all.

It doesn't look like there's going to be a choice here.

My wish comes true as Petra leads by example. Or, more likely, just runs out of patience. Without ceremony she picks out her soaps, undoes her towel and steps into the shower like some kind of Viking goddess. There's that ass again. Lilia, whose plump boobs look entirely fake on her smallish body, follows suit. And gradually the herd musters itself to join them. Towels are lost, and now naked strangers tiptoe, understandably coy, towards the hot water.

I hesitate. *Just do it!* I shake my head and unfurl my towel. I hang it up, trying not to notice whether anyone is looking or not. I am nearly the last one in. Nobody has said a word. Meeting a new group of people is awkward enough clothed, and doing it bare only brings on more paralysis. Still, a ripple of excitement takes me by surprise. The naughtiness of it all!

I pick a shower head. They're closer together than I noticed last night, and it appears that there are exactly twelve of them. I'm wedged in between an unusually tall brunette and a cute little girl with shoulder-length red curls. Both are already running soapy hands across their skin.

Only now do I notice the men. Christ, they must have been here all along! How did I miss that? Just above the towel hooks is what amounts to a viewing gallery! There are two men, sitting on plush armchairs. It's beyond bizarre. But you just wouldn't notice them until you were standing under a shower, facing towards them.

Neither of the guys is the man who woke us this morning. They're more casual, in shirts and jackets but without ties, like it's dress-down Friday. I can't see much more than that through the steam. That's probably for the best, because I'm shaking now. Suddenly I want to die.

I look away from the glaring gaze of these shameless male spectators, and catch the eyes of one or two other girls. Clearly they are as surprised as I am, and their reactions mostly mirror mine. A couple are making pathetic attempts to cover their breasts, but we're all rooted to the spot. Only Petra, Lilia and three of the others seem happy to go on as if they couldn't care less. My mind races.

All I am sure of is that I feel more naked than naked. Exposed and embarrassed to a point I've never explored before. But I know there is no place to go. Not if I want to last a morning in this place.

Pretend they're not there.

It's easier said than done, but I begin to wash. It's difficult, because I can't truly forget their probing eyes. I avoid bending over, and face the wall as I quickly run my fingers over my genitals. Just then I notice dispensers on the wall: special soap for just that area. Probably wise, I suppose. I smirk to myself, in spite of everything, and rub down there again. My sense of humour, like my new-found temper, is never far from the surface.

Some of the other girls are slowly beginning to relax. Most have accepted their situation, that they can't hide themselves. One of them, opposite me, is still looking particularly uptight though. I watch her as I wash my hair. She is the most spectacular blue-eyed blonde. She sports a ponytail, toned figure and skin just one tiny shade browner than pale. She's still trying to cover herself, and seems to have lost interest in washing. There's a frightened, faraway look in her eyes.

Suddenly she makes to leave the shower, one arm across her nipples and another hiding her pubic hair, shaking her bowed head. She races to her towel, flings it around her and scuttles out of the room. I notice the gallery follow her with their eyes as she makes for the door and runs out.

What was that about? I'm wary of assuming anything here, but her eyes showed real discomfort. On the surface it looks like this whole thing is already proving too much for one of our number. It looks to me like she ran out of nerve. I'm not sure I can blame her. I can't quite fathom how I haven't done the same.

And yet my own tension is easing just a touch. I watch Petra for direction. She is lathering herself nonchalantly. It's efficient and rhythmic. She must know she has watchers, but she makes no special effort to cover herself. She even bends over as she reaches down to wash her legs. I don't get the feeling it's for their benefit; I just don't think she's bothered. I suspect she may have stripped for a living.

Great, and now I'm thinking about bending over for the men. And I'm soaping up my breasts. *Stop it, girl, what's wrong with you?* Nope, they're firming up. Fuck! Can anyone see? *Think of something else! Anything!* I quickly take my hands away and let the water rinse my tits clean, but a glance down reveals what I can feel: you could hang a key ring off those.

I finish up as fast as I can, switch of my taps and scurry to my towel. I rub myself down quickly, all too aware that those guys are right above me. Other girls are making for the door too, now. I glance up as I wrap up in my towel and let myself out: the two men are unmoved.

I'm sitting on my bed again, wrapped in my towel, just trying to catch my breath. Did I just shower with 12 other girls while two unknown men watched us? I congratulate myself for not being the blonde who ran out. Maybe I can do this. How in God's name did I get turned on at the end? Could that be…a *good* thing?

It looks like we'll have to grow up fast in this place. Will I be up to it? I think again of my ex-colleagues slaving in front of their computer screens, and conclude that I'm certainly going to give it my best shot. Anything but that.

I feel the need to compare notes with someone, but get a sinking feeling when I realise I have only Petra for company. And she's disappeared inside the wardrobe. No doubt picking out some figure hugging dress for the day.

The thought of wearing the school uniform comes back to me. We *were* told to choose anything from that wardrobe. And it *does* make sense. Plus, it gives me a tiny thrill to think of myself in it. And right now any clothes at all are enough to make me want to take on the world. *Let's do it!*

"Good morning Emma, I'm Miss Jackson. I'll be your mentor this week and I can't wait for us to get started. I've heard some good things about you already."

The woman standing across the desk from me can't seem to wipe the smile from her face. She must be around forty, and looks a touch eccentric. Her hair is cropped short and dyed bright blonde. Red-rimmed glasses, a pink blouse and a bulky stud in each ear give her something of a theatrical look. She's pretty slight, with no bust to speak of, and not especially attractive. But she looks truly comfortable with herself, and that commands respect.

She shakes my hand and motions me to sit. I smile back at her, wondering what 'good things' she's heard, and smooth my skirt before taking a seat. I wonder what qualifies her to *mentor* here.

"I like your choice of outfit today," she remarks, looking me up and down as she eases into her chair. "Very appropriate. I think you might be the first of our girls ever to try that on day one."

I try not to blush, but I'm glad to hear I'm doing something right.

"Thanks! It kind of made sense to me…first day of school and all that…"

"My thoughts exactly," she smiles. "And you're very sexy in that, young lady. Now, in your own words, what made you want to come here?"

Oh! This introductory meeting is cutting right to the chase. I cough nervously. In spite of the otherworldly shower experience and her reaction to my outfit, I still can't quite bring myself to reference *hooker* training directly.

"Um, I lost my job a week or so ago…well, I walked out actually. And then…I guess I was open to ideas, and a friend of a friend told me about…you know…this."

Miss Jackson nods encouragingly.

"You can say it, Emma, it's okay. You're training to be a prostitute. A sexy, irresistible and highly-skilled prostitute."

I nod, grimace and look down at my knees. The words still jar. She really enunciates the three t's in *prostitute*, like rapid fire. Just so I'm in no doubt. Is this *my* life I'm living this morning? What on earth has happened to me?

But my mind flooded with images, too, when she said 'sexy' and 'irresistible'. Oh, and my, how sexily and irresistibly she said those two words! I think I see Charles again. *Jesus, Emma! Do you want this or not?*

She interrupts my daydream. "Now, having told you how lovely you look in those clothes, I need you to remove them."

I look up at her, shocked. She's dead-pan.

"Please stand up and take everything off," she says patiently. "You can put your clothes on the chair."

I try not to sigh out loud. They want me naked *again*? I only just got dressed! I think my leg starts to twitch, but I stand up. I feel like a newborn lamb getting to its feet. *You can do this. Don't show her you're scared.*

"Okay." I try to give her a convincing smile. "Any particular order…?"

She waves my question away: "Relax, girl, it's not a striptease. I just need you naked. It's a logical starting point, don't you think?"

Logical? I don't know. Logic, like my whole world, has been turned upside down for me in the past few days, but I nod anyway. And pull off my schoolgirl slipper-shoes. Then the long socks: first the left, then the right. My bare feet feel sticky against the varnished wooden floor. I unbutton my blouse and slip it off my shoulders. I have to force myself to stay facing her. Then I undo the clip on my little grey skirt, and add it to the pile on the chair.

I am down to my underwear now. I've put on some of the lingerie provided in my drawer. As instructed. Lacy white bra and panties, relatively modest. The air feels close in here. Muggy, even a little moist. I reach behind my back and unhook my bra, freeing my breasts. She sits back in her chair, seems to like what she sees. But I avoid her eye as I pull down my panties and place the lingerie on the chair.

And now I try to stand up tall, hands behind my back. And I'm fucking naked again. Probably balancing on the outsides of my feet, like I always do when I'm nervous.

"That's lovely, Emma," says Miss Jackson, oozing approval. "Really, you're quite beautiful."

I feel a tiny wave of calm wash over me. There's a long pause. She's just taking me in, the happiness dancing even brighter on her face. I feel flattered, but at the same time massively uncomfortable.

"You'll get used to this kind of thing, trust me," she says, getting up and walking around the desk towards me. "You're doing well. I've seen girls go to pieces."

"Er, yes. Actually…I think I saw one struggle in the shower this morning?"

"You did, Emma," she says wistfully. "It's a real shame, but Cassie won't be staying with us. She decided it wasn't for her. Pity: as you will have noticed, she is a real emerald. And such a beautiful Irish accent too."

She's standing right in front of me now. I'm kind of glad we have something to talk about that isn't me.

"So...we're down to eleven?" I ask, stupidly looking at her shoulder blades.

"That's right, you're an even more select group now! Okay, keep still while I take a nice look at you."

And with that, she touches my breasts. She brushes her thumbs across them both. I breathe in sharply. Somehow I'm not offended, just taken aback. Her hands are warm, but they feel rough, more like those of a man. She gives them a gentle squeeze, then lets go.

"Ah, Emma, I have a feeling the men will like to have these in their hands. Classic shape and size, and all natural. A surgeon could do no better. Lucky girl!"

She walks around behind me, ever so slowly. She takes in every angle, pauses as if to sniff the air around my body. Behind me now, I hear her take a step back.

"Yes, yes, I can see that they were right. Your reputation precedes you, young lady. Stunning cheeks. Oh, they'll get some attention alright. You have no *idea* how much potential you've got."

If she's trying to build me up and relax me, she's doing a good job. I allow myself a smile, since I know she can't see my face. "Thanks," I murmur.

"Now please bend over for me."

Okay, there goes the relaxation. Nice one, lady. Now I feel like a slave at an auction again. *You can't turn back now. Do you want to run scared like the Irish chick?*

"Let's have your feet apart...that's right...all the way down now, hold onto your ankles. Wonderful!"

I'm trembling a little, but whether it's the awkward position or the newness of it all I'm not sure. And I thought I felt exposed in the shower! My bits must be looking her straight in the eye. I hope she's happy.

"Oh, Emma! I'm lost for words!"

This gets weirder and weirder. I gather she's impressed again. Should I say something? All I can manage from down here is a grunt. Probably not great.

For some reason the office comes back to my mind. If they could see me now, bent double with my naked vagina under inspection! I'm not quite sure if it's an improvement, but it's certainly different. I definitely didn't need to go to South America for adventure.

"Now don't move," she orders, "just spread your legs a little wider."

I do as I'm told, my brain practically in meltdown. But all I hear is what sounds like her taking something out of her pocket. She takes a step forward. I sense her close behind me. I can see her shoes through my legs. *What's in her hand?* There's a pause, but she doesn't touch me. I tense. I'm on tenterhooks, fearing the unexpected. And then I hear her take a step back.

"Up you get!"

What was that all about? I don't feel it's my place to ask right now. I just stand up straight again. She gives me a light slap on the bum as she passes me and walks back to her desk, still flashing a toothy smile at me. I wonder if she might be a lesbian. She does look the part.

"I'd like you to stay nude, Emma, but please have a seat on the other chair."

Clearly I am going to be getting plenty of practice in my birthday suit. But if I keep getting reactions like hers, I might just get used to it. I sit down on the wooden chair, crossing my legs and placing my hands on the arms.

"I like to know exactly what I'll be working with, you see. If all goes well, at the end of two weeks, you'll be ready to do a shoot with a photographer at your agency. Photos that will sell you to clients."

I nod again. Pretend I didn't hear the word 'sell'.

"So Emma, your training follows a loose basic structure. The first four or five days are an assessment of where you're at. That means testing you, seeing how you react to situations. We find this far more useful than asking you to fill out some silly forms."

I gulp. I guess I've had a couple of those tests already, then. And nobody could be naïve enough not to figure out what might be coming next.

"Some of these situations you can imagine, others may be less familiar. We don't believe in preparing you for them, because we want to gauge your natural responses and get a feel for your experience levels. There is no need to try and impress. You won't see me all the time, but I will have my sources. You won't encounter anyone whose opinion I don't trust implicitly."

I shiver a little at the implications of her deliberately vague words. I feel ridiculous, sitting here stripped, cool wood against my bare bottom, listening to such talk. I wonder if I am about to wake up, sweating and wet at the crotch. Because…how could I not be excited?

"Later in the week, assuming all goes well, we'll meet here again and formulate a plan for the rest of your training. That means deciding where we want to focus our efforts, and why. Much will depend on your strengths, preferences and aptitudes. You'll have a full say in which way we go and how we examine you in the last couple of days. Between now and then, though, the important thing is for you to enjoy yourself as much as you can."

All of a sudden I am naked, blindfolded and bent over this very chair. Footsteps heavy with intent, approaching behind me. The sound of a zip.

"Emma? Cuckoo! I like that you're dreaming already. But come back to the room." She winks at me.

Shit, was my filthy daydream that obvious? Suddenly I begin to worry about the state of this chair when I stand up.

"Um, sorry," I say. I can't hide much from this lady, that's for sure. I cross my legs the other way, relieved that I don't feel any trace of moisture. Stopped just in time, I guess.

"Don't apologize," says Miss Jackson. "Now, as I said, we're not interested in ticking boxes at this stage, but a candid chat does help me understand who you are. I'd like to hear about your sex life. In your own words."

Chapter Six

Miss Jackson leans back in her chair, offering me no further guidance. I take it she's all ears. She's after my dirt.

I swallow hard. Suddenly being naked in front of her seems like the easy part. But speaking of my sex life? My, that's a broad question. I hope I'm right in thinking she isn't going to judge me for anything I've done. More likely things I haven't.

"Uh…OK…" I mumble.

She smiles warmly at me, tilting her head to one side. But she just won't offer me the crutch of a more direct question. I say the first thing that comes into my head.

"I suppose I've been…well, it's all been pretty normal I guess. I've been pretty careful, and I don't really do one-night things."

I don't mention the three or four exceptions to that. The times when some guy has caught me in the right mood at the right time. Or the time when it was actually two guys. Why do I feel the need to be modest in front of a whoring teacher? Damn this English repression.

"Go on," says Miss Jackson sweetly.

"So…yeah, I suppose I've only had about six or maybe seven partners."

I look out of the window, feeling bright crimson, not sure what else to say. Is that a good number? Enough? What is she after? Kinky details? It makes sense that she might be.

"I guess I've been open to suggestions when I've been with someone I'm really comfortable with. It hasn't quite been all missionary position…"

Dammit, this chick still won't give me anything. She's just nodding, waiting for more. I bet this awkwardness is deliberate.

"I've tried a few pages of the *Kama Sutra*. And I've done some dressing up." I feel the redness rising in my face. "And I kissed a couple of girls at university. Probably did a bit more exploring than that with my friends when we were kids, but I don't think that really counts."

More silence, so I plough on, hoping that means it'll be over sooner: "I've let a couple of boys tie me up. Mostly just silk scarves at home. A little more, once."

She looks at me with a twinkle in her eye. She raises an eyebrow, leaving the obvious question hanging in the air.

"OK, once we tried strapping me to the bed," I continue, staring at the floor. I notice that I've started squeezing my hands between my thighs. I wonder how far down my bare body my flush has travelled. "He added cuffs too. I was okay with it, I trusted him. He wanted to try spanking, and then he used a belt on me."

My arms are shaking now. Is it the revelation or the memory? It was just the once. And we were in a serious, steady relationship at the time. Surely it doesn't make me a bad person.

But I'm stopping here. No way am I going to tell her how hard I came that morning, or how I couldn't sit down for the rest of the weekend. How I came even harder when he did me up the ass that night, hips slapping deliciously against my striped, punished cheeks as he pumped. Nice girls don't....no, I'm not telling her this.

She's not getting everything out of me. I'll keep that thing about having my nipples bitten hard to myself. I can't speak about how I twist them when fingering my own clit, it's too weird. Or that other thing I *always* say yes to...I just can't talk about that.

Doing it, maybe. Talking about it with a stranger? I'm not ready for that right now.

And finally she lets me off the hook.

"Thank you, Emma. I know that's not easy, but it's handy for me."

I puff out my cheeks as I exhale for what feels like the first time in several minutes. I don't bother hiding my relief.

"You can relax now," she smiles, switching modes again. "Just a couple more routine things. For now, your schedule will not be revealed very far in advance. But I can tell you that tonight there will be a formal opening event for this class, in the main banqueting room downstairs. Dress is black tie formal, and it starts at nine o'clock. You'll know your way around by then, as you'll have a tour of the house and grounds this afternoon.

"Your medical results from your checkup and tests in London last week have come through to us. You're all clear, of course. I need to tell you that anyone you encounter here has been through the same process. This is a medically screened environment and no exceptions will be allowed into the house for the duration of your stay. So you needn't have any worries about...expressing yourself."

To be honest I haven't given that much thought. Probably wouldn't have done until an inconvenient moment. Good thing someone else did.

You're going to be doing an awful lot of fucking this week, Emma Carling.

"I also need to inform you of your safe word. If there's one thing you need to remember, it's this. Your safe word is simply 'Rex'. It's the same for all the girls. If ever you are uncomfortable in any situation, say the word. Is that clear?"

I nod. I'm not really familiar with the concept. But again, they seem to have thought of something potentially useful before I did. This setup is professional. Weird, in every way, but professional.

"It's all in this indemnity document, which I need you to sign. It's only one page, and it's straight to the point. It really just protects the school from anyone trying it on with rape claims and the like. One or two girls have reacted strangely when they failed to make the grade."

She hands me a document typed on thick paper. It's not your typical business paperwork. There's no letterhead, the school is referred to simply as Cranleigh House and the other signatory appears to be a lawyer with an impressive list of qualifications following his name.

It gives little away about who I'm really dealing with, but the contents are as straightforward as Miss Jackson says. Miss Emma Louise Carling authorizes the use of her body for any purposes deemed fit by Cranleigh House, unless she uses the safe word. Miss Emma Louise Carling expects to perform and submit to a wide range of sexual activities, according to the needs of any non-student present in the house, for the next two weeks.

Seeing my full name all over the document hammers home just what I'm doing here. Oh fuck, what if this lawyer knows my Dad? Where's this paper going to end up? I hesitate.

"Take your time," says Miss Jackson reassuringly. "I only want you to sign when you're comfortable."

No, I really shouldn't. Too much thinking about the possibilities is only going to scare me off. Instead my thoughts wander to the 'wide range of sexual activities'. And all that that entails.

Fuck it, Emma, you only live once.

I sign away that life of mine.

I'm back in my school uniform, and I'm outside for the first time. Actually, all of us are. The remaining eleven trainees have just had a light, sunny lunch on the terrace. Now we're awaiting our tour of the house and grounds. Lunch was pretty much the first time I've seen any of them with clothes on. And I still have no idea if I fit in.

I look around the group. After what Miss Jackson said, I'm not surprised I'm the only one in uniform. But it's clear our wardrobes are all very different. One girl sports a wispy see-through dress I certainly don't have in my selection. She wears a dark bra and panties beneath. And I thought *I* was brave with my choice.

Most of the others are more modest: tank tops and denim shorts or miniskirts seem the most popular first-day option. Makes sense, in this boiling weather. Needless to say, scanning the terrace is like looking out over a sea of sexiness. This place is so artificial it's not funny: where in the real world would you find one hundred percent of the women are perfect? And suddenly I'm not surprised I've encountered some bitchiness already.

There wasn't a lot of chat over lunch. We were left to ourselves, bar Wilfred's comings and goings to serve us salmon and bruschetta, followed by a fresh, scrumptious Caesar salad. One of the confident ones, exotically beautiful with green eyes, suggested we all stand up and introduce ourselves. I didn't take in many names, truth be told. I'm looking at their sleek, gleaming bodies, and pinching myself at the thought that I belong in this company. If indeed I do.

Petra sat at the end of the table with her compatriot Lilia. At least she was ignoring everyone else the same way she ignored me. I made some effort to get to know the girl opposite me. She's also blonde, but she actually had a smile on her. She's particularly tall and it turned out she's Dutch: good, no wonder she's warm. I like the Dutch. Her name's Simone and apparently she's been flown over here by a sponsor. Is this the world's top whore school or what? I wondered if I was the only English one here, but do hear a couple of home-grown accents further down the long, cloth-covered table.

Now a dark-haired woman called Miss Jillings is about to show us around. I gather she is another one of the mentors. Like my own, she is not especially attractive but has a certain something about her. It's not the warmth of Miss Jackson though. This one radiates frigid authority more than anything.

I'm looking forward to this tour. Hopefully I can just take things in for a change, with nothing being demanded of me. I'll feel a lot more settled once I know where I am.

"I hope your lunch was satisfactory, ladies," Miss Jillings says curtly. "Please follow me."

We descend the stairs from the terrace, to the sumptuous kidney-shaped swimming pool. More than generous in size, it's an outlandish thing to see in England, but this is one of those rare warm spells when it might come in handy. It's surrounded by elegant stone paving and enough sun loungers for us all: certainly it is more set up for recreation than Olympic training.

I'm starting to get a feel for where we are. This is the back garden, so the road we came in on is away to the right. I only know this because I hear a car in the distance: the hedge is particularly thick and tall all along the edge of the garden. We're some way below the main house, but the enormous grounds seem to flatten out at this point.

"I am sure many of you will enjoy the pool if the weather holds during your stay here. I trust you can all swim."

She doesn't wait for an answer, but moves on down the manicured grass. Away to the left I notice a lawn tennis court, and a life-sized chess board. This place really does tick every country house cliché. Croquet too, perhaps? It takes us a couple of minutes to cross the expanse of lawn, and I'm startled to see how far away the house appears when I look over my shoulder.

I want so badly to tell Mum about this amazing place and the treatment we're getting. Since I got dressed in Miss Jackson's office it's been a thoroughly respectable lunch and walk about the grounds! I have almost forgotten what I'm here for. But of course I can't tell Mum. She'd flip out. No, actually, she wouldn't even understand what I was saying. My parents are English decency personified.

The vegetation thickens now as we move lower down the garden. It grows more haphazard. There are a couple of large elm trees, and a couple of mulberry bushes with reading benches beneath. Away to the left, a couple of magnificent, aged oaks. Suddenly I'm not sure which way to look.

"That wooden building up against the hedge is a sauna," announces Miss Jillings. "The fire is always burning and it's particularly pleasant at night, even in summer. You just need to throw some water on the coals to make them hiss. Please note that swimsuits are not allowed inside, in keeping with European hygienic tradition."

"Just like home," Simone murmurs to me. I'm sure we're allowed to talk, but nobody seems quite that comfortable yet.

I raise my eyebrows and give her a genuine smile. Yeah, not surprised to hear Dutch saunas are naked. And naked seems to be a recurring theme around here too. I notice a couple of utterly exposed outdoor showers on a paved area just outside the sauna.

"Ladies, we do guarantee your privacy here at Cranleigh," says Miss Jillings in a louder tone. "At least insofar as outsiders are concerned. You will note the high hedges around the garden. They are very thick and nobody can see through them. The outdoor area is totally safe."

We pass more medium-sized trees: there are a couple of hammocks strung up between them. I notice a swinging bench hanging from one stout branch. Chris the chauffeur was right: these grounds really do go on forever.

"This hedge up ahead is not the end of the land here, but it's the last area you can access," continues Miss Jillings. I notice how thin her lips are. I think I like my own mentor better. "This is the start of the Cranleigh maze. The entrance is at the end over there. Eventually it backs on to some of the estate's grazing lands, but I'm sure they're of no interest."

My draw drops just a little. A *maze?* In this day and age? And this is no miniature either. Its width occupies the entire width of the garden, which is easily a hundred yards. In fact, this far down, all I can see is trimmed hedge. Tall hedge to the right, presumably with the road running beyond it. Tall hedge to the left, presumably with fields beyond it. And, ahead of me, hedge – lower than the boundary fences – marking the front wall of this *maze*.

In the far distance – perhaps a couple of hundred yards away – I can see a slightly taller wall of hedge, which I take to be the lower boundary she mentioned.

"The maze is not to be taken lightly. It has been crafted by experts and is rarely navigated with success by a novice. We do not recommend entering it when you are hungry or impatient, unless instructed to do so. Having said that, the first of you to find the end of it may find the reward pleasantly surprising."

She does not elaborate on this. I notice Petra whisper something to Lilia, who chuckles and glances at me. *What exactly is their problem?*

The garden tour complete, we move back into the house. The middle of the main wing is dominated by the banquet hall, which gives onto the terrace. The main entrance is from the central hallway inside the front door. To the left of the front door is the kitchen, a WC and a smaller dining room where we'll be taking our meals on cooler days. There's a selection of fruit and snacks on the side cabinet, which Miss Jillings says will be left for us at all times. The oranges, grapes and apples look delectable, and I make a note to do a raid later.

"Follow me to the North Wing, ladies," she says, trotting around the corner into the wing opposite our own. "This is the lounge, which is always open to you."

We gather in the doorway and take in the vast room. In the bottom corner of the U-shaped mansion, it looks onto the rose garden next to the terrace. Predictably enough, it's old school in there. It's bright near the windows and the one French door connecting to the terrace, but darker at our end of the room. There must be a dozen leather armchairs. A fireplace. Three or four sofas, including one of the longest I've ever seen. There's no television, no concession to modernity. I doubt there's much point asking for Wi-Fi access. Are we really going to need distractions, anyway?

She moves on into the wing itself, apparently in quite a hurry now. "Here is the library, whose door is also open. On the right are three classrooms, which you'll be getting to know next week. You're free to spend time there whenever they are empty. Beyond these, as you'll know from this morning's interviews, are the offices belonging to myself and the other mentors. Miss Honeywell and Wilfred's quarters are at the end of this wing. All of these are, of course, private and off-limits."

She stops suddenly, turns, and clears her throat. "Now," she says, making stern eye contact with each of us before continuing. "The rules are clear. You may roam the house and grounds as you please. The rooms I have just shown you are common. But rooms with closed doors are absolutely out of bounds, unless you are invited in after knocking, or instructed to visit them. Primarily this means the top floor of the North Wing and the ground floor of the South Wing. Are we clear?"

All of us nod politely. I notice that even Petra manages it.

Closed doors. Oh, there's that curiosity again.

"Very good. You are dismissed until this evening's function. Nine o'clock in the ballroom. Dress code is formal. Be prepared for dancing."

Chapter Seven

I'm deep into the getting-ready process. I've just showered again, this time without company and without the audience. Even the two chairs the men were sitting on this morning were gone. I'm starting to wonder if it was all a dream. I'd ask my room-mate, but she's just so damn unapproachable. She pretty much acts like I don't exist. Fine. Two can play at that game.

She stalks out of the room in her towel. I suppose she's heading for a shower too. I'm glad she's out for a while: this room needs a chance to warm up. And I've got some thinking to do. What am I going to wear? What exactly is tonight all about, and where is it going? Every answer seems to lead to another question.

I'm excited, and intimidated, by all the choice in my wardrobe. And that I'm going to a ball! Time is on my side. The full-length mirror in my corner of the room catches my eye. I have an idea. *Show me what you've got, Emma.*

I throw my towel down on the bed, turn on the light and step up to the mirror, my hands on my hips. It's a long time since I've been able to check myself out like this: my mirror at home is tiny. I smile, because I do like my reflection. Especially when there's nobody here to compare it to.

My eyes are drawn to my breasts. I've always thought them my strongest feature. You couldn't fail to notice ripe, lively nipples like those. They seem darker than the last time I looked. They protrude ever so slightly upwards, like strawberries leaning toward the sun, from bouncy coconut-sized mounds that scream vitality and youth. Any bigger and they'd be trying to droop, but these tits are just right. I cup them in my hands, smile at myself and nod.

I cock my head to one side, pleased with the naked girl before me. She's a tiny bit paler than I'd like, but that's being English for you. The flip side to that is that she doesn't much in the way of tan lines. Down there, I've got my usual landing strip. South of that, I'm freshly waxed. All very tidy, and I assume Miss Jackson approved of my efforts. She certainly seemed rather impressed.

I turn around and look over my shoulder. Yes, this all looks very nice too. I can't wait to see longer hair flowing down my back, but we're looking good. My skin is having a good summer: it's nearly flawless. My ass isn't as tiny as, say, Petra's, but it fits my average proportions well. It melts pleasingly into my thighs, which taper down into knees and calves a little more gently than some of the girls here. I'm not one for the anorexic look: there's some healthy substance to me. More than one boyfriend has told me he liked that, so I'm okay with me being me.

Maybe I can live with the rest of these women. We all have our pluses and minuses, I'm sure. Petra and her miserable friend can fuck off. Whether I will perform as well as they can when push comes to shove, I have no idea.

I'm not waiting for Petra. Lilia has come to prepare with her, and they are still fiddling around in our room, finishing with their makeup. I don't sense excitement, I sense two women going through the motions. I smoke a calming cigarette by the window – my first one since leaving London – watching the two of them do their thing at the dresser. I hope they've noticed how little I needed to tart myself up to look knockout. Yeah, my confidence is holding.

I bump into Simone as I head down the hallway towards the stairs. I figure she must be our neighbour. And doesn't she look great! She's gone for a red dress, pretty conservative really, cut at the knee and only exposing a bit of neck. But she's working it: it really suits a tall woman like her because there's still a lot of curvy leg on show. Especially in those high heels.

"Hey Simone, you look great!" I tell her. She smiles back at me. I can sense she's genuine.

"Aw, but you look better!" she says in her near-perfect English. "Blue really suits you."

I hope she's not just being polite. Picking out clothes isn't my strong suit, and I'd have been wasting my time trying to get an opinion from Petra and Lilia. I've gone for a figure-hugging number. My hem is higher than hers and this dress leaves my shoulders bare. It's backless too.

I feel sexy in this shiny new piece, and Simone just made me feel sexier. I'm such a sucker for a formal evening do. Which is just what this feels like. For now. But part of me thinks we'll be asked to strip before the starters are served. And I'm nervous about that idea.

We walk towards the stairs together, each clutching our little handbags. Needless to say, I found an impressive designer selection of those in my wardrobe too. Butterflies begin to dance in my abdomen now: I haven't had a feeling quite like this since high school.

"Kinda weird, isn't it?" I venture. "It feels like we're going to the prom…what with this being a school and all…"

Simone laughs. "Yeah. Only in this case we don't know who our dates are!"

"And we don't know if this is quite going to turn out like a normal dinner-dance…"

"No," she grins. "They don't like to volunteer information, do they? But take it easy, I'm sure we'll be just fine whatever happens. Just enjoy it and go with the flow."

Easy for her to say! My confidence is ebbing away, and we're outside the banquet room now. Wilfred ushers us in.

"Miss Carling, Miss Veenstra, good evening and welcome. Please come in."

Before I can even take in my new surroundings, a man steps forward.

"Hello Emma, I'll be your partner for this evening. My name is Rupert. The pleasure is all mine."

My first instinct is to snigger. *Rupert?* Is everything going to be like time-travel in this place? But when I look at him properly, my smile is replaced by a gape.

The first thing I notice is his eyes. Emerald green, with flecks of chestnut brown. *Wow.* A day's worth of stubble adorns his chiselled chin. He's in the region of six foot. *Ooh, you'll be snug tucked under his arm!* His hair is dark brown, faultlessly tidy around the fringes but long enough on top to run your fingers through.

My handsome date fits the cut of his tuxedo like a glove. It's the broad shoulders that do it. I can see he is the just the right amount of muscular under that suit of his. When I gather my wits – which I'm not sure I'm going to – I want to stroke his arm. Just to feel the definition I know is there.

He's probably around forty, and I'm close enough to smell him. It's intoxicating, yet a completely new scent to me. A mix of earth and spice. He looks at me with dark, soulful eyes and I melt.

I don't get thrown like this very often at all, but then Rupert is film-star attractive. I can't help thinking that this is beating my school prom by miles already.

He takes my hand and kisses it. Old school. Of course. *Mmhmm.* I'm lost for words. Then he holds out an arm to me. This man knows what he is about. He has an air confidence, but it's on the right side of arrogance. He knows what he wants, but he's still a gentleman.

And this ball is the real deal. I look around the room as he leads me into it. It's been transformed since the last time I saw it. Gone is the long dining table, replaced by a handful of round tables around the edge of the room. These tables stand on fine oriental rugs, peach their dominant colour, but the centre of the room is cleared. I surmise that it's the dance floor. The only thing that doesn't quite ring true is how small the crowd is. It won't exactly be heaving in here, but the setting is spot on.

The thick auburn curtains are closed over the French doors that lead onto the terrace. Soft candle-holder lights around the walls complement the chandelier centrepiece, giving the whole place a cosy, warm ambience. There's a pianist playing incidental welcome tunes on a luxurious-looking grand in the corner. It all feels like an intimate wedding reception: there's nothing to suggest we're at a school for budding whores. The sort of place you can tell your mother about with a smile on your face. I'm just not sure how long that will last.

The room is already fairly full. I recognise Miss Honeywell and Miss Jackson, chatting together, champagne glasses in hand. There are other females, presumably mentors I don't know yet. Or could they be agents, like the one Charles brought with him? Is this like an industry networking thing? There are eighteen or so men, all dressed to the nines, and those who aren't escorting one of our group are chatting with each other or the mentors. I get the feeling they're well known here, and wonder if they're where the money comes from. *Maybe one of them owns this place.* I'm excited by the mystery of it all.

Several of my fellow students are already here too, each with her assigned date at her side. I notice right away that not all of them have been as lucky as me. Though all the men are groomed and dressed to perfection, and most seem to radiate a certain assurance, some of them are considerably older than my father. Not all have my escort's attractive features.

A couple of gorgeous waitresses clad in black and white circulate the room, offering drinks. I don't recognise them as members of our group of trainees. I take some bubbly. I can only imagine pretty waitresses and endless Moët and

Chandon is a big part of life in this privileged world. Fortunately it's a drink to which I'm rather partial.

"Come and meet my friend Harry," commands my companion. "We do a lot of business together and travel all over the world."

An odd opening line, really, but I follow him obediently to a couple standing a few paces away. The man I take to be Harry is handsome in a different way. His hair is longer, almost shoulder length, but he's young enough to get away with it. He carries an extra day's worth of stubble. And his dark, penetrating eyes are appealing, almost challenging.

He looks a little more ripped than my date, and still hot as hell in a tuxedo. I can smell him, too, and it's something a little more familiar. Invictus! I only know it because it's my number one favourite smell on a guy.

And when he opens his mouth to speak, I know he's a Scotsman. I've got all the time in the world for that accent. His is a thick one. Yet cultured. Not Glasgow, for sure. Highlands, I'm hoping. Maybe his family runs a whiskey distillery in the hills…*wake up Emma!*

With him is an English girl I've yet to meet properly. I can't help noticing her red, kissable lips and the way they contrast with her fair skin. She's strawberry blonde, and she's just tall enough to be cute rather than short. There are just a couple of light freckles on her nose. Her accent is posher than I've ever heard in real life. She must be that English Rose so many foreign men seem to crave. Harry introduces her as Jane.

She shakes my hand without warmth, says, "Oh hello, pleased to meet you," with a smile that's obviously fake. I have a good sense for duplicity, and I'm getting a strong feeling of it at this moment. She avoided my eye all afternoon at our tour of the premises. I bet she's forgotten my name already, and I know instinctively that we're not going to hit it off. She strikes me as too stuck-up to be a hooker…but who am I to say? I don't know if I'm going to cut it either. At least this Jane *pretends* to be friendly. Unlike some people I've come across.

I begin to relax and enjoy the evening. It's the first time anything has felt remotely normal in this house. Not that miniature embassy balls – there can't be more than 35 people in the room – are an everyday experience for me. Nor is being on the arm of a handsome, confident stranger who looks after me all night long. But I feel beautiful, and I feel wanted. I think I could get used to this.

I'm glad to finally have the chance to mingle properly, especially since my room-mate seems a lost cause. The alcohol helps, of course, and I'm well into my third glass of champagne by the time our creamy asparagus soup starter arrives. It'll take more than that to get me drunk, but it does help stop me over-thinking where I am and what this is all about. Maybe I've stepped into some kind of time machine, and none of this is real. But so what? The champagne and my date make me inclined to just enjoy it all.

As luck would have it, Petra is at my table. I'm amused to see that she's drawn a short straw with her date. Her man, Ralph, is well past sixty, and his weather-beaten look suggests he's enjoyed his life up to this point. If she's annoyed to be paired with him, she doesn't show it. She's civil to him, but doesn't volunteer much either. Watching them across the table, I see a hooker for the first time. Nothing less could explain these two being wedged together, especially her air of disinterest. I can't imagine he'd be too thrilled by her company, but I dare say he couldn't dream of anybody so gorgeous without the help of his fat wallet.

And yes, she is hotter than ever tonight. I mean...*wow*. She'd be well worth the money for any guy. I don't think a ball gown is really her style – she's made for a miniskirt – but her face would be worthy of any magazine cover. She's clearly put time into it, though, with those trimmed eyebrows and big lashes. And her skin is probably more picture-perfect than that of anybody here. Her pointy little ears really define her doll-like cuteness, especially with her hair pinned up tight as it is tonight. If only the woman would smile, she'd be a princess to capture a nation!

There are three other classmates at our table. One of them is the tall brunette next to whom I showered this morning. And she is *really* tall. I always thought men avoided women of that stature, but maybe she brings something else to the table, as it were. Her name is Carrie and she's also English. She wears black lipstick and a dark palette of makeup; her voice has an irritating nasal aspect. She's from Sussex, I discover, educated at a rather strict convent school. She's spent some years in the police force.

Carrie is happy enough to chat, but she has an annoying way of cutting people off when they're talking to her. Even her date, who is half her height and receding. It's almost as though she's familiar with all of this, and feels as though she's in charge. Where are her nerves? I try to probe a little into her presence here, and she candidly tells me she has been working with a mentor of her own for several months since quitting the police just after her twenty-eighth birthday. She hasn't done 'paid work' yet, but keeps mentioning 'the scene'. I only have an inkling of what she means, so I just nod as if I understand.

The most interesting chat I have is with Latifa. I think it was her whose zippy firm figure and perky tits I noticed in the showers earlier. I thought then that she was tanned, but now, on closer inspection and hearing her name, I suspect she's just plain exotic. I try to guess from her skin tone, which in truth is neither tanned nor Mediterranean. It's more caffe latte, but with an extra dash of milk. And those intense green eyes…they're not from around these parts.

"You'll never guess," she says to me, laughing as she confidently takes the hand of her fine-looking companion, Edward, under the table.

"I guess not," I say. "I'm thinking your background is a little more interesting than mine?"

"Well it's pretty unique," she chuckles. "My mother is Omani but my dad's Irish!"

My eyes go wide. "Oh, wow…that's a really interesting combination!"

It comes to me now. I know exactly where I've seen that look before. It's the beguiling mélange you get when you mix Arab with North European. I've had a couple of colleagues of exactly that ancestry, and both of them were drop-dead stunners.

"So…your English is perfect, but your accent is pretty hard to place," I continue, fearful of inadvertently causing offence. "Did you grow up in this country?"

I can't imagine she'd be here if she'd been raised in a conservative place like Oman.

"Nope," she shakes her head forcefully. "I'm pretty much Omani born and bred. Fully Muslim." She winks at me when she says this.

"Wow!" is the cleverest response I can manage. "Then this is…er…especially naughty for you, isn't it?"

"My parents allowed me loads of freedom of thought – my dad was a big part of that. I went to a typical local school, veils and all the rest of it. But at home, my sisters and I were never censored. And we travelled a lot. I've always known what's out there in the world."

"But this…coming here is a big step all the same. For all of us, I mean."

She shrugs.

"It's something I've been thinking about for a long time. I saw things in Dubai and I saw things in Amsterdam. And…I enjoy being with a man. Who doesn't?"

She smiles into her date's eyes as she says this. He melts visibly. If this was a client…he just got half his money's worth right there. This girl knows how to work it.

"My parents might be liberal but they sure as hell wouldn't like to hear about this," she continues. "As far as they know I'm studying in Newcastle. Which I am…but we're on a term break and I thought this would be a fun way to spend it!"

She's warm with her escort in a completely unforced way. I can totally imagine she'd genuinely like to make love to him, and that she'd be spectacular at it. Her hair is long and gently curled: I'm really envious of it. And I already know she has a body to die for. I'm not jealous, exactly, but I admire her for her looks and candour. Above all, though, for her easy manner. I can't bring myself to be so flirtatious with my guy, even though he makes me weak at the knees.

I'm constantly aware of him, though, and constantly aware that I've surely got the hottest date of anyone here. It brings a quiet smile to my lips every so often, especially when stony-faced Petra and her man catch my eye. More so when I think of the lacy red g-string and bra I'm wearing. But there's so much else to take in.

I spend some time looking at the table of 'unattached' men on the other side of the room. I make out that one of them is the man who woke us this morning and sent us to the group shower. He has a stern look about him and doesn't seem to engage the others much. Are these people all too powerful to get close to each other? Are *these* the men who can afford £1000 for a girl's services?

Occasionally some of the men glance in our direction, and once or twice I get the feeling I might be the subject of their chatter. I try to ignore the rising pride in my belly, but that gets a little harder when Rupert takes my hand under the table after dinner.

The booze is taking effect on the room and on me. The whole scenario is making me a little giddy. I'm itching for a snog at least. It's been months! But I'm just plain confused. I know what the old Emma would do: she wouldn't be shy to encourage her chosen guy, but also wouldn't rush into bed with anyone either. I'm pretty sure I know what Emma the booked escort would need to do. But Emma the escort-in-training? She has no idea what's expected of her. So she waits for something to happen.

And now, dinner done, a band has replaced the piano. Couples move to the dancefloor. Rupert and I are among the first. I feel right at home here. It's mostly waltzing – what else? – but I know where to put my feet. So, inevitably, does Rupert, who leads like a real gentleman. There's literally nothing I'd change about him. It's a magic summer's night, straight out of a storybook.

But I *would* like to know a few things. What is his business here and how did he get to be my date? What does he do when he's not here? Is he the boss of a huge company? He seems the type. He's made me curious all night by asking me all about *me*, while giving almost nothing away about himself. I press him again when we're close on the dance floor, but he hushes me by putting a finger to my lips.

"Don't be a curious girl, Emma," he says in that public-school accent that I associate so strongly with success and power. "A lady does not ask too many questions. She should relax and let herself be taken care of."

Fuck, that's a good answer.

My tongue wants to dart out and touch his finger. I only just stop myself.

Close your eyes, Emma.

I can feel desire having its way with me, as the relentless music takes hold of my soul. And it has nothing to do with why I'm at the school. It's the ball, the drinks, the dancing. It's Rupert.

We dance for what feels like hours. And now we're on the terrace. Champagne still flowing. It must be gone midnight.

Just Rupert and I. Somehow the rest of the party doesn't exist. We're looking out over the pool. He has his arm around me.

And still he wants to know all about me. My schooling. My parents. My relationships. Where I learned to dance. The job I've just left.

But he won't give anything away. Except that Rupert is not his real name. He says it with a tiny smirk and looks me dead in the eye.

It's a starry night, warm by English standards, but I'm glad of his body warmth pressed up against me. A few other people are also outside now, but I'm so wrapped up in myself now that I've no idea who. I've forgotten that I might be under observation. My yearning for a kiss is off the scale now: I've resorted to just looking up at him, my pout speaking louder than any words could.

Any moment now, surely.

But suddenly, Rupert yawns and takes his arm off me.

"It's been a wonderful evening, Miss Carling. You're an absolute delight for a gentleman, let me tell you. Alas, I must turn in now. And you shouldn't stay up too late."

I gape at him, but he doesn't seem to notice. He just takes my arm, leads me into the room, then bids me good night with a peck on the cheek.

Where did I go wrong?

I toss and turn, a million miles from sleeping. *Damn* him, that Rupert, he's made me like a coiled spring. The whole day has. Twice I've been naked and watched. And then the dance party, where everything was so right, so *fucking* right, only for it all to peter out. I'm mad.

Here I am in a whore school, so fucking horny, but I don't know what to do about it. I shake my head, wonder if tonight was supposed to be some gigantic tease.

I feel my own hand burrow under the lining of my little shorts. It seeks out my desperate button and I shudder as my middle finger brushes it for the first time.

Seriously, Emma, not now! You're not alone.

Not sure if Petra is awake or asleep. It doesn't seem like she got action either. It seems everyone got sent away like I did. Why on earth would they build us up like that? This place is downright cruel.

I dip onto my slit, rubbing gently up and down its lips. I can't believe I'm actually wet already. The stress of work has deadened my libido for months now, but today and tonight seem to have revived it. Big time.

You'll get noisy. You know you will.

I push two fingers inside my hungry pussy. I feel my shoulders curl as I throw my legs open beneath the covers. Rupert is kneeling above me, poised.

Why are you teasing yourself?

The voice of reason is shouting too loud. Reluctantly I yank my fingers out, flip over, bury my head in my pillow and groan softly. Pure frustration. I hate this so-called school already. Do they think we're training to be nuns?

The thought of finding relief in the bathroom crosses my mind. Or the garden. Hell, maybe even that sauna. But surely going out alone will be scary. And I might get in trouble. Although nobody *said* anything about a curfew.

I resolve to do the English thing and suffer in silence. I wonder if Petra is lying awake, thinking the same thoughts. But I guess not – she's dead inside, isn't she? Pity: I'd almost consider turning for her right now. I hate her with passion…but she is one of the most attractive women I've ever met.

Every now and then I catch a whiff of the scent of my own cream that coated my fingers as I jabbed them inside of me, and have to force my thoughts elsewhere.

It's a long, long time before sleep finally takes me.

Chapter Eight

My mood is even more terrible when I wake up. Now I'm not just frustrated, I'm tired too. My first response to the morning is to frown and sigh.

The Colin Firth-lookalike rouses us again, pulling back the curtains to more blazing sunshine and birds chirping merrily. I notice that it's an hour later than yesterday, but the lie-in doesn't seem to have made much difference. I've got a faintly fuzzy head after the champagne.

I wonder if today will be another never-ending tease.

I begin to think it'll be exactly that as we hit the showers. We have an audience again, but this time it's Rupert and Harry. *Uh oh.* That's my *date* watching me. It makes the whole thing tougher than yesterday, when the watchers were strangers. I simply can't bring myself to make eye contact, and finish washing as quickly as I can. Thinking of how much I want him isn't going to help right now. So of course, my mind insists on thinking of nothing else. And when I strain the corners of my eyes to see where he's looking, I swear it's at me.

It could be my imagination, though. I'd love a penny for his thoughts.

Back in our room, I find the bed has been made. The housekeeping is pretty sharp here, I'll give them that. If life as a...well, if my new life involves never making my own bed, there's something to be said for it.

I also notice an envelope propped up against the freshly-plumped pillow. On it, written in black ink, is my name The cursive script is beautiful. It screams education and upper-classness. *Miss Emma Carling.*

My first feeling is one of concern. I glance over to Petra's bed. No letter there. Nothing for the pro hooker? My trepidation builds – are they kicking me out? Did I do something wrong last night?

I sit down, my big, fluffy, luxurious towel wrapped around my body. I tear the envelope open. My fingers clutch at something thick and smooth: it's some kind of photographic paper. There are two pieces. I pull them out of the envelope. And I gasp.

It's *me*. Yesterday. Bent over in Miss Jackson's office, baring…everything. So *that's* what she was doing behind me, the sly little woman! She must have used a phone, because I hadn't heard a shutter click. Incredible.

I look at the second picture. *My God.* This one is a close-up. I feel my face blaze bright red, even though I'm alone in my room right now. I can only suppose these body parts also belong to me. Two cheeks the frame, and between the cheeks I can clearly see, well, every detail. Laid bare.

I'm a mix of curious and offended. I'm not thrilled she took these pictures without my knowledge. Yet I'm also kind of fascinated to see how I look. I've never seen myself from behind, at least not like that. It's never occurred to me that bending over reveals quite so much.

Of course it has, you've seen porn! You just didn't want to think about what you were showing.

Yeah, I have seen porn a few times. And come to think of it, I compare quite nicely. My waxing girl did a great job. There's no trace of a hair from this angle, and my puckered little rose of an asshole is bald as can be. My sex is neat and pink. The labia are welcoming but don't dominate my vagina. They're like friendly ushers, pulling you to where you need to be.

I'm fascinated by the smooth sliver of pink nothingness between my two holes. Sure, I've been licked there a few times, but never had much idea of how it looked to another. Now I can see it all: pussy, perineum, anus. I feel slightly turned on to think that these things are mine. I shake my head. This whole adventure gets more surreal by the hour.

I switch back to the first picture. There's no doubt it's me, even though I can't see my face. (A relief, come to think of it. These photos could go anywhere!) The pose looks just how it felt: a girl with her hands around her ankles and a dark halo of hair dangling down around her head. Toned legs and tight ass, all the tighter as the muscles strain and stretch in their taut position. I can see my school uniform on the chair in the background.

Yup, that's me alright. I'd better stay on Miss Jackson's good side.

Suddenly Petra bursts through the door. I didn't hear her coming down the hall – must've been too tied up in my reverie. I quickly try to stuff the photos away.

I'm not quick enough.

"What is that?" she says, a little spicily, her voice huskier than ever. She's also in a towel and no more.

I don't really want to tell her. Much less show her. But I'm dying to know if she's had something similar, so I pay the price and share what's happened.

"Erm…I just found these on my bed. Someone put them here while we were in the shower."

I hand over the photos, which she takes with interest. And I feel an ocean of blood rush to my face once more.

Emma, what have you done?

"This is you?" she asks, curtly. "When did they take this?"

There's no fooling her. May as well spit it out.

"It was…it was during my mentor meeting yesterday morning. With Miss Jackson."

"Oh," says Petra. "I have her too."

"Oh cool. Did she…um…make you strip?"

"Yes. I did. But she did not go behind me. I did not see her take pictures."

This is turning into far and away the longest conversation I've had with Petra. She looks across to her bed. Am I imagining that trace of hopeful on her face? I see her brow furrow when she sees there's nothing.

She forgets all about our little chat, and starts to walk away to her side of the room. She looks a little perplexed. I watch her as she goes to the window, her wet hair straggled out across her neck, stray strands splayed across her shiny shoulders like rays of sunlight.

So, am I the only one to have received a porno selfie delivery? I shake my head once more, and suddenly I think to check the envelope again.

There's a note. Written on thick, barky paper. The same elegant handwriting.

Dear Emma,

I thought you might enjoy these. You photograph beautifully from behind. I would like you to report to the Lachlan Room at midday. North wing, second floor.

Miss Jackson

Fuck, I wish they'd tell me what's going on for once! How was I supposed to choose an outfit for yet another mystery appointment? But I figure I can't go wrong in the brand-name pink tank top, dinky denim shorts and flat white tennis shoes I've chosen.

The uncertainty is getting on my nerves, which are still jangling with desire after last night. Back home, I would have long since gotten over myself by now, distracted myself with something – probably the latest work crisis. But it's different here. There's nothing else to think about. There's no hiding from my horniness as I walk the dim hallways to my destination.

They keep building me up, then taking me down, that's the trouble. The balls, the showers, the kinky photos. I get the sense of a brooding sexual storm in the air. This *is* a sex school, isn't it? I just don't want to think too much about what this appointment might be. Expectation. It definitely won't be a good thing right now.

I stop outside a door. Just another big, solid wooden door, like all the others in the house. Or maybe not. This one has my heart beating something supersonic. It's labelled *Lachlan Room* in gold-carved lettering. The letters are high enough that I have to look upwards to read them. I feel timid, cautious, on high alert. I knock.

A male voice invites me in. I've heard that voice recently. *Very* recently. Can it be…?

Rupert.

He's sitting in a broad, red-leather wing-back armchair. There's something in his hand. He looks very, very comfortable and pleased with life.

"Hello Emma. Shut the door behind you."

I do as he instructs. And I look around. It's like a spacious hotel suite, this room, albeit one from several decades ago. There's a four-poster bed, several chairs similar to the one he's sitting on, and even a fireplace. The smell is of wood and leather. There's absolutely nothing feminine about it.

My focus comes back to him. How it ever left I'm not sure. He's stunning. And here I am, standing in front of him, with my hands behind my back.

"I trust you've enjoyed your photographs as much as I have, Emma," he says with a broad smile. He holds up copies of Miss Jackson's subtle photographic efforts. "As teasing previews go, this is right up there."

I want to disappear. I can't believe she's given him those pictures. I bite my bottom lip, because I can't think of anything positive to say. I am mortified.

Rupert puts the photos face-up on a small, rectangular coffee table, takes a final look at them, and stands up. He walks towards me and gently cups my shoulders in his big hands. I turn to jelly.

"You did well last night, Miss Carling. I found your company most ladylike. Even though I could see you wanted more at the end of the evening. Sometimes restraint will be something you need."

I bite my lip once again. I can think of a lot of positive things to say now, but it's like someone hit my mute button the moment I walked in here.

I feel the warm breath of his nostrils on my face. He's a good few inches taller than me. Still smells superb.

He moves one hand to the back of my head, and gently cradles it.

God, if this is another tease…

"You had that hungry look in your eyes," says Rupert. "You didn't need to say anything. It's a look I know well. Leaving you last night was not easy. But we had our instructions on how your training should proceed."

I gulp and decide to stop looking at the floor. I raise my eyes to his, smile a little.

Don't let yourself go, Emma. I don't know where this is going. I mustn't think too much here.

He moves a little closer. Not touching, but close enough to send me his warmth. It's almost as near as we were on the terrace last night. There's something very likeable and comforting about his proximity.

"I've thought of nothing but you since seeing you in the shower this morning. You made a fine sight, even in such stellar company."

He drops his other hand to my bum and squeezes it.

"Do you have an idea of what I'm going to do to you now, Miss Carling?"

Shit, does he want me to answer? *Please no.* But please.

Only two words come to my mind. Over and over. And over. He's still waiting. I look away, then finally summon some power to speak.

"Fuck me?" I whisper.

There. I said it. My eyes flick up to his, worried. But Rupert's face lights up with a soft, caring smile.

"Yes Emma. That's right. I'm going to fuck you," he whispers back.

Oh God, it's happening at last. I'm afraid, still so afraid. Afraid that it might get taken away.

Sometimes a girl wants to make love. Sometimes she just wants to be *fucked*. And right now I'm in no mood for foreplay. My pussy aches too much.

Rupert seems to read my thoughts. *Yes!* He springs into action without further ado.

"I want you naked, right now," he says heavily, yanking my top over my head to bare my braless breasts.

His eyes stay rooted to my nipples as he undoes my shorts and tugs them down to my ankles. My inky-black g-string doesn't last three seconds as he slips a finger inside its hip and simply tears it open. It must have cost three figures, that, but he doesn't seem the slightest bit bothered. Shamelessly wasteful. But what a turn-on.

"Up you come," he says hoisting me into his arms, cradling my butt with one huge hand and supporting my back with another. He kisses me, softly yet urgently. *God, it's good.* I wanted that so badly last night. I feel he did too. He doesn't need to say a word.

His hardness prodding the bottom of my spine tells its own story, as he carries me across to the bed in nothing but my tennis shoes.

He lays me down as gently as his obvious arousal allows.

"Open your legs and wait for me," he commands. Now I'm gone. If they take this away now, I *will* explode.

I brazenly follow his orders and watch him unbutton his shirt. The man is ripped, but not to excess. Just as I'd hoped. I twitch. Now his belt and trousers come off. Oh please, hurry, please. This girl needs *fucking*.

Rupert steps out of his shoes, slower than I would like. He throws away his socks and is finally naked. Eyes fixed on mine, then darting between my legs, and then back to my eyes, he absent-mindedly plays with himself. It's magnificent, fully erect for me. Fuck, *hurry!*

My core is burning with emptiness.

Thank God he is on the same page as me. Without another word the handsome Rupert is on top of me, his everything plunged within me.

You really can let go now, Emma.

And I do. I forget where I am, why I'm here, even *who* I am. All I know right now is that this amazing male and I are one. I think I cry out as he begins to pump, and forty-two hours of erotic tension begin to unfurl from my being. I'm going to give in very quickly indeed.

I keep my eyes open, but see only his vast, powerful shoulders as they work up and down. I throw back my head so I can see the man who is fucking me. It's magnificent. I groan louder as he fucks me harder. *Yes!!*

I feel abandon like never before. Even at home I'd worry about making noises that neighbours might hear through the walls. Not here. I probably should, but I'm in no state to care. I start to writhe at the pleasure I'm feeling, my head jerking this way and that, my mouth wide open as I pant like a dog on a summer's day.

And now words find me. "Yes, *God yes*…fuck me Rupert! Don't stop fucking me!"

I see his mouth curl into a little smirk as he takes heed of my plea.

"Harder! Deeper! Come on!!"

I'm not usually a talker, but I'm delirious now. The part of me that fears this magic being taken away is putting desperate words in my mouth.

"Oh yes…like that…fuck my pussy, fuck it hard…HARD!!"

I think I'm getting louder. And he's definitely listening. The bed is squeaking. I don't care.

"Go on, go on…keep going…yes, yes….YES!!!"

I don't often come on penetration alone, but it's totally going to happen right now. This torrent of desire inside me, which started as a trickle, has been building for too long.

I can't believe he can go harder, but he finds another gear. He's grunting with the effort now. I try to wrap my arms around him but I can't. He's too big and he's moving too fast. So I throw open my legs, wide as they can go, spread my arms out wide. Like I'm making a snow angel.

The feeling is delectable. I am owned right now, and, scarily, I *love* it. He's filling me, and every time he rams into me he seems to fill me more. Can he still be getting harder? It feels like he is.

"Shit…you're so *fucking huge*. Give it to me! Yes….yes….f-f-f-FUCK!!"

Somehow my orgasm surprises me. I knew it was coming, but its speedy arrival is one almighty ambush. I explode and shatter. My pelvis keeps thrusting and convulsing as my pussy spasms around him. He unleashes a great hot wave just as I begin to slow my squirming.

And now, as he too slows, I wrap my legs and arms around his mighty body, still pulsing and breathless.

That was worth the wait, Miss Emma Carling.

Chapter Nine

"I will keep these items, Miss Carling. You won't be needing them in the near future."

It's barely two minutes since Rupert pulled himself – still at full length – out of my sopping sex. And now he's telling me to get out – with all of my clothing bunched up in his fist. He's even snatched up my crumpled panties off the floor. *What is happening?*

My mind is addled with a churn of mixed emotions. The euphoria of my orgasm, that wonderful release, is still there. But it's receding fast. Rupert is busy shaking it out of me like sugar dropping through a sieve. It's like someone flicked a switch in him. He's turned nasty.

The harshness has me shell-shocked. I haven't been allowed a moment to recover. He's had his way with me, and now, even as his seed still swirls around inside me, he's pointing to the door with a set jaw. It's barbaric.

I stand and stare at him, glazed and uncomprehending. I feel dirtier by the second. Suddenly, I have been shamelessly used. I am nothing but a pound of flesh to this animal. Is it so much to ask for a few moments to recover, perhaps a sweet nothing or two? Will it always be this brutal? Will they always build a wall afterwards? And now he wants to keep my clothes? Why? To make me feel more humiliated?

I fight back the welling tears, and I crave a cigarette.

"Miss Carling, I *will* not ask you again. You have no further business here," he barks. Fuck, this is a nightmare. "And Miss Jackson has sent word that you're to remain naked until further notice."

He turns away and begins to put on his shirt, fastening his cuff links. Where in God's name does he need to be so soon?

The awful thought crosses my mind that another of the girls is waiting outside. Christ.

Why are you surprised, Emma? This isn't playschool. You're in hooker training. What else did you expect?

I don't know how to answer myself. But somehow I didn't expect to feel like shit quite so soon.

I'm not sure how much time passes. Then he turns and frowns at me over his shoulder. Fine, I don't want to be here anyway. But…

"Rupert," I croak. "Do you really have to keep my clothes? Why…will I be the only one…?"

He frowns again. "I don't know what programme or dress code the other trainees are on. But if you want to pass then I strongly suggest you do as you're told. No bathrobes, no towels. Now go."

I heave a loud sigh as I feel the stroppiness rising within me. I must fight it.

This is just another test, Emma. And Emma Carling doesn't back down from a challenge. I wasn't getting paid to take shit in my last job. In this one, maybe I am. Fuck. And this is some heavy shit. But I'll show them.

I turn my back on him, haughtily as I can manage. I open the door and step out into the hallway. Cautious. And not one stitch of clothing covers me.

This wing of the house seems dark and deserted. What is everyone else up to? I want to scurry to my room, but I also want to avoid meeting anyone. I walk slowly, listening for signs of life.

Somewhere in the distance, I hear something. It sounds like a girl…enjoying herself. Much as I just did. Oh, wait. Is that a note of angst in her cry? I think I hear a cracking sound! But maybe I'm just imagining it. I no longer trust my instincts. Everything is upside-down here.

I move closer to the sound and pause outside a door that stands between me and its source. The noises are clearer now. They're those of a woman receiving some kind of beating. *Oh, fuck, run away.* Real-world Emma's instinct, especially when she's pissed off, like now, is to storm in and scream at the bastards. But real-world Emma is already in retreat. This is a new world, and it needs a new Emma. *You're probably next in line.* I shudder.

I gather my wits as I turn onto the central wing of the house. I can't think where to head besides my room, but am I going to camp out there indefinitely? I can only think of how ridiculous this is. I can get used to the group showers, but walking around the house alone like this? Having meals in the nude while everyone else is clothed? Are these people serious, or are they having a laugh at my expense?

Footsteps on the staircase. Miss Honeywell. *Act cool, girl. Cool.* She's coming my way with a bundle of bed sheets. Probably destined for the Lachlan Room, I dare say. How am I meant not to blush?

But if Miss Honeywell notices – and how could she not? – she doesn't flinch as she stops in front of me. She really is a treasure! Nobody here can put me at ease like she can. I almost feel clothed again.

"Miss Carling!" she beams. "How are we today? Wasn't last night wonderful? You looked magnificent!"

"Er, thanks, I'm fine, thanks," I say, feeling a tiny bit more comfortable. "How are you?"

"Well, you know, keeping busy," she winks, patting the bundle of fresh linen. "It might have passed you by, but it's gorgeous outside! If I were you I'd get out to the pool pronto. You never know if the sun's going to last.

"And I think," she says, running her eyes admiringly up and down my body. "You'll look even more angelic with an all-over tan."

Not everyone can reference my mild paleness quite so inoffensively, but she's just managed it. I give her a smile, for lightening my load.

"You're right…I might just do that!"

We go our separate ways and I scuttle back to my room without running into anybody else. Petra is there, as my stinking luck would have it. She's wearing one of her trademark miniskirts.

She looks up in surprise when I walk in, then smirks. Why can't she be like Miss Honeywell?

"What?" I say grumpily.

"Did they tell you to go like that?" she enquires.

"Yes. And so?"

She doesn't answer. I grab a cigarette and walk over to the window. I suppose I might get away with covering up my nudity in here, but I don't feel like giving her an inch now. And anyway, it was expressly forbidden by Rupert, and I wouldn't be surprised if these walls have eyes. Can't rule anything out in this place.

"What have you been doing the last couple of hours?" I ask her. I'm fishing for something as humiliating as what I've experienced.

"I had to fuck two guys. From last night," she says bluntly.

"Oh." I'm taken aback at her matter-of-fact response. "Which ones? And…what was it like?"

She looks at me with narrow eyes, as if I've just asked her a silly question.

"What do you think? It was just a normal fuck. It was not *like* anything."

Jesus, this woman's…possibly onto something. She just takes it all in her stride.

"Mm, okay," I respond, genuinely pondering her words.

The room goes quiet for a while as she folds a few clothes and I contemplate my toes while the calming smoke fills my lungs and my head begins to clear. The gentle breeze creeps in from the garden and dries away any trace of those tears.

After a few minutes, I feel refreshed enough to break the silence. "Anything lined up for this afternoon?" I ask, suddenly feeling confident enough to look Petra in the eye. I've been fucked as good as she has.

"No appointments yet. So I will go to the pool."

Always one step ahead, this bloody Petra. Fucking great. And with that she dashes into the closet, emerging a minute later wrapped up tight in her swimming towel, her miniscule shoulders shining like beacons.

Fine, I'll do it! I tell myself I'm not scared of anyone, least of all her. Let her look! We've all seen each other with our kit off already, and I've switched into I-don't-care-anymore mode now. Besides, Miss Honeywell is right: there's no better use for a summer's afternoon. I grab my sunglasses and towel, then follow her out of the room without a word.

She keeps on walking a couple of steps ahead of me. Typical. She knows I'm there. It's like some kind of power thing. Like she's laying down her territory or something. Why can't…oh, never mind.

But once again, just like that first day on the stairs, I am captivated by her moving in front of me. It's her pretty little feet I notice now. So young and full and creamy. So shiny and well looked-after, with cute, healthy toes. They're just right, perfectly in tune with her proportions. Like everything else about her. I watch their confident steps along the cool hallway floor. Left, right, left, right.

I'm lost in that reverie when I realise that she's leading us through the lounge. Through the far window I notice a few people seated around a table on the terrace. And one of them is Rupert.

And his words come flooding back to me. *No bathrobes. No towels.* I start as I realise I've unthinkingly wrapped up in my towel. I've got to drop it before he spots me. I pause in front of the fireplace, suppressing the tiny tremor of thrill that's been threatening to hit me ever since I lost my clothes.

It doesn't seem right, me having to do this. Why should I listen to him, the asshole? Why should I parade naked like I've done something wrong? Should I just leave this crazy house? I just wish I had someone I could talk to. But it's silent in here, and I'm sure as hell not calling my mother. The grandfather clock ticks, as if impatient for me to get through this moment of self-doubt.

Self-doubt? Is *that* what this is? I feel the fighter within me awaken once more. *Emma, you don't doubt yourself. This is a test, not a punishment. Now go!*

I flick open my towel with new resolve, exposing my bare body once again. My towel is in my hand just in time for Rupert to look up. I think he's spotted me through the window. Yes, his eyes don't leave me. Even as the glamorous Petra stalks right past his nose on her way across the terrace.

I avoid his gaze as I pass through the French door. I'll look anyone in the eye, but not *him*. I see a mix of mentors and gentleman enjoying tea on the terrace. Miss Jackson is out here too.

"Good afternoon Emma," says the woman who, lest I forget, very recently photographed all my privates close-up and then sent me the prints. "Wow! That looks just as stunning as yesterday!"

"Thanks," I say to her, making a point of not sounding too thrilled with her. "I thought I'd do some work on my tan."

She nods and smiles, and I gather I needn't stop for another naked conversation with my mentor. When I reach the top of the steps, though, I feel as though all the world is watching me. A few of the other girls are already soaking up the rays, and I swear I see their heads turn at the sight of nude Emma Carling.

And then it hits me: I'm not the only naked one. I'm thrilled and relieved to see Simone stretched out on a sun lounger, relaxed as can be in her birthday suit. Petra has claimed another of the loungers. She's already lost her bikini top and is now casually climbing out of the bottoms. *Uh oh.* They've done this before. No tan lines. Suddenly I'm very aware of mine. It feels like they're stark and pronounced, even though my brain knows they're barely visible.

Still, the nudity levels make me feel a whole lot better as I go down the stairs to the poolside. Who else is down here? There's that uptight Jane girl, looking rather overdressed in a frilly one-piece. And Carol, the pretty but quiet Singaporean who was also at my table last night. She's seemingly asleep in her pink bikini.

As I reach the lower terrace I notice a firm, juicy pair of breasts in the near corner, previously hidden to me. Those melons could only belong to Latifa. Anyone can see they're fantastic. She's in nothing but a purple thong with pink sequins. Next to her, also topless, is the blonde girl who wore that mad see-through dress yesterday. All of a sudden I feel empowered, braver and bolder than the ones in swimsuits. I feel like I'm winning here.

I spot a lounger next to Latifa and see-through-dress girl. I make for it and spread out my towel.

"Hey, girl," says the confident Latifa. "Welcome to the fun corner! I'm not sure if you've met my room-mate Alyssia…have you?"

"No, hi," I say, offering her my hand. I smile as I do so, because it's so weird. Being formal when she's topless and I'm nude. A handshake seems, well, not quite right.

"How ya going?" she says with a warm and distinctly Australian twang. She's got one of those cracked, salty surfer-chick voices, and sounds like someone who's spent too much time singing along at rock concerts. But her deep, golden-brown tan – only a little lighter in tone than Latifa's, but clearly not something she was born with - makes sense to me now. She's clearly spent half her life on some Aussie beach, and judging by her seamless bronzing, she's had her tits out most of the time.

It turns out Alyssia is another of the friendly girls. Really down-to-earth and no bullshit. Alyssia is in the UK on a working holiday and trying out the school just to 'see what happens'. I don't say anything, but figure she must have a fair bit of money in her family to be able to come here just on a whim. Charles never told me any numbers, but I got the impression that the fees here are astronomical. Sure enough, she mentions that her dad's a mining boss, and doing pretty well for himself.

As I wonder whether she's actually told her family what she's up to over here, I discover that she's about my age and hails from Perth. She tells me it's known as the sunniest city on the planet. I make a note to include it on my travels…if I can really bring myself to do…the kind of work that buys plane tickets.

I nestle back in my semi-reclined deck chair as I talk with Alyssia and Latifa. I'm feeling good again. The sun usually has that effect. So does pleasant company. Then there's silence for a couple of minutes, and I begin to doze.

"Come on Emma, don't be so bloody English!"

It's Alyssia's voice that rouses me. And I'm puzzled.

"What do you mean?" I ask.

She sighs with mock exasperation: "You *need* to put some sunscreen on. Do you want skin cancer? Who's gonna want to root you when you're peeling?"

Shit. She's probably right. Of course I haven't thought to bring any on this particular trip. In my defence, nobody packs sun lotion for a trip to England.

"Hah, I knew it! She hasn't got any! Probably like your English friend over there," says Alyssia, jerking her head at

Jane across the pool. "She's gonna go lobster in a minute, but I'm not saying a thing. I don't like her."

"Really?" I say, innocently. I don't mention that Jane didn't give me a great vibe either when we spoke last night.

"Yeah, there's just something cold about her. She's totally fake." Alyssia isn't particularly bothered about keeping her voice down.

"I know what you mean," Latifa chimes in. "She thinks she's better than us, but she's not a very good actor!"

"I guess you'll get a bit of that here," I venture. "I mean…my room-mate's not exactly a sackful of fun either."

"You're with that blonde one, right?" asks Latifa, gesturing towards Petra.

"Yeah, and it's not great. She doesn't have time for me either, but she doesn't even bother acting."

The girls are quiet for a moment as they contemplate the Bulgarian blonde across the water. Petra's reading a book, apparently oblivious to our conversation.

"Jesus, but she's not bad to look at," says Alyssia, taking in the petite youngster. "I could always go for a tight little body like that."

"I bet you could," Latifa sniggers. Am I imagining the double entendre? Or is it really there?

"Back to the sunscreen then!" says Alyssia dismissively, handing one of her bottles of factor 15 to Latifa. "Don't think you can distract us with gossip! You just lay back Emma. We'll take care of it."

"Er….really? I mean…I can…"

"Shhh! It's easier for someone else to do this, you know."

"Yeah," I protest. "I know, I mean, if it was my back…"

She just gives me a look. It silences me as she stands up and rubs some cream in between her palms. I've realised she won't be taking no for an answer.

"You take the left and I'll take the right, okay Latifa? That way we don't miss a spot!"

Seriously, these girls want to cream me up? I sigh. Fine. We're all practically fucking naked, so how weird is it really? I'm not going to argue with a pampering. I close my eyes, let go, and start to feel like the queen bee.

They start with my legs. And they're true to their word. The four warm, liquid-lathered hands really don't miss a spot as they massage the cream into each of my toes, my feet, and all the way up to my knees. No sun-ray is going to have its way with me, that's for sure.

And this is nice. The four hands are moving their way up my thighs now, inside and outside. I wonder if I'm making a spectacle of myself, but remember that we're hidden below the terrace. The other girls at the poolside might have an eye on me, but so what? Everyone needs sunscreen.

I can hear and feel their breath on me as their stooped bodies work their way up mine. I flinch as Alyssia's thumb brushes near my clit while she works the top of my legs. They give my pussy a berth, but not a wide one, and I take in a sharp breath once or twice when they get close.

"Hey, don't worry, we're not going to finger you girl!" says Latifa.

"Not yet anyway…" adds Alyssia. My eyes are open long enough to see her wink at her Arab friend. It's impossible to know if she's joking or not. And impossible for me to know if I want her to be. Do I?

God, what a day this is turning into.

Their fingers splay their way across my tummy as they move up and over my little patch. I love how it feels when their fingers trail in the wake of their hands, one at a time, like a slithering snake working its way along my sides. Especially the way Latifa does it. Alyssia is a little rough, slightly masculine in her movements, but Latifa's a natural.

And now, my sides and tummy fully coated, their slick hands glide onto my breasts. No wide berth here.

Back and forth go their hands. Around and around, swirling and swooping across the soft flesh. *OK, this is a first.* But I don't say anything. Instead I hold my breath. It seems the polite thing to do.

My eyes are shut again, and I become intensely aware of the sun beating down on my forehead while their hands apply the cream. I swear I feel a little pinch on my left nipple as Alyssia's hand retreats for the last time. *Something* makes my toes curl, anyway.

"Nothing worse than burnt tits, hey?" Alyssia says to the world in general. Did the two girls take a little longer than necessary on my chest area? "Gotta take care…especially when they've not seen the sun before. Your nips would sting like hell if we didn't cream them up."

Latifa chuckles and I sigh: enough now! The girls finish up with my neck and shoulders.

"You can do your face," says Alyssia, handing me the bottle. "But I'll be watching you!"

"Alright, alright, I won't cheat, promise!" I smile.

"Yeah don't miss a spot now, not after all that effort we put in."

I give my face a gentle layer of sunscreen while the girls settle back into their loungers.

"Thanks guys," I say. And I just stop myself from adding 'that was nice'. But it was. It really was.

The sun beats down on us and conversation peters out again as we all get a little drowsy. Even though my mind is spinning so fast that it's crying out for a shutdown. It's lumbered with so much: the slight hangover, the whole thing with Rupert, having my clothes taken off me. And now the weirdly cool feeling I had when Latifa and Alyssia worked their hands over my body.

I expect myself to dwell on some of today's more trying moments, but instead it's the good times that push their way to the front of my thoughts. Lying here in the sun with my legs slightly ajar, I can't help but think how good that fuck was. Even if the ending sucked. This place is pushing me, yes, but I think I'm going to find a lot to like. If I let myself.

And that's the last thought I remember thinking before I drift off.

Chapter Ten

Something's not right. I'm groggy, probably half sun-stroked. At first I don't remember where I am. Someone is saying my name.

"Emma. Wake up. Wake up immediately."

It's a male voice. Insistent, laced with urgency. There's a vaguely familiar Scots twang. And a note of authority that startles me into full consciousness. Where have I heard that note before?

My perceptions erupt into life. *You're naked at the poolside, remember? You must have fallen asleep.*

But I'm in shadow now. The sun has sunk lower. A man stands above me, one leg either side of my reclined deck chair. He is naked.

It's Harry. And his cock is barely three feet from my face.

Erect.

Latifa! Alyssia! They were with me!

I look left and right. The Australian and the Irish Omani are still there. Each of them is propped up on an elbow, facing me, intent and watchful. Oh great. What happened to my vocal helpers? Has someone torn out their tongues or what? Looks like I'm on my own here.

"I want you to suck me, Emma," Harry says crisply. "Do it now. Take my cock in your sexy little mouth immediately. Give me a blowjob."

Everyone must be watching me. I can't see much past his sculpted torso, but maybe the terrace crowd has gathered at the railing, above my head, to have a look. And I bet Petra is still there across the pool, taking all of this in. Probably ready to judge my technique.

I'm hesitant, of course I am. But like hell am I going to give her the satisfaction of watching me struggle with my inner prude. Fuck it. Shirk at this, and I may as well pack my bags this minute.

"Yes, Sir," I hear myself say.

I have no idea where those words came from, but somehow I feel like they absolve me of all responsibility for anything that might happen. I feel lighter as I sit up straight, and come face to face with his tautness. I notice there's a large tattoo running down his left side. I can't quite make out what it depicts, as it stops just where his V begins. I get the feeling it's something tribal. I like tattoos. But I have more pressing concerns before me.

I am going to tackle this. I find myself wrapping my right hand around its base, steadying my naked body in a seated position, and plunging him into my mouth, deep as I can.

My sexy little mouth. That helped.

God, he tastes fucking phenomenal. I can smell his manliness even as the buds on my tongue pick up his musky flavour, tinged with perspiration. And I hear him groan a little as he slides his fullness between my lips.

It feels sexy that I have my legs so wide open, one foot either side of the chair as he stands between my knees, awaiting my service. Some part of me stops myself looking up at him, but the physique in front of me – and my memories of last night – remind me that I'm working on a fine specimen.

I didn't tell Miss Jackson how much I love a cock in my mouth. But I do. It's an amazing, spectacular feeling. I am truly awake now.

Though the feeling of his arousal on the roof of my mouth has me in rapture, I'm acutely aware that I'm being watched. That this is *weird*. The sensible side of me is surprised that I'm carrying on with this. It's shocked to see me begin to work up and down his shaft, nibbling gently on the flesh as I pause at my limit, then sucking hard as I pull back up him for another lap.

I move my hand to cup his balls, and I hear another response as I lightly jiggle them in my hand. I also feel his hardness rise on my palate, where I taste a new taste, a drop or two of early excitement. And to that I respond with a firm groan of my own.

And yet I can feel the eyes on me, especially Petra's. Somehow I know that the more evidently I arouse Harry, the better I will feel in her piercing gaze. *How do you like this then, you judgemental, superior bitch-cow?*

I'm dimly aware of movement in my peripheral vision. Alyssia is sitting up straight now, and Latifa has risen to her feet. A moment later, I feel her hands on my shoulders. That silky, light touch again.

Not a word is spoken as Harry begins to lean forward. I guess I tilt back a little, still gobbling on his rigid flesh. I feel Latifa's body against the back of my head, and roll my eyes up to see their silhouettes kissing against the bright, blue afternoon sky.

I sense him reaching out with his right hand to caress her breast: he steadies himself with his left hand behind my head. I'm happy she's there. It's no longer just me in the spotlight. I feel her stomach press closer against the back of my head, keeping his hand in place. We three are connected. My brain is racing: envy, pride, lust. Uncertainty. Was she *asked* to do this? Does it matter?

Minutes pass. Maybe seconds. He begins to thrust in my mouth and there's a helpless need growing between my legs. So soon!

And now Alyssia wants to join in. Through the gap between Harry and Latifa's bodies, I spot her move.

"Come on, big boy," I hear, laughter in her voice. The brazen Australian. "Give me that."

And gently, so gently, her hand brushes mine out of the way and takes hold of him. Pulls the straining sex out of my mouth. I'm not indignant, but I purse my lips as I realise what's happening, dragging it out as long as I can.

I sit up, confused, aroused and expectant. I think she is going to try and take him in her mouth too, but instead she puts an arm around his waist and begins to work him with a deft hand. He straightens up now, leaving Latifa's lips. I feel her hands gently tilt my head back.

Oh, fuck, I know what this is about.

I've never…

Alyssia's going hard now, and talking to him.

"You gonna come for me, yeah? I feel that spunk coming. Go on! She wants it in her face. Come on her face!"

"Open up, baby," says Latifa, gently stroking a cheek with one hand.

Harry says nothing. He doesn't need to. His wet head is growing purpler by the second as Alyssia jerks his base without subtlety.

Now, at last, I forget the audience. This moment is so intense, so new. So captivating. I don't want it, but I want it. I forget to breathe. And I wait with my eyes closed.

"Fuck yeah," says Alyssia. "You're so hard in my hand, Harry! Oh yes, there it is, you're coming, you're coming…"

Splat.

Above my left eye.

Splat.

All over my upper lip. I hold my mouth still. It trickles down, thick, and oozy.

Splat.

He's painting a line across my right cheek, up and over my nose. It's hotter than hot. Summer spunk.

Drip. Drip. Drip.

He's releasing the last remnants directly into my mouth. I'm paralysed now, unsure all over again. I lick my lips but I'm afraid to move.

"You like that taste, don't you Emma?"

It's Harry speaking, at last.

Do I?

I think I do.

I swallow the seed that's in my mouth, and nod. My eyes still closed. I swear I hear a couple of approving murmurs from somewhere in the distance.

"Don't you touch your face now, Emma," he commands. "Not till showers tomorrow morning."

I nod again. I don't know what I feel. The buzzing in my pussy has suddenly subsided, and now shame rises inside me. I have semen running down my face. That makes me a dirty slut. Right…?

Of course I am. But for *here*…I know I must have done the right things. I must have been a good little whore. Not even Petra can say otherwise. And Rupert, well, he can go and get fucked. Double entendre entirely intended.

I'm quiet at dinner. The clouds keep their distance and it's another soft, pleasant evening, so we dine on the terrace again. But now I am not only naked, there's a streaky white crust on my face too. I feel a soiled mess, a freak show. I keep my head down and concentrate on navigating my lobster. I haven't had much practice with those.

I do notice that Jane has similar facial markings, which comes as a huge relief. Logically, everyone here knows that we are all subject to certain happenings and instructions. My brain tells me that nobody is judging any of us. But logic doesn't always win out in my head. I'm embarrassed on multiple levels, especially after what I did by the pool.

Evidently, Jane is allowed to wear clothes. Alyssia and Latifa remain topless – and chatty – at the table. Latifa messes around with a severed lobster claw, tweaking Alyssia's nipple with it. Fuck, this is surreal. None of it makes the slightest bit of sense. But their underdressing and tomfoolery takes the heat off me a little.

He said not to touch my face. And I haven't. Just like an obedient little tart. It feels nasty and ridiculous, though a tiny part of me is proud to have been chosen for the treatment. Not that that I really let that thought in. I want my face clean.

I'm allowed to visit that sauna, aren't I? I wouldn't be *touching* my face, strictly speaking. If I sweat it off, that's just one of those things, right? Plus, it's a great hidey-hole where everyone has to be naked. I'm pleased by my clear thinking. I just want to chill.

I head for the sauna as soon as my dinner has gone down. As I tiptoe down the garden steps in the evening cool, it hits me that I'm utterly drained. After the late night yesterday, so much emotional turmoil with Rupert and so much sun, it's no surprise. The sex and the blowjob sapped me too. And I still have a hint of a headache.

Just let me lie down.

I cross the paving stones outside the sauna, enjoying the cool feeling they impart to my feet. I push the door open. It's not empty inside.

Sigh. *Petra.* Is there no escaping her?

She's stretched out on her back, facing the door. She lifts her head a little as I enter, but loses interest when she sees it's me. Wordless, she goes back to eyes-shut mode.

I sit down for a moment, in a corner as distant from her as I can find. I'll ease myself in: the surface of the wood is quite hot and will take some getting used to.

I just can't help my eye resting on the naked Petra. Again I feel seized by a kind of unwilling fascination that I'm struggling to deny. Her pale ivory skin has become a golden glow inside the semi-lit sauna. And she wears it so tight. Her ass and breasts and stomach and thighs cling to her with a kind of tenacity you have to envy.

There's something about the ensemble of her skin. So smooth and hairless, apart from a little runway patch similar to mine. It has me jealous…yet it draws me in. Why do I keep thinking about brushing my lips across her satin belly?

She wiggles her petite toes and clears her throat. I look the other way.

Fuck, this can't be happening. *Not her.*

Surely it's just the heady sexual atmosphere of this place messing with me? I've never been attracted to a woman. Yes, I had a couple of girl kisses, but that was just drunken curiosity…who hasn't done that? A bit of student playfulness, that was. But this? All these years on? I keep telling myself it's not there.

But it's there. Holy hell, I have a crush on this bitch. But I hate her too. It's a crush I have to crush.

Cross with myself, I lie down and try to stare at the ceiling. A minute later Petra stands up and leaves the room without a word. I open one eye and watch her cute little bum cheeks, taut like tightropes, make their way out of the door.

Finally I am alone, replaying the day's events in my mind. Rupert seems so long ago. Boy, the end hurt, but I needed that fuck. I smile at the recollection, but my brow furrows when I remember how I felt when he made me leave his room immediately, and naked.

Then there was the poolside blowjob. I thought I handled the surprise well, held my own. I can't pretend I didn't enjoy it. Much to my surprise, I wasn't shy performing in public. But the spurting in my face? Walking around stained and shamed? Will the demanding, careless treatment those men dished out be an everyday thing in a hooker's life? Can I handle it?

I'm not sure. Maybe I can. Everything gets easier with time, right? But do I *want* to be good at this kind of thing? My mind's eye roves across the open-plan office I've so recently abandoned. Row upon row of rat-race drones, enslaved by their e-mail. Tight suits, tighter personalities, conflict everywhere. Hmm. If you told me I'd never have to work in an office again, I'd hug you.

I don't remember lobster, sunbathing or creamy hands rolling across my breasts as part of a typical day back in London, either. If I can only make peace with the rest of it…

I start as I hear the door open.

"Hey Emma – us again!"

It's Latifa and Alyssia. They drop their towels without a care and find spots to lie down. It's a spacious sauna.

"Oh…hey guys. Sorry!" I don't know why I'm apologising. It's this weird thing we English like to do. "I'm just gathering my thoughts here. I've had just about enough of today!"

"Bit knackered, are ya?" grins Alyssia. "Me too. We've all had a busy one. You especially. You were bloody good out by the pool, you know that?"

I feel myself going red. Ridiculous.

"Oh, was I?"

I can't seem to think what to say next.

"Did you mind us joining in?" asks Latifa.

"Yeah, that was fine," I pause for thought, and ask the question that's been nagging at me. "Did someone tell you to do that? I mean, I didn't hear anything said…"

Latifa chuckles.

"Er, no. That was just something we *wanted* to do. Kind of spontaneous on our part, wasn't it Liss?"

"Mm-hmm," Alyssia murmurs. The sauna must be getting to her.

"Oh," is about all I can muster. I'm not entirely sure I wanted to hear that.

And again, I'm lost for a response. Latifa rescues the silence as only she can.

"Look, babe," she says. "We're horny women! We wanted to get involved. Just because there wasn't a specific instruction…well, we figure they're not going to be mad at us for being enthusiastic, are they?"

"Well, no," I admit. "The opposite, I would guess."

"Exactly!" I can almost *hear* Latifa beaming. "I mean, we'll happily do as we're told, but going above and beyond is probably going to be a good thing."

"Yeah, and it's fun too. So it's hardly a chore," Alyssia chimes in. "Everyone's a winner. I can't get enough cock."

"Or pussy…" teases Latifa. "You great big lezzer."

"So I like it both ways!" laughs the Aussie blonde. "Shoot me then!"

"And I like women too, Emma," Latifa says, turning her head slowly towards me. "Just so you're not in any doubt on that point. I sense you're a little uncomfortable with girl-girl stuff though?"

Looks like not much is off the table in this conversation. And I'm not sure I know the answer. I mean, yes, I *am* uncomfortable about it. But can I deny that I might be kind of interested? This Petra thing is playing on my mind. And closer to home, my eye falls again on Latifa's ripe tits.

I can see the appeal of her exotic mix and vivacious, perky boobs, topped as they are with nipples that I've only ever seen stiff and taut. I clear my throat and shift my gaze to Alyssia. I can't help thinking she does nothing for me. Or at least, her body itself doesn't.

The brazen Aussie girl was so eye-catching in her wacky see-through dress yesterday, so comfortable in her skin, that I hadn't really noticed her plainness. I run my eye over her now: her breasts are too big. They're just a tiny bit bottom-heavy and they splay out to the side as she lies on her back. She's got the odd speck and freckle down her torso, and her legs are a little too muscular to be ladylike. She fits the overly-sporty bisexual beach chick stereotype just fine.

She's not exactly hot, I wouldn't think. She just doesn't seem to be in our league. Did she get in on personality alone?

Suddenly my stupefied brain remembers Latifa's talking to me: "No…I mean, okay, it would be something a bit new. But we're pushing ourselves to experience new things here. It might be okay…"

"She doesn't give much away, does she?" Latifa remarks to her friend. "That's okay, girl. I know you English are a bit repressed! Us two have experienced quite a lot and we just love it here already. We're actually sharing our bed – didn't get much sleep last night to be honest! And then this morning…" she pauses. "Oh my, did we get a hard seeing-to! This place rocks!"

"Yeah, my arse hurts but it was so fucking worth it!" Alyssia adds, blunt as always.

There's two ways I can take that, but I decide not to pursue it. I'm repressed, after all.

Latifa gets up and moves closer to me. She sits down by my feet and puts a hand on my leg.

"We both really like you, Emma, and we're going to help you. We all know there are some cold ones around here, but you're not one of them. You're sexy and it's not hard to see how much you like the filthy stuff. You try to hide it sometimes but I've got a sixth sense for these things."

She smiles. And I think back to how I screamed and moaned with Rupert inside me. She probably has a point.

"You'll be missing out if you can't learn to really let yourself go. Embrace it all. Even the spunk in your face," she leans over and runs over my now-sweaty cheek with her thumb, decrusting it just a little.

I'm really starting to like these two. They're like young, sexy Miss Honeywells. It's like they've been here for years, done this before.

"You'll get the whore treatment at times. But remember everything, *everything,* that happens to you happens because it gives them a raging hard on. And that's all down to *you*, lovely! Keep telling yourself how much they want you. Once you're out of here, the money will remind you of that.

"When there's spunk in your eye and something huge up your arse, that's Emma power right there. Think about it! And once you really let your guilt go, you become twice as powerful. They will love that you love it. When you get that part right, you will be so turned on."

"I know you're right," I reply with a sigh. She ought to know a thing or two about overcoming repression, after all. "It's just easier said than done! Hey…you two seem to know a lot about how to play it here. You're sure you haven't done this before?"

"Not at all Emma! We're rookie hookers, promise. But we are randy bitches and we know how the world works, OK? I want to see the randy bitch inside you come out, because when she does, Emma is going to have a wicked time!

"This stuff is easy if you only let yourself enjoy it – learning the skills will then be a breeze. You'll have to try some new things here, but it's all about attitude. I think this life can be for you. Anticipate the thrill. Crave the excitement. And let go."

The last two words roll very, very slowly off her tongue, dangling in the thick, roasting air of the hothouse. They hover there until I snatch them.

Okay then. *Let go, Carling*.

Chapter Eleven

I *still* don't know his name. That guy who wakes us up every morning. Him and his goddamn bell. It's hump day today. In every sense of the word, I'm sure.

"Miss Carling, Miss Stoycheva. Good morning."

Yeah, yeah, yeah. Get it over with.

I feel the clammy sheets resting gently on my skin. Then I feel skin on skin: my thighs pressing together. With a sudden fright, I remember that I'm naked.

But at least it's a tiny but less of a shock today. I'm getting used to it now. And have I heard anything other than admiration for my body? In the cold light of day, there's only one answer to that. The compliments are good for my nerves.

I'm well-rested. Yesterday's exertions and emotions, followed by the hot sauna, had me out like a light. I'm glad I wasn't called upon for anything last night.

I stretch as Mr Firth-face moves to open the curtains. It feels just a little sexy to know I'm not wearing a stitch beneath my sheet. Does he know? I bet he knows everything. Before I know it, I'm imagining him lifting the covers for a peek at me. And then climbing into my bed.

God, it doesn't take me long to get going in the mornings these days! A slight chill heightens the thrill – and a glance out the window tells me the weather has broken. It's raining. More the English summer I'm used to. No sunscreen games today, I think to myself.

"Ladies, you have new showering instructions this morning," continues our impassive and smartly-dressed waker. "From now on, room-mates will be responsible for washing each other. Thoroughly."

With that, he turns on his heel and leaves us.

Shit.

My heart begins to race as his words sink in. After my pep talk in the sauna last night, I felt ready, even excited, for most things today might throw at me. Except Petra. I've learned to ignore my room-mate most of the time, but that's going to be tough if I've got to soap her up and down.

My fingers rub gently together at this particular thought. *That's weird.*

I still don't want to admit to myself that I'm attracted to that wench.

And I'll bet there'll be an audience.

My throat tightens.

"You know what to do, right?"

Petra's talking to me. That's quite an event in itself. We're on our walk down towards the shower room. She's wrapped up, but I've remembered my instructions and am ambling along completely naked. Somehow it gives me a strange sense of superiority now.

I can't quite place her tone. It's somewhere between helpful and mocking.

"I'm sure I'll be fine. You wash me and I wash you. Why don't you do me first, OK?"

She replies with her trademark shrug, which I assume must be a yes.

Miserable fucking whore.

And yet…those shoulders. Peachy. Curvy. Straight out of a soap advert.

Sure enough, there's a gallery today. As we step into the shower alongside the other girls, I glance over my shoulder and recognize some of the other gents I met at the ball. One is Jack, another is Frederick and the third has a name I can't remember. He's one of the older, less attractive ones. Also, Miss Jackson is up there.

We're last in. Latifa is well into running her soapy hands up and down Alyssia, and both wear broad smiles. Carrie, the tall one, is paired up with Diane, the cute little American redhead. Jane is uncomfortably pawing at the firm skin of her room-mate Simone. Lilia and Carol have settled in beneath a gushing shower head, and Sarah, the artsy English girl with the red-dyed hair, is showering solo. I guess she must have been sharing with the Irish one that ran out.

Lucky thing. Wish I could have my own room.

I'm so glad Petra's going to do me first. Just when I thought I had my brain in order, my thoughts are awhirl once more. I drifted off to sleep certain of myself last night, buoyed by the encouragement from Alyssia and Latifa. They could bring men, they could bring women, they could bring whips and chains, and I was going to love it.

But this…I just don't know how I feel about this. I've been slightly horny ever since I woke up naked. And I'm antsy at the thought of being touched again. Particularly by…no, I'm going to keep fighting this. I'm not going to let myself like anything that sullen Petra does to me.

She's rubbing her hands with soap now. Her face is expressionless, like a hairdresser getting set to shampoo another client's hair. At no point does she catch my eye. She moves round behind me.

She starts with my shoulders, works her way down my arms. Clinical. Her tiny hands massage the soap into my arms. Right down to my hands. Her fingers lock into mine: she will not miss a spot. Up the inside of my arms she goes, thorough but without tenderness. It tickles a little when she brushes my armpit.

You'll handle this, Emma.

Similar things are happening to the other girls receiving. Latifa and Alyssia, of course, are having a great time of it. Alyssia's head is thrown back now, as Latifa's hand lingers between her legs.

Others look more awkward. I notice that Carrie, in front of me, is kneading Diane's breasts a lot harder than necessary for cleaning purposes. Diane looks just like I feel: she wants to let go, but something is stopping her.

The steam is rising now, and I forget the audience again. All my energy is on getting through this without...*oh, fuuuuuck, hold your breath Emma, think of something else now. Don't think of her hands on your boobs. Don't think of her hands on your...*

This is getting hard. It's the second time in as many days that I've had a woman fondle my breasts. And yes...it's still nice. I look down at my toes, trying to forget everyone and everything. She's pressing against me now as she traces a soapy trail right across my stomach, up and down my sides. Onto my hips.

Close your eyes. No, don't! Damn you butterflies!

I can feel her rubbing my butt now. Her fingers glide down the side of each cheek in symmetrical unison, one by one doing a u-turn as she cups the meaty part of each one, pulling them gently towards her.

It still feels businesslike. She isn't lingering. She's doing her bit for what I assume is the show, that's all. Oh, but the touches are enough to get me going. And as I look down, I can see her sculpted feet, either side of mine, and they're so darn pretty. I have this weird thought of her in red heels.

What's happening to you Emma, for Christ's sake? I try to think of what a bitch she is.

She takes her hands away for a moment. I feel her turn my shoulders to change my position. She's got me facing the gallery now! Oh, Petra, why? Why does it have to be her, of all people? I feel their impassive eyes on me, and yes, it's doing something to me. Who knew I could be *this* okay in front of a crowd?

My breathing gets heavier but I look straight ahead, burrowing my gaze into the mundane, lifeless towels on the railing. It's no good. She pushes her foot between mine and twists, prising my legs a little wider. God, I think I know what's coming. I gulp. I want....*no, shut up!*

Now she's pressed up behind me again, her left arm holding me steady and her right arm...descending. Down, down, past my belly button and straight along my runway. I steel myself, keep looking ahead. *Close your eyes. Yes, OK, close your eyes.* It's fucking Petra, okay?

And now her glistening, soapy hand is over my bone and dropping. Her hand slows now, as it reaches my pussy. *Oh!* Her middle finger rolls down my clit with the accuracy of a tracer bullet. *God, yes!* I mean, no! Down, down, down she slides, that middle finger settling neatly between my lips as her hand descends.

And up she comes again. I am literally holding my breath. This is so good, so fucking erotic, everything heightening everything: the steam, the naked girls, the audience....Petra. No! *Not* Petra! *She's not on the turn-on list, you silly girl!*

She grazes my clit again, and takes her hand away just before I lose my cool. I seize the chance to breathe out. I'm aware of the gallery, Miss Jackson and the men, in my peripheral vision, but try desperately to forget. I cannot let this turn me on.

I hear Alyssia giggling: "Oh yes, girl, right there!"

This isn't helping. How the hell are they so brazen? Was I like that at the poolside yesterday? I wonder.

Petra's back, a fresh stock of soap on her finger. Now she presses even harder against me. Her curled hand pushes between my thighs again, but it bypasses my pussy this time. *Thank God for that!* But she's going for my ass. Of course she is. It's that middle finger again. It rubs the soap into my anus. Round and round, firmly. *No! You do not want her to slide it in!* I try not to think of how easily her cute little digit would enter me there, all soapy and wet. I fail. She doesn't. *Fucking tease.*

Now she pulls away from me. The trial is over. No more sensitive areas. She squats down and finishes the rest of me, lathering my legs and feet one by one. My neck wants to give in, but something tells me to keep looking ahead. What are they thinking? If only I had a different partner, I'd do the Alyssia thing, I swear I would. I *think* I would…wouldn't I?

"OK, finished," says Petra, rinsing off her palms beneath the water. Her tone is that of some snotty kid who's just solved a maths problem before anyone else in the class. My eyes narrow, but I say nothing. I can't believe I let this miserable creature take me so close. I'm glad I held firm.

So I guess I know what to do. I follow her lead. I'll do exactly as she did. I am not in the mood to be creative or give her pleasure.

When my hands touch her cunt and her breasts and her asshole, it's the first time I've ever touched those parts of a woman. It's a curious experience, but to me it doesn't count. It's too easy, too fleeting. Above all, it's Petra, and if I'm going to touch a woman's privates then I want it to be someone I don't actively dislike. So for me, this is all in a day's work. Her way will be my way.

And yet, despite myself, I feel something else when I'm exploring her finest asset. Her skin. I'm intoxicated by that cloak she wears. Oh, Jesus, it's so smooth. So slippery-soapy smooth. This is my indulgence, not hers. *Just because I take pleasure from your sleekness doesn't mean I like you, OK?* Her little doll's butt still has me in its snare, and I have to force myself to move on, to stop myself squeezing its teeny-tiny cheeks a couple of times.

And what the fuck is it with her feet? I have never had a thing for feet. But hers, boy, they're so damn gorgeous. I finish up with them, as she did with mine. I take my time, loving the feeling of wrapping my hand around her perfect heel and soaping up between each of her shiny-capped toes.

And yet I'm also loving that I've got her standing uncomfortably on one leg, too.

I can feel vibes of thunder coming from above, but I hold my ground. I linger on each foot, justifying – and doubling – my pleasure with the annoyance it gives her.

At last I let go, let her stand, and clamber to my feet. I catch her eye for a moment. I imagine I see a trace of a smile start to come, from this woman whose pussy I just rubbed and who just rubbed mine. But it doesn't quite come. If it was there at all.

"Ok, finished," I announce.

I feel good about myself this afternoon. I feel good that I handled that shower session reasonably well. And I feel good about my body – I am beginning to forget my nudity, even though I'm the only naked one at lunch. And I'm feeling excited. As long as the next challenge doesn't involve Petra, I'll be able to succumb to the rising horniness that gripped me this morning. I can't wait to do that.

And the next challenge is upon me now. Naked little Emma is outside the door of the Jennings room. It's actually the room directly beneath my own. The door swings open when I knock. I expect a man or a woman, perhaps two people. But I'm taken aback to see more. Two men. Miss Jackson. And Miss Tottingham, another of the mentors. All are seated, facing me as I enter. To the side stands Sarah, the girl with the freakish red-dyed hair. She wears a traditional French maid's outfit and black heels.

I assess the men quickly. I've seen them around, but I don't know their names. Thank God they're among the decent-looking ones, although nothing like as special as the two I've, ahem, encountered, so far. Both are dressed in thick bathrobes, no more. They're without shoes. The two mentors are as breezy as ever.

"Hello Emma," says Miss Jackson with her disarming smile. "Please go and stand next to Sarah. That's it. Now put your arm around her waist. You too, Sarah."

I begin to wish this was Latifa. I haven't really spoken to this Sarah much yet. Hardly at all, really. She seems OK, a little scatty, quite out there, perhaps a dramatic type. All we really have in common, from what I know of her, is that we're both English. Which is something, I suppose.

Sarah seems relaxed, though. I feel the crisp fabric of her outfit against my side, and there's something comforting in the way she pulls me close. She rests her left hand lightly on my hip bone. I shiver suddenly. The temperature has plunged today, and suddenly the side of me that's not pressed up against her feels acutely cold.

"Don't worry, you won't be chilly for long, dear," continues Miss Jackson. "I'm not sure if you've met Miss Tottingham, have you? She's in charge of anal sex training here. We'll now leave you to the instructions of George and Robert. You will do exactly as they say. Gentlemen."

I begin to shake. It's the cold, the mention of anal sex – *oh my!* – and the excitement. My nipples are already standing to attention from the temperature in this high-ceilinged, sparsely-furnished room. But I swear they harden further as flashbacks from my sexual memory bank blitz across my mind. Did I tell my mentor if I'd done anal before? I am pretty sure I didn't.

Whatever. The truth is it's been a while.

I feel Sarah's fingers tighten on my side as we await our instructions. I'm facing towards the massive window. It looks onto the driveway area, which is all gravel and bright-grey sky, framed by the sentinel trees that keep our secrets within. The trees sway – it's windy today. I hear a crow squawk in the distance.

Inside the room is very little besides built-in bookshelves filled with tomes, a couple of drinks cabinets and the chairs on which the staff sit. The most striking feature is the furry rug, grey to match the day. We're standing just off the edge of it, but I can see it's fluffy and soft. A pool of long-haired comfort. The chairs are arranged around it.

"Miss Carling, kindly strip Miss Smith," instructs Robert, a man with hawkish features and blonde hair. I notice a bulge appearing in the groin of his robe.

"Of course," I smile. I surprise myself with my readiness. The speed bump that was showering with Petra has come and gone, Latifa's words from last night still ring in my ears once again. Anticipate the thrill. Crave the excitement. *Let go.*

And I've been anticipating like crazy since I got the message to come up here. The craving is beginning to take over. So then, it's just a question of letting go. I don't have a clue what's coming, but I think I'm ready for whatever it might be.

I've never unclothed someone before, but instinctively I stand behind her so I won't block the view. Hell, I must be a natural! I can smell the scent of her shampoo, which I've noticed she spends a long time using in the shower. It's coconut and vanilla, heavenly scents for me. Her short red hair shimmers bright before my eyes. It seems to have a life of its own.

I unhook the shoulder braces and let them drop to the floor. This is easy! I start to unbutton the blouse from the top down, and as I do so I notice the smell of her perfume mingling with that of her hair. I forget what's to come and lose myself in the sensations my nose is giving me. I breathe in deep, once again surprised at how I'm living my role.

I pull the blouse off her and it falls on my feet. Over her shoulder I can see her black and white bra, all intricate and curly patterns, revealed. From this vantage point I can see right down her cleavage, all the way to where the generous space between her breasts loses itself in sombre shadow. Suddenly I felt an urge to run my hands over her bra. *Why not, Emma?* What did Latifa say? Going above and beyond is probably going to be good.

So I do it. I haven't looked at this girl twice since we arrived, and here I am succumbing to the latest surge of horniness. More than anything, it's her smell that has me going. It's like a scent from Eden.

I'm not even sure I'm doing it for the people watching, but I'm aware they'll likely approve. *They'll love that you love it.* And all men like a bit of girl-girl stuff, right? That's what the whole shower thing is about, surely? I feel like I'm ready to go with the flow.

"Stop, Emma."

What have I done?

It's George who speaks. His tone is kindly and soft. He has an easygoing look about him, though he's not classically handsome. He is clean-shaven with jet-black hair, and there's a certain passion in his dark hazel eyes. He's the kind of man you have no reason to argue with.

"I want you to kiss. Kiss each other."

I feel a massive surge of adrenaline, but I hesitate. What's this force that wants to hold me back at vital moments?

You can do this Emma. You want to do this Emma.

God, it's been a long time since those drunken student snogs. I barely remember them. They weren't real kisses. This is going to have to be. And I think I want it to be.

We turn to face each other and Sarah gives me the demurest of smiles. It melts me. Her sharp face, nose stud and all, has left little impression on me until now, but this smile changes all of that. Her mouth splays a little more on one side than the other, and a dimple surfaces on her cheek as one eyebrow raises.

Oh! Sarah won't be short of business with a smile like that. She can charge double. I might pay her myself, the way I feel right now.

Either she wants this too, or she's a fucking good actress. Whatever, it's working on me.

I'm the taller one, so I feel like it's up to me to take the lead. One hand on her waist, one softly on her nape, I probe gently with my lips, nibbling at this girl I've barely spoken to, much less know.

My eyes close but I can feel that she's still got some of that smile as she kisses me back. And my heart skips a beat when I hear a tiny mewl come from her – she *does* want this! And the fact that I care? I think Latifa would approve.

From the corner of my eye, I notice the men loosening the belts on their robes.

My hand roams to the small of her back as my tongue delves between her lips, mingling sensuously with hers. I mewl back at her. Press myself closer. Fuck, I had no idea how good this could be.

Our tongues wrestle, but it's mere love-wrestling. It's soft, lubricated, warm and intimate, this moment. I suck at her salty upper lip, sighing again at the taste of her mouth, her skin. I hear a rustling away to my left, but I'm lost in Sarah.

I'm surprising myself here. Naked, kissing another girl with abandon, so much so that I've forgotten the audience. Yes, Latifa would be thrilled with me.

Robert's voice brings me back to the room.

"Thank you, ladies. We very much enjoyed that."

I'm loathe to pull away, but Sarah pushes me gently back. Then she pulls me close again, arm around my waist as we face them.

My God, their gowns are both open. The bulges are exactly what I thought they were. George is enormous. I've never seen…such girth.

The talk of anal sex comes back to me. I eye his member with apprehension and awe. Robert's less overwhelming length begins to look as easy to handle as Petra's finger might have been. Jesus, my thoughts are all over the place.

"On the rug, both of you. Sarah, you just strip and be done with it."

Robert's voice has taken on an urgent, no-nonsense edge. Clearly things are about to go up a gear.

"How do you want me, Sirs?" I ask sweetly, feeling the tingle between my legs rise at the words. I'm in some form today, it seems.

"I want you on your hands and knees, thank you," says George. "Face away from me, Emma."

I do as he instructs, assuming a doggy position as I look across to see Sarah stepping out of her clothes. Why does being told what to do like this get me so hot?

"Sarah, I want you next to her," says Robert. "Right up close. Touching."

It's beginning to sound like I'm going to have to handle George and his vast manhood. I hope I can. The challenge makes the dampness rise in my pussy, and the nerves jump in my tummy.

She settles in next to me, pressing her side against mine as instructed. I feel very, very keyed up. I look across at her as I hear the men rise to their feet. I see Sarah's plump lips pout, and I steal a kiss with her again. She returns it with passion.

I am shocking myself deeply now. Where did my reticence go? But fuck, I'm so turned on. I have been all day.

"Miss Tottingham? We're ready for you."

It's George who speaks.

I'm surprised at this turn of events, and watch as the 'anal specialist' mentor makes for the drinks cabinet, opens a drawer and fishes out what looks like a container of lube.

And now, my hands and knees buried in the soft fur of the rug as I await my fate, I begin to quiver.

Chapter Twelve

I don't remember signing up for this. Oh, sure, yeah, I *did* sign up for this. But right now, on my hands and knees, naked and trembling, I feel like it's out of my control. They're so strong, so uncompromising. Responsibility for any of this is a distant memory.

And I think I fucking love that.

I can almost feel the shy, repressed Englishwoman scampering away in horror at what's being done to her. While the rest of me shrugs, saying 'so be it, you're at their mercy. You're captive. You're here to serve. It's not *you* asking for these things.'

I wish they'd hurry up. I feel like I'm covered in static, that if I were touched now, an explosive spark would split the room. It's a feeling I haven't had for a long time. That job robbed me of a couple of my best years. Who knew I had so much lustful longing stored up?

Something deeply submissive seems to have come over me since I knelt down. Without even being asked, I drop my elbows to the carpet, pushing my utterly exposed hind quarters high into the air. I bury my head between my forearms as a tiny little growl escapes my throat. Trying to bury the crushing need that threatens to kill me if I don't get some soon.

I can hear Miss Tottingham's pointed shoes cross the hard, polished floor and stop on the rug in front of us. I can smell the leather and feel how she towers above our heads.

"Sarah, please put out your left hand," she says, her voice flat and neutral.

I raise up my head to see what's happening. The mentor bends down and squeezes some clear, jelly-like lube onto Sarah's round, rosy fingers. She takes Sarah's chin gently in her hand. I notice Miss Tottingham has short-cropped nails, and how Sarah closes her eyes and raises her head like a cat does when it wants its throat scratched.

I think Sarah is spellbound too.

Miss Tottingham sinks to her knees and whispers into the space between our ears. Her hot breath whirls in that void. It makes a strand of my dewy hair rustle against my temple.

"I want you to prepare Emma's anus for a man. You know what to do."

I really hope she does.

I can't wait for something, anything in there.

What happened to my trepidation about anal penetration? I'm gagging for it.

Sarah's eyes are wide open again. Miss Tottingham releases her chin. There's a moment's hesitation on Sarah's part, so slight that perhaps only I notice it. I'm noticing everything right now. Every sense is on high alert. Her eyes flick to mine for a fragment of a second. I give her a tiny nod. One that spurs her to action.

My desperate sense of touch feels a deep loss as her skin pulls away from mine. She crawls around behind me, and I drop my head to the rug again. It feels clean and new. I like the way the fibres feel against my forehead.

Miss Tottingham's shoes move away. Then I sense she is also behind me. So are the two men, their tools primed. *Oh God, this is it.*

Some of Sarah presses against me again. She's steadying herself. I feel her forearms resting on my sides.

There's a loud thumping. Is it her heart? Or mine? Maybe both. *Holy fuck.*

My butt cheeks are being pulled apart, stretched by a pair of hands. I rack my brains: does she have long nails? I just don't know.

Fuck, it's been a good couple of years since…

I'm so excited.

But jumpy.

Please let her have short nails.

Instinctively I widen my legs a little, push my butt even further up in the air. I am brazen today! But still my heart thumps. For all sorts of reasons.

Her finger is rubbing at my rim. It's cold stuff, that lube. I flinch a little at the temperature, but there's nothing not to like about this gloopy massage.

I panic for a moment as I wonder if I'm dirty down there, but I remember this morning's shower, and Petra's finger. Fuck, it's the second time since sunrise that a woman has fingered my asshole. And it's nothing to what's coming.

The thought makes my clit swell. Honestly, I can feel it happen. Another first.

Now she pushes in. Oh, so gently! Sweet Sarah. If she has long nails, I can't feel them. I gasp, as I always have. It's a shock nobody can prepare you for.

But even as she starts to wiggle a little, I settle. She takes in what's happening, and goes a little further. She probes deeper. I whimper as she twirls some more. Loosening me, stretching me.

I open an eye and look back beneath my dangling breasts. Miss Tottingham is knelt close to my rear, vigilant. I feel…like a centrepiece. The star of the show.

Another finger. She twists them and turns them. My asshole relaxes, gets less taut by the second as she prepares me. Suddenly I feel I could hold her there all day. But I want to kiss her too! *Oh, Emma, where are your thoughts running to now?*

After a minute or so of probing inside my increasingly warm back hole, I hear Miss Tottingham murmur approvingly to Sarah, and the fingers withdraw from me.

"She's ready, gentlemen."

Which one am I getting?

Beneath my crouched torso I can see Miss Tottingham move away and resume her seat.

I raise my head now, eager to know what's going to happen. I'm startled to see *both* men rise.

Robert walks around and stops in front of me.

I crane over my shoulder and I see George kneel down behind me. Robert has lost his robe completely, but George still wears his on his shoulders. It's open at the waist and his monumental erection is all I can look at.

Hang on, why is the other one here? What am I expected to do? What would Latifa do? Should I take him in my mouth? Questions are flying at me.

But before I can do anything, Robert motions me to kneel upright. I do as I'm told, and as I raise my naked front to his full view, that feeling of total powerlessness washes over me again. It makes my pussy gush.

I feel George's hands pull my knees apart. His own knees are spread too: I can feel them inside mine. I can also feel his terrifying length resting against my spine. Resting with intent. But I still don't know quite where this is going.

"Up," grunts Robert, grabbing my butt so that I kneel in a higher position. I feel like a meerkat now. But so totally wanted it's making my eyes water. George is nuzzling my neck with his stubble. Eyes. Watering.

Now there's a triangular tunnel formed by my thighs and the floor. As far as I can tell, the man behind me is mimicking the position. Robert slides feet-first into that tunnel and lies flat on his back.

Oh.

Wait.

Now I think I know what's happening.

My heart beats with the speed of a butterfly's wings, but crashes like thunder.

Stay cool, Emma. Stay cool.

I've never tried this.

I don't know if I can do it.

But now I feel George's hand push my upper body down towards the floor again. And I remember I don't have a say in any of this. I signed that paper.

My face is now right above Robert's. I'm so turned on. Kissing him feels as natural as not kissing him would feel wrong. I plunge into his lips, no doubt still tasting of Sarah's sweet mouth. The thought thrills me. The action pushes my ass into the sky again.

And now George does it. I can feel his dick brushing up and down my crack, probing for that perfect angle. Sweet Lord, yes! *Take him, Emma, take him.*

But I yelp, just a little, as he shoves. No amount of Sarah fingers could ready me for this. There's resistance from my screaming hole. Not because it doesn't want it. Oh no. It's just too big. *It's not too big, Emma. Take it like a big whore.*

I've stopped kissing Robert for a moment as I wince. He pulls my head back to his.

"I never told you to stop," he says, in a tone you don't argue with.

I respond by kissing him harder than ever, even as my ass feels set to burst. Suddenly I feel that pop as George muscles past that first line of defence, my tiny pink hole simply giving up the fight. I gasp, suddenly a whole lot happier. I feel him pushing slowly in, as far as he can go. Which is as far as I can take.

It feels like he's touching my stomach. He rests there a moment. It feels explosively good. He is hard as a rock and I fucking love that feeling of being filled. His hands come down to my tits, and he pulls me up, away from Robert.

"Come on Jones, your turn now," says a voice somewhere behind me.

Shit, here is it. *Brace yourself now.*

My quim feels stretched and taut, somehow full, even without anything in it. It's that huge cock in my butt! But

Robert, lying beneath me, is nuzzling its lips with his tip. He, too, is on the prowl for entry. I close my eyes as my head swims with a mix of hot erotic cravings and trepidation.

Not guilt so much. Not right now.

George isn't thrusting yet, but I can feel him twitch and pulse, deep inside me. This is the calm before the storm, surely? He nudges my hips forward with his, to give Robert a better angle.

Robert brushes my clit with his tip as he fumbles towards my lower lips. I jump at the sensation. George feels it, squeezes my breasts a little. *God!*

At last Robert presses into me. It isn't easy. George has left very, very little room. Everything feels vacuum-packed down there. Now that he's in, I'm not sure he's getting out in a hurry.

I close my eyes again and take a deep breath. I feel like a princess, utterly fucking worshipped.

Double penetration. *You're actually doing it! Emma, you little porn star!*

Once again I'm being manoeuvred. Pushed down. I'm flat on top of Robert, and George is flat on top of me. I guess this man sandwich is the only way this can work. I spread my legs so access is easy from above and below.

Holy fuck. Double access. *Emma!*

If they start to move, I may not last long.

I begin to kiss Robert again. I need a distraction, or my head will explode from the filling I'm getting.

The thrusting starts. *Oh boy.* One from George. My cheeks fill with air. One from Robert. Fucking weird. Fucking tight.

George. Robert. George. Robert.

Ass. Pussy. Ass. Pussy.

They settle into a rhythm just like that. I begin to enjoy it, this stretched feeling. I'm at my absolute maximum. I can't tell one man from the other. It just feels like one massive thing inside of me, wanting me.

I try to keep kissing Robert but it's difficult. I keep being jerked. But every time I miss his mouth, it gets me off to think of why I missed it. I'm making noise now, a throaty squeal with every hit. Even as I kiss.

This is phenomenally fucking sexy.

It's almost imperceptible how they up their speed. The pattern remains the same, but the pulses get quicker. Robert's doing very well: it can't be easy from underneath. I suspect their balls must be touching. I'm majorly turned on to think they'd do that to have a piece of me.

It chafes. It fills. It hurts. It has won me. *Please don't stop.*

I don't scream words like I did with Rupert. But I don't last long this time either. When I come, my ass is so stretched it feels like you could fit a baseball in there. It makes my cunt feel even more saturated. The thought sends me wild. There is no way I can hide my muffled squeals and tremors as I orgasm in my man sandwich.

I came before the guys again. I don't know if this is the right way around. Sarah, whom I've forgotten, appears at my side and whispers into my ear. Reminds me to keep going. I nod, suddenly aware of what a mess I must look. The perspiration is gathering on my brow as I'm pressed between their warmth, their movement.

It's no trouble, really. I'm still enjoying this. I keep kissing Robert, revelling in the aftershocks as the men pump themselves towards their climax. Sarah's fondling my hair, and I feel bad for her being left out. Poor naked Sarah. She's squatting shamelessly next to my head, and there's no mistaking the creaminess I notice emanating from her denied pussy. She must be gagging for it. I look up at her with punch-drunk eyes.

I bring my mind back to the job at hand. I'm not convinced I don't come a second time as the men unleash into me. First a warm spurt of George in my butt, then a hot spray of Robert in my still-convulsing cunt. Alive as my stuffed orifices are to every twitch, I can feel each of their orgasms distinctly, squirming as I listen to their satisfied grunts.

Hell yeah.

I'm in a daze as Sarah and I swap roles and the gentlemen swap theirs. I'm sweating, reddened in places and still breathing heavily as I put my finger up her butt. I'm barely aware of what I'm doing. I've gone a little slack-jawed, and I'm long past the point of anything shocking me. I find the loosening of her puckered little hole quite therapeutic. A chance to get my breath back.

Miss Tottingham cleans up George with a bowl of soapy water before the switch. It reminds me that this place isn't just fun, it's also a professional setup. And I'm probably being scored for my performance. Forgot about that again. Oh dear.

"Sit on the floor, Emma," Miss Jackson chimes in. "We don't want you dripping on the carpet." Oh yes. It must be like Niagara Falls down there. Hmm. I sit cross-legged on the varnished floor.

Sarah gets similar treatment, although she doesn't have to take quite so enormous a shaft in her rear. Robert enters her first, his prick still sodden with my juices as he presses into her ass. For a while he bends her over in a standing position. She looks at the floor, and I wonder what's going through her mind. Does she fight the same English demons I do?

It's weird watching, but as I come to my senses I begin to get turned on again. I hug my knees now, but it no longer even crosses my mind to be conscious of my nudity. I'm still in the moment, and barely perceive the two mentors watching as, finally, Sarah gets put in a man sandwich too. She's on her back, though, her anal attacker below and George playing missionary above. It doesn't look quite as comfortable, I think to myself.

I'm not quite sure she comes. The men certainly do, and who could blame them for that? Sarah seems confident at times, but shy at others. I can't quite place her. I make a note to ask her later.

The mentors look pleased enough when it's over, though they don't say anything about our performance as they dismiss us.

"Thank you, ladies, you may go and rest," says Miss Jackson. "Sarah, leave your clothing here and remain naked until further notice."

I see her mouth twitch with a trace of alarm, but I smile inwardly: I have forcibly stripped company at last! In this warped new world, that feels like a reward of sorts.

Nobody offers us a chance to clean up. I'm not surprised any more. And so we walk out of the door with unmistakable evidence of intercourse streaming down our thighs. That, and a curious gaping feeling inside my butt. I'm not sure either sensation bothers me anymore.

It's a different feeling walking down the hallway this time. We don't meet anybody, but today I'm not dreading the prospect. For one thing, I have solidarity in Sarah. She makes me feel like the confident one as she hangs slightly back and keeps her arms folded across her. She walks with her legs squeezed and her toes pointing inwards, as if that will somehow make her generous vanilla patch less visible.

Reminds me of me yesterday.

Weird how you can let yourself come while being fucked by two men, in full view of three other people, then be shy about something like walking around naked. Why is that?

I find myself taking Sarah by the hand.

"Come on," I hear myself say. "You'll get used to it in no time! I was shy yesterday but I'm past it now."

It's confident Emma saying these words, and I'm happy she's still with me. This is the Emma who is proud of her prettiness and doesn't take shit. Self-awareness isn't really my strong suit, but even I can't fail to recognise the change that's come over me today.

"Thanks…" says Sarah, flashing me that English grimace-smile. I can see something like concern in her eyes, almost like she's welling up.

"You want to talk, maybe?" I ask her gently. This sensitivity is another thing I like about confident Emma.

Sarah sniffs a little and nods as we stop outside her door.

"Shall we go in here?" she says, her eyebrows raised. "I'm…I don't share with anyone."

"Sounds good!" I'm tempted to suggest a swap. But she's done nothing to deserve that.

She opens up the door. It's the first time I've been into one of the other rooms, and straight away I see that this place isn't a hotel, where every room is the same. Hers is laid out differently, with three-quarter beds standing sentinel on either side of the window. It doesn't seem to have a bath, but it's got a little lounge area instead.

I'm not sure we should be sitting on those expensive-looking chairs in this state, though. And I think Sarah has the same thought.

"Um, how about we sit on the spare bed? Probably better to, ah, drip on that?" she suggests.

I nod and smile at her, amused now by the ridiculousness of it all. Two grown women, not a stitch of clothing on their bodies, unable to sit on chairs because of the sticky semen leaking from their vaginas, and, er, elsewhere. Because they've just been double-fucked. On a Wednesday afternoon.

And I smirk to myself once more as I think of the office chair I'd be virtually chained to right now if I hadn't given those assholes a piece of my mind. Despite the rollicking I've just had from Robert and George, my shoulders sure are a lot less tense than they would normally be by midweek.

Sarah hops onto the bed and sits, shyly, with her legs folded in front of her. I surprise myself by sitting cross-legged, without a thought. *You were kissing this girl a few minutes ago…*

"You were amazing back there," I tell her truthfully. "Why the worried frowns? I can't think of any reason…"

"Oh, I know," she sniffs. "It seemed right in the room but as soon as we left, and I didn't have my clothes, I felt really self-conscious and a bit guilty."

I ponder her words. Why am I not feeling that any more? Have I really been hardened quite so fast?

"Hey, that's normal, Sarah…I think! You've had it easy. When my clothes got taken off me I had to walk out of the room all alone. You've no idea…"

"It's kind of dumb, isn't it?" she says, her features brightening a little. "I mean, we do all those things behind closed doors, and then…"

"I was just thinking exactly the same," I interrupt. "I guess it's a responsibility thing, don't you reckon? Like…I don't know about you, but I was brought up in the innocent English way and this stuff is, you know…not what nice young ladies do."

"Oh yes!" she exclaims, sitting up a little so that her firm, peaked tits are difficult not to look at. "I know what you mean. But then, when we're kind of being *made* to do stuff, we feel like it's not our doing, and it's okay."

I nod.

"Until we walk out the door and the people making us do stuff aren't with us. Then we have doubts again."

"Exactly."

She chuckles quietly. We seem to get each other completely. No free-spirited Aussie would understand us like we do. But that passion that came over me in the room, when I kissed her with such burning lips, seems to belong to another time. I can tell she's super-cute, pretty in a girl-next-door kind of way. Like me, I suppose. But it seems like that moment we had just belonged only to that scene. It's kind of weird. Or is that me flipping back to my old self again?

I'm curious to know if it's just me. I probe her a little.

"But did you enjoy everything in there? You didn't seem too introverted…"

Her eyes widen and I see them light up. Just the mention of our encounter seems to have her going.

"Hell yeah! I did it once before but there's nothing much not to like, is there? I feel a little torn in two right now, but in a good way. And you?"

She puts her hand on my knee: "You were a wonderful kisser, Emma. I…I…really did like that."

She cocks her head to one side, as if seeking approval.

"It sure was good," I agree. Her hand tickles the inside if my knee. She really has perked up a lot since we got in here. I gather the spirit of that kiss is still with her. But I'm just not ready for more lesbian talk right now. Too much has happened today. *You'll handle this, Emma.*

I lean back on my hands, trying to cool the situation off just a little.

Nice one, Emma. You've just shown her your dripping pussy, you genius.

Now confident Emma resolves to keep the spirit of honest conversation going.

"Fuck, I really lost myself in that kiss…but the feeling has kind of gone away now. I don't really have any, erm, history with girls."

I avoid catching her eye, but hear her giggle. I feel like a bomb just got defused.

"Oh, *now* who's the shy one?" she grins.

We both laugh as she takes my hand off my knee and we change the subject. I think we're going to be friends. At least.

We stay there, just talking, for much of the afternoon. It's nice to simply hang out, and not have to endure my painful shared room. We really do have similar upbringings. We're both city girls, and we're both at a bit of a crossroads in life. She's graduated from drama school but having a tough time finding any work.

As I get to know Sarah, she begins to add up for me. No doubt someone who wears her heart on her sleeve and enjoys attention. Drama must suit her in that way, but does she have the necessary confidence to handle its knocks? I think the outrageously dyed hair and the body piercings – belly and a nipple – mask a naturally shy character.

Ultimately we've got a lot in common. I think Sarah has to work to bring out her inner minx. So do I. But when our switches get flicked, the minxes are pretty compelling.

We never discuss George or Robert. What we thought of their looks, their ways. The men who just drilled themselves inside each of us don't come up in conversation. Only much later does it hit me how odd that is.

Chapter Thirteen

When I get back to my room, I find a note on my bed. What *now?* I'm feeling good right now, kind of glowing after making friends with Sarah. These letters tend to be unsettling. I just don't know if I need that right now.

Petra's not there. Probably out on a fucking assignment. She's a whore.

So are you, Emma...

I slap that thought away. Suddenly it annoys me. Yup, the English prude in me has turned up again. Just hours after I kissed a girl and took two cocks. How positively annoying!

I sit down on the bed with a sigh, crossing my legs for nobody in particular as I unfold the latest piece of paper. The message is simple.

Miss Carling, you may get dressed. If you wish.

Best wishes,
Miss Jackson.

I stare at page, blinking at the good news. I've almost forgotten about being naked. But it *is* good news. Isn't it?

I digest what it means. At last, I can go to the wardrobe and pick out something to cover my modesty. No more feeling like some kind of warped Eve. An Eve who ate the apple, felt shame, but still walked around nude anyway.

Then I think of Sarah, who has just been stripped and instructed to remain bared to all. All those eyes. Jealous female eyes. Male eyes that would blaze her tight body up and down with their longing stares. Poor Sarah. I know she'll enjoy the solidarity if I stay bare with her. We just spoke about it.

If you wish. Getting dressed is quite clearly optional.

I unfold my legs, lie back on the bed and close my eyes. I crook my arm and rest the back of my hand on my forehead. It's my this-is-too-much pose.

I can't believe I'm thinking about whether to get dressed or not. What has this place done to me? Yes, it really is a bit too much.

I'm out in the garden, alone. Nobody is around. It's a dry evening, but chilly, so I've put on jeans and a black blouse. I wanted a jumper, too, and, miraculously, I found a woolly jersey tucked in the furthest corner of the closet. I'm not convinced it hasn't been left here by accident – but I'm grateful to find it.

I've got no underwear on out here. The rebel in me wants to cling onto that as she fights to stay naked. She accepts the clothes, but only because it's cool outside and she knows I need to think with a clear, head. One that isn't clanging with sexy sensations like the gentle wind whistling across my nipples. One that isn't attached to a body being ogled and inspected and sized up. She reckons it's only temporary, because it's chilly and I'm alone. I think I'll stick to naked when I'm with Sarah and the others. Just to help her.

I don't understand myself at all right now. Do I even know what I want? At all?

I'm sitting on the swinging chair at the bottom of the garden, looking back up towards the house. It really is deserted, and I wonder if some of the resident gentlemen come and go from the house. Do they even sleep here? I think some of the girls are eating inside, but I'm not hungry right now. And I don't feel like talking.

My shoulders are hunched forward, my palms pressed down on the simple wooden plank. The willow fronds swish all around me as I stare absently at the ground. There's something insistent about their constant to-ing and fro-ing. It gets to me. Maybe because it reminds me of me.

I feel completely and utterly overwhelmed. Everything has caught up with me this evening. Sunday seems a lifetime ago, and I struggle even to order the things I've done, the acts I've committed. It's an almighty swamp of experience, emotion and embarrassment. I don't know how I feel about any of it.

I've had my highs, my lucid moments. Times when I've thought I've broken through. But I keep coming back here, to this shy, guilty, confused Englishwoman. Why can't I be like Alyssia? This must be so simple for her!

I find myself wanting Rupert. Where did he go? I know he's capable of holding me, making me feel like a comforted little girl in his arms. Last time we spoke, though, he'd fucked me like an animal.

What if *I* want more of *him?* And how could he dismiss me like that? Why did I just go along with it? Is this how the game will be? *How can you want more of him, Emma!*

I feel the tips of my ears pound with redness as I think of how much I loved being fucked like an animal. Yes, it was as wonderful an orgasm as I've ever had. Not even the prude in me could deny that.

Yet I don't even know the guy. And I'm mad at him. Cause he told me to clear off, and left me. When he knew I liked him.

I sigh again as I look to the pool and see the spot where I did *that* to Rupert's friend. Sprayed, in front of everyone. Who knew I had it in me? Do I *want* that in me?

It's all very well for Latifa and Alyssia, with their fine words of letting go and their open legs and weird lesbian banter. I just don't know if I'm *like* them. I'm not the life and soul of the party. I think too much. I'm…

My inner rebel is jumping up and down, though, clashing deafening cymbals. She startles me with the memory of kissing Sarah today. Of being anally penetrated by a strange man. While being fucked in my pussy. A pussy that had no need of lubrication. And of completely falling into the tail-spinning world of pleasure that came with all of it.

She has a point. Maybe I'm a born whore.

The thought makes me cross. I frown. What road have I come down, and is it too late to turn around? There are things I don't like about this place. Mostly that means Petra. And her bitchy friend Lilia, who hasn't said a word to me all week. Then there's the humiliation. Having to be Petra's personal body washer. The way I've been *used*. And made to walk around naked.

And yet part of me wants to keep doing the naked walks, and not just for Sarah. There's a titillation to it I can't deny. Part of me would pay all the money in the world to not miss whatever is coming next. I'm feeling sexually sated for the moment, but for how long? It seems that I'm discovering a new Emma – or perhaps a buried, long-forgotten Emma – who gets switched on at the slightest erotic hint.

Why am I denying this new Emma, and constantly judging her the moment the dust settles on her fun? *Leave her alone!*

I think of how comfortable my bed is here. How plush the car was, and how sumptuous the food. How pretty the girls are. How hard and how often and how well I've been…seen to. I flush inwardly as I think of my responses. I want to slap myself for being a dirty slut. And slap myself again…*it's a school for dirty sluts and you came here by choice!*

But I don't know how I'm doing. What was it Miss Jackson said? Something about gauging my natural responses? I swallow hard. I think I've 'responded' better than I expected to. But would that show through to *them?* Or have I been too shy? Too keen? Too reluctant? Over-sensitive? Too noisy? The thought hits me that maybe I'm not supposed to come when I'm doing this for a job.

I just don't know what's normal. Does Petra come when she's working? I can hardly imagine so. Is she anything other than mechanical when she's with a client? Does she enjoy anything except smoking and being a cow?

I have absolutely no idea about any of this. God, anything for some feedback! Sometimes, with so much emotion and stimulation buzzing around, it's hard to remember that this is a school at all. Probably because it's the weirdest school I ever did see.

But what happens when I get an ugly man? Can I bring myself to do it? Petra would shrug and get on with it, wouldn't she? *Is that you, Emma?*

I think of the work that had me in its snare until last week. It's gone eight o'clock right now, but half of them would still be in the office, too scared to go home until someone else did. Nothing, absolutely nothing, could be worse than being back in that office. I smile just a little, and suddenly the swishing willows seem to calm me.

I've only been here three days, but feel a lot less alone than I did on Sunday. I have Latifa and Alyssia looking out for me. I'm not sure they quite get me – they're too extrovertly strong. I'm more feisty in a don't-mess-with-me kind of way, but only when pushed. I've never gone looking for trouble. Or fun, come to that. Though everything's been turned on its head here.

But I like that Latifa and Alyssia are on my side. Then there's Sarah. Oh yes, that was some snog. I breathe in sharply as I recall my first girl-kiss in years. How I lost myself in it, how our wrestling tongues made me feel like I was floating on air. Maybe it was just one of those in-the-moment things. It passed once we were out of that room. But I feel she's someone I can open up to.

My eyes narrow at the thought that she might be naked in the hallways, or at dinner, all by herself. I feel guilty for leaving her. Who else will take her hand? Not Petra, nor Lilia, that's for sure. In no time at all I have come to feel sisterly about Sarah. Petra...not so much. And yet there's this kind of fascination with her. A bizarre, warped kind of desire that I can't shake.

I don't even want to think about that.

I run my mind through the others instead. Simone seems nice enough. I haven't really spoken to Diane the American redhead or Carol the pretty, petite oriental. Jane is a false waste of time I want nothing to do with. And Carrie…well she seems distant, but there's something else about her too. She's a mystery that needs solving. I don't know what she's all about.

I can't believe so many girls are even *here*. I can't believe only one of them ran out so far. Are we all natural-born prostitutes? I can't be the only one struggling, can I? Or am I? Or…am I doing just fine, maybe?

I feel thankful again that I've got Sarah to talk to now. She's shown me a human side that Petra and Lilia totally don't have. Latifa and Alyssia are a little *too* human, intimidating in their enjoyment of…things. At least I have one person on my wavelength. As for the rest, we'll see what the rest of the week brings. No doubt our paths will cross sooner rather than later.

I heave another deep breath. *Just get through a couple more days, Emma.* That's right. Didn't Miss Jackson say we'd know where we stand after the 'reaction testing'? I think she did. And it hasn't been all bad. Stressful enough to give me a headache, yes. A frustrating tease beyond measure at times. But the pleasures I've had…*oh my*. In the moments they have felt exquisite. It's only afterwards that I've over-analysed, and wondered at myself.

And now, just as I'm gathering my wits, I think of my mother. And what she'd say if I confessed where I really spent my time away. Once she understood – which would take a while – she'd cry. My father would be uncomprehending. He'd just gawp at me like a goldfish, shaking his head. If I go into this line of work, will I have to tell them? *God no!* But secrets are hard work. Will I have to make up an entirely fictional office job? Tell them I'm moving to Australia?

Everything about it makes me want to cry.

And I find myself wanting Rupert here. Here with his arm around me, making it all better.

Chapter Fourteen

I sit there for some time, blubbing and sobbing like a child. And when I think about why I'm crying, it makes me want to cry more. I feel trapped, like I've swum too deep and I'm caught in a rip. It's reasonable to be overwhelmed by all this, I guess, but falling apart at the seams is not a response I'm proud of.

I bet Petra wouldn't be getting all hung up on a 'client'. She wouldn't be torn to pieces about her vocation. She's probably never cried in her life. How could a heart of stone produce tears? Somehow that thought makes me choke up again. What a mess.

But the very notion of professional Petra handling all this better than me is enough to make me sit up, wipe my running nose and blink the tears away. Because the idea of her being better than me at something – even if it's harnessing her chilliness to her advantage – is not acceptable to me.

Come ON Emma! Stop moping – this isn't you! So I fancy the pants off Rupert, but how can I get like this? We had one date, one shag. I'll definitely need to be tougher than this out in the real world. Even if I'm never a hooker, actually.

But it's easier said than done. I doubt I can dismiss him from my thoughts at the drop of a hat. But I sure as hell can stop with the crying and try to do something positive. If I decide not to be a hooker, it'll be because I choose not to. Not because I can't.

I look around for some kind of distraction. Some sort of fresh start.

It's twilight, and it will be for some time. Even though it's a grey day. I'm somehow feeling even less hungry than before. There's still no sign of life. It's almost as though everyone has gone off somewhere without me. Or…are they all fucking?

At that thought, and unexpected twinge of jealousy seizes me for a second. Where did that come from?

I stand up. I feel like exploring on my own. Walking will clear my head, right? And I haven't really had a good look at the lower reaches of the garden.

I set off further away from the house, feeling the grass get steadily wilder beneath my tennis shoes. This feels naughty, and I'm not sure why. Is there somewhere I'm supposed to be? They *did* say we could roam free in the garden, yes? Christ, I could be naked right now if I wanted to be.

I slip my fingers defiantly into my back pockets, my thumbs hooked over their sides. I'm heading for nowhere in particular, just enjoying the cool breeze as I drink in deep swigs of clean country air. It calms me, and I start to feel human again.

I zigzag down the garden, meandering aimlessly through the mulberry bushes. I drift beneath a couple of magnificent, stately oaks, all the way over to the ivy-entangled hedge at the left edge of the garden. It's very shady down here. It's like the big, aged trees have conspired to bring night to this nook of the garden early.

There's a sudden gust of wind, and momentarily I'm a little spooked. Being clothed and alone has brought back some of those silly doubts. Have I imagined this whole school business? Did any of *that* really happen? Have I been set up for something awful? I do wish my brain would stop it. This is just a walk in an English country garden!

A sheep bleats in the distance.

The soil looks damp underfoot. I suspect it never really dries out down here beneath the leaves. The sun's rays won't penetrate here. It must be permanently damp.

Penetration. Dampness. *Emma…!*

I keep moving towards the bottom of the garden, then start as I spot a uniformity in the vegetation up ahead. There's a green wall. Shit, the maze! I'd forgotten all about it. I raise an eyebrow in its general direction.

The rebel in me has an idea.

What was it that scary mentor woman said? I rack my brains. I'm not sure I was paying much attention that day, whenever it was. I spent most of it being shocked by Alyssia's outfit, and generally gawping at all of my new surroundings. But hadn't there been something about a treat at the end of the maze?

I think there might also have been a warning about not going in alone. Or hungry. Or in the dark.

Either way, this is clearly *not* a good time for the thought I'm failing to push to the back of my mind. Darkness isn't a million miles away, after all. My pulse begins to pick up. What sort of treat was she talking about? What sort of prize would a group of trainee escorts expect? A giant dildo? Surely there can't be a man down there twenty-four seven...can there?

The more I think about it, the more I'm puzzled. I guess that's the whole point of a maze, isn't it? But I feel like some outdoor excitement will do me good now. And if it isn't *necessarily* sexual, that may not be a bad thing.

Rupert's whereabouts flash into my mind, but I do my best to send that thought packing. Instead I gulp as I make my way towards the gap in the hedge that must surely be the maze entrance. It almost feels good to be doing something that's a new, pure kind of irresponsible. This may be unsafe and ill-judged...but at least I could tell my mother about it.

I'm cautious as I reach the entrance. Right away, I'm confronted with a choice. Left or right? Already this maze is beginning to feel like a metaphor for my life. And I haven't even started yet!

I try to remember the movies I've seen and the books I've read. What is it that you're supposed to do? Leave a trail of string behind you? Yes, that makes sense. If I do that, then at least I'll find my way back to where I started. No harm done. But where will I find string?

I look down at my clothing. *My jersey!* There's several sheep's worth of woollen thread in that. I wonder if the idea I've got would get me in someone's bad books…but there's no shortage of clothing in this place. Off it comes. And I tear it open to access the start of the thread. It doesn't resist.

Wow, I'm feeling some kind of reckless.

I tie the end of the thread around the neck of the garden statue – a naked woman eating grapes, of course – that flanks the maze entrance. She doesn't resist either. She'd get on well in this place, I think to myself.

I'm good to go. It's fair to say I'm not warm. Probably another ill-advised move, but I feel safe now, because I can't get lost. I look down at my feeble little blouse. No wonder I'm chilly. I can see my own appetizing cleavage as I peek down the inside of the fabric. I'm slightly turned on. *When did that become normal?*

One way or another, I can feel my nipples tightening.

I take the left fork and lose myself in the maze. I'm steadily unravelling my jersey, trying to keep up my pace for warmth. Three or four turnings in, and I have no clue where I am. That lady's warnings were not out of line. I'm thankful I have an escape route.

What's disconcerting is that the hedges are so high. I can't crane my neck to get the bigger picture. This isn't made for fun. It feels claustrophobic in here. The hedge walls tower at least a couple of feet above my head. And it's narrow enough that you'd have to squeeze to get past someone.

Am I going to meet anybody? Surely some curious and confident soul like Latifa would have tried this days ago?

Nobody's mentioned it. I stop and listen. No footsteps. And I think I'd hear them on this crunchy gravel pathway. There's a breeze up there somewhere, I know, but I can't really feel it down here in the hedge tunnel.

I hum softly to myself, trying not to let spooking happen. Chris was only kidding about that ghost, wasn't he? Anyway, ghosts don't live in gardens!

This is just a little stroll, I tell myself. I can't get lost. I look behind me as I reach what must be about the fifth junction. I give a tug on the woollen wire. It's still tense. I'm a touch relieved. I'm okay.

I turn this way and that, running into dead ends every so often. No matter. When that happens, I go back to the last junction. I have nowhere to be. Twilight is starting to fade, but I'm on a mission now. I've dismissed any doubts about what I heard from Miss Whatsherface. There's a treat! That's all I'm choosing to remember.

What do I want my treat to be? Rupert? Petra suffering some kind of comeuppance? I'm not sure which I want more.

Crunch. Crunch. Crunch. My footsteps. A pause every now and then as I realize I've hit a dead end. You can't see they're dead ends until you're right upon them. Every time it's *not* a dead end, I get a surge of adrenaline, sensing I must be closer to getting somewhere.

All of a sudden, something makes me jump out of my skin. A whooshing sound and a shadow. My heart leaps into my throat and I freeze in terror. Then the bird gets into my field of vision. I breathe again. Terrified by a passing owl.

Okay, fine, I'm getting spooked. What next, bats? I feel my heartbeat thudding in my neck. I listen. Nothing. Even the wind has stopped. No birdsong. I shake my head, and press on.

The twists and turns of the maze are relentless. My glances over my shoulder grow more nervous, more frequent.

Suddenly I'm paranoid someone will come along and cut my safety rope.

It feels like I've been in this weird world of hedges at least half an hour already, but I've probably lost all sense of time. I'm beginning to lose all sense of hope, too. It's getting darker and I'm scared. Forwards or backwards? I'm less and less sure.

Then I round a corner, and something is different.

Chapter Fifteen

Somehow this is not quite what I expect. At the end of this particular hedge corridor is what looks like a long rabbit hutch. Of the various images I've had flailing around my brain on the way here, this wasn't one. I look over my shoulder once more, half-expecting another all-seeing staffer to appear via some secret entrance. But I still appear to be entirely alone here.

I puff out my cheeks and walk closer. I've got goosebumps now – partly the cold, partly the thrill. The rabbit hutch, in fact, turns out to be a squat wooden contraption divided into twelve smaller compartments. The kind of thing in which I imagine they'd keep a bunch of unhappy pigeons. There's wire mesh across the front of each compartment.

The whole thing stands on tiny legs, and I have to kneel down to see anything at all. There are labels. Yes, each of these little doors has a name on it. They're engraved in cursive on brass plates. Nice touch. I read. Miss Stoycheva…Miss Veenstra…Miss Carling!

A delicious rush of excitement seizes me as I see my name. Already this little maze jaunt seems entirely worth it. So *this* is where you have to come to get that childhood Christmas feeling back!

Okay, so these are pretty much just little letterboxes. We had pigeonholes at the office, and they never excited me the way this is doing. But they never held promise like these. What secrets do they hide? Now that I'm closer, I can see that the wire mesh has a dark sheet strung across it, so you can't see inside any of the compartments. What I *don't* see is any sign of a lock system.

My heart thuds and my fingers tremble as I tug on the tiny handle affixed to the frame of my own personal door. For some reason I feel proud that I'm third in line as you read from the left. I don't think the names are in any particular order, but, still, it makes me feel like I'm well thought-of. Of course, it pisses me off that bitch-face is number one.

But I've still got that Christmas feeling! What will my treat be? I look over my shoulder, suddenly feeling guilty. Like I've spoilt Christmas Day by rushing downstairs too early. Is this really allowed?

Still nobody.

I *must* be allowed. My name is on the box!

The door is a little sticky but I get it open. All I can see is an envelope. I stick my hand in and pull it out. Immediately I'm hit by a scent. Perfume. *That* perfume. This can't have been here long. I shiver suddenly, my imagination running amok. I'd swear I'm being watched.

I close the door and kneel upright. I could totally open all these doors! I guess it's an honour system here. Honour among harlots...is that a thing? The thought of nosiness doesn't stay with me for long. There's enough anticipation in my own envelope.

I slide my finger under the flap and gently push it up. I've always been neat like that. I pull out a thick, folded piece of paper and unfurl it. The writing is in thick, black ink. Tidy, posh public-schoolboy cursive. I begin to read.

Miss Carling,

I have no doubt you harbour certain resentments towards me following our last encounter.

All along, I have been aware that I deserve to be punished for my conduct.

So, I want you to punish me.

You will find me in the same place you found me previously. Come. Now. Hit me.

*Yours,
Rupert*

My brain spins into a whirl as I read. Of all the…*did he read my mind?* Rupert knows he did wrong! He wants me! But…punishment? Is that a *treat?* I've got a fair idea of what he might have in mind. It's not something I've ever experimented with. I'm not sure it will come naturally.

I purse my lips, suck in some fresh air, and shake my head slowly. Whatever. This is a command to get back to him. The details will take care of themselves. There's quite simply nothing to think about.

I'm out of breath when I reach the door of the Lachlan Room. I am so, so thankful for my escape yarn. It worked a treat. I dashed out of the maze in three or four minutes, then ran all the way up the garden. I leapt up the terrace steps three at a time. It's like there was a burst of energy in that envelope too. And in a way, there was.

Now I'm paused, just for a chance to catch my breath. And I can't wipe the smile off my face. Clearly I have some way to go before I can 'be more Petra' with clients, because the pep talk I just had with myself is far from my thoughts. I was in tears the last time this door closed on me. Now I'm wet with anticipation. And struggling to feel angry. But he wants me to have my way with him. *Okay then, Mister Rupert…*

Should I knock? How do I know he's here? Oh, who am I kidding! They're always one step ahead of you in this place.

The thought crosses my mind to try my best with the dominatrix thing from the off. I should burst in, slam the door behind me, put my hands on my hips and yell at him to get on his knees. *He'll like that.* Will he? I shake my head at myself, at the way I'm getting all excited like a teenager, thinking I know all about this man.

Still, they like initiative here, don't they? Yes, they do. Right, no more timid Emma.

So I don't knock. I straighten up the shoulder straps of my thin little top, pull up my jeans, and grab the door handle. I imagine it's the day I quit my job again, and push it open with my best impression of an angry woman.

One instant later, I don't need to act any more. I *am* an angry woman. Because what I see chills my blood.

He's kneeling on the bed, eyes closed and breathing heavily. He has a mighty erection, but I can't see all of it. Most of it is buried in Petra's mouth.

Fuck! Fuck fuck fuck! I've forgotten everything beyond these four walls. The school, the training, the invitation: they all vanish from my brain. And they're replaced by pure, blinding green-eyed rage.

She just carries on, the slut, like I'm not even here. Ever the pro. Her nonchalance drives me even madder, watching her head go back and forth on him like that. His knees are spread and she's sitting with her legs between them, flat on the bed.

Rupert is naked, but she's wearing his shirt, a pair of panties and blue stilettos, with blue lipstick and eye-shadow to match. Nothing else. Her get-up is ridiculous, and it makes me seethe. Everything about this has me boiling. I'm here to punish *him*, and then only reluctantly. But the daggers in my eyes are all heading the way of my room-mate right now.

He looks over at me and smiles. The moment he does that, my fury switches to him. How *dare* he hurt me again? And to *grin* about it…? My eyes narrow and suddenly everything comes into very clear, sharp focus. *Fine, I'll play that role you wanted, Rupert.* It's going to come very, very naturally after all.

I feel a lot like I did the day I stormed out of the office. But something has changed in me, because I feel like I can channel this a lot better. I'm going to do something with it. I won't be going away to flop on a bed. But I'm not going to fly off the handle either. These two will only chortle at a hysterical girl-fit.

It takes everything I've got not to lose it. My energy goes into standing up tall and folding my arms in *most* disapproving fashion. I'm proud of how quickly I've adapted. Even when he's still there, *smiling* me into a rage. Even as her hand moves to cup his balls.

I speak as sternly as I can manage. "Rupert! You've been *very* unwise."

He raises an eyebrow at me, then goes ever so slightly submissive. He bows his head and moves his hands from his hips to behind his back. Oh Christ, does this mean I'm doing it right?

I notice that I'm tapping my right foot as I continue with my non-specific line of accusation. "You have shown an *extraordinary* lack of judgement, young man. I have been sent to correct you."

To my surprise, I don't hear my voice waver. But I notice that Petra's lips somehow seem to curl into a smile even as she carries on her awful work. I want to rip her face off. The ongoing sex act ignites me and kicks me into another gear.

I bellow louder at him now, "Where the *fuck* is your belt, you slut? Answer me! And remove yourself from that whore's mouth right now."

Even Petra is stilled now. I'm surprised by the note I've hit. Rupert is straight-faced once again. And he obeys me without any argument. He wriggles backwards, springing free from her lips without changing his position. *Holy shit!* It's working!

It's hard not to get distracted by his erection, so I look him in the eye as he says, softly, "You will find it still on my trousers, Miss Carling. They are at your feet."

This is not supposed to be so natural. But what I've seen has just slipped me into a zone. An intense place where the words somehow just come out right. I'm winning. Petra is leaning back on her hands, seemingly lost in thought. Let her. She's good for motivation.

I continue, though I can't believe it's me saying, "You think *I'm* going to bend down for it? You're a worthless peasant. You'll prepare your own punishment. Come and get the belt. And don't look me in the eye again. I'll be sick."

Rupert keeps his hands behind his back, though I haven't asked him to. And he keeps his head bowed. *Interesting.* Then he slides off the bed and takes the couple of steps towards me. He squats down without looking up once, and retrieves his belt at my feet. I can smell him again. It's the same scent as the letter.

I look away, for fear of melting, and see Petra sitting there like she owns the place. My anger comes flooding back at the sight of her.

"Give me that!" I command.

He stays on the floor as he reaches up and hands me his expensive-looking leather belt. It's got a well-polished silver buckle, but apart from that it's a relatively safe strip of high-quality leather. It has that smell.

Then I bend down and speak to him in a low threatening tone I never knew I had. "I want you to crawl over to that fancy armchair of yours and bend over the arm."

I spin round to my left and watch him go. He does it wordlessly. He is still glistening and large after Petra's efforts, which makes me want to hit him more. He does just as I ask, totally the opposite man to the one I thought I knew. Meek and yielding, Rupert paws at the arm of his chair and pulls himself over it. He grabs the opposite arm so that his torso is suspended over the seat.

I remain standing with my arms folded. I think I succeed in looking emotionless. Even though I want to grimace as I see the way he's pressed against the chair leg. It has to hurt. His legs don't seem to be taking any weight and I'm not sure how he's holding himself in this position. But his butt is at the perfect angle for a lashing. I guess he's done this before.

Suddenly I wish I had those stilettos she's wearing. They would make a far more ominous sound on these floors than my tennis shoes. But I'll be damned if I so much as acknowledge Petra, who seems to have lost interest in the situation. She's lying back now, staring at the ceiling with her knees up.

Well, this is it.

I've never hit anyone in my life before. But I'm not sure I've ever been this furious before. My last day at work included. Fucking worm! With *her*! Ugh!

Outside-world righteousness wells up in me once again and I step towards him. I'm surprised to find that my legs aren't shaking. I'm not sure I'm going to enjoy hitting him, but I can do this. And I think I might enjoy the build-up.

"You know what you've done, don't you Rupert?"

"Yes mistr...Miss Carling." *Did he almost call me 'mistress'?*

"Good, then we're getting somewhere. Would you care to elaborate?"

There's a pause as he takes two deep breaths. Momentarily I'm distracted by the rise and fall of his muscular back, just a tiny hint of damp with perspiration. No two ways about it, he makes a fine sight. Even from this unusual angle.

"Miss Carling," he begins. "I've treated you disrespectfully. I was not a gentleman after we made love the other day."

Made love? My poor brain. It's on fire. It's hard to keep my focus. I have no idea what I'm feeling any more. I know the burning rage is still there, but I keep on softening when he says the right words. And is there also something *sexual* in my emotions right now? Surely not.

And yet…I can't deny the warm juices I can feel in my crotch. How can that be? I've just been hideously betrayed. What could be less sexy? But then I run my thumb across the cool leather of his belt, and look once more at bared cheeks, which I'm going to punish for his wrongdoing.

And suddenly I'm not so sure of anything.

The whole situation is so alien. It's a heady mix of enmity, jealousy, anger and desire. And it's very, very potent. I very much doubt the Emma of last week would have done anything other than run away. And if it's not bizarre enough, the bitch at the centre of it all is still here, watching.

I look across at her once more, and that loathing shoots to the fore again. I find myself whipping my head back towards Rupert's rear end.

"AND…?" I tap my foot impatiently.

He speaks softer now, somewhere between a whisper and a wheeze. "And, I have taken liberties with a wanton harlot, allowing her to pleasure me inappropriately. I should be punished, Miss Carling."

Suddenly I snap. It's not just the admission, but the arrogant note in his voice, even as he asks to be punished.

"You're fucking right you will be," says a voice that isn't quite mine. "You womanizing prick."

I take a step forward, slide my hand halfway down the belt for control, draw back my arm, and land a surprisingly swift, accurate blow across his buttocks.

CRACK!

I plough on, while both my rage and my nerve lasts.

CRACK! CRACK! CRACK!

I absolutely rain down the belt blows on him. My aim is good. He doesn't complain and doesn't move. I take a step closer, and experiment with a higher backlift.

CRACK! CRACK! CRACK!

He's grunting a little with each hit now. Tense, and straining his legs against the floor. What kind of grunt it is, I can't say. His face is still buried, and I don't know what this perverted freak might be thinking. He could be smiling, for all I know.

The thought spurs me into another volley of whips. One way or another I'm going to make him rue messing with me. He asked for this, in more ways than one.

I pause after what must be the fifteenth blow or so. "Are you *sorry* yet?" I'm standing with my arms folded and the belt dangling menacingly from my right hand. And my voice drips with sarcasm.

"Yes, Miss Carling," he gasps. It sounds like he might genuinely be feeling some discomfort now. "I'm truly sorry."

I feel like I've made my point. His ass is now blushing pink. *I* did that! Am I proud? A little, maybe. I pause a moment as my wrist brushes my nipple through the thin fabric of my blouse. It's rock solid. *Holy hell!*

I can't say I felt sexual excitement doing that. But I did feel powerful, and it did get something out of my system. I believed with all my heart that he deserved that punishment, and I didn't hold back. I threw my heart and soul into his strapping…and it seems I've got ice-breaker nipples to show for it.

And now that I think about it, my panties are wetter too.

I don't know what I'm supposed to do now. The ticking of the clock is the only sound in the room. I've got a naked man, beaten red, draped over an armchair. And I've got a half-naked Bulgarian blonde bitch lying on the bed. It feels like it's down to me to manage this further.

My thoughts go crazy again. So maybe I *am* kind of turned on. Yes, okay, part of me wants to stand him up and help make it all better. But no *way* is he getting a treat from me so soon. I only have to look at Petra to remind myself of that. I have to stay in punishment mode right now.

I'm feeling good about that. Nobody's questioning my authority in this room. Even though Petra's body language is that of a slouchy, disinterested, disrespectful schoolgirl. Am I going to walk out now, and let them get back to it? Or what?

And then words just tumble out of my mouth. Maybe the power has gone to my head. "Fine. You are done, Rupert. Now that slut of yours needs punishing too."

Chapter Sixteen

My mouth runs dry. I can't believe I just said that! Where the hell did that line come from? Petra needs a lesson, and I'm on the warpath, but I seem to have forgotten that she intimidates me. Am I planning on taking the belt to her, too? *Shit!* I can't turn back now!

Something really has gone haywire inside me now. It's reminiscent of drunkenness. It must stem from the attack I've just dished out. I feel as liberated as I did the day I stormed out of my job. *Yes! You did that!*

The voice of reason is faint inside my head now, but I can still hear its distant echo. It suggests I'm probably not allowed to beat a classmate. I wonder if I can even take *that* for granted in this fucked-up place.

No way am I dropping the idea now. My anger is back, redoubled, now that I've turned my attention to her. And I'll not lose face. But fine, I'll at least make sure I don't act alone. I'll use my man-slave.

"Get up, Rupert," I bark. "She's not getting away with this either. Part two of your punishment is helping me set her straight." The tone of voice is one I've only ever heard from myself once before. That was on the day I quit.

I'm amazed at myself. I'm feeling like wild tempest right now, but one spitting out plans that might just work. Has my thinking ever been this lucid? Is that what life as a 'mistress' does to you?

Petra doesn't seem to have heard a thing I've said. If anything, there's another trace of a wicked smile on her face. Rupert pushes himself upright once more. I notice that he's still fully erect. I flush with pride at the thought that my beating might have turned him on. Just like him beating *me* might turn *me* on…

He resumes his low, hands-behind-back submissive position. Thank God, he's on my side still. How long will that last?

"Okay, it takes two to tango, Rupert," I say, pulling his belt suggestively through my hands without even knowing I'm doing it. "That wench needs punishing too, for whoring herself out like that."

Even in my heightened state, I don't fail to notice the irony. But I motor on, starting to relish the thought of teaching Petra a lesson. I know that as a fellow trainee she can fight me, but she surely has to obey Rupert. "I want you to bring her over to the chair and hold her down for me. I'm going to stripe her ass. Now DO IT."

I flare my nostrils as I notice that Petra is finally paying attention and sitting upright. In fact, she's swung her legs over the edge of the bed now, as if she's planning on running out. I pray Rupert will act in time.

Petra springs to her feet like a frightened cat. "Go, Rupert! Move!" I roar in a voice I didn't know I had. I've started this mean queen thing, and whether I succeed or end up looking silly is, in this knife-edge moment, down to Rupert. I'm banking on success. This is his chance to repay me.

Rupert responds just in time. He morphs back into the large, powerful man I've come to know. And two strides is all he needs to intercept Petra's attempt at bolting. He grabs her by the elbows, locking her in place. She knows it's pointless to resist his strong hands, and goes limp.

"You heard Miss Carling," he says as he moves around behind her, never losing his vice grip. "You're to be punished now, Miss Stoycheva."

"Fine," is all she says, tossing her head and avoiding my eye. I guess she's back to shrugging mode. No doubt she's been through the punishment routine before, seasoned tart that she is. I notice that her lipstick is smudged after her sucking frenzy. Shameless.

I regard her, standing there in Rupert's shirt, which hangs open so her little breasts poke out, looking right at me. Her belly button joins in their defiant gaze, like some kind of freaky third eye. She's breathing heavier than I've seen before, her tiny, flat tummy rising and falling as she awaits our next move.

I can't believe I've let myself get aroused by this woman. Well, that was this morning.

"I don't want her wearing your shirt!" I scream. "Get it *off* her. And she can lose the stupid slut shoes too. This isn't meant to be fun."

Rupert holds her right elbow firm and starts to tug at her opposite sleeve. She wriggles, pulling it out angrily, thrusting her tits towards me as she does so.

"Stop it," she says. "I'll do it. I'm not fighting you."

Does anything shake this woman? Does she just take anything? I can't help wondering, as she squirms out of the shirt when he relaxes his grip. Then she kicks off the heels, and casually folds her arms. Sullen. It drives me berserk.

When I let rip at my boss last week – was it only last week? – her response was to gawp at me like a goldfish. This indifference is far less satisfying.

"Put her on the chair this second!" I scream. "She's got a fucking attitude problem and I'm going to beat it out of her!"

I have well and truly snapped this time. Everything she does just makes me insane. My eyes are wide and I'm snorting fire as I watch Rupert take her by the neck and steer her towards the chair.

"Face down," I order him. It's true that I don't want to see her face as I do this. Mainly because the sight of it really, really makes me sick. But also because part of me is scared it'll turn me on.

At my command he lifts her up and lies her flat across the chair. She's so tiny that she balances perfectly over the big, wide seating area. Her armpits rest on one chair arm and her knees on the other. Her arms dangle in resignation.

Her miniscule butt hovers in mid-air. It's perfect. Too perfect. My eyes narrow.

I don't think she's going to run now, but I still feel the need for approval and support on this. It's important that I'm acting with Rupert, who is some kind of staff associate, or tester, or whatever he is. The collusion will give licence to my frenzy. So I instruct him to hold her legs down.

Only now do I remember that she's still wearing her panties. Simply no good for the damage I have in mind. I want her total humiliation. For that she must be stripped.

"Right, these are coming off," I say, and find myself tearing the hip string and yanking. It gives, but I'm so irrational right now that I can't take in the need to break it elsewhere to get it off. I hate having to put my hands on her right now, and never mind our shower routine.

I tear wildly at the broader piece of fabric covering her right buttock, hoping like hell she's hating this as much as I am. Eventually it tears right across, and I pull up roughly from between her legs, hoping she gets some chafe. I hear her click her tongue, but her head stays down.

The most secret part of that panty fabric brushes my hand as I gather it up and toss it aside. And for all my fury, I can't help noticing that it's dry as a bone.

But all I can think of right now is tanning this bitch's ass till its crimson. And then some.

I start to smack her before I chicken out.

CRACK!

She's horizontal to the ground, which makes it that much easier than it was with Rupert. Gravity is entirely with me.

CRACK!

Also, my fury with her is deeper, more white-hot, than it is with Rupert.

CRACK! CRACK! CRACK!

This is so depraved.

CRACK!

She doesn't flinch. Just floats there.

CRACK!

I can sense her rolling her eyes, and it makes me find an extra gear.

CRACK! CRACK!

I'm in the zone now. Her tiny ass is taking on a delicate rouge hue in the places I've hit her. It's no work of art, this pattern I've made. The inch-wide stripes zigzag this way and that across the peaks of her buttocks.

Good. I'm spreading the pain.

CRACK! CRACK! CRACK!

At last she begins to writhe. No sounds, just a wriggle. I'm not having that.

"Keep her still!" I yell to Rupert, my weird passion still at fever pitch as I push deeper into this unknown world. I'm terrified by what's come over me, but I know I'm not done.

Calmly, Rupert walks around the back of the chair, keeping one hand on her skinny legs and placing one on her back. He's so much stronger than her, she's locked in place. His long arms let him stay upright enough to keep out of harm's way.

I like that she's locked down like this, by *my* lover. Yes, that's what he is! We're punishing her together for leading him astray. It's delicious, exquisite, to be the one dealing out the justice. Just me and him, together, putting things back the way they were.

CRACK! CRACK! CRACK!

I attack with renewed vigour, trying to hit the paler patches of her skin. Yes, it's *me* with the power now. What goes around, comes around, doesn't it Petra?

I realise that I'm pouring with sweat. There's still a whisper of arousal in my nerves, but the thought of taking off my top quickly passes. I'm not ready to show Rupert my body right now. I'm still pissed off with him, though less so with every stroke of the belt that hits Petra.

Yes, it's like she's his scapegoat now. I lose count of the blows, but I've gone way past the number of hits I gave him. I feel I can lay into her more, because in some twisted way she's taking Rupert's punishment as well as her own.

I can see her muscles tensing. Her fists have clenched, just like her buttocks. It's like she's trying to squeeze the pain out. Maybe she's human after all? Not a whimper from her lips, though. She's a tough cookie, this one. I'll have to give her that.

And still I thunder the blows down upon her.
CRACK! CRACK! CRACK!
Me, who has never hurt a thing in her life.

I stop, flick some stray strands of hair back behind my ears, and meet Rupert's eyes. He's looking up at me, softly disapproving now, yet wordlessly so. *Those eyes*. Suddenly I feel the tears knocking at the back of my eyes.

Rupert doesn't move, he just keeps looking at me. I take a step back, and survey the wreckage of my savagery. Her ass is *bright* red.

I have inflicted some very serious pain on this woman. She's motionless, passive, and in an instant I feel like an unspeakable bully. There's a rising lump in my throat, like a light has just come on in my brain.

I have no idea how to end this, but I know I need to get out. Now. I'm getting the sniffles, and can feel the emotion gearing up to flood through me like a torrent. A quick escape is all I want. I need to round off this act pronto, before all of my control falls apart.

My voice wavers now. "Consider yourselves punished. Now don't let me see either of you any time soon."

I drop the belt on the floor with a clatter. It's my last statement. I have to force myself to avoid Rupert's eyes. I turn and walk out of the door, slamming it behind me. The harsh crash of its wood echoes through the empty corridor as I leave them there.

I scuttle down the hallway as fast as I can, my heart racing and the tears in full flow. Thank God I don't meet anybody. I'm a tangle of all the feelings a woman can know, but mostly I am just upset. That was one hell of a ride back there, from anger to megalomania to pride to jealousy to lust. And back again.

No wonder my head is in a spin. All I know is that I don't want to go back to 'our' room. I don't want to see her and I don't want to know how long it will be before she comes back. If she's blowing him again, crimson ass and all, I just don't want to know. What I need is somewhere to unwind.

I find myself heading for Sarah's room. She's on my side. She's got a spare bed. I'll close my eyes, and when I do all this will go away.

I knock, whimper my name, and she calls me in. She's sitting on her bed, reading a magazine, like a normal person might. Sanity in an ocean of madness!

She looks up, concern all over her face, and says, "Hey you, what's going on? What's with the crying?"

I shake my head. "Oh Sarah…I can't talk about it now. I just want to curl up. I'm spent. I can't go back to my room and *her*. Please can I stay in the spare bed?"

The warmest, most caring smile lights up her face. "Sure thing! Whenever you're ready. You just take it easy now and get some rest."

I nod, wiping my nose gracelessly with the back of my hand. She holds out a tissue box from the bedside table. I give her a feeble smile and take one. I blow my nose and dab my eyes.

"Thank you," I mumble as I crawl under the covers into the bed's warm embrace. I'm fully clothed. She's still naked. And

I'm so completely spent that I don't care. This day has been so long, I don't even remember its beginning.

She smiles back at me and flicks off my bedside light.

Chapter Seventeen

I wake up early. I must have fallen asleep right away. That always happens when I'm upset. But it wasn't a pure sleep. Dreams haunted my night. Whips cracked in my head. Fury bubbled and burned. None of these visions were pleasant. It feels like I've only been half-asleep all night long, and I'm more exhausted than ever.

As I come to my senses I realise that Sarah is wide awake. She's lying on her side, looking at me with concern in her eyes. When she sees I'm joining her in the waking world, her face breaks into a smile. It's the kind of wake-up I'll never get in my own room.

Speaking of which….*shit!* Showers! I'm going to have to wash *her* again! Either that, or rebel completely. I sigh and curl up into a little ball. I don't even want this day to begin. I hate it already.

"What time is it?" I whisper from underneath the comforting duvet.

Sarah giggles and says, "It's only seven! You can go back to sleep if you want!"

I groan. "Ugh. But I won't. I don't even want to think about today. I'm going to pieces." And then, "I'm so happy I could sleep here, Sarah. You have no idea what a lifesaver it's been."

She clears her throat and says, "Well, no, I don't really. But I do know that I like having you here. Stay as long as you like! You're a great distraction. And you've got to tell me what's going on now!"

Sarah throws back her covers, runs excitedly around the front of my bed, and crawls in with me. I'm too taken aback to say anything as she spoons up to me in her bright red pyjama shorts and plain white t-shirt. The little rebel's sneaked some clothes on in her room!

She puts her arm around my stomach and says, "I've had enough of shouting across this great big room. Now won't you tell me everything?"

This feels nice. Comforting, warm and almost motherly. All the things I won't get from *him* or *her*. If there's a girl among us whose looks are an acquired taste, it's probably Sarah, but maybe that's why she's a decent human being. She needs friendship and support, so she's learned how to give it. Positive vibes are simply flooding out of her right now. I feel better already.

I bring her up to speed on my first few brushes with Rupert and Petra, blushing when I skip through the sex session. And then I tell her the whole story of last night, from the maze to the letter to the thrashings. She listens to it all without interrupting. Just the odd murmur in my ear to tell me she's listening. I'm surprised, but it feels super-nice to have her hold me like this. I must be a wreck.

"And that's why I'd rather not do today," I conclude. At least my sense of humour is coming back. "Can I call in sick for showers?"

She snickers and says, "I dunno, maybe you can? Or you could just do me." She gives my tummy a playful pinch. "I don't have a shower partner, remember?"

I ponder the idea, which sounds far more pleasant. But then, I think Petra will go through with it. So me switching to Sarah would be me backing down. Emma Carling does not lose face any more.

"Don't like that idea?" she says, sounding disappointed. She's nothing if not flirty with me. I remember suddenly that we can have no secrets after our double-man experience the other day.

"Don't be silly," I reply. "It's just that it would be letting her win."

"You fancy her, don't you?"

Her words are like a punch to the stomach.

"No! Stop it!"

"Haha, I bet you do! Who wouldn't? And tell me you didn't feel a bit turned on during the beating…"

I don't know *what* to tell her any more. The beatings were an emotional tumble-dryer. Was I aroused at certain moments? I vaguely recall something like that. It certainly isn't my dominant memory. And if I was, was it *her?* Him? The act of punishing? Being the punisher?

"I can't really say," I reply crossly. "All I know is…I'm not really sure of anything. I can't say I feel like seeing either of them. As for sexy beatings…I don't know about that either. Maybe if it's a bit less personal next time, then I'll have a better idea."

"Less personal is probably what we're looking at in this line of work, so I guess you'll find out soon enough."

She cuddles up closer to me and holds me tight. Gosh, this Sarah really likes me!

Petra ignores me in the shower, even as we rub our soapy hands all over each other's bodies. So what's new in that? Don't mix business and pleasure, huh? Or pain and pleasure, as the case may be. It's back to normal. Neither of us cracks. I don't think we'll be talking again.

I do allow myself a moment of satisfaction as I note the rosy tan on her backside. I even take a step back for a second to admire the remnants of my handiwork. In the clear light of day, my guilt has taken a back seat again. Although it doesn't look like anything the Emma I know would ever have produced, I'm strangely proud of that criss-cross of two-inch-wide pink strips.

Maybe it's because they tell me I'm getting kinda liberated in this place. And they remind me that I am strong. Not to be messed with.

There is still a part of me that feels repelled. But if this is a kinky rite I had to go through, well, I can't think of a more deserving recipient. (Apart from my ex-boss, of course...*my* that would be nice!) And yes, it's a little bit sexy to think that it was me who painted that scarlet picture. I can't understand that part...I never knew I had it in me. But there you go. I'm learning new things about myself every day here.

I think the other girls all notice it too. You can see the marks from several paces away. Latifa winks at me over Alyssia's shoulder. Sarah watches us, unashamedly fascinated. Lilia catches my eye with a cold glare. Petra, in fact, seems to be the only indifferent one in the room. Are we the number one storyline here? Surely the others have had their adventures too...haven't they?

Rupert is nowhere to be seen. Funnily enough, it's just Miss Jackson and another mentor, the glamorous Miss Ridgewell, watching us from the gallery.

I'm famished, but I nip back to my room to fetch some clothes. Petra still seems no more grumpy than usual. She certainly has no interest in where I might have spent the night. I find myself unconcerned about what she may have done with hers. We ignore each other. Every girl's played this game, and honestly it's not that difficult. It's easier than pretending, I always think.

Then I remember my resolution to stick with Sarah in her time of nakedness, so I just head off to her room in my towel. She's thrilled when I drop it, explaining that I won't see her isolated and want to support her.

I grab her and we report for cooked breakfast entirely in the nude. I'm far less bothered now that I'm not the only one, and the other girls barely seem to notice our state. Maybe they're quiet because they know their turn will come. Miss Jackson pauses in the doorway, and gives me a smile. I rather hope she likes my 'initiative'.

But never mind naked – I'm only thinking food this morning. Last night's unexpected exertions played out on an empty stomach, and I can feel it now.

Wilfred obliges me with poached eggs (who even knows how to make those?), bacon, fresh fruit and creamy yoghurt. Sarah's a little more restrained, and I feel like a pig. But I'm lucky that I've never been one to put on weight. All I ever did was lose it, courtesy of work stress.

At times like this, being waited on hand and foot with brilliant food, I can't bear thinking about failing at this thing. There's no downside to this kind of perk. As for other aspects of the game, well, I'll keep working on those. The fundamentals of it are sexy and fun. Surely it's just a case of getting used to it?

The opportunity to push myself further comes in the afternoon. It's new territory for the group: everyone is going to be involved in something at the same place and time. The life-sized chess board at three o'clock, to be precise. I gulp as Miss Ridgewell announces the plans to us at the breakfast table. She has a twinkle in her eye.

All the trainees are instructed to wear black. We're told not to wear anything tight, but it's stressed that we're to put on enough to be 'identifiably black'. The weather is warm again, though breezy. Alyssia's see-through thing would do the job, I think to myself. *Life-sized chess.* They're not short on imagination here.

Rummaging through the Aladdin's Cave that is my closet, my eye falls on the weird backless dress. The *really* backless one. It's jet black. Sexy in its own way. It's definitely loose. Dare I? I think I've got the guts, but what if the whole event is perfectly respectable and I end up the odd one out? Those doubts again. What a yo-yo my mind is!

Respectable seems highly unlikely, but I compromise and wear a pair of reasonably substantial – yet silky enough to make you groan – black panties. At the last second I decide to add a bra.

It's quite a collection of outfits that gathers on the lawn alongside the chess board. There's leather and plastic. Robes and miniskirts. A cape and a cloak. Some *very* high heels. Well, you can always trust a bunch of girls to get into the spirit of fancy dress. If this was a test of our creativity and daring, I'd say we've all done well. Although our stuffed wardrobes certainly make that easy.

I stare at Sarah. She's not been granted leave to dress yet. Someone has used body paint on her instead. Strategically. Only her sex and breasts have been spared the black brush. It's…compelling.

Then I notice the gentlemen. Most of the faces are familiar to me by now. I try to stop myself seeking out one in particular, but it's only a moment before I notice him. Rupert, like all the others, is resplendent in a creamy white dress suit. The men are identically tailored, down to their red pocket handkerchiefs and silver cufflinks. To a man, they look like they're on their way to one extremely exclusive wedding reception.

They ignore us as we gather, and continue to mingle amongst themselves. They help themselves to drinks, mostly of the sparking variety, from an immaculately laid-out side table, where Wilfred is in attendance. Miss Jillings calls us together and hands us bottles of water. She instructs us all to drink. I can feel electricity brewing already.

Finally Miss Jillings sets us up. Most of us fill the second row on our side of the board. It's a long time since I've played chess, but I surmise we must be pawns. And then it finally dawns on me why we're all dressed in black. The girls are all on one team. My square is near the edge of the board. We're all told to stand upright – hands in front of us - with our legs slightly apart.

Alyssia, Carrie and Simone are given roles as knight, rook and bishop respectively. The last five places on our team are taken by women I don't recognise. Generally they seem a little older and wiser. Beautiful, of course. They seem unperturbed by the mystery of it all, and share jokes amongst themselves as they assemble. The uncertainty in our trainee group is palpable though. Even Alyssia and Latifa are quiet as the men take their places.

Apart from the morning showers on day one, when we were all too shocked to have any thoughts at all, this is the first time our group has faced a collective new challenge. Maybe I imagine it, but for once I seem to feel a blanket of solidarity over us as we contemplate the two ranks of white suits before us. *All* of us. I don't think any of us wish it on any of the others to be the first to have to make a move.

And what happens when one of us is...*taken?*

At last we are all in place. A voice cries out for a pawn to advance, and Robert takes two paces forward in the middle of the board. I start in the direction of the sound: it's our mysterious daily waker. Not for the first time this week, he's lording it over us in an elevated position – this time a chair on the terrace – and I haven't noticed. Looks like he's calling the shots for the white team.

As for team black, well, none of *us* gets a say. There's another equally authoritative looking man sitting next to waker guy. I'm pretty sure I haven't seen him around the house before. He decides where and when we will move. In effect, we're just actors in a giant game between two overgrown boys. What kind of a thrill are *they* getting out of making us their puppets?

It's not long before I find out. I'm quickly plunged into one of the most shocking afternoons of my life. Incredible and indelible. If there were any inhibitions in this setup before now, they take a pounding today. I can't imagine a more intense test for our group. Or a better bonding exercise.

I watch, mouth agape, as the first capture is made. Their knight – a balding man with a cigar in his mouth – takes our pawn Carol. She awaits her fate with admirable courage. She must know the eyes of nearly forty people are locked on her as she goes limp and lets him pull her skimpy dress off her shoulders, dropping it to the floor. She must know we're fascinated and powerless and riveted as she follows his instructions to bend over in nothing but her heels.

Not ten yards away from me, on a bright afternoon in an English country garden, the oriental beauty is vigorously fucked in the middle of the chess board.

I doubt she comes, but she whimpers and cries out as he gets closer and then releases into her. Then, bent over with her eyes closed and breathing heavily, she is given her marching orders. She gathers up her clothing and walks off the board, white liquid streaming down her legs. Her expression is blank. *Jesus.* My heart starts to thud at the thought I could be next.

Is it a good thing that I'm a fringe piece? It's a long while before I am moved. I watch as Lilia the pawn is taken by Frederick, whom I remember mainly for his intense stare while he watched us shower. He demands a blow job. She unhitches his trousers with ease, and delivers what looks like expert service. He comes in her mouth. I can't tear my eyes away. Except to catch Sarah's now and then. She looks worried again.

The game is not entirely one-sided. The female team has its share of success, and when one of our team takes a white piece…the man evidently submits to the woman's desires. Holy crap! I think I like that idea even less. But Alyssia seems to revel in squatting above Jack, exhorting him to lick her ass and pussy. She comes in loud and ear-splitting fashion. Bloody extroverts!

My heart beats faster and I fervently hope I'll be taken, rather than a taker. I can't have *desires* in front of so many people. Can I?

Oh, but…I *do* have desires. Whether I like it or not. I feel seepage in my loins as I watch as Simone has her loose catsuit ripped open and is thrown onto her back…*oh my*…right in front of me. I don't know the man's name, but he's ripped. He thrusts hard into her, and I think she comes. *I want that.* But how can these people let go in public like this?

I pray for someone to struggle. Petra doesn't. She takes Rupert. Of course she does. My worst nightmare is replayed again. What are the chances of that? Her version of having her desires is…sucking on him again. I find that odd. But, like watching a car crash, I just can't look away. I swear he glances across at me as he walks off the board. He likes these games. In every sense of the word. That much is clear.

Can it get any more depraved? I notice Miss Honeywell watching from the terrace. Clearly the sweet old lady does not offend! Because Lilia is made to take a fairly sizeable dildo in her back hole, which she then has to hold in place with one hand while pleasuring her captor with the other. I cringe and flush at the same time.

Latifa has her way with the mightily-endowed George, taking obvious pleasure in riding him inside her cloak. I find myself thinking how much nicer it would be if her full, bouncy breasts were bared to the afternoon sunshine. What a magnificent image that would be!

She is onto her second capture before I have even moved. The game must be nearly two hours old now, and it's getting uncomfortable standing in this odd position. Though the time has flown, such has been my incredulous wonder. This time she does remove the robe – the harlot! – and makes the guy suck her nipples. *Fuck, I want mine bitten. Hard!*

But it's never an orgy. It's strictly one at a time, always following the game's structure. For long periods, it's just moving and thinking. The terrace puppeteers seem in no hurry, and seem serious about winning. Then there's an exchange of pieces, and an explosion of sex ensues. I'd be lying if I said I knew what to make of it. I frequently burn up with jealous desire, but I'm also scared of being in the game. At least that decision is out of my hands.

Jane ends up as almost the last line of defence. She's Frederick's third capture. She's the cape-wearer, with just a bikini for modesty. I've never seen anyone look so vulnerable. He pushes her roughly down to her knees and guides her head onto his manhood. I'm jealous and I'm not. He fucks her standing up. She catches my eye a couple of times as he jerks through her and spasms. It's a glazed look, one that chills me. I wonder if I've looked like that in my sessions this week. It's surely not a good look.

And though I don't like Jane, I feel some solidarity with her when I see those taken eyes. I wonder if this afternoon will turn out to be a bonding experience for our group. As icebreakers go, public sex acts outdoors must be pretty near the top of the list.

I'm paying no attention to the actual game, of course. Even with only six pieces left on the board, I'm still being shocked to the point of going slack-jawed. The crowd, the submission…it's taken things to a whole new level. That, and doing it outdoors. I glance at the sky, and note with relief that there are no low-flying planes about. My, what sights they would see!

I still can't believe any of this is real. And I note with some satisfaction that I've forgotten about Rupert and Petra. My mind has been consumed by other things. Mostly shock and astonishment. And need.

The captured sit on the grass at the side of the board, our team's fallen remaining in whatever state of undress they left the scene, watching the final battles. I have long since forgotten my own ridiculous attire. All I've done, apart from watch, is advance a couple of squares in the latter stages. Just to remind them I could become a queen. If I go all the way.

"And, checkmate!"

That's us!

I didn't see our victory coming. What now? What happens to the, um, unfucked among us? Our queen – a busty, raven-haired woman in suitably regal robes, is the one with the honour of sealing the opposition king's fate. It's Harry the Scotsman. She smiles a watery, evil smile as Miss Jillings materialises without a word to hand her a strap-on and a multi-strand whip.

I have to admit she plays her role with skill. She strips him and whips him mercilessly with what I later discover is known as a cat o'nine tails. He actually cries out, but I notice he's aroused. Then she instructs him to stand up, unclip her robe and attach her strap-on.

Then she fucks him in the ass. I'm rooted to the spot, wincing. It's the most deeply shocking of all today's scenes. And yet...he seems to enjoy it. In fact, there's no doubt he does. On the strength of this submissive, painful act, and with nobody touching his hardness at all, he releases into the ground. It lands with a tiny splosh.

Then she makes him lick her clit until she comes, right there in front of everyone.

Game over.

After all that, I have been untouched.

I flop down on the grass next to Sarah. I've never seen such scenes. My legs hurt. I'm spent, even though I've done nothing but stand.

Sitting down in this dress, I feel ridiculous.

A little unwanted, too.

"You OK?" I frown at Sarah, whose paint is now decidedly smudged after she too was taken and defiled. I can't help smiling at the get-up.

"Yeah," she grins. "It was weird but...nice."

"Hmph," I say, tossing my head. "I wouldn't know."

She gives me a knowing look. I've noticed this with Sarah – sometimes we just don't need words. I know she knows what I'm thinking. Which is that I might need a little time alone with my middle finger.

"And I need to get this gunk washed off in the shower," she snickers.

We both burst out laughing, and head towards her room.

Chapter Eighteen

Sarah's room remains my sanctuary. Nothing bad or awkward ever happens here. I flop down on the bed I've started to make my own, my legs leaden and aching from all that standing up.

My brain hurts too. Not for the first time this week, I feel mentally bulldozed by the rollercoasters this place gives me. I'm fatigued beyond words again, yet somehow still tense. There's a weird jealousy thing going on in my head after I wasn't 'taken' in the game, and it's eating up my energy. It's a bit like when a guy teases you for weeks with his mixed messages, and you spend all day obsessing about it.

And it's nothing if not mixed messages, this place. One minute you're a slave, the next you're dishing out the whippings. You never know what you're going to get; whether to get keyed up or not. That's the most draining thing about it all. But I guess all that not-knowing does make the orgasms pretty intense when they come round.

Speaking of which, my coiled stimulation hasn't gone anywhere. I'm lying untidily on the bed in the backless dress, feeling the comforting sensation of today's freshly-changed linen nuzzling my back. There's a mild frustration creeping up on me.

Sarah is standing up near the window, looking dishevelled and helpless. Obviously she can't lie down in her smeared coat of body paint. The poor girl desperately needs a shower. I wonder if they're going to let her put on clothes again soon?

She seems to read my thoughts. "Guess what, Em? I can get dressed again! I just found a note on my pillow about it!"

"Hah, they like their little letters around here, don't they!" I chuckle. "I think you might need a thorough scrub-down before you go raiding the wardrobe though…"

I curse my choice of words. Was I asking for trouble with that suggestion? I see the answer as she flicks her eyes onto mine. I've walked into something here.

"You volunteering to help me?" she asks, with an over-the-top pout she must have perfected at drama school.

I'm already swollen with sexual energy. Excitement rushes through my body as my mind paints pictures of her depainting. I need release very, very soon, and my affection for Sarah is growing. And yet I can't bring myself to say yes. I baulk and stutter. I can't agree to rub down another woman in the shower unless someone's told me to. *Can I?*

And I'm not a lesbian…right? So would it be fair on her? She wants something, I know she does. Even though she got plenty this afternoon. She's obviously got a real thing for me.

I realise that the comic-looking Sarah, a cacophony of mussed-up red hair and black body paint, and the bright white orbs that are her enquiring breasts, are all still looking at me in search of an answer.

"I, um…" are the pearls that escape my lips.

I want to do this! Why won't I let myself?

"You know you want to!" she says, gaining confidence, putting her hands on her hips. It makes my eyes drop down to her little bush, where the paint runs out. It makes me think. "Come on! Please?"

And there it is: my trigger. Someone *telling* me to do it. Pleading with me to do it. The responsibility of deciding melting away as I hear the words I need. I'm just helping someone out. I'm still a good girl, really.

But my heart thuds with excitement as I smile, shrug as casually as I can and swing my legs off the bed. "Okay, alright, you win!"

I know I'm letting my pulsing clit have its way with me here. But I'm just helping a friend – letting her win – right? A friend who no doubt wants some girl-girl excitement. A friend who is looking prettier by the minute. A friend who thinks I'm *hot*. I'm having flashbacks to that kiss we had.

"Aw, thanks Em!" she says. "I'll try and make it worth your while!"

I gulp, and she pulls me up off the bed by my hands. "Come on, lazy legs! I'm the one who should be tired after chess, not you!"

"Yeah but you…I mean, I didn't get…"

She just winks at me and hands me a towel. And I decide to give up speaking for a while.

The streaming water makes light work of Sarah's body paint. Obviously they've used the best stuff you can buy. They don't cut corners on quality in this place. In truth, she doesn't need much of a helping hand.

But she's standing expectantly in front of me with her arms aloft, black streaks of dying paint tumbling down from her neck and shoulders, gently tarring her breasts with tiny, inky waterfalls.

And wow, her boobs are quite a sight when she stretches like this. So firm and self-sufficient, all they've done is glance upwards at me. Her nipples are looking quizzically in my direction, challenging me where Petra's angered me.

We have the shower to ourselves, thank God. My nerve's running away again. I don't know why this is so hard. I do this with Petra every morning! But that's when everyone knows we've been made to do it.

"Come on lovely," she encourages me, closing her eyes and taking a deep breath through her nose. "I can't wait another minute to be clean!"

Fuck, she's picked just the right words again. I'm just washing her off. It's okay.

I join her under the warm jets, standing close in front of her, almost nipple to nipple, but not quite touching.

A little tentatively, I start at her nape. I simply run my hands over her skin, watching the blackness vanish as I work my way from her shoulders to her throat, her collarbone and then – oh fuck it! – her breasts. Her skin feels delicious, and it's satisfying to see my good work taking shape as her natural colour begins to take over.

I do a first and a second run down each part of her body, and I swear her nipples are harder the second time than on my first passing.

I find myself lingering there, tweaking a nipple and rolling it gently between my thumb and forefinger.

I gasp at my own audacity. She gasps at my touch.

I take her other nipple and do the same, doubling her sensations in an instant. She opens her eyes now, and looks punch-drunk. She closes them again, arching her back and moaning a tiny moan.

Something makes me look over my shoulder. I check the gallery, always expecting to see someone materialize there. But it's empty. And the door is shut. We're alone.

I start to fear that I might get into this.

I pinch her nipples a little harder and her mouth drops open. This woman is completely at my mercy, her nipples hard as diamonds. It scares me that I might have this kind of power. I don't know what to do, but I know I'm turned on. *Can I do this?*

Suddenly it's as though she can take no more. Her eyes open again and she steps into me, pressing up close, so close that she's got my toes wedged under her feet. And we're having that kiss again, our naked breasts squeezed against each other this time as our tongues lock in the warm rain.

It's heaven. It's better than before. *Holy hell this is hot!* It's wet and steamy and this girl can kiss like a Roman goddess. She bites my bottom lip and gently sucks it in, and my breath hitches as my control ebbs away. I can feel her hands running down my back now, across my bare ass.

It's pure and beautiful discovery as we keep on kissing and roaming our hands over each other's bodies. I sense – I *know* – neither of us wants this kiss to end. And neither of us can stop ourselves taking in every inch of skin we can reach while standing pressed together.

I'm sure all the body paint must have left her now, but the washing pretext is long forgotten anyway. We're too busy trying to burrow deeper into the other's mouth, dancing on her palate and slathering over her taste buds. Oh, this is *really* good.

The kernel of doubt and guilt inside me feels like it's slowly getting slain. So what if it turns out I like to do things with girls? So *what?* Emma Carling does what she wants!

Suddenly she pulls away from me, takes my hands and gazes deep into my eyes. That intoxicated look is still in her pupils. We're both naked and dripping warm water. And it hits me again. She's a *woman*.

My nerves start to fray again, but she has no idea as she sinks to her knees, pushing me towards the centre of the shower stream so that I'll be warm while she...*oh!*...shoos my knees apart and runs her hands up the outsides of my thighs and brings her face, parted lips, closer to…

No!

I feel my hand jink towards my centre, that old defence reflex. She stops her approach and I shake my head stupidly, hating myself. It's like my switch has been flicked again, the other way this time.

"I'm sorry…I can't…I'm not ready…" I mumble without catching her eye, slapping my own words across the cheek as they pour out of me like the tears I know aren't far away. I'm being so unfair to her. I know how much she wants this. I know how much *I* want it. But that *fucking* voice inside my head still shouts to get her way, to stop my fun, and right now I'm letting her.

"It's okay, hun…" she coos from down below, her voice all chocolate strawberries. God, she's going to make me cry if she's so nice about this. I can feel the sniffles coming on already as I step out of the shower and grab my towel.

She follows me, her brow furrowed with concern. I've been so mean to this sweet, pretty thing! I don't deserve…

"We can take our time, Emma, don't worry," she says, putting her hand on my shoulder. "I know you want this. It's not easy. I struggle too you know. We'll get there. It's been a big week for us both."

I bite my lip as I try to stop the tears, nodding because I can't agree more. This week has been nuts. The last ten days have, in fact.

"Sorry I'm such an idiot, Sarah. I've ruined it…"

"No apologies, babe," she says. "I'm more worried about your need right now. You must be dying to get there."

Oh, yeah, that. Now that she mentions it, I *still* haven't come this afternoon. *And whose fault is that, huh?*

"Look," she continues, her tone dripping with concern. "I won't be offended if you need me to leave you here for a bit of time to yourself. Maybe you can imagine how we'll pick up where we left off. Next time."

She winks as she says it. I feel that fire rising in my belly again, and I have an impulse to pull her face onto mine. I fight it off, of course. Because nice girls don't fuck other women – or random men – unless they're told to. I can see the delusion, but won't respond. *Idiot!*

Instead I just nod. She gives my bottom a playful slap and leaves the room. It's just me now, and the only sound is the *drip-drip-drip* of the cooling shower.

I'm standing there naked, with my towel in my hand. And then it hits me that my reflex to wrap myself up is no longer there. It hasn't crossed my mind. Hmm. My thoughts flick around to the positive once again. I may not be winning every battle, but in the war against myself, I'm slowly gaining ground.

Cheered by the thought, I lock myself in one of the toilet cubicles and spread the towel over the closed lid. I sit down, lean back against the sturdy, old-school cistern, and splay my legs wide.

I slip a finger inside myself, and find I'm still astoundingly wet. Soon I'm busily working my clit. For the first time this week, it's physical pleasure where I'm in charge and nothing's new and nobody's watching. When did I forget I could do this?

I take Sarah's advice and imagine where things would have gone if I hadn't gone crazy and run out of the shower. My mind takes me to some very pleasant places indeed, and before long it's her tongue down there, not my finger.

It's not long before a shuddering climax hits me like a bomb. Not a moment too soon.

Chapter Nineteen

I'm too shy to return to Sarah's room tonight. So I slink back to my designated quarters, where Ice Queen and I ignore each other. It's a full turn of the clock since I whipped her, and I'm dying to see if the marks I left are still there.

But she doesn't give me the satisfaction, staying clothed throughout the evening. And since asking her to show me would involve talking to her, I make a mental note to look out for it at showers tomorrow.

Sarah doesn't bother me all night. I hope she doesn't think I'm mad at her. I'm totally not. I'm mad at myself, and just need a little me time. I try to read before bed, but it's hard to quieten my thoughts for more than a few paragraphs. It's been the most intense week of my life, hands down. Visions from it keep swimming before my eyes. Focus is impossible.

Next morning, I wake up with a clear head, and make sure to catch Sarah as we head into the showers, this time with about eight people up on the gallery. My mentor, our chess queen from yesterday, Rupert, our waker, George…it seems the whole world is watching.

I'm so much less bothered about it than I was at the start of the week. It's startling. I'm actually switched on enough to put my arm around Sarah as we head towards the water. She looks like she hasn't slept much. I bet she worried last night, despite her brave words. I feel bad.

"Hey, just in case you're wondering, we're good!" I murmur in her ear. "Sorry I messed up, I just needed some time to myself. I guess maybe I'm just not there yet."

"Aw, thanks Em," she whispers, no doubt feeling the umpteen eyes on our conversation. "It's cool. Take as long as you need." And then she puts her arm around my waist and adds, "Just remember I'm first in line when you are, okay?"

I give her a smile and tell her it's a deal.

We disengage and I head for Petra, who is already standing under the shower, arms folded and tapping her foot with the impatience of a spoilt princess awaiting her make-up artist. I roll my eyes, and giggle as I notice that the grinning Latifa caught me doing it. It's lovely to have a few girls on my side.

I go through the now-familiar motions on Petra, as always shutting down my senses as best I can. I know how fun this lesbian shower lark can be, but I won't let it be fun with her. I note with satisfaction that the stripes on her bottom are turning dark purple.

And I'm well aware that Rupert is watching. He knows how those stripes happened. I wonder what marks *he* is bearing today? The whole thing is kind of a turn-on.

I'm not quite sure what to do with myself after breakfast. It's Friday, and we've been told there's a chance to get out to the pub tonight. I'm all for that idea. I need to escape this madhouse for a few hours: good call, staff. I can't be the only one nearing breaking-point as the first week ends.

Apart from that, I can't really understand what I'm supposed to do today. But something is bound to turn up – it always seems to. One thing's for sure: I'm definitely too proud to go looking for Rupert. I knock on Alyssia and Latifa's door, but they seem to be off…somewhere. Sarah's occupied too. Am I being left out again?

I mooch back into my room for a while, throw on some plain jeans and a t-shirt. Petra doesn't seem to have made it back from breakfast. Momentarily I toy with the idea of going through her things, just to be a bitch. But I drop it just as quickly. Bitchiness just isn't a game I want to play. I'm not going anywhere near her level.

Looking for stimulation, I grab a newspaper from the library and take it through to the lounge. Before I sit down in one of the broad, manly armchairs – I should have a pipe! – I stare out of the window for a moment. I can see the chess board, where so much went down yesterday afternoon. I can see the willows at the bottom of the garden. I can even see the entrance to the maze.

It's a bright but breezy day, clouds scudding fast across the sky. I wonder if I should brave the pool deck, but decide I'll be more comfortable in here. I can't believe I've made it as far as Friday. Nearly halfway! I truly can't wait for my assessment with Miss Jackson. She promised the mysteries would stop after that!

I'm about to turn away from the window, smiling at that happy thought, when I notice a movement at the bottom of the garden. It's the unmistakeable, shapely figures of Petra and Lilia. And they've just emerged from the maze. I feel my brain click into overdrive and my pulse quicken.

It hasn't crossed my mind to go back in there, but suddenly I want to know if I'm missing out on something. What's *she* getting? Will her 'treat' be the disappointment I got after finding that envelope laden with promise? The fact that she's with her partner in crime makes me doubly suspicious, curious and jealous in equal measure.

They're closer now, and – yes! – they're holding envelopes. They're not running and skipping like I did. You can't tell what they're thinking, really, from the way they amble along, smoking, like they own the place. I've forgotten all about my newspaper. I want to see what happens.

They don't see me watching as they cross the terrace and enter the house. I'm quite sure of that. I'm going to follow Petra, or I'll go insane with curiosity. I creep into the doorway and peep out, fugitive-style, as I hear them having a conversation in the front hallway. I've no idea what they're saying, of course. Eventually Lilia heads upstairs, and the miniskirted Petra trots off towards the hallway beneath ours. Uh oh. That floor is the south wing. South wing, ground floor. That's where *things* happen.

Fortunately, she stops and knocks on the first door, so I don't lose her around the corner. I see her push it open, but from this distance I can't catch a glimpse of anyone who might be waiting inside. *Now* how am I supposed to find out anything useful?

I guess I won't. I tiptoe down the hall, apparently forgetting that I'm perfectly entitled to walk in it. But the house is strangely quiet today, and it makes me jump when I hear a door slam in the distance. Yep, there's plenty room for ghosts in this mansion.

I'm pretty sure it's not good form to eavesdrop, but I've got nothing better to do right now. And I'm bubbling green with envy. I won't be happy unless I hear cries of pain coming from in there. So I find myself at the door, barely breathing, trying to listen. I'm ready to spring into a casual walk if I hear anyone coming.

At first, I can't make out a sound. They must be pretty solid, these big wooden doors. Would I hear a sound if there were any to hear? Minutes pass. Is nothing being said or done in there? Something must have been said after she went in, but I hadn't arrived yet. Would I have heard it if I had?

I strain my ears. Is that panting? Heavy breathing? Or am I imagining it? Then, a male voice. "I love that, Petra, play with your pussy some more for me. Keep your fingers wet at all times."

Holy fuck. The sound carries just fine if a man talks. I can't place the voice, but it's one of the regulars. She's...playing with herself for him?

Wow, she must be a good actor, because I don't think she plays with herself in real life. She's got no soul, after all. Hey, but as long as *he's* enjoying it.

Then again, she's not making much of a sound. Maybe she's not such a good actor after all. Even drugged-up porn stars make a noise when they get busy. Isn't it part of the show? Maybe not in these circles.

"Take a vibrator now, Petra," the voice insists, more urgent now. I'm surprised this kind of thing is so exciting for a man. "Lie back. Spread your legs wider for me. Push it inside you. Again and again. Do it now."

I don't hear her voice. I assume she's simply doing just as she's told.

Wow. It sounds like nobody is so much as touching her. Interesting! I feel better now, but who knows where this is going? I'm dying to know.

"MISS CARLING!!!"

I jump at the bellowing voice behind me. It comes from the next room along, whose door has just crashed open without a moment's warning. It's Geoffrey. I've had nothing to do with him so far, but vaguely remember being introduced to him at the ball. Though not particularly good-looking, he's insanely tall. Heavy-set as well, like an international rugby player.

He looks pretty scary right now.

I want to disappear. I have no place to hide as he strides towards me.

"Eavesdropping, are you? That's most unladylike, Miss Carling. Country houses such as this expect discretion, do I need to tell you that?"

I shake my head and squeak a no. "I…I'm sorry," I stutter. I hope and pray I'm going to get off with a warning.

But instead he shakes his head too, and grabs me by the collar of my orange blouse. "Evidently you need reminding, you ridiculous girl. Come with me. Move!"

He pushes me roughly down the corridor, squeezing my collar so tight my top button is starting to strain. *Oh, fuck.* What have I done?

I can feel his snorting breath bellowing down on my scalp. Either this gigantic man is also a good actor, or he's incensed beyond words.

Moments later, I find myself in Miss Jackson's office, naked once again, and hanging my head.

Geoffrey left the room immediately after depositing me with my mentor. She already seemed to know my crime, and wore a stern look. She was not alone. Carrie, my intimidating co-student, the one who used to be in the police, was with her, looking mighty comfortable in the chair in which I sat on Monday morning.

Miss Jackson sighed after Geoffrey left, and told me to strip immediately and await further instructions. So here I am, head bowed, hands behind my back, my clothes already stashed in the cupboard by Miss Jackson. Am I going to be turned loose naked once again?

I'm wondering if what I've done is an instant dismissal offence. Maybe I just don't belong here, I think to myself, trying to blink back the tears. I breathe deeply and try to keep as calm as I can.

"Miss Stafford will take your punishment from here, Miss Carling," says Miss Jackson, her tone even and low.

Great. First I get caught like a rookie, and now I get my punishment from my freakishly tall classmate. *Why couldn't you just read the newspaper?*

My mentor leans back in her chair, and out of the corner of my eye, I see Carrie stand up.

"Right," she hisses through gritted teeth. "You little fucking spy. Your mistress is going to set you straight, so you'll not behave like a gossiping shit in future."

I begin to tremble. She may be a classmate, but she's acting on full authority of staff. And her tone is pure venom. I'm terrified. And I don't know what to do. For a second I wonder if I was anywhere near this scary for my session with Petra and Rupert.

"And now you say 'yes, mistress'. Unless you want to double your punishment, that is. And you will keep your eyes down. To the floor."

There's silence as my brain computes what's going on. I don't know this 'scene' of hers. A helpful cough from Miss Jackson rouses me.

"Y-y-yes...mistress." I splutter.

"Very well. Wait there."

I hear her black shiny boots – they're all I can see with my eyes downcast – trot over to the cupboard. The door opens, and she gather some items. I hear her come closer again, then she stops at my side.

I smell leather.

I hear metal. Something like a chain.

She clams something tight around my neck. *Oh.* I've been collared. Like someone's pet.

Some of me is curious and wants to know what will happen next. Most of me wants to scream with fear.

"Turn around!"

God, she could freeze your blood with that tone. I'm beginning to sweat already. I do as she tells me, of course.

"Get on your hands and knees, you nosy little cunt. Quickly!"

Wow, the language. I'm tempted to say 'alright, alright,' but somehow manage to spit out the magic words before it's too late. "Yes, mistress."

I sink onto all fours. Do people actually get turned on by this kind of treatment?

Her high heels are next to my eyes now. The chain tightens with a sharp jingle, and she yanks me forwards, towards the far end of Miss Jackson's spacious office. To the rug in front of the fireplace.

I crawl along with her, never quite able to keep up with the chain enough for me to breathe easily. I'm quite sure that this is no accident.

The fireplace comes closer to my face. It's clean, but the cradle for the wood is still there. Carrie pulls my head right inside the fireplace, then reaches up and hooks the end of the chain around something within the chimney.

"Put your head in the cradle, you dirty miscreant. You're lucky if I don't set you on fire."

I'm humiliated now. I'm naked, collared, on my hands and knees like a pathetic animal, and now my head is actually inside the fireplace. I rest my chin on the dark, thick, burnt metal. I smell smoke and oak and winter and ash. Male smells, like everything in this house. Thank God the hearth has been well-swept.

"Do we need to restrain your hands, bitch? Can we trust you to take your punishment?"

I hesitate, unsure of what the truthful answer is.

"Yes, mistress," I murmur. She asked me two questions, but this is an answer she seems to like. I just want this over with, whatever it is. Let them send me home. Whatever.

"I'm not sure," she barks. "Better safe than sorry." And with that she grabs my wrists, cuffs them together and affixes them to what must be the bottom rung of the chimney sweep's ladder. It's just above my head, but I must keep my chin down. I can't rest my elbows at all. It's barbarically uncomfortable, and I feel totally helpless now.

"That's good. She won't move now. I think ten hits with the riding crop would teach her a lesson, Miss Jackson."

I have no idea how good or bad that is. I haven't been hit with anything other than a hand, well, ever. And then only for a bit of fun. So now I really do start to shake. Brave Emma can't do much in this position. And it's about to get worse.

"One last thing, young whore," says the voice behind me, softer and more threatening now. "I want you to spread those legs. I need to see that mischievous gash of yours. Bottom up, knees apart."

I wriggle into my most demeaning position of the week, wheezing my 'yes, mistress' for this horrible woman just in time. I sensed an ugly vibe from her the moment we met, and it seems my instincts were bang on.

This is ironic, I think to myself. Things have come full circle. I was dishing it out on Wednesday, and there was a certain twisted pleasure in that. Now I'm about to be on the receiving end, and there's absolutely nothing to like about it.

"Hmm," I hear Carrie murmur. "There's a certain level of moisture there. Clearly being naughty excites this devious little snake. I haven't even hit her yet. This is worth noting, Miss Jackson."

Wet? Now? *Me?*

All I can think, as I press my forehead into the metal and feel the blood draining from my hands, is that I simply don't know who I am anymore.

Chapter Twenty

The first bite of the riding crop makes me wince and grit my teeth. It's vicious. It really hurts. I don't know if I can take ten of these.

Crack!

Carrie really puts her back into the second blow, and it seems to sting more. I don't know if this is as painful as what I gave Rupert and Petra, but it's definitely enough for me.

Crack!

My top-heavy body convulses and sways. I don't know if I can last in this position, with my hands going more numb by the second. The loss of feeling there only heightens the sensation in my burning backside.

Crack!

It feels like a short strip of leather she's using. It concentrates the pain where she hits me. She alternates strikes between my left and right cheek. I feel completely and utterly pathetic.

The physical violence goes on, and my trembling doubles as I feel a bead of sweat roll down my face. *My head is in a fireplace; I'm bound; I'm naked. I'm being beaten like small child.* These thoughts continue on a loop.

But there are no more spiteful words. Carrie lets the riding crop do the talking, for now. Does she think she's turning me on or punishing me? Both? I can't really think about any of that, because tears are forming. The strain is getting too much. How many to go?

Crack!

Surely that's ten, now? I don't hear anything. *Oh God, please be done.* I wiggle my butt as invitingly as I can, just so it'll be over quicker. Fuck, I've never felt so completely open, such submission.

Crack!

My breathing turns short and rapid-fire. I'm desperate to be let off the hook, literally. I'm coiled spring and caged animal, and my ass cheeks are burning like crazy. I must look an unbelievable sight.

"Last one," she announces coolly. She's in no hurry, and it's torture.

I spread my legs wider and push my head even deeper into the hearth. I'm not sure why I do this.

CRACK!

Extra effort went into the finale. Are we done? That's all I care about. But she leaves me hanging a moment. I'm breathing heavily, and dying for release. I'm aching all over.

At last, she leans in and releases my hands. Mercy! I let them fall to the hearth, just letting my circulation return. I don't even think about moving. I'm not sure if I am supposed to, anyway. I'm not sure of anything.

"And *what* do you say?"

Uh oh. I have to guess.

"Er…thank you, mistress?"

"Say it like you *mean* it."

I take a deep breath. This is the last thing I want to say.

"Thank you for my punishment, mistress," I say, trying to sound more sincere. "I won't eavesdrop again."

"The fucking amateur is learning," she says, evidently addressing Miss Jackson. "Now turn your body around. Keep your head where it is and keep your legs spread."

Clumsily – there is no other way – I do as asked. I'm looking up the chimney, but I'm terribly aware that I am as exposed as it's possible for a woman to be.

In my peripheral vision I can see her boots standing between my legs. The riding crop is there too. I flinch in surprise as I feel what must be its leather part probing my lower lips. Is she going to hit me *there?*

But the movement is a gentle caress, no more. It's…pleasant. She probes inside me with the tip of the instrument, and I gasp. I'm not sure if it's the shock, or something else. I'm definitely wired. And the stinging beneath me has barely subsided at all.

"There's no doubt, Miss Jackson. Look at this! My crop is soaked with her lubrication. We have an excitable little sub on our hands."

I try to take in what she's saying. Am I really wet down there? It's the second time she's said it. I just can't believe this punishment is doing anything to me. I don't understand.

"You need to taste this," continues Carrie. "Taste your arousal. Taste why you have to thank me."

And with that she traces the leather tip across my cheeks. Oh God, it's leaving a moist trail. She wasn't kidding. Holy hell, that's embarrassing.

Now she prods my lips with it, pushing them apart. "Suck it," she orders. I do as instructed, genuinely curious now. I taste leather but I taste the moisture too. Yes, it's that dewy nectar I've supped from my fingers so many times.

The association with arousal is so strong that I'm inflamed. No doubt about it this time. I can't stop myself. It's beyond weird, but I want to dip my fingers down there once more. I don't suppose I should do that right now.

Carrie speaks again: "This isn't about *your* pleasure, you know. Stand up, you selfish slut. We're not done yet."

I wriggle out of the fireplace, barely hearing her abuse now. It's a relief to stand upright again, though I'm exposed, giddy and feeling a little sooty.

"Your response has excited Miss Jackson, I believe. You'll need to take responsibility for that, just as you will for all of your misdemeanours. So now, lick her pussy until you bring her to climax."

Nothing shocks me any more around here. Deep down, I think I knew this wasn't going to end with my physical punishment. This latest twist barely makes my heart skip a beat. I think I'm going to be okay with it, though I'm not really sure where to look.

Miss Jackson smiles her warm, comforting smile at me as she gets up from her desk, but says nothing as she unclips her skirt and drops it to the floor. She's wearing red panties. Keeping her blouse and shoes on, she moves around in front of her desk and sits on it.

She beckons me to come over. "Thank you Carrie, you may sit now," she says.

It looks like my moment of truth cannot be delayed any longer. What I couldn't contemplate with the lovely Sarah, I am going to have no choice but to do now. I may not find Miss Jackson attractive, but at least I'm feeling aroused.

I try to think positive thoughts as I cross the room towards my mentor. Miss Jackson is sweet and makes me feel comfortable. I wasn't expecting to perform a sex act on my mentor herself, but it's far from the biggest surprise I've had this week. She's smiling, and that calms me.

I'm sure I'll figure out what to do when I'm up close. It'll come naturally, right? I'm a woman, I should surely know what's where. This moment has been coming for a couple of days now. I'm curious, and, after what I've just been through, I feel ready. Getting thrashed with your head in the fireplace puts things nicely in perspective.

"Take your time and take charge, Emma," Miss Jackson murmurs. I nod, nervous but feeling brave. I feel my breathing quicken, but it's a long way from the I-can't-possibly kind of hyperventilation I would have felt a few days ago. I'm about to go down on my teacher!

It's kind of exciting.

My first woman.

She motions to the spare chair, and I pull it up so I'm sitting at a comfortable height, within easy reach of the edge of the desk. She places her feet on the chair arms, spreading her legs wide in front of me, and wriggles towards the edge. She leans back, taking her weight on her hands. I think she's done this before.

Right. I can do this. I couldn't ask for a better angle. She's tilted her hips up towards me, and all I need to do is lean in. Is every measurement of every piece of furniture in this place perfectly calculated for sex?

I take a deep breath and nose gently towards her centre. The red fabric is still there, but I can smell her arousal. My nose touches the material and I breathe in the scent of a woman. I've never been so close to it. I…like it.

I find myself nibbling, sucking and biting at the wet cloth that stands between my lips and hers. Despite the audience and my general uncertainty, it seems I want to savour this. I hear her sigh softly as I lick lovingly up the warm strip of red, then kiss gently on the inside of each thigh.

I must be dripping on her chair again. In my head, I'm shaking my head. Not a single one of my friends, family or colleagues would ever believe this if I told them. And I grin out loud at the thought. It makes me sizzle.

These panties must come off now. Yes, it's time I stop denying. I want a pure, unfettered pussy experience for my first time. That's right, *pussy*. I want to taste a vagina.

I begin to paw at the straps, wondering how I'm going to get this done with any grace at all.

"It unties, Emma!" she says helpfully.

Aha! That's good news. I find the tiny clasps on the sides, and the whole thing disintegrates. The front drops away and she tilts her hips towards me a little more.

And wow. Miss Jackson may not be a supermodel, but she has an undeniably gorgeous womanhood. It's classically neat, a model pussy. It's entirely waxed, and looks as appetizing as a classic Sunday lunch. I can see all of her slit, right down to the bottom, where a tiny bud of wetness is poised. Soon, surely, that will be a trickle. I can't wait to put my lips to it. *That's where I need to taste.*

This, now, is as much about my pleasure as hers. Everything has changed for me. I remind myself, over and over, that I'll never have a first time again. This is big.

I run my hands down the backs of her thighs, and gently grip the sides of her buttocks. At this, she arches her back a little further, and I pull in as close as I can. My own legs spread to full width so my knees don't crash into the desk, and that makes the whole room get a ton sexier. What is it about throwing open my legs that always drives me so wild?

And that pain in my ass? If anything, it seems to be heightening my lust right now.

Something makes me close my eyes as I move in again, memories of my first kiss stirring in the depths of my mind. I stop with my tongue an inch from that spot where her nectar hovers, and the smell sensation spirals. Mmm, yes, that, right there, is the smell of sex. I fill my lungs with it, let my tongue cascade a little further over my bottom lip, and sink into her.

And now my thirsty tongue drinks. Just a tiny tickle at first, her wetness on its tip, and an enormous shudder of thrill passes through me. Of everything I've done this week, this feels the naughtiest. Not only is my tongue brushing a woman's darkest place, but it's my teacher too. And my legs are open, and I'm naked, and I'm being watched. Holy hell, does life get any sexier?

I pause on my tiny *amuse-bouche*, tickling, teasing us both. I felt her breath hitch, and it hasn't yet unhitched. I smile to myself between her legs, as I dance on just that spot, tiny circles, like a honeybird grabbing every last drop
of nectar.

I moan quietly, taking everything from this moment, imprinting every smell and taste sensation on my mind. And then I find myself really moving.

She sighs with satisfaction as I grant her all of my tongue, one full lick moving all the way up her length. Along her wet crack, no concessions, diving in wherever it can, tasting the sweetness of her crevice. It's divine, sensual and my own legs feel weak. I reach her clit, and my own begins to burn.

I return to where I began, and lick all the way up again. And again. I can't take this smile off my face, and my eyes open again. There is nothing but pussy in my face. It's a reminder of where I am and what I'm doing. *Wow!*

I take my time, switching from long licks to deep probes inside her. I move my hands, pulling her wider so I can lap up more from her core, before exposing her clit to my eager, curious tongue.

My suspicions were correct. I know exactly what to do. I'm guided by the sighs and groans of another woman; guided by what I know I'd want. Add in the dash of intense passion I'm feeling, the drunkenness I'm drawing from this beguiling drink, and I seem to have a woman close to the edge. Two women, actually.

Finally I focus on her clit, nibbling now and then, kissing and sicking occasionally, but mostly just little hits with my tongue. I'm giving her exactly what I'd want right now. I slide my finger inside her squelchiness and she responds in sounds and breath and movement.

I thrust gently, surprisingly myself at how natural it is to keep that rhythm while holding my tongue's delicate pulse. She clearly loves it. And I can feel myself beginning to seep. I have no shame.

She explodes loudly around my face, and I grin as I keep working, allowing a second wave to hit her, and then a third. She is not a talker, but her groans and yelps tell me everything. I have made my teacher ecstatic. My punishment is forgotten – surely?

I pull back in satisfaction, and all I see is Miss Jackson, head thrown back, eyes still closed. Suddenly I am acutely aware of my own need. I am only barely aware of Carrie sitting next to me. The warm feeling in my belly dominates everything. It has slain the pain.

A minute goes by. She gathers her breath, and stares right at me. There is a dazed look in her eyes, but also a twinkle. I'm not sure what happens now. I'm burning up inside, that's all I know.

"Thank you, Miss Carling," she says to me without moving. "You may dress and leave."

But…what about me? Another crush of disappointment. This place!

I sigh, perhaps not as quietly as I might, and nod. I'm a little indignant, but resigned to do as I'm told. I don't let her eyes catch mine as I rise, make myself appear respectable, and let myself out. My pride won't let her see the need I can't hope to hide right now.

Chapter Twenty-One

Thank God Sarah is in her room. I go there without even thinking. Lust churns in me like a bubbling whirlpool. I am so ready, so desperate. I appear in her doorway, and I give her a look.

And she just knows. It's a girl thing. I don't want to look her in the eye either. Because I feel bad at how I ruined things yesterday. It should have been *her*, it should have been *us*. I've already taken another girl, but she could have my own virginity.

"I'm ready…oh, Sarah, I'm sorry…I need…"

She hushes me, pulls me into the room, and closes the door behind me. It no longer even crosses my mind that the bedroom doors don't lock in this place.

"Please…" I whine at her, panting like a desperate puppy, "Just please…"

"I know," she smiles. "Shh, calm down now, Sarah's going to make you happy."

How does she *know?*

A minute later I'm flat on her bed, minus my jeans and panties once again. Beyond the whiteness of my t-shirt, Sarah's pretty head bobs between my splayed knees. She's working my folds with gusto.

I curl my shoulders and close my eyes as the tickle begins to build into something more. I don't think about the thrashing, or how I licked Miss Jackson. I think only of the impossibly delicious sensation coating my vagina. But what happened in the last hour has played its part. I'm not going to be able to hold on for long.

It doesn't help when she starts moaning with pleasure just at the same moment I do. The pleasure of exploration…I know it all too well. Only this time, there's a mutual affection thing going on. It suffuses my feelings with a syrupy extra dose of warmth.

It's bizarre to hear womanly moans coming from the one pleasuring me. Bizarre in a good way. A super-good way. It's a double-dash of wicked naughtiness that ignites me and takes me closer.

My orgasm takes me by surprise. I squeeze her torso with my knees as her deft tongue-work sends me off the edge of the cliff and I soar out into space, my joy like the free flight of a gull riding the sea breeze. It feels like it won't stop, this long wave of pleasure carrying me forth.

It's beautiful, it's exhausting, and it takes me a long time to return to earth. I actually forget where I am for a moment. When at last I open my eyes, I feel like I've woken with amnesia. Then Sarah's face swims into my blurry vision, and I'm overwhelmed by gratefulness and the need to kiss her deeply. Over and over.

We spend several minutes, our mouths locked together, and then I push her down on the bed and we swap roles. Yes, I've done this before. Her eyes shine in anticipation and thrill as I grin at her, then feast on my second pussy in the space of half an hour.

I feel nothing but thrill and pride (*where did that guilt go, Emma darling?*) as I bring her to climax with my now shameless tongue. A tongue that, today at least, no longer knows what depravity is. I'm glowing.

We lie and cuddle for a while. She tells me of how she blew four of the men for her morning assignment, who then came on her face as one. Rupert was one of them, but I just giggle at the notion. She returns the favour as I tell her of my adventures with Carrie and Miss Jackson. I grumble that it's all Petra's fault for making me get caught.

"Move in with me," Sarah says, suddenly earnest. "What good is she doing for you? Any at all?"

I think for a moment, then pull her closer. "Okay, okay, you're right. Sold! Let's stop pretending, huh?"

She just smiles back at me, and we snuggle some more.

I feel like being indulgent this afternoon. Things are starting to fall into place. My jealous flame for Rupert seems to be dying, and I've got this lesbian monkey off my back at last. And what's more, I feel somehow stronger and prouder after my beating in the hearth.

Most importantly of all, I'm out of the hell-hole that was my room with Petra. Not sure if this room switch is strictly allowed, but I think they'd surely approve of my reasons. If they want to beat me again, so be it. Apparently it turns me on! My butt sure does feel bruised though.

Have I started something serious with Sarah? The looks she gives me suggest she's fallen hard for me. I think I might be heading that way too, but I'm wary. I've already been burned once in this place. It's good to keep things in perspective. It's the end of the first week, and I resolve to enjoy my remaining time with her without overthinking it. I'm sure next week will have its own twists and turns.

There's a group lunch on the terrace, now that the sun has come out. Miss Tottingham appears before we're served, and addresses all of the trainees.

"Ladies, you've made it to Friday lunchtime," she smiles. "Congratulations, you're doing well. I trust you're all a little sore, for all the right reasons."

I can't help smirking as I catch Latifa's eye. Petra, sitting with Lilia at the far end of the long, white-clothed table, doesn't even seem to have heard the joke.

"It's time to unwind," Miss Tottingham continues. The staff will be clearing out for the weekend, and we'll leave you in the safe hands of Miss Honeywell. On Monday morning, you'll all meet with your mentors to review your first week and map out your second week's training. You'll be spending more time in the classrooms, and things will get more practical and specific. There'll be fewer surprises."

I'm relieved to hear that again. This week's salacious activities would have been exhausting enough without so many of them being unexpected and against the run of play. I never knew how much intensity that could add, and it's left me mentally shattered.

"Between now and then, you all need to recharge," she goes on. This is as sweet as I've seen any mentor since we arrived. I hope it means the fake aloofness is on the way out. "This afternoon is for relaxing, and with a bit of luck the sun will stay out. Tonight, Christopher is at your disposal to drive you to a local pub. I suggest you take the chance, as he'll be away Saturday and Sunday. It's a classy cocktail place, so do glam it up a bit.

"Take it easy on the weekend, girls. The grounds are yours to explore as always, and if you wish to go out walking in the surrounding countryside, Miss Honeywell will let you out and provide you with packed lunches. A little exercise never hurts in your chosen profession."

She winks, and I gulp. It hits me just how deep a hole I've dug for myself. I'm halfway to being a *qualified prostitute.* For the very first time all week, it actually seems possible I might go through with this life change. From here, it's downhill all the way.

I look out at the spread in front of me: the flawless grapes, the fancy cheeses I can't name, the thin-sliced salmon, the dazzling salad. I've never eaten as well as I have this week. I've never used gleaming cutlery like this. I think of my infinite wardrobe, and the fine, expensive lace I can feel nuzzling my butt cheeks. I think of chauffeurs, and butlers. And the life-changing sex.

My heart beats a little faster as I think about how I'm going to hide this from my parents.

We've been tricked again. The *bastards!*

Cocktail bar? Christ, that was a bald-faced lie. The eleven of us have just tumbled into the country pub to end all country pubs. About a dozen old men, mostly with a pint of dark ale in their hands, turn around and peer at us. A couple of them are actually smoking pipes.

There's a Labrador tied up next to the bar. He's lifts his head from where it rested on his paws, and gives us a quizzical look as we spill into the room. Even the animal knows there's something not right about a group of gorgeous young women, mostly in heels and tight black dresses, coming into a place like this.

I know this kind of joint. The carpets smell of beer and there's a copy of every major newspaper in the rack. Terrific on a Sunday afternoon, in jeans and a t-shirt. But on a Friday night? After good-mood Emma dressed up in a daring red number that went pretty bold on cleavage? Thank God I'm not alone. Safety in numbers.

"Jesus, really?" says Alyssia, turning to us. "They've brought us to the wrong place! Has Chris gone already?"

We all turn and peer out of the window. In the dusk, we can see the limo just pulling out into the road. He's not due back for three hours.

So we're trapped. Sarah and I raise our eyebrows at each other. Jane screws up her nose, making herself look really ugly. Carol looks like she wants to crawl into a hole and hide. Petra is looking around the room, like a house buyer determined to find signs of damp. Latifa bursts out laughing.

The positive Simone is the first to make a move, pushing her tall frame towards the bar. "Hey, at least we have free drinks guys! Let's make the most of it!"

That much is true. Chris did tell us our tab would be picked up. I think I'm going to need something pretty strong, pretty soon.

She orders a shot of vodka for all of us. Not exactly classy, but nobody objects. Not even Latifa. Not sure why I thought she'd be a good Muslim girl when it came to alcohol. She's so naughty!

Nicely warmed up, we order the pub's most expensive bottles of red and white wine. Someone suggested champagne, but a place like this was never going to have any. We're lucky to have something that isn't beer.

We find an alcove in the corner near the front door that's big enough for all of us. It's the best we can do to make ourselves feel less conspicuous, but it's hopeless really. A dozen glamorous trainee hookers, dressed up as if they're hitting London's clubs, are like an alien landing party in this kind of establishment.

I wonder if the regulars here *know?* We're about a 20-minute drive from the house. Country people love to gossip. They know things. And if someone from the school is picking up our tab, surely the landlord here must at least wonder…I try not to think about it.

But I struggle not to think about it. How embarrassing it would be if these people know that we're a bunch of professional sluts in training! I gulp my wine faster than usual, and somehow feel glad I've wedged myself into the corner with Sarah, Alyssia and Latifa.

These are the girls I'd choose to hang out with, and with my back to the wall, I feel a tiny bit shielded by them. Before long, with a glass of wine on top of my shot, I've forgotten that this is supposed to be awkward. Conversation is flowing nicely between the four of us.

"So, what's up between the two of you?" smirks Latifa suddenly, giving me a wink.

My stomach jumps, but Sarah grabs my hand under the table and it calms me. I hate quizzes like this, especially from sharp people who can spot the glow and chemistry between us a mile off.

"Nothing much," Sarah smiles, "we're just getting to know each other, aren't we Em?"

I nod in exaggerated fashion. Good answer, Sarah! And the four of us burst out laughing.

"I've slowly started to take your advice on board, guys," I admit to Alyssia and Latifa, feeling myself blush furiously. "Thanks…"

Alyssia offers me a high-five. Are we turning into boys, with celebrations like this? But I guess, come to think of it, a bit of a male attitude to sex is just what's needed around here.

"And Emma's moving in with me," Sarah goes on, jerking her head at the far end of the table, where my Bulgarian friends are camped out as usual. "She's much better off without all that negativity around."

Everyone nods in agreement. The thing with Petra isn't just me, after all. Nobody likes her. But I've had the worst of it as her roomie.

The four of us really begin to gel as we get stuck further into the wine. It's *really* good to be away from the house, tittering as we compare notes on the week. Sarah gets into dramatic mode as she recounts how she felt during the chess game, and has us in stitches. Latifa and Alyssia don't hold back as they tell of their sex adventures, though even they keep their voices down.

Then it's my turn. And it's hard, even with the alcohol loosening my tongue. I skip over how I got jealous about Rupert – they'll laugh at me, surely! I twist the story of beating him and Petra accordingly, and everyone likes the part where she gets lashed. Then I admit that I felt kind of left out during the chess game.

"I could see it in your eyes, girl. I was watching you!" says Latifa. Dammit, she reads me like a book.

"Well, it's been good since then," I admit. "It took a while but eventually Sarah…well, she's good! Mind you, I had a bit of pain first."

"Oh really?" chime Latifa and Alyssia as one, leaning forward, eager for more.

I recount the story of how I got caught eavesdropping, and thrashed by Carrie, whose eye I've studiously avoided catching all day. I'm not really mad at her. I figure she's got a role to play. And she played it well. But it seems a bit much to actually be chummy.

"Really?" says Latifa, eyes wide and shiny. "Wow, we've not had any of that beating stuff, have we Liss?"

"No...but I've not done multiple blow-jobs like Sarah," I reply. "I mean, we've all had quite different assignments, haven't we?"

"Hmm," says Alyssia, "I guess we wouldn't be very good at that submissive stuff. Maybe they don't think it's for us at all, so they don't test us on it?"

"Could be," says Sarah. "I think it may look pretty random, but there's a fair bit of thought gone into it. They're clever, they are..."

"They are," I add, "but then why did they make *me* do stuff I've never done and have no idea about?"

Latifa's reply is instant: "Because they see your potential. You can do absolutely everything, Emma, even if you don't believe it yet. People like me and Liss, we're a bit one-dimensional. They're probably happy that we stick to our strengths. Maybe we're too vanilla, huh?"

I flush bright red, and hope this nook's gloomy light hides it. God knows why I care in present company. Sarah's hand squeezes my thigh. "Maybe you'll be top of the class come next week, huh Emma?"

"Don't know about that! Hey Latifa, how do you know? You've only seen me in action, what...once?"

"I have a sense about these things, Emma. You're a wonderful little all-rounder. And as for seeing you in action, I hope I'll be seeing you perform more very soon...now that you're a randy little bi lady like the rest of us!"

Her foot's up my skirt! She's quick as a cat! She sits back and takes a sip of her wine as she wiggles her toe deep between my thighs. And she doesn't seem to care if anyone knows. In fact, she's looking at Sarah, and grinning.

I feel a bit bad, like I shouldn't exclude Sarah from something like this. I'm probably overthinking things again. We've licked each other out once, that's all! But anyway, I grab her hand and guide onto the bulge under my skirt, just so she knows.

And I'm relieved to see her grin right back at Latifa.

Still, it's getting a little out of hand. I'm starting to squirm. We're supposed to be having a break from all this tonight.

Latifa senses it's enough for now, and pulls her foot away. I puff out my cheeks and sigh. Sarah withdraws her hand. I feel curiously naked.

Chapter Twenty-Two

The wine does wonders for that self-consciousness of ours. Another bottle arrives, and then another. We forget how out of place we are, and the giggles keep coming as the honest tales from the week begin to flow. I can almost see the release as our tension ebbs away into the room.

This may not have been our venue of choice, but a few drinks are exactly what we all needed. Few of us have been much good at being ourselves this week. Most of us have played as cool as we can, but, apart from maybe Latifa and Alyssia, we've had a hard time of it. It's been intense on so many levels.

It's been difficult to be friendly when we've felt there's an element of competition about things. I suppose nobody actually *told* us we were up against each other, or that diplomas were limited or anything. But it's a bunch of girls living together, being graded on how they satisfy a handful of strong men, while some of us still don't want to admit just how 'liberated' we've become. I guess civility is about the best you can hope for, come to think of it.

And that's before you add the sparks of lust that have been flying between some of us girls. I shake my head and wonder how any of this can be real. It all seems so unlikely, so not twenty-first century. I've been without my phone for a week, living in a house where everything's an antique! As for what I've been getting up to, well…I really didn't expect it to be as wild a ride as it has been. No wonder we've all turned up here a little dazed.

Now, though, alcohol is doing its magic, and we're learning to laugh at ourselves and each other. For tonight, at least. It strikes me that so much of this week would have been easier if we could have pulled together a little more. Easier said than done, of course. I promise myself I'm going to spend a bit more time around the drinks cabinet in the lounge. I feel so much looser tonight, and I like it.

I spend some time getting to know Simone and Carol. Both pleasant girls, and beautiful in their own very different ways. Simone is tall and Dutch and confident, and I can totally see her living this life. But Carol really impresses me, because I can tell she's naturally demure, and this has been a big step for her. She's got that Asian flush going now, thanks to the booze, and giggles shyly when Simone points it out. I can see how appealing the little Singapore sweetie might be. I wonder if she's too nice for this game.

Though there is much hilarity, I'm impressed with how we manage to keep our voices down. A handful of honest, plain country women have joined the early-evening male drinkers since our arrival. When I steal glances around the room, which still smells of smoke after years of cigarette ban in England – all I can detect is disapproval from the women and eager curiosity from the men. After a while I have to admit that I quite like the feeling.

It seems we've all had that whole discretion thing impressed upon us rather well. And most of us have it in-built anyway. I don't suppose the school could expect a group like ours not to attract attention – all we can do is carry ourselves in a way that offers more questions than answers. Come to think of it, that would probably make our stock go up. A vision of a cattle auction musters in my mind's eye, and suddenly I shudder. And then I laugh as I whisper my thoughts to Carol.

I don't talk to Jane, because I still don't like her fake, awkward way. I try and chat to Diane a little, because we really haven't spoken this week. The American redhead seems nice enough, but doesn't offer much. I'm not sure she's all that smart. She doesn't navigate conversation all that well, but maybe she's just shy. I wonder if I was like that at the start of the week. I'm quite certain I've changed. I think most of us have.

Even Carrie speaks to me for a while, offering me a rare smile as she slides into a seat opposite me. I can't really hold her eye, and I just cough and nod as I look down at the table. What do you say to a woman who only a few hours ago tied you up naked in a fireplace and tanned your hind quarters? I'm suddenly aware that there's still a tingle in my bottom.

"Hey, Emma," she says with a warmth I didn't know she was capable of, "you know that thing I do is part of a persona I work with, right? I don't hate you or anything."

I look up at her, encouraged by the words but still unsure what to say. I notice she's only drinking lemonade.

"Actually I quite like you," she chuckles. "You really turned me on in Miss Jackson's office."

I raise my eyebrows, curious now. "Er...I turned *you* on? Isn't it...I mean..."

Christ, I know so little about her world.

"Of course you did! A dominant like me gets a kick out of the power and the caning, but only when she has a super little submissive to give her the right vibe. You, darling, are a super little submissive. And from what I hear, you can go the other way too."

Oh. I guess she must be referring to my caning session with Rupert and Petra. She's giving me a knowing look that tells me, as if I didn't know already, that nothing stays a secret for long around here.

"As for your treatment of Miss Jackson," she goes on, "all I can say is that it made me want to scream with jealousy! You weren't the only one who was wet after your beating, you know. But I didn't want to overstep her authority. Hopefully my act had you fooled, but I'm still a student here and can only do what I'm told. For now."

She winks and I soften, even while blushing. So the lemonade-drinking Carrie Stafford is yet another one who isn't quite what she seemed, and clearly it's not alcohol talking. What next? Am I going to find that Petra turns into an angelic, cheerful kitten tonight? No, that seems a little too far-fetched.

I've forgotten about her for the last couple of hours. Last time I checked, she was keeping herself to herself – herself and Lilia, that is – at the far end of the table. No interest in talking to any of us. Nothing new there.

I glance across to my left again, and this time something has changed. My eyes go wide at what I see.

Petra and Lilia are deep in conversation with two men. They've moved away from us to a neighbouring table. Neighbouring, but most definitely separate. Carrie and a couple of the others follow my gaze. It seems none of us noticed this happening. Too busy sharing salacious tales and getting drunk.

What the *actual fuck?* The men are both about thrice their age, I'd guess. Both are drinking pints of dark ale and dressed in country style. There's a hint of tweed about both of them, and neither is particularly groomed. One's rather red-faced, the other has hair growing out of his ears. They're model customers for this place.

Even if this were a pub for pulling members of the opposite sex – and it most certainly isn't – I can't think of a less likely match than these two and *those* two. What in the world could they possibly be talking about? Even the dog at the bar is looking on in astonishment.

Petra and Lilia are both leaning in, resting on their forearms, but neither of them are smiling. They seem unaware that a couple of us have started watching them. I exchange a glance with Sarah, who shrugs as if she doesn't much care. I shouldn't care much either. I mean, these are *not* men to be jealous of! And yet…I'm dying of curiosity again. Sharing a room with her has twisted my perspective.

And now I've got an excuse to stare at her.

The glow of the wall lamp reflects sensuously on her shiny lip gloss.

What is she *doing?* How did this conversation begin?

The men's body language is curious. They look at ease and entirely satisfied. They don't have that desperate, over-interested way about them that boys my age tend to have when they're trying to chat you up. Maybe age cures that? Or maybe they're just being curious, friendly locals, wondering what this odd group of women are up to.

And yet, Petra and Lilia seem more interested in this conversation than the two granddads are. Especially Petra. I've never seen her so talkative. It's like she's deep in discussion with a lawyer about her share of a great aunt's estate. It's very strange. I wish I could lip read.

Simone offers to refill my glass, and I barely acknowledge her as I push it across the table. I'm transfixed. I mumble thanks, and, just as I raise it to my lips again, Petra's conversation seems to come to an abrupt end. She nods, Lilia smiles, and they both stand. Without so much as a glance at the rest of us, they walk out of the pub.

Ever so slowly, with a stretch here and a sigh there, the men rise to their feet. They stroll to the stand in the far corner and retrieve their hats. It's still too warm for anyone to need a coat. Then, nodding politely at our table as they make for the door, they let themselves out, donning their hats as they go.

Some of the other girls are still too busy drinking to have noticed any of this, but again I give Sarah a look. Sharp Carrie has seen it too. I'm too flabbergasted to move, but Carrie gets up, steps around our table, and parts the curtain to look out of the window.

"They're all getting in that guy's car," she says matter-of-factly, staring out dreamily. "Did they not say anything to anyone before they went?"

"I'm pretty sure they didn't speak to anyone all night," I mutter, insane with not knowing what to think any more. Diane nods, and Simone shrugs. Sarah just raises her eyebrows at me.

There isn't much will to go after them. If they get in trouble for going AWOL…I can't imagine too much sympathy from the rest of the group.

But where? And why?

And why do I care so much?

"I'm going to look for clothes," I slur in Sarah's general direction a couple of hours later. Thanks to Chris and our limousine, we're safely back in my newly-adopted room. It must be long past midnight. Country pubs like that don't worry about traditional closing time.

My head is spinning. Simone made us do a couple more shots before we left, and I'm not feeling great. Yet the Petra thing is bright and bold and clear as a vivid nightmare, gnawing away at my brain.

"Sure you are, you curious cat," she grins. "I don't know if she's coming back, but go on. And then *please* come back." Her grin turns to a naughty pout. I frown, unable to think about sex right now.

Moments later I stumble through the door of what is officially my room. She's there, sitting on the bed with Lilia. They look up, startled.

Petra makes no attempt to hide the cash in her hand.

I make no attempt to pretend to look for clothes.

The addled cogs in my brain wheeze into action and start to compute. Hang on a second. She's. Counting. Money. *Holy fuck.*

Her hair's a little mussed-up, but basically there's only a hint of just-fucked about her. I don't even see Lilia.

I feel entirely intimidated again, but drunk enough that I can speak. "How much do you have there?" I ask.

I expect her to snap that it's none of my business, but she gives me a challenging look that has an infinitesimal trace of a smile about it. It has a superior quality, but it's the nearest thing to a smile I've seen from her, anyway.

"Three hundred fifty Pounds," she says, her tone flat. She gives a tiny sigh, as if to say it's not a very exciting amount of money.

"How long have you been back?"

"Maybe one hour."

Jeez, they couldn't have done very much in that time, those two. It must have been straight down to business. There's no glow, no flush, no sated look. Wouldn't you be a little *happier?* Money and sex. I think I'd be smiling. Especially if I'd just weaselled some bonus freelancing ahead of everyone else.

Resourceful…certainly. Against school rules? I'm not sure, come to think of it. What about discretion? I'm so confused. And why couldn't I do that? Why didn't I even *think* of that? And why can't the one who *did* do that at least look like she hasn't been shat upon by a seagull?

Why does she even want to do this, if she doesn't want to do this?

Fuck her. I turn on my heel, walk back down the hallway, jump into Sarah's bed. I let her have her way with me in the dark. And I make sure I come hard.

Chapter Twenty-Three

The weekend is so, so welcome. Even though I come down with a minor cold. This always happens when stress is suddenly lifted from my life. And this week has been nothing if not stressful. But more because the highs have been so high, so intense, and because I've had so many new experiences. Not because I've had a load of pointless meetings and impossible deadlines.

Every time I used to go on vacation from work, I'd get ill too. At least that's one thing that doesn't seem to have changed in this new life of mine. The other thing is the presence of an evil bitch. I can't believe it's taken me this long to realise just why Petra grates me so much. She's a darn sight better-looking than my former manager though. It makes me shudder. Especially now I've had to admit that I must be a little bit bisexual. But I think that after Friday night's performance, my crush is beginning to fade.

It feels strange waking up with Sarah in my arms on Saturday morning. But more than anything it feels nice. No group showers, no wakers. Not for two days. We're both a little fuzzy-headed, and I've got a cough that hints at more than just a hangover. With a reluctance that surprises me, I move to the other bed for the rest of the weekend, so she won't catch anything.

Only when we're getting ready for breakfast do I get round to telling her about Petra and the money. The bitch's mercenary, business-like way hit me hard in my drunken state and made me crave some hot, human sex. It drove me straight to Sarah's flesh. I wanted to revel in the joy of her touches, and I did exactly that. It was my way of taking a stand of sorts.

Now Sarah is wide-eyed as I tell her what I saw in my old room. "Wow, so you think they actually did business last night?" she asks.

I shrug. "It's what they do, isn't it? They're both already working. I guess they know how to spot an opportunity."

We're silent for a moment, pondering.

"I didn't even see that conversation begin with the two old guys!" she muses. "I don't understand how they made it happen. How do you begin a chat like that?"

"I haven't got the slightest clue, and I don't think it's me," I answer, dragging on my favourite pair of tracksuit pants, one of the only items I'd brought from home. "I got the impression that if I do this work, it'll be booked appointments. No touting."

She smiles back at me. "You're gonna do this work, babe. You're too good not to. You can be honest with me."

She's right. But can I be honest with myself? Maybe not just yet.

"We'll see," I shrug. "What about you?"

"It's still a weird thought, you know. I'm like you, Emma. I can't really do the extroverted thespian thing the whole time. I'm shy and I wasn't brought up for this kind of thing. I want to get better though. And at least I knew I liked girls before this week!"

She winks at me, and I go red again.

"I've enjoyed everything so far," she goes on. "It's been hot, hasn't it? Nothing not to like. Okay, we're very exposed and that's been weird. I'm not really as confident as I'd like, but I'm getting used to it. I dread the idea of a first assignment in the real world. I think I'll have shaky knees. It'll be so tough. But I think I do want to give it a go. I like to see things through. And my acting career…it's not happening right now."

"Ah, well, acting might come in handy," I grin. "I mean, what if it was *you* with those two geezers last night? They'd have had to be pretty good..."

"Yeah, true! Although from what you've told me, I can't imagine our friend down the corridor does much pretending. And she seems to do okay."

I think for a moment. "I suppose…but does she really? I mean, if those two are that wonderful, then why are they here for training?"

"Good question, Em…good question!" Sarah shrugs, slaps me on the bum and steers me towards the doorway. Soon we're tucking into a superb fry-up thanks to Wilfred and Miss Honeywell. The creamiest scrambled eggs and crispiest, juiciest bacon. Fresh-squeezed orange juice washes it all down a treat.

My illness is nothing major, but I stay in the room for all of Saturday. I think I'm just tired and run-down more than anything, and something's attacked me while my defences are down. Sarah takes care of me, bringing me snacks and drinks all day long. I wouldn't mind a television to flick through, but I must admit watching the news would seem a little odd in this time-travel experience.

She even brings Miss Honeywell to me at one point. The kindly woman looks concerned, and somehow I feel embarrassed. She could be my mother, but she's seen me naked and watched us all take part in an outdoor orgy. She's handled my cream-soaked panties and dealt with the linen from the Lachlan Room.

None of this seems to trouble her matronly way. She tuts and sticks a thermometer in my mouth.

"Nothing serious, thank goodness!" she says when she retrieves it. "Rest up, hopefully you'll be fine by tomorrow evening. Have yourself a couple of these pills after you eat. We need you fit for Monday, so let's not take chances!"

I nod and smile at her, and my stomach knots as I wonder what Monday has in store. Despite my state, it's a good kind of knot.

It's still there when I wake up on Sunday morning after a solid ten hours of sleep. My throat's a little sore but my head's almost back to normal. As for that knot, it grows and grows throughout the day. At least that probably means my body's defences are up again.

It takes most of Sunday to work out what the knot really is. It's a little thing that's been nagging at me. Something I don't want to say out loud to anyone, much less to myself. But as I take a sauna on Sunday evening to sweat out any remaining ugly stuff in my system, I'm forced to come clean with what that thing is.

Cock.

Is it an accident that I haven't had a man since the middle of the week? Probably not. But with everything that went on with Sarah – and Carrie and Miss Jackson – I kind of forgot about that in the midst of all the lesbian firsts. The last time I had a chance at penetration was the chess game. The game in which I was never taken. And that was Thursday.

Rupert, and the double-penetration session with the other two guys, seem like months ago. I sigh to myself as I own up to my surprising need for a man between my legs. I want to be taken!

It's not like I haven't come several times, and come hard. It's not like I haven't had more action this week than I'd normally have in a year. I'm amazed at how strong and insistent my desires have become now that they've had a taste of regular feeding.

Much as I have started to think about tonguing Sarah's pussy again, I'm pleased that the urge to feel a good length in me is so strong. I really don't want to turn into a full-on lesbian. Girls are new and fun and good...but it seems I do want the best of both worlds. Probably a good thing for…business.

I'm alone in the sauna as I start to think about something very substantial pushing roughly in between my legs. I close my eyes and let myself imagine that feeling. I've come so much this week that I don't feel the need to touch myself. I just go for the ride with my mind. It's amazing what a feeling of fullness I can conjure up with nothing but my thoughts.

After a few minutes, another odd things hits me. The shaft I'm imagining is attached to nobody in particular. I think that might just be a first. All I'm thinking about is the sensation, not the man. Rupert would have been part of the scene even three days ago…have I forgotten him already?

I'm confused suddenly. I remember myself flirting with Wilfred as he served me tea and sandwiches this afternoon. Sarah was out walking with Latifa and Alyssia, and I had nobody for company. Wilfred! Our butler must be 65, and he proved entirely professional in deflecting my *double entendres*. What was I thinking chatting him up?

Well…at the time, he was the only man in the house. Hmm. The only pair of trousers with something inside them. Clearly something in my subconscious, ravaged by five days without a man, took that on board, and it came out in behaviour utterly alien to me. Has one cock suddenly become as good as any other to Emma Carling?

Am I turning into a man, ready to fuck anything with the right body parts? Christ almighty! Well, hang on…I didn't actually fuck Wilfred, after all. That would be ridiculous! Although…perhaps no more ridiculous than what I presume Petra and Lilia did with those two pub regulars. But my mind is doing odd things.

I can still picture Rupert, and I still know he's wonderfully handsome. Yeah, of course I want to have him again. He's had his punishment from me, and, more importantly, the thrashing broke my own bonds with him. I no longer feel worried about what he does. If I can have him, good and well. There'll be better lookers, worse lookers, dildos. I'll get my filling one way or another. He's just one way of many.

It seems I'm changing rapidly, especially now I've had a quiet weekend to take stock of everything. Maybe the illness was a blessing. By all accounts I missed out on a pleasant stroll and a good swim with the girls this warm afternoon, but it would have been non-stop chatter. Maybe more.

I wonder, too, if Latifa and partner will end up getting her way with me this week, or if they tried it on with Sarah this afternoon. Oddly, I'm not bothered either way. I'm happy with Sarah for now. We're a personality match and we get each other. It feels good to be taking my fledgling girl-girl steps, not to mention my fledgling hooker steps, with someone that shares a connection with me. But jealousy seems to be a feeling I'm losing.

The burning need for male anatomy pumping me, though, has gone nowhere. My body feels back to full health by bedtime, but that little knot in my tummy is growing at an alarming rate. Add that to the nerves I feel about the week ahead, and I struggle to sleep on Sunday night.

Chapter Twenty-Four

School's back in session. It's nine o'clock on Monday morning, and I'm sitting in Miss Jackson's office once again. This time, though, I am neither naked nor bound. In the absence of specific instructions, I'm wearing a black skirt and white collared tennis shirt. It feels pretty sexy.

I'm freshly showered. Just went through the motions with Petra again. It's like a non-experience now. I feel healthy again, and I'm actually looking forward to this briefing. Miss Jackson's smiling at me, and the vibe is different from the trying circumstances of my last two visits. We were promised more clarity this week, and I hope Miss Jackson is going to be completely open with me about the programme.

What I really want to know is how I'm doing. I've heard mostly good things from the girls, but last week was so tumultuous and secretive that I still feel I don't know where I'm really at. I'm hoping my mentor will give me some serious feedback. She's sitting upright in her chair, looking far more professional than she did the last time I was here. So far, so good.

"I hope you had a good and restful weekend, Emma," she beams. "It sounds like you didn't have much choice in any case! Are you feeling better now?"

"Yep, I think I'm all good, Miss Jackson," I reply chirpily.

"Good, because you're set for another busy week. And a fun one, of course!"

I nod and smile, trying not to look too enthusiastic. Although that twist of need in my stomach is still pulsing away inside me.

"So, you've made it through the first week, and believe it or not, Emma, you had a good one. I'm very happy with how you've come along. There is certainly work to do, but nobody has a perfect first week. We've looked for natural aptitudes, and we've found plenty with you, young lady!"

"Thank you, Miss Jackson," I say, hoping that this is the right answer.

"Okay, you can relax a little this week, dear. Last week we pushed you in all sorts of ways, and it was important to see how you coped with an element of surprise. Or to put it another way, to see how you reacted without having had time to prepare.

"This week's going to be more traditional schooling. You'll know what you're working on and why. And where. And when. We'll be running classes. They *will* be highly practical. Expect demonstration and participation. I think you know what I mean?

I *know* I know what she means.

"Not all the girls will be in all the classes. The sessions will focus on specific skills, so it all depends on the individual. One of the things we'll do this morning is map out what you need to work on this week.

"First, though, I want us to look back on last week in some detail together."

I nod. I want that too.

Then Miss Jackson does something I didn't expect at all. She reaches into her desk drawer, pulls out a remote control, and flicks on the flat screen television affixed to the wall behind her desk. She swivels her chair around so we're both facing it.

Holy fuck.

The black and white image that first comes onto the screen is someone I know very well. I'm lying on my back, looking up at the camera. I appear to be naked, and there's a man on top of me. I recognise him straight away. It's Rupert. *I know that scene.*

My heart thuds like a drum as I try desperately to think of a reason why this isn't what I think it is. There's a date and time in the corner, and it corresponds pretty much to the moment I first visited the Lachlan Room. The film is rolling, and his powerful hips are thrusting hard. Their rhythm is familiar. I'm running out of ways to explain this away.

I'm flabbergasted, and fortunately Miss Jackson speaks first. "We couldn't make it obvious, of course, but we did film everything last week. It's essential for the purposes of reviewing your performances in a natural way. Don't you agree, Emma?"

"Um…I suppose..." But I just want to crawl into a hole. The girl on the screen – me – is making a lot of noise now, even though there's a distant quality to the sound on this playback. Oh, but that girl is really, *really* enjoying what's happening to her. Ouch. Of all the embarrassing moments of the past few days, I think this one is making me reddest. I think I look really silly.

"We'll go through your main encounters for the week with a little critique. It's a really good exercise for you at this point. For a start, I really did love your reaction here! You come across as a girl who is really enjoying her sex. And I don't think that was acting, was it?"

"Erm, I don't think I'm a very good actor…" I mumble.

"No, and that's okay, because we are *not* looking for actors here. We're looking for enjoyers. And with some work, I think you're going to be one of the best of them. You can start off by snapping out of this embarrassment."

She flicks the pause button and fixes me with the most serious look I've seen her wear all week. It's sterner even than the one she gave me when I was hauled into this room as a guilty spy on Friday.

"I've watched a ton of these, Emma. It's just sex, and like all sex, it's beautiful. Beautiful enough to make me jealous, okay? I can't have you going red at the sight of you getting it on. Blushing is a bad sign in an escort. *Nothing* makes a quality prostitute blush. And I truly do want you to be a quality prostitute."

I nod, and try to look relaxed. I sit back in the chair and try my best to focus on just how much fun that fuck was.

"I'm going to criticise you now and then as we work through this, Emma, but don't take it the wrong way. Nobody expected you to be flawless last week. The reason we're doing this is so that you are clear on what was good and what wasn't. It's entirely constructive.

"Anyway," she goes on. "I've got a fair idea of just how much you've come along since the week began. I think most of these scenes would be different if we filmed them again this week, wouldn't they?

I nod, thankful at the chance to say something more general. "I'm pretty sure of that – I've changed a lot. The learning curve has been more like…well, it's been vertical!"

She chuckles and rolls the film again. We join the action just as I scream my unforgettable orgasm. Yeah, it's a good memory. I'm trying really hard to shake off the years of English piety right now.

"He's a bit special, isn't he?" she muses.

"Well…yes, I suppose he is."

"You certainly showed it. There will be times when you won't want to climax quite so easily in the company of a good-looking client though. That will come with time and experience. Also, be careful with your language – not every client will appreciate the four-letter words. But I'm more concerned about what happens next."

We're coming to the part where Rupert abruptly shoved me out of the room like…well, like a whore whose services were no longer required.

"You get very upset at this point, Emma, and that's totally understandable because you come from a normal background," she remarks. "This was not a test we expected you to pass first time. It's not something likely to happen all that often in the real world. But you need to be hard-hearted enough for this kind of scenario.

"The notion of an emotional bond with any client needs to leave your head. Unlikely though it is, you need to be ready to be kicked out of bed like that. You need to be ready for it to happen without you climaxing. This is very important, Emma. Are you with me?"

I nod, not particularly happy that she's kicking romance in the guts like this, stabbing it with her high heels. But I know she's exactly right. This isn't a flowers and kittens game.

"Don't frown, girl," she laughs. "Remember we're preparing you for worst-case scenario here. Nine times out of ten you are going to have the most fantastic time. Like you just did on screen. And nobody can really ask you to leave their house naked, I assure you. But you've absolutely *got* to keep what happens with a client in perspective and enjoy it for what it is. Never get ahead of the moment."

"I know…and I think I'm getting there," I tell her, thinking back to my musings in the sauna last night.

"I don't doubt that for a moment, darling! Now, let's take a look at this DP assignment…"

"DP?" I give her a blank look.

"Double penetration! Oh dear, you really are an innocent one aren't you? Well, maybe uneducated more than innocent…because you made me proud with your attitude that day. Some girls get pretty freaked out when two men enter them for the first time, but you seemed to have a wonderful experience. And it *was* your first time, right?"

"Er, definitely! I think I'd remember that if it had happened before!"

I'm totally transfixed by the screen now. Shame has turned to disbelief. That's *me* having my anus penetrated, right there. *Oh my.*

I'm beginning to feel a little bit wet.

"Another thing, Emma. You and Sarah…it was a privilege to watch the chemistry building there. An absolute privilege. It took everything for me not to get up and push in on that kiss, but it would have been very wrong to interfere with something so natural."

She shakes her head in a slow, dreamy kind of way.

"I had a hunch you two would go well together, that's why I paired you. And I understand you've been doing some extra practice with her?"

Am I in trouble? But the corners of her mouth are turned up in a knowing smile. I think she approves of my extra-curricular activities.

"Oh! News travels fast around here…"

"It's my job to know these things, Emma. By the way, if you're wondering, your rooms are the one place where there are no cameras. They're private in that respect. Everywhere else is covered. Soon we'll see your little fingers doing their magic in that toilet cubicle."

"God…" I bury my head in my hands, my fingers clawing at the perspiration around my hairline. But then I come back up smiling.

"That's better. Laughing at yourself is the first step in your walk away from cringing at yourself. All this may seem bizarre, but remember your office desk in London was on CCTV as well. And I think you'd be having a lot less fun there, wouldn't you?"

Well, she's one hundred percent right on that. Monday morning is PowerPoint presentations. Yep, they'll be in the nine-thirty meeting right about now. My smile broadens. "Absolutely! Maybe you should stream this film into conference room 14C. That would wake them up!"

She laughs out loud. I like how the mood is lightening. "It certainly would, Emma. But remember, at this level we are a very discreet game. Girls like you don't hang out on street corners or put their cards in telephone booths. You're exclusive and you're confidential."

We move on to the most intense moment of the week: my thrashing of Rupert and Petra. Miss Jackson goes serious again, but after the laughter I feel relaxed. As I watch events unfold, I expect to feel self-conscious about my swearing and aggression. I expect it will look lame and pathetic. But even I can't deny...I look pretty convincing. I suppose it helped that the anger wasn't fake.

"First things first," she says as I start hitting Rupert. "You're a natural at this too! It's extremely rare to find a lady who can give this kind of thing as well as receive, but you've done both extraordinarily well this week. Remember what I said: we don't look for actors. You've done well because you *are* those roles when you're in them. Ultimately, your skill set will mean more demand...and top dollar for you."

For the first time, I smile at the mention of money. Hell, I'm *good* at this stuff! Or at least some of it. It's time I started to feel blessed.

"Of course, there are aspects to correct. This worked as a trial for you as a dominant, because I engineered a situation in which your emotions bubbled up. It wasn't hard to see you'd fallen for Rupert, and the coldness between yourself and Petra was obvious. And understandable, I think."

Oh, does she think Petra's a bitch too? But she doesn't dawdle on the topic. Pity. I'd love to explore it some more.

"I was pleased with how it worked out. Your emotions took you to places your clients will find sexy. And *you* find it sexy...I can see your nipples from here! Not to mention the clear arousal on your face. The trick now is to find that sexiness without the need for emotional stimulation.

"Perspective and a cool head, even when you're being hot-headed, you understand? You had no *right* to any of this. It was, in fact, a fine line that you walked, but I've let it pass because it was an important moment for you sexually."

I nod, but I need her to piece it together a little better. Fortunately she does.

"In the context of this school, you can't beat Rupert because you feel wronged. He owed you no apology for anything. He may have played the guilty one, but if a client does that you must *always* be aware that he is playing. As a staffer, Rupert would be entitled to turn on a whim and strap *you* down. You see that, don't you?"

Her point of view is starting to come together. Not the sweetest thing to hear, but, as always, I can't fault her logic.

"It's good that you got into the role as you did. That much was perfect. If it helps you to imagine that you've been wronged, or to concoct a story, that is perfectly fine. But you must always, *always* keep in mind that it's not a real punishment. Live your role, but without delusion. You need to be ready to roll with changing situations and switch roles seamlessly. It will happen."

I'm laying into Petra's peachy little bottom now. Miss Jackson coughs.

"Similarly, if you're working with another girl and you feel your client will appreciate such a course of action, you can do this kind of thing within pre-established limits. Again, you can use whatever mental stimulation you need. Again, always enjoy it. No acting, like I said.

"BUT," she says, pausing the video and raising a finger in front of her nose, emphasizing the enormousness of the 'but', "you have *got* to remember who you are. No matter how much you get into it, you're not doing it for you. It's extremely important, Emma.

"Bringing personal relationships into play on a client assignment is exceedingly delicate. Many will love to see your passion for Petra or your passion for Sarah, very different though those passions may be. That passion is almost always a plus. But use them positively, and be prepared to switch them on and off, or switch them around.

Because there may be a day when you'll have to make soft love to your Petras and whip your Sarahs."

It's a lot to take in, especially now that we're moving onto a montage of my shower sessions with Petra.

"There's somewhat less positive passion going on here," she smiles. "You're getting there. It's something we'll work on this week. Enjoying a pretty girl's body in front of your clients is something you'll do a lot. You'll get used to it. You may not like all the girls personally, but – unlike some of the male clients you'll get – they will invariably be beautiful. One focus this week will be to teach you to love a girl's body even if you don't love her soul."

She pauses. This Petra thing is becoming an elephant in the room.

"I can't discuss another student in detail with you at this stage, Emma, as it wouldn't be fair. I want you to focus on the constructive criticism I give you this morning, and make of that what you will. And remember you can learn something from everyone. I am okay with your room move, but in keeping with what I've just said, be ready for further encounters this week. And you'll still be shower partners."

Further encounters. Fine. It's just work. There's no more crush, right? I'll try and fake it.

"You can't try faking it, Emma," says Miss Jackson, interrupting my thoughts with her eerie mind-reading. "Enjoyers, not actors, remember?"

"I get it," I murmur, nodding. "I think. But…then how do I not enjoy it *too* much sometimes? Like with Rupert?"

She smiles. "You'll become an expert at that. It's about feeling the situation and knowing the client. You'll usually get notes on your clients before an appointment, by the way. Anyway, never suppress your enjoyment unless you're asked to play something like a rape or kidnapping role. *Always* enjoy. Control of orgasm is a separate skill, and we'll work on it this week."

I nod and my eyes flick up to the screen again. There I am licking Miss Jackson, in this very room. We've gone well beyond the surreal now, and I blush furiously.

"Good memories," she murmurs. And then scowls at me when she sees my shocked face. "Gracious, Emma, not that again. Please!"

"I'm sorry…it's just…I feel like I'm watching myself in a porn movie!"

"That's exactly what you're watching…and so? Do you know how many girls would kill to be porn stars?" She rolls her eyes quite unashamedly. "I think you've still got too much stigma stuff planted in your head. Your parents made you think sex is ugly and bad.

"And in spite of your clear enjoyment of the actual sex itself, I feel you're not always secure about your body, perfect as it is. And there are still moments of hesitation. I saw it when we had you naked around the house, and I saw it again out by the poolside. There's still the odd moment of doubt, where you're thinking *this is wrong.* It's normal enough for a first week, but we need to get you thinking more like, say, Alyssia. You've got to one hundred percent love what you're doing.

"The beauty side of things is pretty much a given in this game, up to a point. But it's not enough. Always remember, it's your attitude that earns more than half your fee. Not your looks. There are some relatively plain girls out there pulling in the cash because people pay for their spirit. There's at least one in your group with that potential."

She doesn't mention the name again, but I suppose she's still alluding to Alyssia.

"A bored, disinterested prostitute never gets called back, no matter how gorgeous she is. I don't think you're going to have that problem, but clients also don't like traces of guilt or insecurity. They're clever, successful men and, they can sense those things from a mile off. You're moving away from such a mindset, certainly, but I think I know what will take you past the point of no return. It will shout down your subconscious angel."

She opens her drawer and ferrets around in it for a moment. Then she pulls out a handful of DVDs. Porn.

She pushes the discs across the desk at me, and I inspect them. *Hot Wet Lesbians. Sordid Secrets. Anal Pleasure.*

"It's quality stuff from one of the world's best production studios. Absolutely hard and uncensored, yet beautiful – the sexiest porn money can buy. These are going to help you shake off those guilty feelings about sex.

"I'll have a television and player brought up to your room. I want you to spend time watching these thrice a day this week. That is your regular homework. And I want you to masturbate while watching."

Chapter Twenty-Five

I stare down at the piece of paper in my hand. I think it's actually been typed on an old-fashioned typewriter! The ink is still fresh on the thick, sweet-smelling paper. It's a summary from my meeting with Miss Jackson. Sarah and I are lying on her bed, comparing notes.

    Miss Emma Carling

    Aptitudes & Skills you can offer:

    -Straight sex
    -Group sex (MMF, FFM)
    -Fellatio & associated oral sex
    -Subordinate BDSM
    -Dominant BDSM
    -Sex shows including solo masturbation
    -Anal sex
    -Double penetration
    -All role play

I wonder what 'associated oral sex' might mean. Could it be *that* thing? The thing I can never turn down? I wouldn't put it past Miss Jackson to read my thoughts.

This is quite an exciting report card. Yet somehow morbid. And I'm glad there are no instructions to hand it to my parents. We read on:

    Areas for classroom treatment:

    -Basic technical skills in the above areas

-Reading situations
-Emotional detachment & focus on physical pleasure only
-Enjoyment of giving pleasure as much as receiving
-Control of orgasms
-Self-esteem
-Guilt

Phew. It sounds like I'm going to have quite a week. The 'school' part of this whole thing is really coming to life. Although 'control of orgasms' definitely wasn't on the menu at my secondary. And what's this about giving pleasure?

"Hmm, do they think I'm selfish in bed?" I muse.

"Oh Emma," Sarah sniggers, elbowing me playfully in the ribs, "they might have a point you know!"

Do they? I guess I do get a little inattentive when I'm enjoying myself. Maybe. I don't like to hear it. I drop the paper and fold my arms, feeling defiantly apologetic.

I mumble at Sarah: "Oh, sorry...if I've...you know..."

She kisses me lightly on the cheek.

"It's okay, babe. You're halfway there. You definitely do need to enjoy yourself, and show it. You've got that right! And besides," she pauses, licking her lips. "I could taste you down there all day long. It sure beats ice cream!"

"Yeah, well, lick Petra out and ice cream is probably what you get!" I chuckle.

"Ooh, witty!" Sarah laughs. "And bitchy! I like it!"

I suppose it *was* a rather clever joke. Maybe I'm relaxing.

"But I'm not allowed to take bitchiness into the bedroom," I groan, running my hands through my hair. "I was told that in no uncertain terms this morning."

"You're gonna be fine, Em! Here, let's look at mine."

Sarah unfolds her little report card.

Miss Sarah Smith

Aptitudes & Skills you can offer:

-Straight sex
-Group sex (FFM)
-Fellatio
-Subordinate BDSM
-Anal sex

I can't help noticing her list is a lot shorter than mine. I put my hand on her thigh, in case she's upset.

"See, I *told* you you were the superstar!" she says. "I guess none of us have ticked all those boxes you have. It looks like you've got the full monty."

She's putting a brave face on, but looks a little down. I'm surprised role play isn't there, or sex shows. I mean, she's into drama after all! And double penetration is conspicuously absent, which seems odd after our hot session with the boys.

"I guess they decided I'm too tight or something," she murmurs, as if thinking about loud. "It *was* a squeeze, but I didn't think I showed it. Looks like I'm not down for threesomes with men. I wonder what I did wrong?"

I put my arm around her, hook my leg in between hers and try to think of something to say.

"I don't think you did anything wrong, lovely," I murmur softly. "Maybe they just don't want you to hurt yourself. They seem pretty all-knowing around here. Or maybe they just want you to take it slow for now. I'm sure this list isn't cast in stone forever.

"As for shows," I go on. "That seems pretty unfair on you. Do you think they judge that on the showers? You haven't even had a partner to play with!"

She says nothing and looks out of the window. Then, "Yeah, but…I was called for a little performance with a toy on Wednesday. I guess…I guess they weren't impressed."

Her eyes are a little cloudy, as if a storm of self-doubt is gathering. Acting is meant to be her thing. Her career, even. But judging from her report card, it looks like she's failed in exactly that area this week.

"Come on!" I say, picking up her piece of paper again. "Look how much fun stuff *is* on here! Never mind what's missing – you're still gonna get paid hundreds of Pounds to play in a threesome with a guy and a girl, aren't you? It'll beat rehearsals on a Tuesday morning by miles! Who knows…we might even work together some time?"

I see her face light up considerably at that thought.

"I'd like that," she smiles.

There's a small glass of gooey white liquid perched in the inkwell holder in front of me. It sits there, layered like cooling lava, patient yet expectant. Like a medicine you know you have to take sooner or later.

"Miss Carling, please show the way," says Miss Littlefair, a pretty mentor with a cute, rabbit-like face and blonde curls. "Drink up."

My heart pounds. Straight into the deep end in our first classroom session. Up at the front, in large letters on the chalk board, is one simple word: fellatio.

Every one of us is in this class. As Miss Littlefair, oral sex specialist, explained when we took our places at the scratched, slanted wooden desks after lunch. "This is as fundamental an art as exists in your trade, ladies. At the high end, there is no such thing as a fellatio opt-out. It's as much a necessity as having a vagina between your legs.

"Same goes for swallowing. If anyone has a problem with it, I suggest you put up your hand right now and let me know.

Because we'll need to work on some spectacular skills in other areas if you want to have any clients."

She looked around the room, and everyone's hands stayed down. I noticed a few nervous, darting eyes, though. Latifa, of course, was smiling broadly.

"Before we go into any technical skills," continued Miss Littlefair. "I want to isolate the taste and swallowing experience for you. It will help those of you who have little experience in this area. Trust me."

And so my mouth fell open as Wilfred entered the room bearing a tray of eleven little glasses of...yes, really. They're double shot glasses, in essence. Gleaming with white.
Oh God.

"Our men have been working hard this morning," she smiles as Wilfred distributes the cocktails, impassive as ever. "This seed is all from the gentlemen of the house, whom you met last week. Whose it is doesn't matter. It's important that your default is never to care whose it is. You must simply love the drink itself."

She caught my eye as she said this.

And now, since I was dumb enough to sit in the front row, I'm going first. Wilfred has let himself out, and I can feel the eyes of the class on me. Apparently I'm the teacher's pet now. Lunch over oysters seemed to prove Sarah right – as far as I could tell, my list of 'skills and aptitudes' was longer than anybody's.

Still, it didn't have this level of detail on it. I suppose I shouldn't be surprised to be learning the art of swallowing. I'm not a complete stranger to the sensation, though it's been a while. I just didn't expect it in a glass.

I look up at her as I take the vessel in my fingers. She's smiling encouragement, but silent.

Okay, here goes. I can almost *hear* the sweat pouring out of me. But let's pull this bloody trigger.

If memory serves, this isn't going to flow like water. So I lean my head right back – rather like we're back at the oyster table, in fact – and tip the glass upside down.

The liquid dribbles heavily onto my tongue and then back onto my throat. It's cool; I think it's been refrigerated. I fear my stomach might turn, so try not to think about what it is as I swallow once, then twice, then a third time. It's impossible not to think about what it is. *Holy fuck*. I am a naughty girl!

Hooray, though…my stomach doesn't flip at all. I handle it. It's…soothing. The taste is familiar, but more abundant and salty and powerful than I've known before. I've never had this kind of quantity, this much to go on. I even find myself swishing the last mouthful around like mouthwash, before letting it slide down inside me.

I think somebody notices, because I hear murmurings and then, finally, the sound of clapping. I turn around to see Latifa and Alyssia leading the applause, and I smile bashfully as I wipe my mouth and replace my glass.

Not everyone joins in the ovation, of course.

All the girls pass the seed tasting session…although I'm not sure about Jane. I'm getting a better feel for the characters in our class, and I'm less and less convinced she's cut out for this. She can't help herself screwing up her nose when she's halfway through, and she coughs at the end. Like everyone, there's a round of applause, but some rounds of applause are warmer than others. This one isn't a ringing endorsement, and I see Miss Littlefair make a longer note for Jane than she made for the rest of us.

"Well done, ladies," she says, resuming her strut around the front of the room as Wilfred clears the glasses away. "Now which of you absolutely *loved* that?"

Latifa and Alyssia don't hesitate sticking up their hands. So, to my surprise, does Carol, the naughty little thing. Though it was quite arousing in a vaguely submissive kind of way, I'm not sure I'd go quite so far as to say I loved it. So I keep my hand down with all the rest. I suppose yes is the right answer, but then again, I don't want to be too much of a teacher's pet.

"A good prostitute is greedy for semen," says Miss Littlefair. "She picks the right moment to show that greed of hers, but doesn't rush her client before that moment has come. So to speak.

"I want to help you develop the taste this week. It helps when you're giving a blow-job. Obviously having a man – maybe two – in your mouth is terrific. But knowing that something extra nice is coming for you will help you do the necessary to take your client all the way.

"It may be that your client prefers to let go on your face or on your breasts, perhaps even more unusual places. You will all hopefully reach the point where you'll want to scoop some of it up and put it on your tongue. And though our clients have many and varied tastes, it's safe to say none of them will object to this.

"It's rather difficult for us to source you a glassful every day, but your watchword for this week is to taste and swallow at every opportunity. This week we are here to teach and guide, not to force things or test you, so I suggest you take that responsibility. For the reasons I've just outlined, it is in your very best interests. Any questions?"

Nobody speaks. The air is thick with anticipation.

"An excellent start, ladies. Let's break for a glass of water, and return here in ten minutes. For the rest of this afternoon, we'll teach you the art of sucking."

Chapter Twenty-Six

Miss Littlefair flicks a switch, and the projector sprays a diagram onto the screen. On it, the unmistakable likeness of a man's penis. At the top is a flaccid one, beneath that, a drawing of one that's most definitely aroused. It's getting more classroom by the minute in here. I'm getting flashbacks to sex education.

A couple of giggles ripple around the room, which seems silly. Looking at a harmless drawing from an anatomy textbook is far and away the tamest thing we've been asked to do on our sojourn in this house. Somehow, though, the more formal school-like setting makes it all seem a little outrageous. I can sense the embarrassment welling up inside me already.

"Ladies, this is where you come into your own. Your intimate, specialist knowledge of one of these, and how it works, is what will set you apart from a regular woman. Looks will only get you so far in this business. And there's not much you can bring to the party when you've actually got your client thrusting inside you. If there is one thing that affects your stock more than anything, it's your abilities with one of these.

"Women think it is easy. Maybe *you* think it's easy. Get on your knees and suck, right?" She stops, looks around the room, and shakes her head. "Get that out of your minds, young ladies. Most girls simply have no idea. I hate to tell you this, but you've probably all given mediocre oral sex in your lives. Just because a man is hard doesn't mean you've sent him to heaven.

"When I started in this business, there wasn't a school like this to help me. I actually had some complaints about my technique. I really didn't have a clue. I took that as a challenge, asked a lot of questions and did a lot of practice. By the end of my career I was taking 750 Pound bookings for blow jobs *only*."

The *end* of her career? The woman only looks about twenty-eight! She seems friendly, and I want to stick up my hand and ask her if she really meant that.

But Alyssia beats me to it.

"Miss, did you just say your career is *over*?" asks the Aussie, her tone of voice curious and hopeful.

"Indeed I did. You see, I've retired. Three or four years of high-class prostitution were enough for financial independence. There were days when I made upwards of twenty thousand Pounds."

My brain freezes. It's a while since I've thought about the money, but this incomprehensible piece of information has me completely dumbstruck. Visions of an endless, carefree trip around South America, funded by the interest in my bank account, swarm into my head. They sit there and ripen, like heavy air brewing a firecracker Amazonian thunderstorm.

Her voice shakes me back into the room, which is now thick with promise and competition: "I like to give a little something back, so I was delighted to say yes when I was asked to help out as fellatio expert here for a few days each year. But this teaching is about the only work I do nowadays. I want you girls to have the same opportunity I did. Which is why you need to pay attention to *this!*"

She swipes at the penis on the screen with her pointer stick. "This, dear girls, is your cash cow. And what's more, it's a great deal more fun to play with than a keyboard and a mouse. Once you're hooked on a regular diet, believe me it's really hard to give it up. Fortunately I have a wonderful boyfriend now, and he's always ready to indulge my greedy mouth. Life is good when you love cock."

"Amen to that," cackles Alyssia. "Tell us everything we need to know, Miss!"

I wish I could be that forthcoming. All this talk is making me feel closer than ever to being a *prostitute*. I still don't know if I like the thought. But it looks like I've got the week to get used to it. And…what she said about the keyboard and mouse! An excited little shiver runs right up me, from my toes to my ears, as I think about entertaining a client at my old desk. Right in front of *her*. Wow, that would be poetic.

I sit upright and clear my throat, all attention now, as she launches into technicalities.

She talks us through the internal workings of the penis, then takes us to our work surface. Nerve endings and epicentres and sensitive bits. I've never heard of half of these places. She teaches us how to find them without fail, even though there are so many shapes and sizes out there.

I think it's safe to say we're fascinated. I can't believe any of us knew quite what a complex device a penis could be. It sure doesn't look easy. Suddenly I feel a little empathy with those boys who kept falling off my clit.

"This may look intimidating, ladies, but with intent, imagination and spirit you are halfway there. Remember, your client's needs come first, but within that framework, it's your own enjoyment that really shines through. Pick your spots with him in mind, but take joy in tasting each of them."

She looks around the room, and I wonder what she's thinking. I guess she's seen all the notes our mentors made on us last week, and I wonder if she's talking to some of us more than others. Petra looks stony-faced.

How much do *I* like it? Come to think of it, I only took one man in my mouth the whole of last week, out by the pool in the sunshine. I'm not sure I let myself enjoy it, mainly because of the audience. But I've gotten into the sucking thing in the past. I'm sure I can again.

Then Miss Littlefair thrusts into detail about how it's not just sucking. It's slurping and it's licking and it's kissing. She passes giant boiled sweets around the class and gives us three minutes to suck them to oblivion.

"No biting or chewing, ladies, I want your saliva glands to do this job. Wrap your tongues around the sweet. Swirl it into your cheeks. It'll keep the moisture flowing. Hear that swish. Let all those slurps and sloshes out. He will almost invariably love the sound, and the wetness that goes with it."

I look around the room as I take on the furious challenge of making the sweet go away in one hundred and eighty seconds. I laugh at Latifa and grin at Simone. It's kind of sexy to be doing something so innocent, yet which represents something so filthy and devilish – you could practice this on a bus and nobody would have the faintest idea! Petra's looking out of the window as she works her sweet. What a funny assignment!

"One minute to go!" cries Miss Littlefair. "Remember what I said, no teeth! And it's exactly the same with your man, by the way. Only the kinky ones want your choppers scratching them. So work on doing this with your mouth as wide as can be inside."

Her words sound strange, but make perfect sense with the sweet inside my mouth. I roll it around and around, keeping my teeth apart and consciously using all of the space available. I think I might just be getting stimulated by this…who knew boiled sweet could be this erotic? Latifa, who is just across the aisle from me, points between her legs and makes a face. Guess it's not just me then.

None of us quite hit the deadline first time, but Miss Littlefair is unperturbed. "It took me a long time to get that right. It doesn't really matter too much, it's just about teaching you to make the right moves. Still, it's a fun challenge for you girls to work on this week. You'll get one of these after lunch and dinner each day, so have some fun with them!"

Then she returns to her diagram, and explains how to take long, deep draws on a length without irritating the often-sensitive tip. We should only work our lips up and down in the area beneath the base of the tip, and only activate our tongues once we're travelling lower. The sensation of depth, she says, comes from how far down the shaft our lips travel, and how we suck when we get there. Not from maximum up and down movement.

I never knew there was this much to think about. Wow. Do we really live in a world where getting this stuff right is worth as much as she says it is. Craziness!

She teaches us tricks and spots with the balls, impressing on us the need to give this area plenty of attention.

"Most girls forget them completely," she says, shaking her head, as if ruing the youth of today. "Don't let me see you fall into that trap. Even some men don't have the imagination to want you down there, and even lower, where his balls meet the perineum, but then it's your job to show them that there's another level of pleasure, isn't it?"

Most of us nod energetically, thoroughly captivated by her style. Like all the teachers here, she could probably do rather well at leading a dictatorship if it took her fancy. But she's sticking to what she knows for now.

"As a very general rule, save the serious sucking for the end. You'll need to read your client (and any pre-notes, if you're given them) to know what to do. Talk to him, even. Much depends on when he is hoping to come. They may not want to overdo your oral sex work if he only sees it as foreplay. The strategy is quite different if he does. In that respect, common sense will be your guide.

"Now, your mouth has one very important ally in all this. Who wants to tell us what it is?"

To my surprise, Lilia and Petra both answer this one. "Hand," they say, in a flat, almost impatient tone. It sounds like they're rolling their eyes as they say it, as if it's the most obvious thing in the world. But they do flash each other a little smile after answering in unison.

"Correct, you two," says Miss Littlefair. She holds up her palms to the classroom and wiggles them. "Hands! It's rarely a good idea to waste them! Amateurs do exactly that. You're going to know better. You're going to stroke his balls while you work the shaft. Or you're going to gently stimulate the base while you're moving up and down."

She teaches us how a well-worked hand can push a guy over the edge. How it can only add to the stimulation down there. And then she adds something I never thought of.

"Don't depend on being able to use hands *every* time. A lot of clients are going to want your hands tied behind your backs. You can imagine how arousing it is for them to watch, can't you? We'll practice that."

On whom? When?

She impresses on us the need to read the situation and follow feedback from the guy. Our ears, she tells us, are our most important source of information. We should listen out for the little increases in noise and breathing that tell us we're doing something he likes. And each time, she says, we should file it away. If we enjoy giving that pleasure, she stresses, it won't seem a chore.

Read situations. Enjoy giving pleasure. Sounds like my report card. I'm starting to hanker for the chance to prove myself. Will there be a practical exercise? It certainly sounded like she had one in mind.

Miss Littlefair rounds off the lecture with some wise words on the sixty-nine, the mere mention of which makes me go red. It's seriously indulgent, utterly naughty; but the reason I blush is because I can't deny I like it. Actually, come to think of it, I haven't even had one this week!

"A lot of clients aren't going to want to lick you down there," she informs us. "They might think you're not safe, although of course at your level nothing could be further from the truth. Good agencies will have their full-time doctor inspect you at least once a week."

Inspect. Oh, fuck, how has a simple word like that become so damn sexy? All this talk has made my world a high-voltage place. And it feels as though I might trip.

"When you get the chance of a sixty-nine, grab it! No matter how rubbish a performer your client may be – though a lot of them are surprisingly skilled, believe it or not – you're getting extra pleasure whilst you work. Channel that pleasure into what you're doing, and it'll be more fun than ever for both of you."

After a little more technical talk about how the challenges of angle posed by a sixty-nine, she fixes us with a glare that's almost stern. It looks like she's daring us to argue with what she's about to say.

"Girls, you will be amongst *extremely* few women in the world who can have their pussies licked and call it work. Stop and think about it!"

True to her word, she stops. There are a couple of chuckles behind me, but I do actually stop and think about it. Yes, she is right. In fact, she's hit a nerve, because I used to have a little fantasy about James from ads doing exactly that under my desk while I typed emails. But that's the thing – it would only happen in fantasy. Until now

And if last week taught me one thing, it's that in this surreal new world of mine, I don't need to count on fantasy. I can have reality. And never worry about money again. I start to feel a little woozy as desires and moisture and images sweep my soul and body. I'm aware of my lips dropping open like a dopey idiot.

Not for the first time, Miss Littlefair brings me back into the room with a sharp bark. "Enough talk, girls! It's action time!" My heart seems to stop for a moment. "I'm sure you're all a little hot under the collar, so let's break into groups and try out what you've learned."

Chapter Twenty-Seven

Four men sit in front of me. One of them is Rupert. Another of them is George, and he's every bit as massive as he was last week. I don't know the names of the other two, but recognise them from around the house. I think they look okay, but my eye is more interested in the impatient-looking bulges in their underwear.

They're all wearing just shirts and boxers. Though George's pair isn't quite able to contain his excitement, some of which peeps out over the elastic. The men sit on reclining chairs that look comfort personified.

We're in another of the stately suites, the McDonald Room, having been told to strip down to our underwear and leave our clothing in the classroom. Inevitably, Petra is in my group. We're joined by Carol and Simone, who towers above me to my left.

Beyond her is the window, which looks onto the rose garden. I see Wilfred, the subject of my fleeting weekend lust, pottering around watering the flowers. He could surely see everything if he glanced this way. I'm a lot less bothered about that than I would have been a week ago. There's a feast before me!

I don't even recognise myself any more. There's Petra and there's Rupert and I'm supposed to be worked up again, aren't I? Not to mention outraged and embarrassed and mortified! Maybe another time. Right now, all I can think of is what's in front of me.

I want to tuck in, and, though I scratch around trying to find some shame within myself, I am not sure that I care who knows it or sees it.

But there's one thing I have to keep in mind. That thing about enjoying giving pleasure. I'm going to enjoy myself, but in a way that coincides with pleasing the man. I must try all of Miss Littlefair's tips and tricks, and take my own pleasure in that ride.

"Miss Carling, you will start with me," says one of the men whose names I don't know. He's probably in his thirties, has green eyes, a five o'clock shadow and a rugged crop of curly chestnut hair. Not bad. "On your knees."

This is as expected, along lines that were explained to us before we came to this room. We'll rotate through the men, trying different positions and exploring the unique challenges of each. My first task will be to pleasure a seated man. Then we'll all switch places, and I'll have to kneel before a standing man, working without the use of my hands. After that, I'll take a passive lying-down man, then finally it will be sixty-nine time.

"Yes Sir," I smile at my guy, hoping this is the right sort of response. The rest of the girls are then called forward. Simone to the thin, grey-haired guy with the goatee. Petra to George, who lies down on one of two futon beds drawn in close to the chairs. And then Carol goes to Rupert. We're all within a circle of perhaps fifteen feet. My, this is going to be…communal.

And so the depravity begins, with barely a word spoken. Just when I thought things couldn't get any more salacious, I am swept into a scene from somebody else's life. Somebody (bisexual, apparently) who goes to orgies, maybe? Four young women are sucking the cocks of four men, without even the decency to retire to the furthest corners of the suite. And I am one of those women with a cock in her mouth. Yes, me, Emma Rosemary Carling!

Amid the slurping and the girly sighs and the manly groans, I feel like I'm doing something amazing. I conscious that I'm on an adventure. I know it will take some getting used to, but this is a journey that precious few women will ever dare to take. It's a privilege. I'm staggered at what I am doing, but deeply proud of myself. Purely because I'm doing it. I can do anything.

All this, though, is just foggy thought at the back of my mind. I am aware of the acute indecency of the situation. Aware how fucking hot that acute indecency is. But I can't exactly look around. My man needs my focus. And that's exactly where I want my focus to be. Because for all of the fun I've had with Sarah over the weekend, I so need my mouth filled.

He tastes pleasant. In fact, he's clearly just showered, and I'm grateful for the scent of apple-infused soap and the smoothness of his skin. He's kept himself nicely trimmed, so I can savour every sensation. I remember the boiled sweet, and I'm absolutely thrilled when I hear his breathing quicken as I simulate the confectionary trick. Hmm, is that the pleasure of giving right there?

Shit, did I mention this was amazing? I lick him up and down, using the man to try out all those subtle zones Miss Littlefair mentioned. I love every minute of this exploration, really I do, and I'm not sure I care whether I know his name or not. What matters is working magic with this special part of a man. I'm totally wrapped up in the challenge of it. Though my mouth moves with our classroom instruction in mind, everywhere it travels on its journey is a thrilling new sensation in itself.

I lick his balls. No, I never did try that before. It feels incredibly naughty, and makes me feel warm to the core. He tightens and sighs as I cup them in my hand and then lick long, slow strokes from there all the way to his tip. There's an impossibly beautiful mix of power and pleasure in me. I am losing myself in this.

I look up at the man, and he looks down at me with…could it be awe? How could he feel that for some girl he just met?

It's like he's in a gallery, marvelling at some beautiful work of art. Can I inspire so easily? What a thought that is! I feel my own juices beginning to gather in my crotch. Inevitable.

I want to do even better for him, to make him come. But then he pushes lightly on my head and whispers, "Enough."

I withdraw dutifully, and sit back on my heels, licking my lips. I am smiling a little, while his features bear a benevolent, mild look. Between his legs is all arousal, glistening and slick from my mouth. *My* mouth.

I look around at this scene of which I am a part. Just in time, I see Petra bring George to an obvious climax. I notice she uses her hand on his ample base whilst deep-throating him. She seems to swallow some of his seed, but pulls away quickly and lets the rest of it drip down his shaft.

Fuck...am I supposed to make him come again so soon? I haven't thought about this. Surely these guys haven't got it in them to come four times in quick succession, have they? No, surely not. Miss Littlefair said they'd be mainly looking at our technique and our responsiveness. Didn't she?

Simone and then Carol are told to stop, and it doesn't look like their guys came either. Carol just gave Rupert a blow job! Oh well. He hasn't even caught my eye yet. Whatever. Water under the bridge and all that.

And so the lust-laced session goes on. The four wanton, incorrigible girls move to their next assigned men, and fall onto their cocks. I wish I could watch the others more closely, but I guess that's what my porn assignment is for. Still, I'd love to know who is doing what, to whom, and how well she's doing it. But the man in my mouth is more interesting. Way more interesting.

It's weird moving to an already-wet manhood. I inherit Simone's Dutch saliva, but it's kinda sexy. It takes the tone even lower, makes me feel even dirtier. Fuck, bring it on. *Only real women could do this.* Even as I take his glistening length in my mouth, I think about someone taking me from behind. Very soon.

I finish what Simone started, and make him come quite quickly. For the second time this afternoon, I swallow. Well, that *was* lesson one, wasn't it? Still quite new for me, but I think of it as the taste of success. *I* did that!

The others are still busy, so I stroke my man gently as I stay kneeling, feeling the tiniest slackening of his erection as he comes down whilst in my hand. Oh my! Who's next?

The lying position is my favourite, although I enjoyed the servile feeling of being on my knees. George seems to have recovered by the time I reach him, and he's back to full size. I remember now that I've had him in me, and how good it was, and I keep having to stop myself from sitting on him. My pussy is absolutely burning beneath my panties. I don't know how much more of this tease I can take.

Then it's Rupert's turn, and I walk over to him with confidence and poise. As with each round before, he is wet from Simone, and, I suppose, Petra and Carol before that. A little something in me makes me want to outperform Petra here. It's not about Rupert. I look across at her sleek little body as it kneels before standing guy, and feel a little twitch in my nose.

"Please go on top first, Miss Carling," says Rupert with that annoying, haughty formal way of his.

Fine. But before I climb aboard, I whisper in his ear, "Did you come yet?"

He nods.

"Petra?"

"Miss Stoycheva, yes."

Fuck, I'll bet the bitch is four from four. She must be good with her mouth.

I kneel above him, then purposefully lower my crotch into his face. I give it a little grind as it gets there. Just trying to tell him something. I don't even know what.

I feel the man pull my panties to one side and begin to lick. I'm kind of glad I don't have to look at him right now. It might just awaken the things I've buried. I take him in my mouth, and decide I am going to outdo my former room-mate come hell or high water.

I tickle and I tease and I suck and I lick and I bite and I kiss. I remember every last scrap of our lesson. I do the boiled-sweet thing, slurping like crazy. My hand joins the party, fondling gently down below. He's not giving much away with his voice, but I can feel him growing stouter and I can feel him losing interest in his own end of the bargain.

Well, okay, it's not a bargain. *He's paying you!* Whatever. I can enjoy this either way. But it's interesting that he's not very good. Or at least, only good enough to get me feeling even more desperate for something very substantial between my legs.

A couple more minutes of wet slurping has him close, but then he wants to switch and be on top. Quickly – since I'm desperate not to lose momentum – we rearrange. He resumes his long, lazy licks on my sex, which slow to a trickle as he slides into my mouth and, quite frankly, leaves me very little to do.

He begins to pump me, and all I can do is try to keep my tongue moving and my mouth juices flowing. Because there's no trouble with juices flowing down there, which must be gushing like a waterfall. I create a tube around my lips with my palms, to give him an extra something to rub against. Another of Miss Littlefair's tips. Although this, quite frankly, does not feel like doing very much.

It is, however, very sexy. And it's sexier when he jets his salty stream into my throat. I cough a little as some of it catches me awkwardly, but still feel thrilled and on edge.

More than anything, though, I'm desperate.

We're all done now. I put my underwear to rights as I stand, and my fingers come away completely soaked. The first guy I was with catches my eye, and it's a sympathetic look he gives me. He holds my gaze as the others file out back to class. I'm rooted to the spot, transfixed by his still-hard member. Someone must have run out of time on him! Ooh, I could use that right now.

I slowly make my way towards the door. The other men go past me, on their way back to the feedback session. Rupert gives me what must be a funny look as he slips by, but I don't catch his eye. Instead, I hover in the doorway, hypnotised by my runaway desires.

I need to be fucked. Like, *now*.

I'm going to ask. I can't take this anymore.

"Would you like to fuck me, Sir?" is what I come out with, though what I really mean is *please, please, please can you fuck me this instant.*

He motions to the futon, and I feel my time has come.

I want it from behind, deep and hard and fast.

I take a chance and get down on my hands and knees, wiggling my ass hopefully.

Jesus, what am I doing?

I don't even know this guy's name.

I'm dripping wet. I need it.

He nods and moves in behind me. The relief when he slides in is beyond words. It's like getting to a loo when you've been holding it in all day. That kind of relief.

I drop my head and push my hips into his. I just want the unknown guy to go for it. Like he's never gone for it before.

He reads me. Or maybe he just knows we're both due downstairs in a minute. Whatever. Forty-five seconds and a few dozen thrusts later, I'm coming all over the place like a crazed wolverine.

Thank God the wait is over.

Chapter Twenty-Eight

I'm dishevelled and breathless when I get back to class. The others are just about finished dressing. My guy follows me in afterwards and joins the other men of the house at the back of the room. I dress quickly and quietly, avoiding eyes. I'm not sure I got rid of all the evidence running down my thighs. Oh God. They're not going to be fooled.

I sit down as inconspicuously as I can. Petra's hand shoots up in the air.

"Miss? Is it okay to stay and have sex with a guy after an assignment is over?"

I studiously look into space ahead of me, but I can feel she's got her eyes on me while she poses her snide question in front of the class. Her first contribution of the day, I might add. *Fuck you!*

I can feel my jaw tightening and my fist clenching. Is this her way of taking revenge for the beating? Belittling me in front of the class? What a witch!

Miss Littlefair seems to know what she's getting at, of course, but our teacher doesn't look my way at all. "If a girl wants to go the extra mile, Miss Stoycheva, then she should be commended, should she not?"

She's silenced my slight Slavic friend. Who, I am most tempted to yell out, did a spot of freelancing of her own on Friday night.

"If a girl can get caught up in the situation, carried away if you will, then nine out of ten clients will love it. As long as it's not a strict dom-sub client request. And as long as she is prepared to change course for the client should he wish it."

She reluctantly unglues her judging eyes from Petra, and slowly sweeps her gaze across the room. "And that goes for all of you ladies. Don't let enthusiasm and abandon become forgotten arts. Though you must always couple these with intense awareness."

Hurrah for Miss Littlefair! Carling one, Stoycheva nil! Suddenly I feel refreshed enough to throw Petra a triumphant look. But the blonde, of course, is looking out through the giant glass panes of the window.

I relax through a lengthy feedback session, in which each of our techniques are picked apart at length by the men and Miss Littlefair. Our teacher even does a couple of demonstrations, and my, she really *is* good. Also, she seems to enjoy it as much as the orgasmic men she's pleasuring.

We're called up at various intervals to work on this or that aspect of fellating a man – and our test model keeps changing. This is getting seriously hands-on! I can tell that embarrassment has all but dried up for most of us, myself included, but Jane's body language still indicates a level of contempt for what she's doing. Sarah's a little shy today too, but then she's always a bit up and down like that.

I barely even notice whom I am working with. I'm sated for once, and I'm actually able to focus on the technical skills. I guess they planned it that way. I focus hard on the folds and the special veins, my sucking depth, tongue work and nibbling pressure. I have time to feel amazed and thrilled at just how interesting and fun my life has become. Training seminars were never like this in my last job! To think I used to get nervy about doing a presentation…!

It's an exhausting afternoon, and we're all gagging for dinner when it comes. The kitchen has gone oriental tonight. I virtually inhale my spicy lobster soup, then tuck into some exquisite sushi. Even before I reach the tamarind and coconut mousse dessert, my eyes feel ready to close.

Sarah elbows me in the ribs and reminds me that I've got to watch my evening porn before I fall asleep. She lapped up the on-screen fornication earlier in the day, which only helps I guess. Tonight, when we roll a boy-girl-girl threesome film featuring a blonde hunk and two incredibly perky brunettes, I already feel closer to their world than I did this morning. Maybe even a part of it.

The scene begins to smoulder and I feel Sarah's hand roaming along the inside of my leg. I forget that I am probably the only one who had the chance to come today, and anyway, I feel ever so mildly horny watching this. Without warning, then, I whip on top of her, pin her down and kiss her deeply. Then I slip my fingers into her, and my thumb onto her clit, kissing her all the while.

In no time her day's stimulations come pouring out of her, and I smile maternally as I watch her writhe in ecstasy.

The next day we begin to break into smaller, specialist groups. Nobody was going to get away with not perfecting their blow-job technique yesterday, but now it's about getting into the specifics of our training programme. Miss Jackson tells me that because of the length of my speciality list – and the things I need to work on – I'll have to do some extra evening sessions.

Tuesday morning is all about that emotional detachment thing. I think I've come a long way in this area, but Miss Jackson says there's another exercise that can help. She runs a small group with myself, Sarah, Carol and Diane. I guess we're the girly, emotional ones then. The four of us are stripped, blindfolded and told to sit cross-legged on the floor, which has been covered with beautiful, velvety mats.

"Ladies, you're going to have a very interesting morning of completely detached sex acts," says Miss Jackson. "You will be joined in the room by some other individuals now, and I'll be instructing you. Since you can't see them, you're going to learn to focus purely on the physical thrill of the sexual contact."

I'm totally switched on again and begin to shiver with excitement. And gosh, her blindfolds are top-notch. I couldn't see through this red cloth for a million bucks. It's tight around my eyes, but its lower edge caresses my cheek bone gently, and I like how it feels.

She's not wrong: it's a very interesting morning indeed. The door keeps opening and closing, but the only voice I ever hear is Miss Jackson's. Three times my pussy is licked, but I have no idea by whom. One is definitely a man, because I can feel his stubble brush me, but I don't know who or what the other two are.

The sensation, the not knowing, is unbelievable. It's like one of those silly restaurants where you go and eat in the dark, so your taste sense is more switched on. I feel like not being able to see has got my clit in turbo mode.

Miss Jackson makes me crawl up to someone and perform oral sex. Her terminology is deliberately vague, which makes my newly bisexual tummy do cartwheels. I hold my breath to prolong the tension, so only when tentative, fearful tongue touches the unmistakable wet folds of a woman do I know what I'm working with. Christ, it's hot in here.

It might be a mentor, or it might be Diane. Or Carol. Or it might be Sarah – should I be able to recognise my most regular partner by taste? Who knows? Miss Jackson was right – all I can do is enjoy what I'm feeling.

And orgasm. Twice. Both times when I'm penetrated. Once by a mystery man and once by somebody with a vibrating dildo. Normally I am more of a clit girl, but the blindfold seems to have shifted things. Being fucked by someone I can't see somehow takes on an extra dimension of sexiness. The man feels gigantic on top of me, but I'm not sure if he really is.

When our visitors finally leave the room and Miss Jackson takes away our blindfolds, we all have dazed smiles on our faces. She winks at me and leaves us to loll on the rug for a few minutes, giggling as we try without success to work out who might have done what to whom.

With the intensity of our days seemingly on the rise, so our food gets more indulgent, though not heavy. I try not to overdo it at lunch time, limiting myself to a couple of slices of sourdough and *foie gras*, followed by a refreshing bowl of fruit salad. It tastes so sweet I'd swear it's just been flown in from Tahiti.

In the afternoon I'm joined by the other girls earmarked for extra-naughty stuff, as we're lectured by Miss Tottingham on anal sex and double penetration. We're all given stretching aids and advised on how to use them safely before and during client visits. We're reminded that all but the kinkiest clients will want us ultra clean down there.

We're informed that it's very common for us to have to loosen up a colleague to prepare her for client entry, like I did with Sarah last week. Our anal mentor is full of tips I'd never thought of, and then we try it out on each other. I'm paired with Latifa and I stick a couple of lube-coated fingers up her butt. Miss Tottingham strides around the room, bending over for close looks.

"We need to be sure you all have the capacity for this kind of act," she muses as she bends over my Arab friend. "Some women are simply too tight. But as far as I can see, you girls are relaxed enough and accommodating enough. It's great news for your earnings, not to mention a ton of fun!"

I think it's the first serious sexual contact I've had with Latifa, and I've barely registered it. I must be getting good at this dehumanization thing! She's certainly purring on her hands and knees as I wiggle my fingers in her. I can almost see her smile bouncing off the floorboards.

Then Miss Tottingham gives me a strap-on and tells me to fuck Latifa. I do it. She nods approvingly as she sees the Omani's back hole stretch to a happy gape. Then each pair switches, and I'm on the receiving end. I enjoy it, and that no longer makes me blush. Though I don't make as much noise as Alyssia, who is clearly thriving on Simone's anal attentions.

The first half of the afternoon passes quickly, in a blur of anal and double penetration. I can't fault the lessons. Solid, useful, practical tips, followed by putting them into practice right away. In ways no warm-blooded girl would be likely to forget. Oh, I guess Petra might be in trouble then.

We break for afternoon tea and cake, then there's a more informal seminar for the whole class, which takes place in the drawing room. Miss Ridgewell, the busty, drop-dead gorgeous active hooker amongst the mentors, announces we'll have a male guest speaker.

And when I see who it is, I want to melt into the floor.

Chapter Twenty-Nine

There's a flash of recognition as he walks into the room. Oh lord, I know this man. I'm just so shocked and dumbstruck that my mind struggles to pick out the right file on him. It feels like someone from my past.

FUCK!!!

This cannot be happening. I'm floored.

No. Please, no. Let this be a dream.

It's the CEO of the company I just left. None other than Mark D. Spurring himself. Known as a prize dick to everyone on my floor.

What are the chances? A million to one? I curse my luck and close my eyes. I hope I'll open them again to find this awful vision gone. No such joy.

I try to keep still whilst my heart goes ballistic and I feel the hairs on my forearms rear up. I unfurl the large collar on my blouse and pull it up to my chin, in the vague hope that it will somehow hide my face.

It's not the brightest room in the world. We're scattered around on the antique furniture, and I'm perched with Sarah on a soft and comfortable, white sofa about half way back. We're just in front of the fireplace, off to one side. Maybe I won't be noticed?

He doesn't do a lot of eye contact as he starts to speak. When his gaze sweeps across the room, it doesn't particularly rest on me.

I am paying absolutely no attention to what he's saying. Something about sleeping with a lot of outstanding escorts, and things a client likes. Instead, I'm racking my brains to figure out if he actually *would* know me.

Let's think about this, Emma. The guy used to strut around our floor roughly once a week. There must have been sixty people on our floor. And our company occupied about ten floors. Six hundred people maybe? Are egomaniac pricks good with faces?

I never loathed him like I loathed my manager, but to me he was the not-particularly-good-looking poster boy for senior management incompetence. Rarely did a day go by on which I didn't think a caustic thought about him.

I don't *think* I ever spoke to him. I was in a couple of meetings he addressed, maybe thirty of us in the room. I responded to maybe three email threads involving him. Was it really enough to have made any lasting impression on the guy? Right now I'm so desperately hoping that it wasn't. I'd do anything for that.

My eyes are firmly fixed on the floor. I'm still hoping against hope that he'll just go away and not know that his very recent employee is a trainee at the hooker school, where he obviously gets a kick out of sharing his wisdom with the next generation on whom he'll spend his money.

At least he's not married. I'll give him that. So I suppose he's entitled.

And he is, today as always, very tastefully dressed. I steal the briefest of glances, and catch his eye.

Crap! His gaze lingers just a moment, and I hope that shadow by the fireplace is super-dark. It's a bright day outside, after all.

I drop my eyes and watch with my peripheral vision. He's pausing on a number of us now, while he drones on about attitude or whatever. Is he just checking out the talent, thinking who he'll want to fuck when we've graduated?

God, there's a thought I'm not sure I wanted to have.

I can feel him looking at me again, but I keep looking away, adding nods just to show I'm paying attention. *There are two reasons he might look at you.* One, he thinks you're hot. Two…he recognises you. Which is it?

I pray to God it's the former. But if he thought I was hot, then wouldn't he have stared at me when crossing my open-plan office?

Well, maybe not. He was never the flirty sort during work time. Too busy being demanding, I suppose. Maybe he's only attracted to hookers, whom he knows he can have any time he wants. My head is starting to hurt.

Part of me is so deeply curious that I want to run up to him afterwards and ask if my face rings a bell. But that's total madness. There's a chance, just a chance, I might get away without being rumbled. Oh, to see inside the man's head for just one minute!

His entire lecture passes me by, and he looks my way a couple more times as I ponder the awful possibilities that would go with recognition. The moment he drives back into mobile reception, every one of my former colleagues could know what I'm up to. I feel myself turning a little bit puce at the thought.

But wait, hang on. Even if he did recognise me, how could he spill the beans on me without having to explain what *he* was doing at a sordid place like this?

I suppose he must have one or two trusted lads on the board who could spread a rumour on his behalf. If he were feeling vindictive. I suppose he might have reason to, given the way I left. But would news of my outburst have reached him in his glass office? Was I remotely important enough to his executive existence? Surely *she* wouldn't have told him. There's no way something like that would make her look good. Right?

I feel completely powerless. If he's figured out who I am, my mother could know about this whole escort thing by dinner time. I banish the thought as quickly as I can, because I would die of shame. If he hasn't, then…onwards and upwards. But seriously, I'd have to sidestep any assignments involving the guy.

My blood runs cold as I begin to think of various other former bosses, professional associates and well-off gentlemen my father knows. Will I not walk into a client sooner or later and come face to face with somebody who knows me as Emma Carling?

His lecture feels like it drags on for hours. I'm dying to whisper something about this madness to Sarah, but chattering in class would only draw attention to me.

At last he greets us and leaves. For a moment I fear he might want to demonstrate something on one of us, but thankfully the whole thing is respectable. Miss Ridgewell takes over the talking, and I don't listen to her either. Instead, it's with much relief that I hear car wheels spinning on the gravel outside. At least the guy isn't staying over.

Then again, he'll find cell phone reception in a few minutes. I tremble to think what might happen, and I'm overcome with a desperate need to check my Facebook. If horrible rumours are going around – and I have a couple of 'friends' who would be only too happy to share them – then I want to know about it.

But I won't be able to get online until Friday. And today is only Tuesday. It could drive me crazy.

It's Sarah who calms me down, of course. Once we get back to our room, I tell her the awful truth. She's wide-eyed, but says she didn't think Spurring had lavished any obvious extra interest on me. I breathe a little easier.

She takes me for a sauna before dinner, which calms me a touch more. She tells me there's no point worrying about it right now, and that, anyway, even if the world did find out, they have every reason to be jealous of *me*. Tons of sex and cash, remember?

I'm still pretty sure I don't want to share my whereabouts with the world all the same, but, surprisingly, she has me convinced enough to settle me for a couple of days. She's right, there's no point even thinking about it. She's rather good at these pep talks.

We shower and dress for dinner. I'm feeling a little bullish, so I go for a miniskirt with my red tank top. Petra stares at me after I whip it out of our closet and take it back to Sarah's room. Well, she can please herself.

I feel that sexy thoughts will do the best job of taking my mind off worldly concerns. If my parents are about to disown me for training as a sex worker, I might as well have all the fun I can now. Luckily, I suppose, I've got a solo class scheduled for after dinner. And it's going to be with the glamorous Miss Ridgewell.

I squeeze in my evening porn-watching homework before I turn up, rather excited, in Miss Ridgewell's office. I've been told I'll be learning about sex shows. I forgot that was on my list, and I'm not even entirely sure what it means. But bring it on, I think to myself.

It's a fun evening. I'm solo because of a timetable clash earlier in the day, so I've got Miss Ridgewell's expertise all to myself. She tells me how I'll often be required to masturbate for the viewing pleasure of my clients, explaining that it can be one of the easiest and most fun aspects of
the job.

"All you have to do is pleasure your own sweet self to the max, and show how much you enjoy it," she grins. "Fun money, easy money, and no acting required!"

She watches with approval as I show her how I play with myself, reminding me only that I can add variety by playing with my nipples and sucking my fingers. I nod, not wanting to tell her that I usually do those things anyway – this shy Emma still surfaces in the strangest of ways!

Then she shows me another trick I really *haven't* ever tried. With the help of some lubricant, she teaches me a couple of ways in which I can penetrate my ass and pussy with the fingers of the same hand. I like thumb and middle finger best, and file it away for future use.

"That will drive them crazy, youngster," she cackles. "And you too, by the looks of it!"

Then she tells me that I'll need to know how to perform lesbian sex for an audience. "It's not the same as lesbian sex for yourself, which I know you enjoy," she winks. "When you're doing a show, the view must always be factored in. You need to lick a pussy whilst getting your body out of the way, because they'll want to see. That kind of thing."

She pauses, walks across to a camera in the corner of the room, and flicks it on. I know what's coming. I think vaguely about rogue sex tapes, but shrug to myself. I may have done all the damage in the world already, so whatever.

"Let me walk you through some of the moves," she says, turning my body to the camera and then standing behind me, kissing my neck softly. "Your audience is in the camera. See how I'm pleasuring you whilst also letting them see you take that pleasure? Natural pleasure is absolutely essential still, but you just need to tweak your positions a bit."

I nod and swallow hard as I feel my heat begin to rise. Miss Ridgewell makes me come twice during our session. There is no way this very tired Emma can bother about her latest worry as she drifts into the deepest of sleeps. I've never felt so wanted in all my life.

Chapter Thirty

The next two days are a whizzing blur of sex. I don't have much spare time or energy to think about Mark D. Spurring, or Petra, or the Pandora's Box that I fear my Facebook might be when I get home. No point.

Sarah is a great help in keeping me on track, my mind fixed on living and learning the sweet pleasures of the flesh. She helps me to stay focused and makes sure I don't forget my porn-watching homework, which I'm starting to really enjoy. Miss Jackson can start unchecking that guilt box. We're beginning to watch critically now, looking at how the girls suck cock, and debating which positions look sexiest to an outsider.

I feel rude and naughty to my very core when we have these conversations, but in a good way, because I know that I'm going to *do* this. These movies are really about *me*. I have a growing suspicion that seeing Spurring has pushed me over the edge of not-caring. Though I still don't want to think about it, the fact is that if my reputation in the outside world *is* in ruins, then this might be the only career option anyway. I may as well stick at it.

Once or twice I imagine some of my more immediate ex-colleagues, the ones who obviously had a thing for me. That blonde guy who wore the pink shirts and once walked into the door frame because he was too busy admiring me. I bet he'd be intrigued to hear about all this. Would guys like him try and book sessions with me?

Hah! But they couldn't afford me! You really would need a CEO's salary to have yourself a piece of Emma Carling. Glory, I feel so powerful.

We're treated to more lectures and more practical sessions. Miss Ridgewell is prominent, just like her magnificent breasts. Most of us are brought into the sessions on threesomes, where we explore boy-boy-girl and girl-girl-boy possibilities. Latifa and Alyssia lay on a superb demonstration that leaves Jack completely stunned and has me leading a spontaneous round of applause.

A handful of us – the elite? – are given group sex training. Meaning foursomes and moresomes. Alyssia, Latifa, Simone, Petra, Lilia and me. We watch *that* scene from *Eyes Wide Shut* and we talk orgies. We can expect one a week on average, Miss Ridgewell tells us, and they're terrific fun. Thankfully, given the scary abilities of some of my classmates, there's no practical. Not yet.

I'm still soaping up Petra in the shower in the mornings. Every now and then, I still catch myself admiring her. In spite of everything. The attraction is chipping away at my soul as I grow in comfort with my bisexuality, though I really don't want to let it. What is my type? Surely not a cold, heartless bitch! I like a pretty, wholesome girl who is smiling and sweet.

And yet, there is still this raw beauty about Petra that occasionally draws me in. Even though she hasn't spoken to me for a week. Even though she makes another cutting remark during Miss Jillings' session on beating, suggesting that 'some people' here can't control themselves.

I redden, because I know everyone knows what happened with me and her and Rupert last week. And I feel gladder than ever that I gave her that thrashing. She's only justifying it more now. Miss Jillings says anything goes if the situation demands it and the client will like it. I'm not sure the situation quite demanded it last week, but then, it wasn't a real client situation either. And anyway, those were the days of emotional, hung-up Emma.

We play around with various instruments of pain, practicing on a dummy. Carrie shows she's way out ahead of us with her high backlifts and a level of passion that's off-the-scale mean. I watch her and I'm pretty sure my lashes aren't quite such a turn-on for anyone wishing to be made to feel like a worm.

"One tip for those of you new to this," says Miss Jillings. "It's a huge help if you can have a certain someone in mind when you're giving punishment. Someone who did something terrible to you. Train your hand to feel like it's hurting that person. It'll be better for everyone, trust me."

Okay, well that's easy. My ex-boss. She will be the one I imagine is getting it if I ever have to do this, even if, as will most often be the case, it's a man I'm hitting. I try it on the second round of practice strokes, and feel my energy for the task skyrocket. It works!

I'm actually seething about my former manager as I wander back to my seat. It's a powerful image, somehow made more so by the fact that Spurring turned up. I guess that's because if my professional life has been destroyed by that twist of fate, I can trace the whole thing back to her.

I ponder this for a moment as I watch Petra. She's really not very good. Even I can see that. I'm not sure why she's been brought into this class. Did she really have thrashing people on her list of aptitudes? I know she can *take* punishment okay, but this looks like an area where you need to at least manufacture some feeling. And she ain't strong on feelings. Plus, she isn't physically strong. Lilia, at least, can get some force into her blows.

And then I have a lightbulb moment. She. Is. Her. I mean, Petra. She's my former manager! I've finally figured out just how it is that she manages to wind me up so much. Why everything she does gets to me. They're fucking peas in a pod, apart from the fact that my boss did a fair bit more talking. But that nose-in-the-air haughtiness, that frigid coldness, that sniping way? Oh yes, they'd get on well.

My boss wasn't gorgeous, though. And the thought of running my hands across her soapy breasts, tripping my fingers over each delicate nipple as they go, is untenable. No, I'll stick with the original cow as my image for giving beatings. Though Petra will always be a handy backup.

I'm not actually sure how much I'm up for this giving pain thing, despite all the tips we get from Miss Jillings. I know I can be good at it if I get into the zone, but will I always be able to rely on a made-up image of my ex-boss? Looking at naturals like Miss Jillings and Carrie, I'm not sure I'm nasty enough. Sarah suggests as much later that night when we compare notes on our day's activities. But part of me is determined to keep it on my skills list.

After all, it turns out I am the *only* girl who sits in both the dom and sub classes. Gosh, I must be quite the all-rounder! Sarah, Diane, Jane and Carol join me in the latter session. The quiet ones, I guess: makes sense. And Carrie's there too, salivating at the chance to practice on us, while Miss Jillings and Miss Ridgewell watch.

It's a fun session. We're all told to find the school uniforms in our closets, as this will be our most common attire in an assignment involving punishment. Carrie makes us pull down each other's skirts before we all bend over the huge oak desk at the front of the classroom.

The beating is lighter than the one she gave me in the fireplace. She uses a swish with a single, stinging strand. The turn-on is greater than the pain, especially as there's a gap between sets as she works her way along her row of five miscreant bottoms. As I knew would happen, I soon ache to come, whimpering as my forehead rests on my elbows.

Carrie won't let us touch ourselves, on pain of a serious caning. Then the gigantic Geoffrey takes over from her. Poetic enough, I suppose: he's the one who caught me eavesdropping. It only makes me wetter and shakier. I'm not sure if the others are as affected as I am. When the punishment ends, and we're all instructed to lie on the floor with our legs open, and Miss Jillings gives us each a little vibrating bullet to play with, I am the first to come.

Miss Ridgewell runs a session for the entire group, this time on the art of holding back our orgasms. She impresses upon us the need to see a few steps ahead in a situation. How long is our booking? Are there any specific instructions about how and when a client likes to come? Are we confident we can come more than once? Can our client? Has he requested to see us come in a certain way?

We'll constantly need to be weighing these things up, she tells us, and evaluating whether we should let ourselves go or not. There are times, we learn, that we'll need to switch on the opposite of blindfold mode. When we'll have to try and dull our senses. Diane suggests we could always fake multiple orgasms if necessary, but that makes Miss Ridgewell turn almost purple.

"Miss Quinn, we are not street whores!" she growls. "Your clients are paying huge money for a real experience. If they want to see good acting, then believe me they can afford box seats at any West End theatre. They want a good time, and maybe some of the warped ones will want to deny *you* a good time, but I can guarantee you that not one of them wants to see fake orgasms. *Ever.* It's one of very few hard and fast rules in this game.

Simone, and the rest of aspiring escorts in the room, are in complete silence now.

"You're worth as much as you are not just for your skills, but because you *love* your sex. It's a turn-on, in fact, that sometimes you have to think of other things to hold yourself back. If these men wanted a diet of grudging, fake enjoyment, they would have gotten married, wouldn't they? Not nice to say, but still true. So…natural orgasms, ladies, and if the timing of that isn't going to be right, then you'll need these holding-on skills, understand?"

Everybody nods, and she plunges into more mental and physical tricks designed to add control to our climaxes.

"It's not like you're going to be doing this all the time," she concludes with a smile. "Many clients will want things to happen organically. After a few weeks you'll find you're dealing with a lot of repeat clients, and you'll know which ones want you to let yourself go, and which ones want things just-so. The main thing is that you can adapt."

After dinner on Wednesday I'm taken into another evening session, with only Alyssia and Latifa. It's Miss Tottingham. Could this be 'associated oral sex'? I've been wondering about that all week.

And yes, that's exactly what it turns out to be. *That* thing. The one thing I didn't want to tell Miss Jackson about on that first morning.

Licking ass. Love getting it, love doing it. I shiver as she runs us through the basics, telling us what a select group we are. I think back to that night in the sauna last week, when Latifa told me to let go. Back then, I couldn't imagine for a second that I'd end up in any kind of select group with her and her liberated friend Alyssia. My, how far I've come!

Chapter Thirty-One

By Thursday afternoon, I am beginning to feel ready. Ready for whatever the world wants to throw at me. I'm exhausted. I've come about ten times this week. And still I want more orgasms. I never could have guessed I had so much wicked sex in me. I can no longer deny, on any level, what I've become.

I still have this deep loathing of Petra. It's all I can do not to slap her when I pass her in the hallway. She's started scattering clothes all over my old bed, which kind of annoys me when I pay visits to my wardrobe. Even though it was me who chose to leave.

I miss the big bath in that room, but bathing with her in the room would be like bathing in a pool of awkwardness. Luckily Latifa and Alyssia let me use theirs for a Wednesday night wind-down. They shamelessly sit and watch me, but I'm cool with it. These girls have taught me a lot.

They're super-excited about their career prospects, though neither is going to be ready to start right away. They've got a few work and study things to wind up first, and Latifa's considering working in Oman rather than London.

"Do they…have that sort of thing over there?" I gawp, astonished. "Wouldn't you get executed or something?"

She chuckles.

"Course they do, babe! There are hookers in every corner of this world, you innocent little thing. Trust me, those sheikhs and emirs are all at it, and they pay top dollar. As you can imagine, they're buying silence as much as anything. And as for Oman, our Sultan is gay, so he can't be too judgemental about bending the rules, can he?"

A gay sultan?

"Well…okay…but I'm sure you'd be safer here, wouldn't you? Come work with me and Alyssia and Sarah!"

"Who says I don't want to go and work back in Perth?" grins Alyssia. "Those mine workers are loaded! But yeah, London would be a good experience, I think. Let's get our shit together and do it 'Tifa!"

"Alright, alright…London it is!" says Latifa. "Let's all try get into the same agency, Sarah too. Deal?"

"Deal!" I grin, excited to think I'll have my friends with me as I venture into this mad world. "If you guys need a few weeks to tie things up, I'll wait. I'll find out which agency Petra's in and make sure we avoid that one!"

Everyone laughs at that, though I'm deadly serious.

"I hope we're right in assuming we're going to graduate," Alyssia muses. "Otherwise we're all gonna be lining up to work at Starbucks!"

God, there's a thought. I really would be a prize fool to let it come to that.

"Something tells me we're going to scrape through just fine," says Latifa, winking at me. I lie back in the luxuriant warm bubbles, delighted with life.

Thursday lunch is the juiciest, thickest steak I've ever eaten, washed down with freshly-squeezed orange juice. I keep having to remind myself I haven't paid a single penny to be here, living this life.

After that, it's into the final formal session of the week. Miss Jackson, my mentor, leads it. The topic is lesbian skills, and nearly all of us are summoned. It seems like girl-girl play is pretty much a non-negotiable in this game. I'm thankful I've tried it out at length already this week. The likes of Jane look pretty uncomfortable.

"Don't think this is only about doing shows and taking part in group sex, class," says Miss Jackson. "That's most of it, and it's key you know how to genuinely pleasure each other in those situations. But there will also be times when you'll be booked by straight couples."

Ooh, really? I hadn't considered that.

"Sometimes it may be that the woman wants to live out a lesbian fantasy, and you will have the massive responsibility of making that fantasy as amazing as she has been dreaming since she was a teenager.

"Very occasionally you will get booked by a solo female, but most often she will bring her partner along. He may just watch her experiencing a woman, or he may want to join in later. This is one situation where you always need to establish the ground rules with both beforehand. I've seen people get carried away, and that's not a good time to have the conversation about boundaries."

She looks around the room. "I believe all of you have at least got as far as licking a pussy this week. I trust you've all liked it, ladies. We're going to perfect the art this afternoon."

It's anatomical drawing time once again. Miss Jackson takes us through a few technicalities, just like Miss Littlefair did with cocks. I feel like I'm a little past this stage, and exchange knowing glances with Sarah when Miss Littlefair mentions tricks that we recognise from our bedroom.

"Vaginas are rather harder to generalise about that penises are," she says, "but learn to embrace that. There's extra satisfaction in getting it right. When you're working in a small, exclusive agency, you'll soon get to learn where and how your colleagues like it. It's a good idea to familiarise yourselves with each other before you go out on any joint assignments. It's the best kind of teamwork, I always think.

"When you're dealing with a female client, all you can do is follow general principles and then follow her feedback, her cues. And for heaven's sake, don't get fixated on pussy play. Whether you're pleasuring a client, or each other for an audience, foreplay is usually a must. People want to see intimacy, feel intimacy. Kissing. Lips on nipples. Hands running up and down her back.

"You're all women and you know what a woman likes, she concludes. It's actually a lot easier than trying to get inside a man's head!"

I'm feeling pretty hot by the time she announces it's time for a practical. I'm up for playing with any of the girls here, and I'm no longer bothered by the audience. A bed has been brought into the room, and it's scattered with blue satin pillows. It looks pretty comfortable.

"I know some of you are quite familiar with certain classmates by this stage in the course," Miss Jackson smiles, "so I'm going to take you out of your comfort zones. Unfamiliar pairings, by my reckoning."

What could that mean?

"The goal, remember, is to provide an intimate, sexy experience to your partner, whilst at the same time losing yourself in the pleasure. Don't worry about the audience for this exercise. This is about thrilling your lady and yourself."

So Lilia and Carol are called up to play together. Then Jane and Latifa, who makes Jane come in spite of herself. I start to think about the remaining permutations. Sarah goes with Simone, and I smile to myself as I watch her squirm under the Dutch girl's caresses.

But when Diane gets paired with Alyssia, I begin to worry. I look around the room. Carrie's not here. I suppose this isn't really her department. Maybe she doesn't do pleasuring people. Anyway, so that leaves...*God no!!*

I know it's coming, but I feel utterly rooted to my seat as Miss Honeywell comes in and changes the sheets after Alyssia left an enormous pleasure puddle before her and Diane even finished kissing.

My temples pound as I watch the housekeeper bustle. I thought I was ready for anything by this stage in the game, but her? I'd love an emergency phone call to come in for me right about now. I find myself glaring at Miss Jackson, because I think she's done this deliberately. She, and everyone else here, knows exactly how I feel about Petra.

I breathe in deeply and close my eyes as Miss Honeywell closes the door behind her. Miss Jackson speaks again. For once I am feeling a long, long way from turned on.

"Miss Carling, I'm not sure if you know it, but Miss Stoycheva is renowned in the trade for her skills in this department. Please come forward and enjoy."

I catch the eyes of my friends as I stand up and make my way to the front, feeling a lot like a lamb to the slaughter. I cannot, and will not, allow myself to catch Petra's eye. We'll blunder through this, but…intimacy? That's going to be hard to pull off.

I can imagine letting her lick my pussy. I can lie back and pretend it's someone else. But kissing her? That's another thing entirely. Oh, boy.

We kneel on the bed, and I feel we're going to circle each other like coy boxers in a ring. Which of us is going to make the first move? I suppose the real question is, who is the better professional?

When I think about it like that, I want it to be me. But before I can bring myself to move a muscle, a funny thing happens. Petra presses go. She crawls over to me like a sexy cat, and starts to take control. She pulls my face to hers, drawing my mouth onto her open lips, and…*oh my*.

Seriously, I forgot that I quite fancy this girl. So consumed was I with desire not to do this with her, I almost convinced myself I didn't want to. But now…*oh she is good…*

I know Miss Jackson said to forget the audience, but there's no way I can be anything but aware of their rapture. They must be enthralled by this, like you get drawn into an unexpected twist in a soap opera. Right now, I suppose, the episode would end, and they'd have to wait until Monday to see where it went.

But it doesn't end, of course. She deftly unbuttons my blouse whilst sucking in my top lip, as if she's known all along what that can do to me. I feel my nipples tightening, but with fierce concentration I stop myself from moaning. Because I'm not going to let the class see that *she* is pleasuring me. That would make her a winner, wouldn't it?

I feel like a helpless dummy. I'm too proud to respond, or to try and pleasure her. Maybe it would be a good idea. Maybe it would take my mind off this insane pleasure, especially now she's chewing my nipple, oh so just-rightly.

But I can't. I'm spellbound, caught like a statue, in a no-man's land between surrendering to delight and trying to remain as cold as her. Maybe that's why she's taken the initiative. She knows her technical skills are good, but she might not do so well at conveying intimacy if I do things to her. She's playing to her strengths, the bitch.

And yet moving isn't possible. It's too good, when she pulls off my blouse, rolls me onto my stomach – thank God my face is off show for a moment – and drags off my jeans and panties in one. I can feel her stripping off her top somewhere above me, and then lying down on my back, in her miniskirt only.

Her tongue is in my ear, loud and warm and erotic, and then it's on my neck, and I can't hold back that tell-tale breathing. She goes lower, biting my ass cheeks and then parting my legs with her hand, rubbing me in *that* place. Face down like this, I can't see her, and it's easier to forget just who it is doing this to me. It almost brings tears to my eyes to try and stop myself groaning.

But...I...Will...Not...Let...Her.

And then my respite is over, because she pulls me up onto my knees, facing the class. *Oh fuck.* I couldn't ask for a more exposed position as Petra – *yes Petra!* – lies on her back and wriggles underneath me, her head right beneath my melting, throbbing, begging centre.

It's like ice and sparks all in one as I feel her tongue below me. She's working in an awkward position, with her feet away from me, and I have no idea how she's getting this right. But getting it right she most definitely is.

Like this, my chances of staying sober are about as good as an alcoholic's in a vodka distillery. If I look down, I see her slender, petite body snaking away from me with that healthy glow of hers, all the way down to her perfect little toes, and I am reminded of what a sexy animal it is that's doing this to me. I can even see half her face, and it awakens the uncomfortable, unwanted thought that she is the most beautiful woman in the house.

I don't want that thought. It will make me come.

But if I look up, I will see my classmates. Alyssia. Sarah. Latifa. Everyone! Even Miss Jackson has moved to that side of the room. The thought of catching their eyes…I honestly have no idea what that would do to me. But I don't like it. I know what they must be thinking. Nothing bad about me, just…wow, being the centre of attention, you know? Like, nobody in this room is thinking about anything other than what's going to happen next.

Anyone else, and I'd just let myself explode right now. But pride has me ensnared, no matter how luscious that roaming tongue is. No matter how…*oh!*…beautiful it feels as it tickles my clit. Fuck, does she *have* to get it so right? I'm tightening all over. Nipples and hairs stand on end. But I keep my breathing zen. And not a sound passes my lips.

Is this a matter of professional pride for her? Is making me come the kind of thing she thinks will make her graduate, if she even *needs* to graduate? I still don't even get why she's here, if she's this good and she's already working. Yes, *this* good. Fuck, yeah, right there…*Petra*.

I'm on a knife edge. I've been holding on for a few minutes. Actually, some of the tricks from that delay-your-orgasm class come back to me, and I clench everything. I know this is not the assignment for those skills. I'm letting my feud get the better of me. I'm being unprofessional. Why not just come? *You've got a thousand volts in your vagina right now.*

I close my eyes, trying to dull the senses and avoid the sight of her semi-naked form beneath me. Maybe it'll look like I'm having a quiet, tiny orgasm. Would *that* be okay?

I sense I can't hold on much longer. There's no let-up from her. The rhythm is perfect, and now she's managed to slip two fingers in. Model student, she is: I am gushing a torrent. I can't just sit here like this the whole time. I've done well, but the girl is going to win if I don't move away.

So I take the bull by the horns, and do what I'd never do with anyone else at a time like this. I spin off her mouth, away from those delicious licks. I'm buzzing with arousal, so much that even the minute graze of moving almost pushes me over the edge. But I get away with my wits intact.

She's surprised that I've moved. Before she can react, I lay down alongside her. I lean in over her and kiss her, pushing my fingers hard into her pussy. So here I am, inside Petra. Holy hell, that is outrageous...*outrageously sexy*. But at least it won't make me come.

I begin to ram my fingers in and out of her, aggressive even in the midst of lust, and listen for any sound of arousal from her. I continue to kiss, but get nothing either. Is she playing my game? I wonder as I drop my mouth and taste her sweet nipples. There's a hint of perfume about them, and I remember all the times I've seen her spray fragrance down her top.

I shudder, because Jesus, they taste good. I'm actually enjoying this. They're delicious, and she's beautiful. And no, I won't come.

Neither will she, by the sounds of it.

But I keep going. For several minutes.

"That will do," says Miss Jackson, calling time on us. She sounds curt: neither impressed nor concerned. You never do know with Miss Jackson.

But I didn't come, and that's all that matters.

Chapter Thirty-Two

That night, our last, we're back in the ballroom. It's another formal function, but our invitation left me in no doubt that this affair won't be as equivocal or as teasing as the last one.

> *Dress is formal evening wear, but you are requested to bring a selection of outfits for play with your hosts in the lounge after dinner. Prepare yourself physically, as you would for a major client assignment.*

Alrighty then. It's not hard to see what's happening here. Last night, last chance to prove ourselves. I'm not sure innocent Emma would have understood what was expected of her one week ago, but now I'm clear on where I stand. There's going to be major group sex in the drawing room…and I'm invited!

We're given heaps of time to get ready, and I feel nothing but excitement. I follow the advice on the invite, and take a long, hot shower. I clean myself thoroughly with what looks like obscenely expensive coconut and vanilla soap. There's no audience and no Petra and no distraction. I wash my hair with rich, oozy apple-scented shampoo from the selection in our room. I feel just plain sexy.

I trim my bush, and let Sarah work the hard-to-reach bits before I return the favour. We agree not to get carried away, lest we need another shower, but I can feel my appetite building just a little. Petra certainly started something this afternoon, there's no denying that.

It's more awkward than ever with her, at least for me. I have to spend a fair amount of time in my walk-in wardrobe picking out outfits, and there's just nothing to say. Now that I'm no longer soaring on the delicate breeze of her skilled attentions, I'm mad that she tried to embarrass me in front of the class. Then again…was she just doing her job?

I want to ask her advice on what outfits to choose, but all I do, of course, is watch her out of the corner of my eye. She's putting some of the more outlandish stuff into a bag. Well, she'd know better than me what you have to bring to a sex party. So I copy her, and in goes the nurse uniform, the backless dress, the long, shapeless black cloak and the tiny pair of denim hot pants.

The skimpy shorts have never felt like they're my style, but I'm feeling like I can pull it off. I'm tired of being surprised about how well my appearance is received. I'm going to wear them, and wear them well, because I left my job and I'm doing this and I'm living a dream I never knew I had. I'm going to be a woman that men empty their wallets for. Whatever I wear.

Spurring flashes through my thoughts and I remember that tomorrow I'll be back in communication with the real world. My body fills with apprehension for a moment. I still have no idea whether he placed me or not. Pretty maddening stuff. But I use the skills we've learned this week, and shout down the thoughts and feelings that aren't working for me. They're no good to Emma Carling right now.

There are no dates or partners for this banquet, and unlike last time, we're all at one long table, adorned with silver-plated candlesticks and little bouquets of irises. The mentors are nowhere to be seen, only the dozen or so men who've been having the time of their lives all week. Oh, and there's the guy I fucked after the blow-job training. Amazingly, I still don't know everyone's name. And I never thought to look up his.

The cute waitresses are back, and even Miss Honeywell and Wilfred keep away from proceedings. There's the pianist in the corner, playing slightly repetitive tunes that serve only to build a certain expectation. The melodies keep gathering pace and then slowing, fraying your nerves and making you think something is about to happen.

The only really curious thing is the table for one in the opposite corner. It's our waker man, who still religiously does his thing each morning. I can see him well from where I'm sitting in the middle of the table. He's dining alone, apparently taking very little interest in us. He doesn't talk to anyone, and only occasionally does he let his eye rove across our number.

Conversation is civil and casual. It's difficult to really warm things up, though the champagne is flowing once again and that does start to help after a while. When it comes to chat, I notice that the men lead all the way. I'm actually dying to ask them some questions, but – and I can tell it's the same for all the girls around me – I get almost no answers. Instead, the men keep steering the topic back to ourselves.

I'm seated near Robert, Geoffrey and a portly, shortish but confident-looking man named Sebastian. Nothing much to look at, but like the rest he has a certain air about him. Like the rest, I can tell he's used to getting what he wants. I'm curious to know what these people get up to when they're not here. What makes them who they are.

Even with Alyssia and Simone seated near me, even with their evident curiosity there to support mine, we just can't make much headway. These men just don't want to talk about who they are. I'm not even convinced they're using their real names. I notice Robert make a slip-up and almost call Sebastian something else.

I suppose I can understand why they might want to be secretive. I can only imagine they're rather important in the world of commerce, maybe politics. Maybe they're even artists. I wish I was a little more news-aware – I probably wouldn't even know it if they *were* famous.

Of course, they won't be drawn. And then I blurt out something: "But none of you boys are married, right?"

I deliberately make eye contact with each of them, because this is one thing I want the truth on. The idea of being a husband-stealer is one thing that still plays on my mind, despite the assurances from that agent woman in London.

Sebastian takes on a stern look, and, for once, I get a clear answer from someone. "That's a shocking question to ask, you know," he says, not entirely jokingly. "You know what we've all been up to with you trainees this week. What kind of people do you think we are?"

I blush more furiously than at any time in this whole stay. More than for any of the naked humiliation, the public sex, anything. I can feel the temperature in my cheeks.

"I – I'm sorry, I just didn't know if…well, I mean…this is all really new to me. I'm sorry."

"Accepted," chimes in Geoffrey. "Though I will make you pay for that insolence after dinner."

A twinkle in his eye. Butterflies. Dancing.

His friends laugh, but I am almost certain it's no joke.

"No agency or institution worth its salt will accept a married man as a client," he adds. "And believe me, they do check. And when it is claimed, as is the case with the lucky Rupert, that a man is married to a highly liberated woman happy to let him play, then these things are checked out with the woman in question."

Rupert. *Taken*. But his lady gives him permission to fuck the likes of me. It makes my head spin. Well…okay.

And then we go back to fielding questions about us. And we must tell them all about our lives, our families, our work. And then, when the pavlova arrives, some of our fantasies and experiences.

I'm as red as the dessert strawberries at some of the questions I have to answer. Even the unflappable Alyssia seems a little coy. It seems unfair that we must share so much, but they seem to be enjoying it as a part of the build-up to whatever is coming. And what's coming is in no doubt.

I just wish I knew something about *them*. Because these men – all of them – fascinate me more and more.

Then again, I can't deny that a little mystery thrills me.

Coffee and cheese. And then the music stops. Harry stands up at the head of the table and speaks in his sexy Scottish drawl. I could listen all night.

"We'll move to the drawing room now. Convene there in five minutes, in outfits of your choice. Ladies, you are in charge of our after-dinner entertainment. You should leave no man unattended."

I'm actually more comfortable once we get away from the dinner-party bit and get ready for the public sex part. I'm amazed that this is so, but I feel like whatever happens in the lounge is going to be less ambiguous and more exciting.

I'm nervous, too, as I drag on my nurse uniform, which seems as good a starting point as any, in the classroom where we're told to get changed. I look around at my classmates and feel proud of all of us. Maybe even…well, okay, most of us. We're half naked for the umpteenth time in the last ten days, and everyone's pretty much just getting on with it. Jane still looks a bit like someone who found Brussels sprouts in her porridge, and appears to feel dirty as she changes into a belly dancer outfit that actually suits her rather well.

Oh well, her guilt is her problem. The rest of us…look how far we've come! I feel something like solidarity with this group of women as we prepare to entertain a roomful of horny men. This must be what it feels like to join an elite army division, maybe. There's a sense of mission, and it draws me to them.

I know that whatever we come up with will be well-received. But I'm not exactly sure how to get the ball rolling. I don't want to walk in there and have the others looking to *me* for inspiration. Who is meant to take charge? I decide to follow the experienced ones as we file into the room. Petra and Lilia. And they're happy to lead the way.

The air is already thick with smoke and whisky when we arrive. It is as manly as anything in life gets. They're indulging in putrid cigars, and all looking very pleased to be where they are. And why not? I'm feeling pretty excited too. My stomach is dancing itself into knots. Is this going to be a full-on orgy?

I hang back and watch Petra, who sports heels, a tiny grey miniskirt and a blouse tied up beneath her breasts. Lilia is in something like a catsuit, which I don't find all that sexy. But I know some men like it, and she does have experience on her side. Anyway, my outfit is pretty silly too.

Petra goes to the far end of the room and kneels in front of Sebastian. Odd that she'd choose him, when there are so many better-looking guys. Lilia takes the next one, and, per our instructions, no man is left unattended. I look up to find myself kneeling before Harry, feeling more submissive and ready to please than I could ever have imagined.

I don't know what to do next. He's wearing a kilt, for a start. If something happens, that's going to be a first for me. A Highland fantasy that may just have crossed my mind once or twice before. Harry is undressing me with his eyes, but rather than anything outrageous, he pours me a glass of white wine and begins to stroke my head. Am I supposed to show initiative now, or do as I'm told?

It occurs to me that no instructions were given because this is all meant to happen in a natural way. Twenty-two highly-sexed adults, reasonably fuelled on alcohol, in a warm, safe and comfortable room together. The men lavishly dressed, the women in attire than can mean only one thing.

Yes, any thinking now is nothing but over-thinking.

I hear a sharp intake of breath behind me, and turn to see Latifa straddling Rupert as he leans back in the middle of a broad sofa in front of the fireplace, which glows with romantic warmth. She sports a *burqa*, something that definitely wasn't in my closet, but I know it's her in there. Who else could you count on to get things going like that? I can see why it would be a turn-on to anyone who knows her background, though. The repressive garment is climbing up her body now, its black hem nestling in the crook of her kneeling knees.

I feel nothing but horny, and I take a swig of my wine. Then I put it down and make a move towards some fun of my own. Still kneeling, I push my head under Harry's kilt, and suck on his cock. It's cosy and dark in here, and I like it. I hear him gasp and wheeze as I take him in. I remember his taste from the poolside, and, yes, it's the best dessert I could ever ask for.

Harry says nothing, but leans back and lets me have my way with him. I don't let him come, because I think everyone wants to make a long night of it. There are no more classes. We're done. *Mmm.*

The depravity takes a natural course from there, and in a matter of minutes I can't believe I gave a moment's thought to who was going to do what to whom. Yes, it's an orgy, plain and simple. Everyone is at it. After the icebreaker of the initial attentions from each girl to each guy, the sex just begins to flow.

Sometimes the impetus comes from the girls, sometimes from the men. The notion that one side is paying and the other paid gets completely lost in lust. I think I might have paid for this myself! The idea that we might be being graded quickly vanishes from my thoughts too. The mentors are nowhere to be seen, and if they are watching on camera, well, they have much to envy.

At times there *are* men left unattended, but only once the party is really swinging, and not without good reason. Like when one of us ducks out to try a new outfit, which is super fun. Or the time when Latifa, Alyssia, Sarah and I indulge each other to distraction on the soft, fur rug in the middle of the floor. Most of the men gather to watch, and the rest of the girls rush to stimulate them – by hand, mouth or both - whilst the boys enjoy our show.

When expressly told to do something, of course, we do it. In the case where Rupert asks Carrie to strip off my hotpants and t-shirt, and bind me to the equally naked Sarah, I oblige with my own moisture almost running down my legs. I'm pressed breast-to-breast and face-to-face with my special girl, expertly trussed up with ropes around our knees, waists and under our arms.

It's *hot*. And it gets infinitely hotter when the guy who fucked me on blowjob day comes up behind me, and Rupert presses up against Sarah's back. They borrow the Jane's unwilling fingers to lube us up, then push rudely inside our asses. They almost lift us as they begin to thrust from behind, squashing us even tighter together as we kiss. It is the single most sexy thing that happens to me all week, and I come just as I feel the guy shoot his own load into my needy backside.

I change into my cape, and get fucked in a more natural way by Robert, and then it all becomes too much trouble, and our clothes just stay shed, and I lose track. My ass gets taken again as George bends myself and three others over the back of the sofa and sodomises us one by one. I'd be lying if I said there wasn't a dark thrill in it.

I lose count of the cocks I suck, the seed that lands on me, in me, the asses I lick, the tongues that probe my pussy. It's thirsty work, and I keep drinking wine that seems to magically refill. The men nibble my breasts and spank my bottom. I am taken every which way, thrown over chairs in all sorts of positions, and I gobble it all up.

The hours fly by, and I can't believe it when I hear the grandfather clock strike three. We've been fucking since eleven. Four hours! No wonder I'm beginning to flag. Just one thing. I've come thrice, and there's a need building once more. What's in this wine? Do I seriously need another release? I've become insatiable.

There's a little lapse after Rupert unleashes inside me for only the second time on my stay here. I look around, breathing heavily, as he nods in Petra's direction.

"I want to see you finish Miss Carling," he says to the gorgeous blonde. And in my drunken state, all I can see is her gorgeousness. I'm tipsy enough to be everyone's friend now. I know she tends not to drink, but she looks happy to take up the challenge. I think I insulted her pride when I held on against her magic tongue this afternoon.

She pushes me into an armchair, her perspiring body glistening gold in the firelight. I let her place a cushion under my hips and I'm vaguely aware of Rupert nestling into a nearby chair with a good view. And I don't mind looking down. *Aah. You can finish what you started now.*

There's a determination to her lapping, and it's as amazing as it was before. I think she wants to finish what she started earlier. This time, I'm not going to fight it. It's our last night in the school, and I'm drunk, and she is insanely attractive. I *want* her licking me there. We'll never want to talk, but her head between my thighs? Yes please.

Maybe *this* is the naughtiest thing I've done all week, I think to myself, as I watch Petra's pretty little head bobbing down there, tap-tap-tapping away on my clit, while Sarah sits on Rupert's lap and fondles his flagging manhood whilst he watches Petra tongue-fuck me.

Oh yes, it's *bad*. And that makes me come hard and fast, crying out without a care. For a minute it crosses my mind that she might be spiteful and stop at the crucial moment. But no, she lets me explode. I don't think teasing is Petra's game.

Is there to be lovemaking? It doesn't seem so ridiculous after all this fine wine. Have we had a *rapprochement?* Should I return the favour? She doesn't seem bothered. Does that mean I *won*? Was I more irresistible than her this week? Fuck, but she's *so* hot. Hmm.

All I really know is, my knees are weak from what she did to me down there. My butt still feels wet and gaping, and my pussy feels inflamed and sensitive. I'm getting flooded with fatigue, and this release of tension with Petra has given me an instant headache.

I look around the room, dopily, and see that the party is winding down organically. Only Alyssia, that Duracell bunny, is still going, riding George on some distant sofa, but even she's doing it dreamily. Other girls and men are dozing, or just gently caressing each other. It's almost sweet.

I'm pining for my bed now. I stagger up the stairs, and throw my naked, wanton body in between the sheets. I feel ready to sleep for a decade. And though a little voice in me says that I could probably be okay with the fuck-free day I'm expecting tomorrow, I'm not sure I entirely believe it.

Chapter Thirty-Three

"Take a look inside," urges Miss Jackson, beaming at me as she hands me another of her trademark crisp, thick envelopes.

It's a big one this time. Size A4. I take it from her, with a nod and a raise of the eyebrows. What could this be? It's our last day and word on the street has been that assignments – surprise or otherwise – won't play a part. I'll be catching my train back home to London later this afternoon.

I hope this isn't going to be one of their riddles. I've let my guard drop. For the first time in our stay, our waker didn't show. After last night's hot exertions in the lounge, we all enjoyed a serious lie-in. When Sarah and I finally stirred at around eleven, a note under the door told us to come down and order breakfast at our leisure.

It was a warm, blue-sky summer's day, like that of my arrival, and we took full advantage by dining on the terrace. I sent Wilfred running back and forth for fruit salad, Greek yoghurt with nuts and honey, and then a full English. We'd made it to the last day, the sun was out, and it was our last chance to pig out!

Some of the other girls came and went, a touch of awkwardness about one or two of them following the evening's drawing-room antics. Even Sarah seemed to want to change the subject away from our most abandoned display of the week. And me? I felt nothing but a deep comfort and a satisfaction that's completely foreign to me.

For me it was something akin to a morning-after glow, I guess, but more than that. Just the release of knowing that I could let go in a different way now. That there'd be no more surprises here. That I could go back to London and let all this madness sink in.

It was like the first day of the holidays after a semester of exams. Three cups of coffee went down good as I sat there in a pair of broad, loose cotton trousers, a plain t-shirt and sneakers. Nowhere to be, and not a care in the world.

And now, another envelope…

There's just one thing inside. It's a single cream-coloured piece of card, almost like a certificate…it *is* a certificate! As I pull it further out of its sheath, a thin border in royal blue homes into view.

This can only be good news, right? I avoid catching Miss Jackson's eye, in case I smile prematurely and look a fool. I read the words, professionally printed in curly French script.

This is to certify that,

Emma Louise Carling

Has satisfied the examiners that she has the skills and aptitudes to satisfy the most demanding clients as a premium escort.

She has passed the summer 2014 course with distinction.

I did it!

And now I look up at Miss Jackson, and I do smile.

"Thank you," I grin. "Distinction? Really?"

She chuckles. "Yes, really! You were the outstanding girl here, don't you know that? We're very excited about your prospects out there in the workplace. We think you may soon command Class 1 fees."

I look at her in expectation, slightly scared of what I may hear. She leans forward and lowers her voice.

"How does earning five thousand Pounds an hour sound to you, dear?"

I very nearly faint. I have to grip the handles of the wooden chair.

"I'm...lost for words..." I splutter. "You *must* be kidding! I don't believe it!"

She just shakes her head. "Your looks and your spirit and your versatility, Emma, are a rare combination. It's not as easy to find that mix as you might think."

I'm stunned. I thought I'd done okay this week. But...Class 1? It sounds like I must have done quite a lot more than okay.

"Don't lose that certificate," she goes on. "It's the ticket any agency will want to see, although we'll certainly be in touch with your patron and his agent to communicate the good news. It would be courteous to give a few months of your time to her, with him as a priority customer, if you're going to go into this business. And I can't think of a single reason why you shouldn't."

I look down at the fancy paper confirming me as a first-grade whore. I most definitely will not be hanging this on my wall. Or leaving it lying around.

I clear my throat. "But...there's not even a name on here. Couldn't anybody make one of these?"

"No Emma," she says with gleaming eyes. "We don't put Cranleigh House on certificates because we don't need to. There's no other school in the world like this. People in the business know *exactly* who issues these. We have our reasons for staying below the radar. Some of the people involved in this school would not want it known.

"As for counterfeit, there's a complex watermark that only our industry partners can scan. Your less fortunate peers wouldn't be able to fool anybody for a second."

Less fortunate peers? "Do you mean that...some of us didn't pass?"

She nods slowly. "It's the reason we don't do a formal prize giving. It would get awkward with such a small group. But I'll fill you in. Only Latifa joins you with distinction. The rest all passed well, apart from Jane, Lilia and," – she coughs conspicuously – "Petra."

My eyes go wide. I can't believe what I'm hearing. I mean, I can. But I can't.

"Really? But...Petra...and Lilia...I thought they already worked as...you know!"

"What you've heard is quite right, Emma. They've both worked full-time as prostitutes in the high-end bracket. But that doesn't mean they're great at their jobs, does it?"

She shakes her head very, very slowly.

"Those two women were sent here by their agency. Kind of a last-ditch thing as I understand it. They've had a few client complaints and their agent thought we might be able to put a few things right. Save their careers, if you like.

"Sadly they're fundamentally unsuited to this work, and we couldn't give them approval. It's sad, because they're truly beautiful girls, skilled in many areas. They just don't have the right attitude. I think you've had a taste of that, haven't you?"

I've never been a gossip, and much as I hate Petra, I don't want to complain about anything behind her back. Especially when, if I understand correctly, her career is about to grind to a sudden halt.

"So you mean, they'll be out of work now?" I venture.

"Certainly their regular agent won't have them back," she nods. "They may find work elsewhere with some maverick start-up, of course. This isn't a compulsory professional certification, but all the top agents and their clients insist on our seal of approval.

"There's nothing to stop them working the streets, either...but their income and lifestyle would be very, very different. And it would be dangerous."

I sit back, trying to resist the temptation to break out into a gloating beam. I mean...I'm top of the class, and she's...out! I'm not vindictive, but, well, it does feel kind of great.

"So…what wasn't right with them…?" I ask hopefully, wondering if I might get told to mind my own business. But Miss Jackson seems to be in a forthcoming mood on our last day together as mentor and student.

"It's really simple, Emma. Those two girls think it's all about achieving a certain result. They see it as a job. Bring the client off, take your money, go home. Now, as I *think* you know, they – especially Petra – are extremely good at bringing the client off. Technical skills? Looks? No problem.

"But, as we've repeated time and again this week, top clients are paying for more than that. They're not interested in a woman going through the motions, really they're not. And they're not interested in actors. They want the looks, they want the skills, but they want to feel wanted too. And you *cannot* fake that.

"In other words, they want a woman who is hungry for sex and as thrilled to be doing what she's doing as the client is. Petra and Lilia have never gotten this right, and they've shown no signs of improvement while here. We've given them every chance, but they continue to see any encounter as an exercise in box-ticking. And letting themselves smile never seems to be one of those boxes. There's just no real drive there."

I think back to Petra's bone-dry panties during my violent encounter with her and Rupert, all those days ago. It adds up. She just doesn't get turned on at all. Yes, she can do what is asked of her and likes to finish the job – her tongue-work yesterday was evidence enough of that.

"We even tried something we've never tried here before," Miss Jackson continues. "Do you remember the pub outing, when she and Lilia went off with those old men? Well, those guys were sent there by us, to give an off-site verdict, as it were. Petra and Lilia took the bait – they're great at spotting a business opportunity – but our feedback was that they left their clients cold.

"The men tried everything to engage them, make them smile, even make them come. They're known as considerate lovers and went to great lengths. But we're told Lilia and Petra just wouldn't play along. They just wanted to satisfy the guys and take their money. Pretty disgraceful.

"It's most frustrating, because those two could go far. But hey, it's people like them that make *your* stock go up."

I suppose she's right. Gosh, am I really going to be doing this? It still doesn't seem at all possible.

"One thing, Emma. I know you haven't gotten on with Petra and I completely understand. But be careful. Agents aren't going to deliberately pair you up with girls you clash with, but sometimes it's unavoidable. If you end up with a Petra licking you out for a client, like you did yesterday, you can't try and hold yourself back out of pride."

Then my mentor softens. "I think the circumstances were a bit exceptional there, though. I'm sure it won't be an issue in your work. Just remember that thing we did with the blindfold. Dissociate the feeling from the person if the circumstances dictate. That said, I was impressed with your ability to hold back your orgasm yesterday, even if it was the wrong time to use it. She's *good*."

And I wonder if Petra also did to Miss Jackson what I did to Miss Jackson. Sitting in this very chair. Her twitching mouth tells me she might just have run that test at some point in the past couple of weeks.

"What about Jane…?" I ask

"Just too much guilt," Miss Jackson shrugs. "We had her watching porn, we gave her books to read, we exposed her to relentless sex. But she was too tough a nut to crack. She's from a posh background and there's just been too much revulsion about sex bred into her. You can see it in her face.

"Of course she's liberated in her own mind, but unfortunately she can't bury the repression – so to speak – enough to fool others. She's done all we asked, but she's invariably passive and struggles to let herself go. We could never give her our stamp of approval.

"And speaking of guilt, young lady, don't think you've completely shaken off that English upbringing of yours. Yes, you're barely the same girl who arrived here two weeks ago, but I have a slight concern that a kernel of repression remains. It's been slain for now, but I worry it may surface after you've had a few days off.

"So I want you to keep the porn I gave you, and *promise* me you will watch it at least thrice a week. In addition, I'm going to be emailing you some files for your audio player. They're basically hypnotherapy meditation. You close your eyes and they talk you into a state of deep relaxation. Then the magic happens.

"I've tried them, and I think you'll like them. They're a very strange experience. I've found myself pretty much unconscious, then suddenly bursting into an orgasm. It's very weird, but very effective in talking your guilt issues out of you. Three times a week too, okay?"

I nod. I think I can manage that. After all, I have no concrete plans for the foreseeable future. It's only been a couple of weeks since I quit my job, and it's still sinking in that this is longer than a holiday. I'm going to have a long chat with Martin, take a few days to think about things, and figure out what I want to do.

My thoughts are back in London, and the real world, and suddenly they run back to Spurring. Miss Jackson seems to know it. Again.

"Oh, by the way, Emma, you seemed to have a fan in Mr Harris this week! He kept asking about you afterwards…I think he's going to be trying to book you…"

"Mr Harris?" Shit. I remember now. Spurring was introduced under that name. Of course he wouldn't announce his real identity.

Suddenly I feel terrified. "He did…?"

"He kept asking for your name, actually. But we didn't give it, as that's not our policy until you confirm you actually want to sign on with an agency."

My mind's doing a land speed record attempt now. Asking for my name...does that mean he wanted to confirm a suspicion he knew my face? Or did he just fancy me, because, you know...I'm a Class 1..."

"Oh..." is all I can think to say.

Well, I'm not volunteering my links to the guy if I don't have to. I want to keep that distance as big as possible. Like hell he's going to book me. I'm going to be sick that day.

Miss Jackson rises from her seat and comes around to my side of the desk. "That's all we needed to go over today, Emma. You're done. And may I say what a pleasure it's been looking after you? You might just be my favourite student ever. Hug?"

We share a warm, long embrace. I am going to miss her. She's been tough on me at times, but her caring has always managed to seep through. She's been a big help. We trade numbers and agree to meet up next time she's in London.

"And I want to hear some exciting stories about your new work," she says, eyes all sparkly and excited.

Chapter Thirty-Four

Some goodbyes are more emotional than others. It's hard bidding farewell to Latifa, and Alyssia, and of course Sarah. We've talked about how cool it would be if we all worked together, but I wonder if this is going to be one of those summer camp things where everybody talks about keeping in touch but nobody does.

I'd like to think my bond with Sarah is deeper than that. She lives a little outside London, but she's pretty sure she's going to give this prostitution thing a go and move into the city. I tell her, with a wink, that she's welcome to stay at my flat, but she'll have to share the bed with me.

She wells up a little, gives me a tender kiss. "I'd like that," she says, and we swap numbers. Then there's a long, long hug before she slings her bag onto her shoulder and heads downstairs to jump in Chris's Jaguar. For some reason we're all booked on different trains out of here, and she's a couple of hours ahead of me.

I'm one of the last to go. We're told the clothes from our wardrobes are ours to keep, and that they'll be sent on to us at home. So many free clothes, it's outrageous! As are some of the outfits…I'm thinking I might need a secret wardrobe in my flat!

Anyway, it means there's precious little packing up to do, which spares me having to go back to my original room. I soak up some more sun and coffee and sandwiches, indulging in a couple of cigarettes as I wait for my five o'clock pickup. I have to hug Latifa, Alyssia and Simone goodbye. It's a strange experience, truth be told. I've come to expect something way more…sexual from these people. Somehow it makes the hugs all the more meaningful.

Of the menfolk, there is no sign. They must have gone home after a nap in the drawing room armchairs this morning. No emotional goodbyes with Rupert, then, and it occurs to me that I haven't even thought about that until now. I really have managed to start thinking of them all as just…men.

Of course, Petra and I are the last to leave, and we have to share a car again. I hug Miss Honeywell and Wilfred, while she doesn't even offer our cheerful carers so much as a grunt. She's even more sullen than usual – if that's possible – presumably after getting news of her failure this morning.

Petra and I make our way to separate carriages without so much as a word. It's bizarre and weird and impossible to think that we did the things we did yesterday. That she made me explode with pleasure rather than rage. But Miss Jackson said it: it's just box-ticking to her. It doesn't mean we're friends. And I'm good with that.

It's a faster train this time, and I'm grateful for it, because I'm a little keyed up to see what's been going on in the outside world. Two weeks since I've seen a text or an email or my Facebook! Now that I'm heading back towards London and real life, I'm suddenly hungry for updates.

I have this insane urge to post my status. Oh, I could shock a few people if I wrote something like 'en route back from hooker school…and just passed with distinction.' I'll have to resist that particular urge. Forever, I'm quite sure.

No, I'll need to be exceedingly discreet. Thank God I have Martin I can talk to. I'm a long way from being able to tell my girlfriends, though I'm really dying to do so. Opening my mouth about any of this business will need some careful consideration.

The other thing is Spurring. Unless any of the staff are indiscreet…which seems impossible…he is the only possible leak about what I've been doing. And then only if he figured me out. Or is he? Wouldn't be hard for a spiteful Petra to look me up, would it? There's a lot to worry about in this day and age. My adventures could be all over the internet at any moment. I think of all that CCTV, and of Miss Ridgewell's video recorder.

I'm seriously twitchy as I wait for bars of signal to appear on my phone, but tell myself I'm being paranoid.

There it is at last! Reception! My hands are shaky as I click my icons. Only a couple of texts appear, since they never come through when your phone's been off for ages. One from my mum, which makes me feel guilty. She obviously wasn't paying attention when I told her I was going to a phone-free island.

Facebook has been busy, but harmless. A few wall posts asking how I'm doing, wishing me well on my holiday. God! I'm going to have to make up a few tales about my island, aren't I? I suppose it will need to have some goats and some olive trees. But I'm a rubbish liar and I'm not looking forward to it.

There's nothing worrying on my personal email or any other networks. Just a couple of messages from recruitment agencies I'd been sounding out. A couple of job ideas from them. They look like more of what I'd just left behind. 'Fast-paced', 'prospects for advancement', 'our busy office', blah, blah, blah.

And the money they're offer? I keep thinking of Miss Jackson's five grand an hour, and calculate me that it'll take me about two months of slog to earn five grand in one of these jobs. That's nine to five, Monday to Friday. Orgasms not included.

Hmm, is there really anything to think about? Apart from the fear of public embarrassment, I'm not sure there is. But I feel I owe it to myself to chew it over. Martin will definitely help. I'm relieved to have survived my return to reception without any scares, be they from Spurring or anyone else. I begin to feel much lighter.

I'm surprised to see my work emails still coming through. Clearly they haven't shut down my mail account yet. I guess that's what happens when you don't follow the standard Human Resources exit script. They get thrown.

I look through them curiously. Nothing of interest. No gossip. Just rubbish from various group lists I was subscribed to. Meeting this, action that, discuss that. I think I would genuinely sooner jump into a fire than go back to all that pointless nonsense.

Yeah, I've got a much better option now! I look behind me, see that nobody is looking over my shoulder. Nope, everyone else sharing the train is in front of me. I pull out my certificate. I hold it in my fingers, admiring the words.

Emma Carling. Distinction. Escort.

They're the business nouns, aren't they? I still can't quite believe I'm reading them. The two weeks I've just experienced are already beginning to feel like a dream, but I hold in my hands the proof that it really happened.

Can I do this? What happens if I cross paths with somebody I know again? Would I eventually learn to stop caring? How in God's name could I ever tell my family? Financial independence in a couple of years…hmm.

But the questions slow to a smoulder as memories of my passions overpower them, peppered with visions of rich food and hot baths and expensive clothes. The train begins to pick up speed as we hit a long stretch of non-stop line. It makes my mind run to the best orgasms I had this week. The first one with Rupert? George and Robert? The time I got beaten in the fireplace? The last one, with Petra?

My mind replays them all to me. In graphic detail. I squirm in my seat. And then I just lose myself in a haze of hot recollections. And I think I'm smiling a faraway smile as I gaze out of the carriage window at the green fields of England. And nobody could ever know what wicked things I'm thinking.

Also by James Grey

Escort Unleashed

Emma's qualified as a prostitute…so what now? To work, of course! The heroine of *Escort in Training* must head back to London and find out if she can really do this for a living.

Will she be as good as her report card suggests? Will she be able to keep her trade a secret from her friends and, above all, her parents? Just what will it feel like to be *this* desired by London's wealthiest men…and couples?

To find out whether it's all plain sailing for Emma in the English capital, and where her incredible journey takes her, you'll need to read *Escort Unleashed*, the second book in this fascinating series.

Connect with James online for launch news, links to this book, and the latest news on printed editions, audiobooks and other platforms.

About James Grey

First, let's get one thing clear: I'm for real. Yes, a male writer of erotica! No unicorns here! Ladies, I have all the right parts in my pants. End of story.

I am in my thirties. I am based in the UK and English is my mother tongue. But I am not British. Yes, this is a *nom de plume*. Yes, I am a professional, published writer in many different fields. Yes, my background tends towards the conservative. So I know you'll appreciate my privacy needs.

Now then, I am an extremely naughty boy. The average guy thinks about sex, what is it, eight times an hour or something? For me, quadruple that. My imagination is a wild place. You'd have a lot of fun there.

So here's the thing: I revere and worship women. I find your scent intoxicating. The feel of your gentle, soft skin is like a brush with the divine. Kissing your perfumed hair makes me close my eyes and silently give thanks.

I love to see you naked, adore it when your hair tumbles down in perfect curls over your bashful, beautiful breasts. When your body glows in the golden light of flame, it dazes me. I am entranced by the bead of sweat that forms on your tender neck, and gently trickles down your bare, tanned back. It's one of my favourite parts of you, your back, because it's your biggest expanse of skin. And that skin – every inch of it – is joy and wonder to me.

You are everything I am not. You fascinate me. I can never get enough of you.

But don't be entirely fooled by the poetry. I am a man. I like sports and lesbian porn. In my perfect world I would have a harem. On the other hand, I don't like beer or cars or explosions very much, and I'm into literature, and I'm sensitive enough to cry at times. So maybe I'm not quite the stereotypical guy. I'm complicated. Just compare my stories *Playdate* and *The Raven*: they're both true tales, and they're both me.

Some of my work is fiction, some is fantasy, and some is honest-as-steel autobiographical. The more you connect with me, the sooner you'll learn which is which.

At times I'll write from your perspective. But what I'll always do best is take you inside a man's mind. When my men speak and think, you have a front-row seat. Nothing is softened for my audience. It's raw, it's real and it might just be an education.

Thank you for buying me, and letting me have this honest outlet for my passions. Thank you for the ongoing feedback and encouragement. The thought that you might be turned on by my words, turns me on more than you can know.

Connecting with James Grey

I hope you've enjoyed reading *Escort in Training*. Your interest is precious to me as an independent author. Your support, both moral and monetary, keep this whole thing going. There are a hundred ways you can join me on my journey as an author.

For more on how you can get to know me, share feedback and meet other fans, please join the James Grey Fan Group on Facebook. From there, you'll also be able to friend me! I'm on Twitter too: @jamesgreyerotic

Want me to keep you abreast of any future releases? Send a note to jamesgrey2205@gmail.com, and I'll do just that.

Looking forward to meeting you!

Printed in Great
Britain
by Amazon